Betty Burton has won acclaim for her novels, *Jude*, *Jaen*, *Women of No Account*, *Hard Loves*, *Easy Riches* and *The Consequences of War*, and for her collection of short stories, *Women are Bloody Marvellous!* She is currently working on her next novel entitled *Long Hot Summer*. She has won several awards for her writing, including the Chichester Festival Theatre Award, and has written for both television and radio.

Born in Romsey, Hampshire, Betty Burton now lives in Southsea with her husband, Russ.

By the same author

Women are Bloody Marvellous!
Jude
Jaen
Women of No Account
Hard Loves, Easy Riches
The Consequences of War

BETTY BURTON

Goodbye Piccadilly

Grafton
An Imprint of HarperCollins*Publishers*

Grafton
An Imprint of HarperCollins*Publishers*
77–85 Fulham Palace Road,
Hammersmith, London W6 8JB

Published by Grafton 1992
9 8 7 6 5 4 3 2

First published in Great Britain by
HarperCollins*Publishers* 1991

ISBN 0 586 20874 7

Set in Bembo

Printed in Great Britain by
Clays Ltd, St Ives plc

For Patricia Parkin

My thanks to Ken Weller for his generosity
in giving me permission to make use of
Don't be a Soldier!, his book on the radical anti-war
movement in North London, 1914–1918.

Betty Burton 1991

Part I

SOUTHSEA 1911

'Otis, if you wish your cards to arrive by first post, then I think it wise to give them to the porter at once – this is not London, and they may not be too swift at handling the mail in a seaside town. You remember your father's experience last year?'

'No, Ma.'

'An important letter to his office did not arrive until third post next day, yet it had been posted in Brighton main post office before eight P.M. of the previous day.'

'They are ready, Ma.'

'Then run along, and take mine with you. And ask the porter if the local paper has arrived.'

Inwardly Emily Hewetson sighed at the prospect of a month of hotel life – the very best hotel, it was true, but

Southsea was not the Côte d'Azur, not even Harrogate. But then parenthood has always meant sacrifice. And there was always Vienna to look forward to.

Otis whisked up her mother's neatly piled letters. 'Oh the *papers*, Ma, of *course*. I forgot, the Lists will be out. I do love to see us in the Lists.'

'Otis.' Mrs Hewetson's voice was low and restrained, as befitted a hotel with marble columns in its halls. ' "Run along" is not intended literally. Do *try* to behave in a more feminine way.'

'Yes, Ma.' Otis walked demurely from the terrace, but could not restrain herself when it came to descending the long, wide staircase, which she took like a youth.

Otis Hewetson was eleven months over sixteen, and an only child. Child is perhaps misleading, for although Otis was not, like her mother, tall and willowy, she was most certainly womanly beneath her girlish dresses. Emily Hewetson was something of a beauty, and perhaps it was for that reason that she kept her round-hipped, neat-waisted and pert-breasted daughter dressed in clothes more suited to a twelve-year-old, for it was quite apparent that, when the time came, it would be the daughter, with her masses of dark hair, wide-set eyes beneath straight brows, and oval face, upon whom eyes would alight.

In some ways, this extended childhood suited Otis, for she had discovered quite enough restrictions because of her femininity as it was.

Perhaps Emily Hewetson was wiser than she appeared, and thought it better to keep her daughter in prints and aprons than constantly have to remind her that young ladies did not do such-and-such – as now when Otis, with the newspaper secured, raced back up the hotel's main staircase. On the other hand, perhaps she was not at all wise, but was instead a rather vain woman who did not want to be seen to have a grown daughter.

Feeling pleased with herself for having resisted the

temptation to scan the Visitors' List in the foyer, Otis asked eagerly, 'May I look, Ma?'

'If only you will not scrunch the paper – you know how your father hates a scrunched newspaper.'

Kneeling at a low table, Otis respectfully turned over the pages until she found the page with the columns of recently arrived hotel guests and boarding-house visitors. In order of peck, their own hotel, The Grand, with its prime position facing the Common and the sea, came first. She read aloud.
' "Miss Lashbrook. Mrs Preston-Jones. Miss Eunita Truscott. Miss José Dubois." (Oh, Ma, do you think she's French?)'

'Otis, do lower your voice. Even if Miss Dubois did not object to having her name shouted all over the hotel, there are others present on this terrace . . . not everyone is interested in the Visitors' Lists.'

Otis gave her mother a look which Emily Hewetson recognized as very like that of her husband's brother, Max. A knowing, teasing look. 'Of course they are interested, Mother. They pretend that they are looking at the Lists merely to see who else is here, when what they are looking for is to see their own name in the newspaper.'

Emily Hewetson's only consolation in having an enthusiastic and lively daughter was that Otis might have been born a boy, who might well have been even more embarrassingly noisy.

Otis read on. ' "Lieut. Bindon Blood." Ugh!'

'Otis!'

' "Captain Bockett-Pugh. Sir Douglas and Lady Brownrigg", and . . . look, look, here it is, Ma, "Martin Hewetson Esq., Mrs Hewetson" and look, Ma ". . . and Miss Otis Hewetson." '

Otis smiled at the fame of Miss Otis Hewetson, who had in previous years been 'and daughter'.

' "Miss Otis Hewetson". Well, Ma, I am now a real person – there is a compensation for being almost seventeen.'

11

'You may well be right, Otis, but I have yet to discover any evidence of it. There are times when you run away with yourself and behave as though you were eight years old.'

Otis's feelings about her age fluctuated. There were times when she wished to be calm and elegant, to not speak loudly and to remember her manners, but mostly she loved to leap and dash and run and to show her enthusiasm for things. Fortunately, the girls' school she attended was run by a woman who appreciated a girl of Otis's enthusiasm and love of learning, and she had gathered about her teachers of her own kind. Otis had no experience of other schools, so took this coterie of unusually broad-minded teachers for granted. The choice of this school for his daughter was that of Martin Hewetson, her liberal-thinking father.

To blot out the rest of her mother's lecture, Otis ran her eye down the other lists of summer visitors to the lesser hotels and boarding houses. Her heart leapt but she managed to take control of her voice before she uttered, 'Look, Ma!' and jabbed her finger at a column which listed visitors who had taken a private residence for the season. 'It's them! Oh, Ma, how wonderful! Who would ever have expected such a coincidence. May I call on them . . . well, will *you* call on them? Could you do it today?'

The urgency in her daughter's voice did not strike Emily Hewetson as anything out of the ordinary. Otis wanted every request or scheme of hers to be put into practice then and there, at once! Today! Emily Hewetson considered herself to be a most understanding and patient parent, modern in her outlook and allowing a freedom that would not have been permitted in her own day. Putting her theory into practice, she inclined her head in order to see where the rudely jabbing finger pointed and saw, 'At Garden Cottage, Sussex Road, Southsea. Inspector and Mrs George Moth, Mr John Moth, Miss Esther Moth.'

12

Otis scanned her mother's face for a sign that she had mellowed or forgotten the Moth episode at Bognor.

She had not.

'I know what you are thinking, Ma, and you may be right that the Moths are not really *our* sort but . . .'

'I think no such thing. Mrs Moth was a Clermont. And even if she were not, I should like to meet the person who could say that I am not the free-est and easiest of social person. I have no time for snobbery. All I ask of any person old *or young* is that they have mannerliness.'

'Well, you really can't blame Jack and Esther for not having had the chance of a good upbringing, as I have. Mrs Moth is very easy with them, and their father is away from home so much.' Otis was pleased with this argument: it had the merit of praising her mother as well as putting her in a position where she could not fairly refuse a meeting with the young Moths.

'If you are trying to butter me up, miss, so that I will allow you to rush to . . . to this Garden Cottage, then it will not work. Your father must be consulted. He was not pleased at having to witness his wayward daughter and her companions being pulled from the sea . . .'

She had not forgotten – not a single detail.

Otis's mind's eye saw Garden Cottage, saw Esther, saw Jack . . .

'. . . to say nothing of an absolute promise from you.'

. . . saw little Mrs Moth and large Inspector Moth . . .

'And you have not heard a word I've said.'

. . . saw Otis and Esther and Jack playing cricket on the beach, taking threepenny trips round the harbour. Oh, this would be *the* most divine holiday.

Otis snapped back from Garden Cottage. 'I did hear you, Mother.' Saved from having to prove the truth by the entrance of Martin Hewetson, smiling and gay in holiday dress and a straw boater. 'Here's Pa.'

'You are not to . . .'

13

Too late. Otis had leapt up from her kneeling position and was flinging herself at her father in what appeared to be one movement.

'Oh, Pa.' She kissed him warmly. 'What do you think, the Moths are here, in a cottage. And I will promise anything you like if you will let me meet Esther. We are both older this year. Honestly, there would never be another –'

'Hold hard. Hold hard.' Good-humouredly, Martin Hewetson unhooked his daughter's arms from around her neck. 'Tea. First, foremost and before anything – tea!'

And Otis knew that she was forgiven the disgrace of Bognor.

Ten Years in a Portsmouth Slum – R. R. DOLLING, 1896.

'. . . *the children ought to have been boarded out. I doubt if any institutions for children are right, but I have no doubt at all that our present barrack-system is altogether inhuman and scandalous.*'

Nancy Dickenson, cook-general for the summer season to the Moth family, was snatching a read from her library book. She stopped and turned back to page ninety-four: on the facing page was a photograph of her dead brother. It was not the first time she had turned to that page, nor yet the first time that Father Dolling's book had been issued to her from the public library. The photograph facing page ninety-four was not only of her brother, Doug, but also of Father Dolling and twenty men and boys. Nancy read, 'Christmas Party, 1893', and rubbed her finger across Dougie's frowning face, in which she could recognize the likeness to her own, straight-browed features.

Nancy's Mum had said that she must be imagining it, that no four-year-old would be able to take in enough to remember somebody dying. But Nancy knew that her

14

Mum was wrong. She remembered. He had died of 'The Dip'. She remembered Dougie being wrapped in a piece of sailcloth. She remembered her Mum crying and saying, 'A pauper's grave. I never thought any of mine would see a pauper's grave.'

Her Mum thought different now: Dad and three others of Nancy's siblings had gone on a cart wrapped in sailcloth.

Since Nancy had begun reading seriously and sorting things out for herself, she had come to the conclusion that poor people could stand having their noses rubbed in their poverty a lot of the time, but not when it came to burying their own. A funeral with a glass-sided hearse and black horses was the only dignity a dead body had. Sailcloth and a hand-cart was disgrace poured on sorrow.

Nancy was a brisk and practical young woman of twenty-four, not normally given to mooning over photographs of the dead, but Doug was the only member of the Dickenson family ever to have his picture taken. In some way this seemed to make him still alive, and still a boy of ten. They had switched places, and now Nancy sometimes spoke comfortingly to Doug as he used to speak to her at times when their Dad had had a few too many and there was a row going on. And not only that, Doug's picture had been put in Father Dolling's book, which had become so famous that for two years they had had to print more and more of them.

There was also the matter of Nancy's reading.

Nancy's great regret was that she had not paid more attention at school: Well, I never saw the use of it at the time. I could read and write enough as I needed to be a chambermaid. I learned to figure up money all right in my head because when I was only little me and my brothers used to go and help my Uncle Alby on the market – you got to be smart there. 'Penny ha'penny a pound, half a stone for eightpence. Save yourself twopence ha'penny.' Figuring has to come into your mind like a flash. But it's not figuring

15

that gets you anywhere. It's reading – you can find out anything from books.

And so, when she was twenty-one, Nancy Dickenson began determinedly slogging at the rock-face of books from the public library. Three years on she had made footholds, and now read anything and everything that came her way, particularly newspapers: I used to think that they was full of dry old things, but that's not true. You can find out things that are going on all over the world, and about new, restorative drinks and special ointments and things for sale.

Whenever she had the time she went to trawl the shelves of the public library, never coming away without having made a discovery.

'You'll be sorry for that later in life, our Nance, wearing your eyes out like that. I knew an old woman that got cataracts from reading.'

'Lord, Mum, half the old women round here got cataracts, but they never read a word in their lives.'

'Well, they must have done something else to wear out their eyes.'

'More likely from turning out shirt collars by candle-light.'

'Don't start on that again, Nance. We don't need nobody to tell us about conditions in the work-sheds. You won't do yourself nor nobody else no good by keep on about it.'

Nancy shut up for her Mum's sake, but she didn't stop thinking about it.

In the corner of her room now were several copies of *The Times*, unread by Master Jack. These she was gradually going through during the odd five or ten minutes here and there.

Her mistress's silver bell sounded, so she put away Father Dolling and Dougie and went downstairs. She went quickly and willingly because she had been lucky to get this job: it was easy and the family was nice and there was only the mistress, Master Jack and Miss Esther. The master would be down for odd days, but that would not be often. The mistress was easy-going and so nice.

Too easy-going with the master by the look of her – she's over seven months gone and she must be forty if she's a day, but it don't seem to trouble her much. Like a cat that got the cream when she sits in the garden.

The money was only average, but the time off was the best Nancy had ever known. Miss Esther didn't play up as only daughters sometimes did, and Master Jack kept his hands to himself, standing aside for her to pass as though she wasn't a servant – very polite. Jolly Jack was the name she gave him in her mind.

SOUTHSEA PLEASURE PIER

Poor Father. There are no p.cards depicting G'den Cott. I'll do a watercolour and send it so that you may imagine us. I think it horrid that you have to be detecting m'derers instead of riding the merry-go-rounds with me and J. Do arrest him soon and come here. It is a sweet cott. with a well. Esther

---

Esther Moth rushed through the cottage with a page torn from the same local paper as Otis Hewetson had kept smooth for her father. 'Mother, look! You'll never guess.'

'And I'm sure that I will not get the chance to guess, because you will have to tell me or burst.'

'The Hewetsons are here!'

'Here, as calling at the house? Or here, as in the town?'

'They're listed in the new arrivals at The Grand.'

'And if I know them, that is precisely what it will be.'

'Mo-*ther*! If you knew them better you would soon change your mind. They are not at all grand. Otis is the best company one could wish.'

'You may be right, dear, but I have no desire to go out of my way to renew the acquaintanceship.' She smoothed her

17

protruding abdomen. 'Or anyone else who may be holiday-ing in the town. We have taken this place so that I may rest.'

Esther Moth pressed her cheek against the equally blooming one of her mother. 'And I shall see to it that you do. I promised Father and I mean to do it.' She had every intention of seeking out Otis Hewetson and renewing their friendship, which had been cut short four years ago. In order to placate her conscience, she went into the tiny scullery and made her mother some fresh lemon with chilly water drawn from the well.

'Mother, would you mind if I went to the pillar-box and took a walk across the Common? I might meet Jack.'

'Just so long as Nancy knows and is within hearing.'

Esther climbed the steep, narrow stairs to Nancy's little room where the servant was on her bed reading.

'I have to go out, Nancy. I know it's your off-time, but would you just keep an ear open for Mother?'

'I was about to go down to start the supper.'

'It's just that a friend I know is staying at The Grand, and I would stroll by on the chance that she's looking out.'

Nancy nodded and smiled. 'Wouldn't they just let you call there?'

'Well, I'm not sure if we are speaking – not me and my friend, you couldn't stop *us* speaking – but our families. There was a bit of a contretemps.'

'It'll blow over no doubt, miss. These things always do. But you're wise to do a bit of a reconnoitre in the circumstances – before going in with both feet, like.'

Nancy interested Esther. She was not at all like any servant they had ever had. She was good-tempered and showed a great deal of concern for Mother. She was polite but not obsequious, and you knew somehow that she would not sneer at you behind your back.

'You've always got your head in a book or newspaper, Nancy.'

'It's the best place to put it, miss. Don't you like reading?'

18

'Only average. What are you reading?'

Nancy held up a cheap news-sheet. 'I don't know as the mistress would approve of me showing you.'

'Oh, Nancy!' Scornfully.

'It's the *Dreadnought* my young man Wally sent me. It's to do with votes for women and that kind of stuff.'

Esther's eyebrows shot up. 'Suffragettes! Mother would not mind, but you had better not let Father see that: he doesn't approve of them breaking the law.'

Nancy smiled cheekily. 'Well, he wouldn't, would he, being a policeman and all? Don't worry, miss, I knows how hot under the collar a lot of men gets – I *mean*, you've only got to ask a question about it and they want to lock you up.'

'You know that my father is in the police force, then?'

'Oh yes, miss. He's a London detective, worked on that murder of the Haymarket prostitute. Anyway, it says Inspector in the Lists.'

Again Esther's brows arched. 'Not so loud, Nancy. I'm not supposed to know words like prostitute. The girl was a music-hall singer.'

Nancy grinned. 'All right, miss. And don't worry, I'll see the mistress is well looked after while you're out. There's six younger than me, and I helped my ma with birthing some of the young ones. She'd probably have had more if my pa hadn't fell down the side of a ship in the docks and drowned.'

The thought of Nancy helping with a birth occupied Esther Moth's thoughts on the short walk to the Common where The Grand Hotel was situated.

Twice she walked the footpaths, keeping her eye on the hotel, but there was no sign of Otis. She thought she saw Jack at a distance, walking along the promenade, but she decided that she did not want his company just now, she preferred thinking about Nancy and what it must be like to birth a baby. Probably quite horrible.

Jack Moth flicked half a dozen identical postcards with their identical messages into the King's Road pillar-box. He and his sister were as physically unalike as were their parents. Jack was over-sized and growing broad-bodied like their giant of a father. Esther Moth, like her faintly blue-blooded mother, had fair, crisp hair and a petiteness that gave her the misleading appearance of fragility. There was a likeness though in Jack and Esther's straight noses, large eyes, fringed with thick lashes, and generous, sensuous mouths.

The music-hall song that went '. . . a'bossin' of a feller who was six-foot-four and her only five-foot-two' might have been written about Inspector and Mrs Moth. However, the lines following –

> They hadn't been married but a month nor more,
> When underneath her thumb goes Jim.
> Isn't it a pity that the likes of her,
> Should put upon the likes of him?

– were not apt. Nobody, least of all the happy-go-lucky and sweet-natured Anne Moth, put upon the likes of Detective-Inspector Moth. She did though, in her own way, usually get him to see things from her viewpoint. And so it was with Jack and his sister.

Once Jack had posted his cards, he sauntered around wondering how he was going to amuse himself for weeks in this place. It was an agreeable enough town with sufficient entertainment for a fortnight, but he would have to see whether he might escape from time to time and perhaps meet a fellow or two. His old school was Winchester, which was only an hour or so train journey, and he had addresses of old boys who had homes in Hampshire. But, standing in for Father, it was unlikely that he'd be able to get away for more than a morning now and then.

So Jack, being practical and uncomplaining about the unalterable, turned his mind to how to fill the eight weeks. A pity there weren't still snipe to be had beyond Southsea Castle – it was all built up there now. He fired an imaginary shot-gun at a passing seagull which fired back, streaking one of the blue stripes of his cream jacket.

'Damn you, bird!' He raised his straw hat at a passing gentleman in apology for his language. The gentleman acknowledged and suggested quickly sponging the mess at the drinking fountain.

The fountain was a fine, cast-iron affair, with spurts for people and little troughs at the base for dogs. Holding his handkerchief over the spout, he pushed the plunger, which responded with a great gush down his fashionable trousers and into his light shoes. 'Damn! Damn!' quietly through gritted teeth.

He dabbed at his trousers until his handkerchief was sopping, he then applied it to the unwanted white stripe down his arm. He became aware that he was being watched. By a young lady sitting beneath a young holm oak only yards from where he floundered inelegantly. As though it mattered not a jot, he abandoned attending to his clothes.

'Would you care to use this?' The young lady held out a large, rolled-up towel. 'It is only slightly used. I tested the sea, but it was rather cold.' Her voice was clear and rather deep and heavy which, he decided when he thought of it later, sounded as though it was lubricated with cream and honey. A singer? A contralto perhaps?

She was very lovely, vibrant, elegant, desirable and altogether the type of woman Jack imagined himself escorting, dining, dancing with, strolling with. She was also older than Jack, and he especially liked older women – particularly beautiful ones. He raised his hat to her.

'That is most obliging of you, but I'm afraid I should soil your towel.'

'That doesn't matter, it has to be laundered. Here, let me.' And before he could protest she had moistened one corner of the towel at the fountain and, with light, pinching movements, removed the seagull mark.

'There! If you give it a brush when it's dry to bring up the nap, it will be like new.'

In the two minutes from the offer of the towel to the final smoothing down of his dampened sleeve, Jack Moth had fallen in love. Not only because she was elegant, desirable, et cetera, but because she had such an unaffected manner. Because she was bold. Jack loved the idea of a bold woman. Forward, would be the description his mother would have given. Modern, Esther would have said. She was all of these. Also, she was an older woman. His entire body twanged with the tension she had built up within him.

Jack Moth was smitten by a bold, modern woman. An older woman. Suddenly eight weeks seemed to be such a short period of time. He must waste none of it.

She began to roll up her towel.

'Please.' He took the towel from her. 'You must allow me to . . .'

'Nonsense, it will go to the hotel laundry.' She took it back.

Jack too must be bold. 'Please. It will give me an opportunity to see you again.' He took the other end of the towel, which unrolled revealing its woven identification. He read aloud, ' "Beach Mansions". Beach Mansions?'

'It is on South Parade. And you, do you live here?'

'Oh, just a cottage for the summer, with my mother and young sister.' Usually he ignored as much as possible his mother's condition, but he felt that he could easily have mentioned it to this woman with whom he was linked by a length of Indian cotton.

'And if I allow you to take it, who then would launder this great thing? You mother, your sister?'

'We have a servant, and a washer-woman.'

She tugged at the towel. 'Then there is no question of it. I shall take it back to the hotel.' She looked at him boldly, maturely. 'Unless you would care to accept a condition.'

A bold challenge. Jack's heart leapt. He grew mature. Suave. A modern man, a man of this modern age. 'I accept your condition.' He tilted back his head and met her eye, smiling.

'Well then, you undertake to launder it yourself.'

Not visibly shaken, he said, 'Done!'

'With absolutely no help from servant or washer-woman.'

'Absolutely none.' He rolled up his prize and tucked it under his arm. 'And I shall return it to Beach Mansions tomorrow.'

'I shall look forward to receiving it. It is unlikely that I shall be there, but you may leave it with the porter.'

Jack's face fell: his purpose had not been to effect an encounter with an hotel porter. 'I should prefer to deliver it directly to you . . . to be sure that you get it.'

'I am afraid that I really do not know my movements. My time is not my own. I am not in Southsea for pleasure . . . no, that is not true . . . pleasure or satisfaction is to do with it, but . . . oh well, never mind. I am likely to be eating a light lunch on South Parade Pier at about midday.' And, picking up the canvas bag that had contained the towel, she began to take her leave of him.

'Wait.' He laid fingers on her arm. Soft, warm, firm within the sleeve of her plain white cotton blouse. A thrilling arm with a surprisingly hard muscle. The arm of a mature woman. The contact was intoxicating. 'I don't know your name.'

Clearly, frankly, boldly, proudly, she announced, 'Victoria Ormorod,' and held out her hand and shook Jack's own firmly. 'And yours?'

'Moth. John. Clermont. Moth. Not double-barrelled – Clermont was Mother's . . . I'm called Jack.'

'Jack Moth. A nice, orderly name. It suits you.' She smiled, and was briskly gone through the avenue of holm oak without a backward glance.

Victoria Ormorod. Miss Victoria Ormorod. That name had existed in the world since the time of his birth and Jack Moth had not known. That copper hair, that wonderful figure, the thrilling voice and the beautiful face had existed in the world and Jack Moth had, until minutes ago, no inkling of it.

Victoria Ormorod. A rallying name, not the name of a singer. Perhaps a model for Womanhood in symbolic marble statues. He imagined her sculpted as 'Justice', or 'Victory', her splendid figure revealed by a breeze blowing her diaphanous drapes. Victoria.

Victoria Moth? Oh, what a depletion of so splendid a name.

Nancy Dickenson had been born in Portsea, ten minutes' walk away from Garden Cottage. A ten-minute walk but, for residents of elegant and wealthy Southsea, an unbridgeable distance. They knew that Portsea existed, of course – why should they not know, seeing that it existed within easy walking distance – but Southsea knew as little of Portsea as Vladivostok knew of Cincinnati.

Much the same applied to the Portsea families, who often spent most of their lives in the dockland area without so much as walking over the boundaries into Portsmouth or Southsea, the large stores and shops of which were only one mile distant. Portsea, Portsmouth and Southsea were, for most civic purposes, a single entity, with a tram service and railway station serving all. It was not, though, a single entity to the people of the Portsea dockland area; to those many long-established families, theirs was an entirely separate community. Generations having lived, worked, married and died within it, never needing or wishing to go outside.

Nancy Dickenson was different. Although she was born into one of those old dockland families, she now found that Portsea was becoming too tight, too restricting. She had dreams of going places and doing things. Nancy worked in Southsea and her Mum lived in Portsea. During the tourist season Nancy lived in. In recent years she had been quite lucky.

'It's a lot better doing holiday-let domestic. I always

hated hotel work, hardly any money in it, if it wasn't for tips. Fetching and carrying, clearing up and laying up from morning to night. Kids bringing in jellyfish and seaweed and hiding them in the po-cupboard till they stink rotten; people leaving sopping towels on the floor. Wouldn't do for my mum, she'd whop your ear smartish. Lord! you should see some of the things I've seen, you would never credit it. They wouldn't do it in their own homes – perhaps they would, though. This mistress is different, about the best I've ever had. People behave better in holiday lets than they do in hotels. I stopped being surprised at hotel guests donkey's years ago.'

How many years ago? It could not have been too many, for by the time that she was doing cook-general work for the Moths, she was still only twenty-four years old. But she had left school at thirteen, so that she had eleven years' service to look back on.

Working for her present mistress suited Nancy just right, for the lady read books all day whilst resting her water-logged legs, and so sent Nancy frequently to the library with a list. Nancy was surprised to discover that many on the list were romantic novels, which Nancy had always assumed only shop-girls and domestics read. Nancy had tried one or two and, though she had quite enjoyed them, had found them to be all much of a muchness, the girl always ending up getting married which, from Nancy's observation, wasn't much of a prize, even though she was really keen on Wally who drove a London tram and had courted her from a distance.

Nancy was concerned for her kindly mistress and her bloated condition. My mum had legs like that every time she was in the family way. It's water that don't get peed out properly. It goes away soon as the baby's born. It was the midwife that told me about water in the legs: first time I helped my mum, and her waters broke, I thought that must be what it was, you know, water coming out of her legs – like a boil bursting.

Mrs Moth liked Nancy.

And even though Nancy was only twenty-four, Anne Moth felt quite secure with her. There were still several weeks before her confinement, which was to be in a London clinic, but should anything untoward occur, then Nancy was the kind of person one wanted around at such a time. There was not a lot of work to be done in the cottage. No fires because it was summer, no range or boiler – the old place had been thoroughly modernized, with gas laid on and good plumbing. Jack seemed to like eating out at what dubious places his mother did not know or want to. So cooking amounted to a breakfast of eggs and bacon, a light lunch for Mrs Moth and Esther, then supper for the three at six o'clock. All of which, plus the employment of a washer-woman and a weekly odd-job man, left Nancy with more time to read than she had ever had before. A kind of bond existed between servant and mistress, both of whom devoured books.

'Your last choice of books was excellent, Nancy. I will leave it to you to select two more for me.'

Anne Moth thought how George would have drawn his mouth down at the idea of having one's servant choose one's reading material, and how Mama would have disapproved, and her sisters would have tut-tutted and re-affirmed the twice-told tale that Anne's behaviour had always been extreme – witness her behaviour when it came to choosing a husband. But George was not here to comment on the easy-going relationship, nor Mama and the sisters.

'Nothing too taxing, Nancy. Something a touch romantic. With a happy ending. Try to find one set in Paris . . . oh, how I loved Paris when I was a girl. How I loved everything when I was a girl.'

When she reached the library, Nancy came across a knot of people in hot discussion with a uniformed town hall doorman who, having realized that he had lost the battle, retreated into the protection of the grandiose public building. His parting shot, '*Sweated labour!* You lot wouldn't know sweat if it hit you in the eye. Clear off or I'll have the lor on you', was drowned by a dozen female voices singing.

As would any servant encountering something interesting when out on an errand, Nancy sauntered to see what would happen.

A woman was issuing handbills to anyone who would accept them. Having read it, Nancy enquired whether they were members of the NUWSS.

'We are!' She spread her arms to encompass the other girls and women. 'The National Union of Women's Suffrage Societies.'

'Suffragettes.'

'Not too much like them. Suffrag*ists*. Universal suffrage. We are for *all* women – the "have-nots" as well as the "haves". Look, we are holding a meeting in Portsmouth, could you come? It's in the evening. We like local women to act as stewards. Would you do it?'

'Oh, I don't know about that.'

'Please. You wouldn't be alone, there are other Portsmouth women helping. The NUWSS is not only fighting for the vote, at this meeting we are campaigning for better working conditions for the shirtmakers. You see naval officers everywhere in this town, but did you know that the girls who make their uniforms do so on starvation wages?'

'Do I know? Better than most. I've lived all my whole life with them, I'd be one myself if I hadn't got a bit of luck and got into hotel work.'

'Perfect! The perfect steward. You *must* join us. You belong with us.'

From her reading of the *Dreadnought* and her association with Wally, she was not entirely ignorant of the women's movement, but it was never wise to let everybody know everything about you first off. 'I wouldn't be no use in chaining myself up or knocking off copper's hats. I've got my living to earn.'

'Of course you couldn't, neither could we. That's the difference between the NUWSS and the Pankhursts: they can afford to pay fines and if they go to prison they have servants to see to their homes and families. I'm not saying that they are not brave, but they are in a position to choose to be. We believe that we can win our cause by public acclaim through rational argument and democracy.'

The young woman's eyes shone, and Nancy felt her own cheeks begin to burn by association.

'We *know* that working women and poor women and women with family duties cannot afford the luxury of martyrdom or imprisonment. But of course with your first-hand experience you will know this.'

Nancy wondered whether the woman always talked as though she was making a speech. Even so, she felt that she was with someone of like mind.

'Women like yourself are the most valued in our movement, Miss . . . ?'

'Dickenson, Nancy Dickenson.'

'You could be invaluable as a member. Come to our meeting, Nancy, we are in desperate need of stewards.'

'All right, then. I will!' Nancy said, thrilled at having committed herself to something that Wally would approve of. 'All right, I'll give it a try.'

After much negotiation with her parents, Otis squeezed an agreement out of them.

'I will go thus far, Otis. I shall send Mrs Moth a note inviting her to take tea on the terrace, and we shall then see what we shall see. But I am making no promises. I doubt that Mrs Moth is over-anxious to make your acquaintance again after two of her children ended up in the sea the last time you were together.' She glanced to try to catch out her daughter in a blush or other tell-tale discomfiture, but Otis remained sanguine.

Otis observed her mother's glance and wanted to protest: All that took place ages ago when we were young. But she knew the tensile strength of her mother's affability and how far it would stretch before it snapped. So she was pleasantly quiet.

Later that week, on receipt of a reply from Garden Cottage, Mrs Hewetson exclaimed in an undertone, 'Goodness, Martin! Mrs Moth is seven months gone with another child.'

Otis, who was assumed to be out of overhearing range, swivelled her eyes so as to watch her father's reaction. 'Good Lord! the woman must be forty if she's a day.'

'And the son is all of nineteen.'

'And Esther is nearly my age,' observed Otis, unable to contain herself at the extraordinary news about Mrs Moth.

Her mother raised her eyebrows. She had given up saying, 'Little rabbits have long ears' – but it was in her expression.

'You'd best do as she requests, Em, and you call upon them. And least said, soonest mended, regarding the other thing. You know?'

Otis knew. Least said about the to-do with the children at Bognor, when Otis had, without permission, gone out in a hired dinghy with Esther and Jack Moth, and they had all been pulled out of the sea without a stitch of clothing on and a very thin explanation.

'Not "them" apparently. Only Mrs Moth is there, alone with the children.' At her father's short tt-tt, Otis noticed that Jack – the son who a moment ago was all of nineteen – was now a child. 'And you know, Martin, she does have some very good' – voice lowered – 'connections. It can do no harm to know a member of the Clermont family.'

Otis of course knew everything of Mrs Moth's connections, as Esther had told her in Bognor. 'Mother's people are the most awful bores. She was a Clermont. They are all Honourables or something. The only thing they like is killing birds and fishing. My mother is supposed to be terribly well-off, not that you'd know because Father will not allow show. I think it's because he's a policeman and he's afraid people will think he married her for her money. But he didn't, Mother threatened to run away when they weren't going to let her marry him. We don't feel well-off, except that when I see the way that other policemen's families live I realize that we are better off – our house, Jack being sent to Winchester and now university . . .'

Otis thought that a love-affair between a penniless policeman and an Honourable must have been terribly romantic. Especially as Inspector Moth was very big and had probably been as handsome as Jack when he was younger.

When Esther had said with candour, 'People can't afford Winchester for their sons on a policeman's income', Otis had been quite shocked, having been taught that it was bad form to talk about money and income and affording things.

31

And getting to know people with connections. Pa, being a partner in a large practice of solicitors, relied quite a lot on connections, but one did not say so. The thing that Otis had loved most about that summer in the company of Esther and Jack Moth was their openness and candour. They could discuss anything that came into their heads, and apparently were encouraged to do so by their mother at least.

It was as a result of this attitude that they had all got into that final bit of trouble at Bognor. It had come about because Otis had mentioned her curiosity to Esther, saying that the only naked male she had seen was in an art gallery.

Esther had said, 'Come out with us. Jack is going to hire a boat. He likes to dive off the side. I go with him. He likes to swim in his skin, he read that that's how pearl-divers do it – they are terribly brave, you know. Jack likes to try out things he reads about. He's never embarrassed about things like that, I don't think boys are; all the boy cousins swim naked at Mere, Uncle Norbert's place. Nobody thinks much of it. I should love to, but Uncle Norbert will never let the girls.'

'I *couldn't!* I should be too embarrassed to look.'

'Rubbish! You know you wouldn't. I *say*, why don't we try it, it would be lovely. Oh *do*, Otis.'

Although she longed to keep up with the kind of tricks that the Moths were always involved in, Otis had blushed hotly at the idea, but Esther argued that if God made the human body, then there could not be anything wrong in looking at it. So Otis had asked herself what could possibly be wrong in seeing a young man's parts in the flesh when she had seen them in marble, and what was wrong with anybody swimming naturally, and had received her own reply: there is nothing wrong.

They had their daring swim. Clambering back in, the little boat had capsized and all their clothes had been lost. They had been picked up naked as babes by some fishermen.

32

And there was quite a to-do in the Hewetson household.

Emily Hewetson, not knowing of course where to put her face for shame, had at once packed up and they had returned to London. Martin Hewetson said that it would have been better to stay; after all they were still only children and children did some wild things. Anne Moth said that they were very foolish children to take out such an unstable boat, and next time to be sure that they told her where they were going. Nobody knew what Inspector Moth said for he was, as usual, working on a murder investigation and not holidaying with his family.

Some good came out of it though. Otis had had wonderfully enhancing experiences. Of waves surging against her naked skin; of linking arms with Jack and Esther and treading water and bobbing about in a circle game; of seeing beneath the water their bodies looking like fluid glass in the filtered light, and of the utmost freedom of movement. She had seen the human body at its best. Buoyed up by water, youthful, healthy and graceful. She was thereafter more knowledgeable about the differences between people that are usually disguised. She began to love the changes that were taking part in her own figure when she saw the common features of femininity in Esther's black pelt and small swellings. And the marble Hermes that had first provoked her curiosity did not seem half so much a work of art as did Jack's warm flesh when poised to dive.

Otis had accepted the deprivation from her punishment and had behaved in the contrite manner her bewildered mother sought, but she had never regretted the escapade – except that it had separated her from the Moths.

Emily Hewetson looked a picture of elegance as she set out on the ten-minute walk from The Grand to Sussex Road. She walked slowly, wonderfully aware of the way her bosom greatly protruded and her waist curved and her hips swelled with the assistance of her new straight-fronted black and blue broché corset. It had cost twenty-three shillings and sixpence but its effect upon her Japon gown with its gauged back made it worth every farthing. If a woman was not blessed with the ancestry of a Clermont, it was possible to compensate through one's appearance. And at the moment, Mrs Moth was in a condition which Mrs Hewetson would have loathed. At nearly forty! The experience of Otis had been bad enough, but to be like that again when one had a son who was a man was beyond anything. Surely the woman had someone to advise her, if it was only a physician. Every woman of class must know that it was perfectly possible to protect oneself and to arrange with one's husband to dispose of his ardour safely.

At first, Otis was to have been left behind. But she eventually persuaded her mother that her present behaviour would be evidence of how responsible and grown-up she had become. She did not look grown-up in her cotton skirt and tammy hat.

They almost passed by Garden Cottage, overborne as it was by a smart Thomas Ellis Owen villa. Hidden behind an iron gate in a high wall and standing at the far end of a stone walkway, the strange-looking castellated cottage could scarcely be seen from the road for the large spread of a fig tree.

Nancy Dickenson bobbed an inch or two of curtsy and said that her mistress was in the garden and would madam and miss come through. The term 'garden' had brought to Mrs Hewetson's mind her own green Lavender Hill garden and, in view of the long approach and its name, she had expected something other than what it was. Mrs Moth was seated, legs raised, on a wheeled wicker, much cushioned, cruise chair, in a tiny courtyard that literally brimmed with true geraniums, climbing roses, clematis, tall citronella lilies, furry pulsatilla, little yellow Welsh poppies and cascading lobelia. It was as though Anne Moth was seated in a bowl of flowers.

'What a charming place,' said Mrs Hewetson graciously, once they had formally greeted one another.

'It is as much as we need. Esther and Jack are out of the house much of the time. George, my husband, discovered it. He has the knack for such things.'

The ladies now being settled, and Otis having presented a bob and having given polite replies to Mrs Moth's enquiries as to her health, Esther was given leave to show Otis the cottage and take her into the front courtyard to drink cordial made with cold well-water.

At first meeting the girls smiled a little shyly as they each weighed up the changes and waited patiently to be free of their mothers' observation of their manners. Now they flung their arms about one another and gave unladylike bear-hugs.

'Esther! You've been and gorn and become a lady.' Otis put on the funny common accent that had so amused them at Bognor.

'Nar I ain't, it's only me cloves.' Esther wasn't as good at it as Otis, who had a good ear for mimicry.

They hugged again, neither of them disappointed by finding the other too different from the memory.

'Come through, there's a nice sunny wall at the front of the house.' Esther led the way through the ground floor of the cottage which comprised a kitchen-cum-scullery, a little dining-room, a study, a small sitting-room and a large hallway.

'What an amazing place,' Otis said. 'From outside it looks like a fairy house, I thought it must be like the weavers' homes we saw when Pa took us to Yorkshire.'

'It's because it's long and narrow. Five bedrooms and the usual offices.'

'Oh, don't spoil it, Esther. I want to go on thinking of it as a magic house – tiny on the outside but large within, like something Alice would have come upon when she went through the looking-glass.'

'Otis. It is so wonderful that you are here, saying your imaginative things. Nobody has said anything interesting or original to me since Bognor.'

Otis made a face. 'Oh, Bognor. That's the real reason my ma is calling on your mother. She's testing the water. She doesn't think that we are a good influence on one another. Does yours?'

'I don't believe she thinks much at all these days about me or Jack. She just sits around holding her bump. It moves, you know.'

'Moves? Her . . . ?'

'It twitches. It's the baby wriggling about. It's called "quickening". If you watch closely you can see little bits of lace on Mother's dress seeming to move of their own accord.'

'I never knew they moved before they came. I thought that they were – well – like new dolls wrapped in tissue-paper in a kind of box.'

'They move all the time. When they are ready to be born, they turn a somersault and go head down.'

Otis was always amazed at Esther's great store of facts. 'How did you get to know? I could never find out a thing like that.'

'Ma doesn't mind talking to me. Mostly I just listen. Father never lowers his voice so that even if one is in the next room it is possible to hear quite clearly what he says.' She put on a sober 'father' face. ' "What d'you think, Annie, that little miss they fished out of the river, she'd been tupped." All one needs then is to look up "tupped" and you find out something else.'

'My pa never says anything interesting. Lawyers never do. Uncle Hewey says that there is no talk as boring as that of lawyers. And Uncle Hew's a lawyer so he should know. Esther, what is being tupped?'

'It's what I told you about before we went out in the dinghy.'

36

'Sexual congress you mean?'

'Lord above, Otis, keep your voice down.'

Grinning, Otis said in a whisper, 'I think tupping is a much better word.'

'Just as long as you don't say it in front of relations or company.'

Esther arranged cushions in a little alcove created by the old garden wall and some trellis, up which grew pink roses entwined with sweet peas and clematis. She poured the cool drink in which slices of lemon floated, and offered cat's-tongue biscuits.

'Esther! you remembered my favourites.'

They caught each other's glance and, holding the gaze, smiled at one another with looks that only young girls who hold one another's secrets sacredly can give one another.

'Oh Otis, I feel so happy. Nothing has changed has it? We are still the same friends we were at Bognor. Four years and yet I don't feel even slightly strange with you. The times I have wished that you were my sister or that we lived close.'

'And I. But my parents would never have let me continue the friendship. They are only doing so now because we are bound to meet one another daily in a small town such as Southsea.'

'Why were they so very upset? You must have disobeyed them before, and every child tells its parents lies once in a while. It wasn't such a terrible thing to do to say that you were going to the lending library but to go out in a dinghy instead. And you wouldn't have drowned, you know, we weren't very far off shore.'

'It wasn't the danger. It was our bare . . . chests and Jack's . . . you know.' She stifled a giggle, feeling childish but unable to do anything about it.

Esther's mouth twitched. 'Don't start that, Otis, or we shall be well and truly banned. There's nothing suggests to parents bad goings-on so much as girls giggling. I give you that gem of information for nothing. What did your mother

37

think Jack was up to that they should whisk you away from us like that?'

Otis put on her very straight face. 'Tupping me I shouldn't wonder.'

Esther exploded and spilled lemonade.

'Hush, Esther!' Otis said, grinning herself.

They were both suddenly sobered and hushed by the clanging open of the iron gate.

'Hang me if it isn't the notorious Otis Hewetson.' Jack Moth whisked off his straw boater, gallantly took Otis's hand, and placed his lips warmly upon it.

'Jack?'

Oh, he was *handsome*.

'As ever was. Was that "Jack" a query? Don't I look the very soul of Jack Moth?'

He was *so* handsome. So tall and manly. And so . . . *handsome*. Such thick crisp curls, such a broad forehead, such large eyes, such wide manly shoulders and long, long legs. *He must be fearfully impressive now, diving from a dinghy.* He was looking so closely at her that she blushed to think that her thoughts might show in her face.

'No . . . No, you don't at all, you have grown into a man.'

'Lordy, Lordy, Miss Otis, and what pray would you have me grow into . . . a big geriller?'

Otis laughed. 'Well at least you sound like Jack.' Suddenly she felt shy of him, of his hand still holding hers, of his inspection of her, of his genuine pleasure at seeing her again. She felt gauche and awkward. Since she had last seen him he had grown from a cheeky and slightly outrageous youth to a young man with grace and a modern manner.

She tried to find a safe place to rest her gaze, but he was a minefield for her, particularly when she could not eradicate the vision of him as he had been, stripped to his white skin and poised to dive from the dinghy again and again. Unembarrassed, a little proud of himself, he had enjoyed flouting convention. Perhaps he boasted of such things to his friends. Perhaps it had been a dare. Unexpected thoughts tumbled through her mind and she blushed even more deeply.

He must have noticed but he put her at once at ease. 'I say, Esther, I'm roasting. Aren't you, Otis? I'll ask Nancy to dig out some of her famous water ices from the ice-box.' Skimming his hat on to the hatstand inside, he went into the cottage.

Otis followed him with her gaze. 'That's Jack? I can scarcely credit it, Esther. I thought you had become grown-up, Esther, but Jack . . .'

'Oh, you shouldn't place too much credit on the outside, that's how they all are at university. He's still Jack underneath. I'll tell you a secret about him. He's in love.'

Dressed as she was in her print cotton, with her hair tied back in a ribbon and a childish tammy on her head, Otis knew for sure that it was not herself with whom Jack Moth was in love. And that knowledge poured vinegar into her wounded, fragile heart.

Suddenly she hated her mother for her vanity. People were not so stupid as to believe that Otis was still a child so that Emily Hewetson could pass for something just over thirty. Girls didn't have breasts, didn't have Eve's curse, didn't feel dizzy with love for a man.

No matter what the cost, Otis Hewetson was determined to be allowed to become as much a young woman as was Esther. At once! Now! She would stun Jack Moth into noticing that she was no longer a girl.

LANDING STAGE, PORTSMOUTH.

Grandmother, The organization here is surprisingly gd. More of that anon. I prepd for a sea-bathe but the Solent Waters are chilly. I know that you set great store by immersion in sea-water, and I promise that I shall try again. Into the fray. I shall not let you down. My love to Aunt K. & all children. Yrs with gt affction, Vicky

'*Voilà!*' Jack Moth flourished the neatly parcelled towel as he presented it to Victoria Ormorod.

'Jack Moth. I never thought to see my towel again and that I should find its cost added to my hotel account.'

He made a funny tragic face. 'Madam, did you doubt my ability to complete so simple a task?'

'Simple to a woman, true, but I know few men who would know how to go about the laundering of a towel.' She indicated that he might take the seat opposite. 'I am awaiting a tray of tea and sandwiches from the pier tea-house if you would care to join me.'

In a flash he cunningly moved the chair closer to her and sat down. 'Nothing would give me more pleasure. Waves lapping, sunshine, the smell of ozone in the company of the most extraordinary woman I ever set eyes on.'

'Mr Moth! Are you always so forward with acquaintances of five minutes?'

'Not forward, but eager. Five minutes or five years, I know everything I ever need to know about you. That you are extraordinary and if I live to be a hundred I shall never meet the likes of Victoria Ormorod again.'

Her eyes crinkled when she laughed at his nonsense.

A small boy with oiled hair dressed in a long white apron brought her tray of tea and sandwiches, went away, then brought another for Jack.

Hungrily he bit a dainty sandwich in two and put the whole in his mouth. 'Tell me about Victoria Ormorod.'

'Two minutes ago you said that you knew everything about Victoria Ormorod.'

'Everything I ever *need* to know. Tell me what I wish to know: where you live, what you like, have you a cat, do you like boiled fish, can you play the violin?'

'Jack Moth, I shall tell you nothing until you tell me what *I* wish to know.'

'I lay the book of my life open before you.'

'What I wish to know is, who laundered the towel?'

He placed his hand on his breast. 'I swear before my Maker that John Clermont Moth did launder the afore-mentioned towel.'

She refilled her cup, exaggerating her expression of doubt as she did so. 'Unassisted?'

'Well, M'Lud, it depends on your definition of "un-assisted". It was necessary for me to take my sister into my confidence and it was she who versed me in the art of twisting out the water. I say, did you know how jolly heavy a towel of this size is when it is waterlogged?'

'Yes, I know very well, having wrung out many a towel by hand.'

'Then you are a laundry-maid by night and a princess by day.'

'Is this a piece of information that you *wish* to know?'

'It matters not one jot. If you are a laundry-maid then I ask only to have the privilege of meeting you here again tomorrow.'

The lightheartedness went from her face. 'I did tell you that my time here is not my own. I have work to do. Don't look so downcast, I have enjoyed our al fresco meal enormously. It seems ages since I had such a jolly companion.'

Suddenly Jack Moth saw the possibility of her walking away from the pier and him never seeing her again. 'Please. Meet me at least once. I must beg at least that.'

'I cannot promise. I often do not know where I shall be from one day to the next.'

'But I cannot let you simply walk out of my life.' He reached out and clutched at her fingers. 'At least give me an address. I haven't the least idea where you are from. I will tell you mine, and my college if you wish it.'

She looked down at his hand and looked a bit perturbed, though she did not withdraw her fingers, and said, 'Jack Moth. Jack Moth.'

'Whilst I am in Southsea with my family, I stay at Garden Cottage, Sussex Road.'

'I must go.'

'May I walk with you?'

She signalled to the table boy.

'Oh, I see that he has put both trays on one bill. I hope that you will not kick and scream if I settle it.' Without waiting for his reply, in a manner that was both masculine and delicately feminine, she gave the boy a florin, picked up a small document case and the brown-wrapped towel, and held out her hand to Jack. 'Thank you for your company, Jack Moth.'

Had any other woman done such a thing as to settle a bill like that, Jack Moth would have been acutely embarrassed and affronted. But this woman, this bold Victoria Ormorod, paid for his lunch as though the action meant nothing. And he let her.

Side by side they walked in the direction of the roadway: she did not look down as women did to make sure that they did not slip between the slats and into the sea; he searched wildly for some way of keeping contact with her. He dropped his bantering manner. 'Look, if I were to write you a letter, where could I send it?'

'Jack Moth.' She scolded gently. 'Just like your name-sake, you are flitting too close to a flame. You will get burnt. Let our delightful meeting stay as one of those encounters – a memory for us to store away and bring out embellished and glittering for our grandchildren, who will never believe that we were once young enough for such nonsense.'

'If it is nonsense to you, I am in earnest. You see me as just a young man who has been carried away, but you have made me wise. If you do not let me have your address, then I shall write to Beach Mansions and they will have to forward it to you.'

She smiled. He watched as the corners of her greenish eyes crinkled. She said, 'Oh, *what* persistence. Very well. Anything sent care of this address will find me.' She handed him an empty envelope upon which was a Hampshire address.

'The Jarrett O'Mahoney Memorial Home?'

'It is an orphanage. My grandmother rules there. Be careful, she eats young men for breakfast.'

He put the envelope into his inner breast pocket, holding it safe from without. 'I shall come here again tomorrow. In case you do come.'

They had reached the front of the pier and were suddenly out on the pavement. 'My hotel is just across the road, I must go, I have some people to meet there.'

Reluctantly he let her go and stood watching the sway of her hips and the movement of her skirt. She reached the roadway, stopped, put her finger to her lips with a pondering action, then she turned and came back to Jack Moth. 'Do you know Portsmouth?'

'Of course, I walk there almost daily, it's scarcely a mile from where we are staying.'

'Next Tuesday I shall be attending a meeting there – the town hall. You may not wish to be concerned, but that is where I shall be.'

He spontaneously clasped her hand. 'Thank you, thank you. Have no fear, I *shall* be concerned if you are there.'

And she was gone, tripping lightly between the strolling parasols, errand boys and carriages.

Once Emily Hewetson had talked with the languid Mrs Moth – for whose condition she felt much pity; had observed Esther's mature figure, dress and demeanour; and had met the mannerly and attentive Jack Moth, she thought that there was not the slightest harm in Otis and Esther going about Southsea in one another's company.

It was, of course, Jack who had the most influence on her decision. If there was one thing, besides his physique, that the son had inherited from the father, it was charm. It was well-known in New Scotland Yard that if one wanted to extract information from a reluctant female witness, then Inspector Moth was the man to do it. He had charmed a confession from many thieves and at least one murderess. He had charmed the Hon. Anne Clermont from the bosom of her family. Add to the charm, the smile, the thickly-fringed eyes in a well-boned face and the full, sensuous mouth, and you began to see how it was that both father and son were attractive to women. And, as women themselves sensed, were attracted by women.

He had gone into the garden whilst his mother and Emily Hewetson were being gracious to one another, and paid homage to Mrs Hewetson's good looks and striking figure with his eyes.

Nineteen years old, thought Mrs Hewetson, and he has the manner of an experienced man. 'You must take great comfort in having such a fine son to care for you,' she said, accepting his homage.

She's not half bad, thought Jack Moth, momentarily forsaking Victoria Ormorod in mind. You'd never believe she could have a daughter of almost seventeen.

Later, after dinner at The Grand when Otis had gone to her room, Emily Hewetson suggested to her husband that there would be no harm in the two girls spending time together, particularly as in any case they were bound to come across one another in such a small town as Southsea, and that he must agree that any other behaviour would be *outré*.

'Mrs Moth wondered whether you would be willing to consult with her on a legal matter. She said that it was only minor, and that she would understand if you would prefer not to whilst you are on holiday.'

'I trust you put her mind at rest on that score, Em.' Knowing that she had already offered him to Mrs Moth.

She smiled at having won her husband this small prize. 'I said that I was quite sure that it would be no trouble to you at all.'

He gave her what almost approached a wink. 'No trouble having a Clermont on the Hewetson, Batt books.'

'You won't charge a fee, Martin?'

'Now, Em. You're off again . . . sprats to catch mackerel, eh?'

'If it is a small matter, and you *do* have the time. And . . .' She smiled archly across the top of her sparkling wine-glass. 'She mentioned that her son and daughter are to spend a week or two in Lyme Regis with an uncle of hers during the period of her lying-in.'

She sipped her wine, obviously teasing with a tidbit of gossip. He played along, puffing a little on his cigar, twirling it between his lips, his eyes half closed. 'And?' he asked.

'Nothing, except that Mrs Moth's uncle is Sir Norbert Clermont of Mere Meldrum.'

'Is that a fact?' He topped up her glass and his own.

Watching the rise and fall of her vastly exposed bosom, he wondered, as he always did, how it was that she managed to stop it spilling over and thus giving the world at large a view of those wonderful fruits. And noting the fat-cat satisfaction in her expression, he knew well that later on he would discover that the pink flush he now observed creeping slowly down from her cheek and neck would have painted and warmed her breasts, puckered her rose-buds and sharpened her fingernails.

If there were too many nights for his liking when she would not accept him willingly, those nights of the pink breasts were magnificent. There was no knowing when those nights would be, it was part of the mystery of that side of their life. He could give her anything, forgive her anything, do anything for her in the knowledge that she could unaccountably reach a pitch of desire when she would rake his spine with her fingernails. He knew also that an occasion such as this was the best time for persuading her to his way of thinking – better far than laying down the law.

'And?' He crooked a finger at her, beckoning her words.

'And, Mrs Moth suggested that Otis might like to visit with them.'

A small frown puckered his brow. 'Ah. D'you think that'd be the thing? I mean, it's never been clear in my mind what those three were doing out in that dinghy. Why didn't they hire a boatman?'

'Let us not go over all that again. That was ages ago. Since this afternoon I am quite clear in my mind that it was merely a foolish, childish escapade. The boy wanted to practise diving, and in their innocence the girls saw no harm in wanting to do likewise. Of course, the boy should have known better, but I believe that his only crime was want of good manners in the presence of the girls. After all, it is perfectly obvious that Otis has come to no harm, and she saw no more than I had seen of my own brothers at that age.'

Martin Hewetson did have to admit to himself that that familiarity had not been a disadvantage: Em had not been overwhelmed at the sight of the male body on their wedding night as other young brides he had heard tell of had been.

'Well, Em, I bow to your superior judgement. If they invite her, let her go.'

Emily Hewetson accepted another refill of her glass. She felt at her best. She knew that she looked her best. Young Jack Moth's eyes had traversed her figure and injected her with a feeling of youthfulness she had not felt in ages.

Now, chinking his brandy glass against hers, Martin Hewetson, the opportunity having presented itself, judged his time exactly right. 'I expect you want a bundle of money from me then. We can't have Emily Hewetson's daughter without the correct wardrobe for visiting country estates, can we? Buy her the very best, the prettiest, the latest fashion, buy her hats and get her hair done. No one will ever believe that she could be your daughter: you are bound to be taken as sisters. In that print and those tammies, they know that she's your little girl, but with lace and pretty boots, your sister.'

'Now then, Martin, a little flattery is always welcome, but don't drown the oyster in sauce.'

He saw that his judgement had not failed him. He had hit the right note at the appropriate moment and managed what he had waited months to do, to get Em to take Otis out of those ridiculous girlish clothes.

'Are you ready, my dear? I thought I would get some Madeira and sponge fingers sent up.' This time he really did wink. It was a joke from their wedding night that meant nothing to anyone but themselves.

She nodded, smiling. 'That would be *very* nice, Martin.' She looked at him from beneath her lids. 'You know how I do *love* Madeira and sponge fingers.'

Madeira and sponge fingers for afterwards . . . after

47

young Jack Moth had felt the rake of sharp fingernails down his spine.

Emily Hewetson went gracefully up the grand staircase, aware of the tingling that her exquisite new corset caused to her warm breasts.

THE ROCK GARDENS — SOUTHSEA.

Aunt Kate, As promised, a coloured picture. This must be quite an old view, as the trees are now much more grown. Yes, the accomm. is gd. Yes, I am takg some time off. No, I am not wrkg too hard. I shall write a long letter after Tues. Hope to hv. time to visit home on my way up country, Vicky

---

Victoria Ormorod was kept extremely busy during the next few days. This was the first time that her work had brought her to the joint towns of Portsmouth and Southsea. Although Portsmouth – with its railway, factories, crammed back streets, and busy shops, noisy market, and Royal Navy dockyards – was the more stimulating, it was the idle, affluent elegance of Southsea front that drew Victoria whenever she had time to spare. Here there was air to breathe. Smokeless, fumeless air that was ever moving, and filled with rustling sounds from the movement of shingle.

Already a watering-place at the time when the old Queen acquired Osborne just across the water, Southsea, with its ever-growing naval-officer population, steadily spread its fine villas into what had a few years before been open coastline. Walking the three miles of promenade – the Isle of Wight as a backdrop, the sea calm and blue, the air refreshing and warm, warships, fishing boats and sailing dinghies sliding or bobbing through the Solent channel for interest – anyone could see why naval officers, who had been quartered in the town, often, upon retirement, dropped anchor there.

But Victoria had seen the other side of the coin. She had visited the huddled terraces of the dockers who serviced the navy vessels and the dank yards of the rope- and sail-makers. She had spoken to women who made uniforms for naval officers and fashioned stays and corsets for their wives.

Victoria Ormorod, who had been brought up no differently from the houseful of orphans her grandmother cared for on charity, had not led a soft life but, compared to those of the stay-makers, it was secure and luxurious.

'Seven in the morning to seven in the evening, miss,' a group of sixteen-year-old machinists had told her during their midday break – Victoria could not think of it as a dinner-break, for few of them had better than a quarter of plain bread and a drink from the factory standpipe – 'Sometimes it's only one-and-six a week that we've took home.'

'That is quite illegal. Don't you know that the Board of Trade lays down a minimum of thirteen-and-six?' Victoria prompted.

'That's for over eighteens and for best work . . .'

'And that's if you don't work in Portsmouth . . .'

'Board of Trade rates don't mean nothing here . . .'

'Most you get over eighteen is half what they lay down . . .'

'Portsmouth is the poorest paid you can get anywhere . . .'

'And what about your unions?' Victoria had asked.

'Join a union, and you gets your minute's notice . . .'

'Tain't fair, but like the master says, there's three other girls waiting to step into your shoes and it's better'n nothing.'

For a moment they had all clamoured to join in, letting their sense of injustice spill over for a few minutes till the factory whistle ordered them back to their machines.

And for a moment outside that factory, as she had done

outside many others, Victoria Ormorod had applied an irritant to their sores of ill-use in the hope that scabs of apathy might not cover those sores. It was not easy for them, but to give in to the system was to make matters worse.

A VIEW OF LONDON. OLD HOUSES. HIGH HOLBORN.

Esther. It has all taken so long. Hwvr Ma is pleased. Otis trnsfrmd. Rather uncomftble. Can't wait to get back to S.sea for our (almost) mutual b'day. Strange to be staying the night at home. All seems dull, except short vst from my Unc. Hewey. Back with you anon. (10 A.M. train). Yrs, O.H.

Thumping the King's green head, Otis secured a halfpenny stamp on her card and put it ready to post so that Esther Moth would receive it by the first delivery. Otis and her mother had spent an entire day in gown and accessories' departments, boot shops, and milliners'. Emily Hewetson had hired a cab for the day, costly but not so aggravating as trying to find one for hire at will. She loathed the grubby, smelly London cabs and their matching drivers, and set out on the shopping expedition for Otis's new wardrobe with some irritation. But, by the time they went for high tea at Fortnum's, her serene face showed her state of mind.

The change had been wrought in a gown shop where a forceful madame had brought out the very latest fashions for Otis.

'No, no,' said Emily Hewetson, looking at the drape and narrowness of the open-fronted skirts and imagining the stimulating way the fabric would divide, giving glimpses of stocking. She shook her head. 'Something more suitable; you know that my daughter is only sixteen.'

Seventeen in a few days, thought Otis, but held her tongue. Emily Hewetson had enough to cope with, accepting this overnight transformation of a daughter from girl to maiden, without leaping into womanhood.

'Ah,' said the clever lady who had had for twenty years the privilege of dressing Mrs Martin Hewetson, wife of *the* Hewetson of Hewetson, Hewetson, Batt and Hewetson. 'Of course, you are right, Mrs Hewetson. What a pity that madam is not thinking of adding to her own wardrobe. These, of course, as you will well know, are the newest styles to come to London. You are right, of course, I shall bring Miss Hewetson some separate items: some pretty blouses and plain skirts.'

She did not, however, take away the new styles, but left them hanging at a seductive distance from the *chaise-longue* upon which Emily Hewetson rested, and from there the desirable dresses hummed siren notes to mature vanity.

In Fortnum and Mason's restaurant, restored with a little salmon pâté, green salad and brown bread, and a *compote* of fruit, Emily Hewetson smiled across the table at her daughter and sipped fragrant green gunpowder tea. 'Well Otis, I think we have done very well this morning. Are you pleased with your wardrobe?'

'I don't like the idea of the stays.'

'This is neither the time or place . . .'

'I like the skirts, and the white blouse, and the spotted one.' As she had tried them on in the gown shop, Otis had imagined the effect the deep yellow skirt and blouse with the gathered bodice would have upon Jack Moth when he saw her wearing them.

'I shall get the Southsea man to come and look at your hair.'

'Oh, Ma, must you? It will just get blown about on the seafront.'

'Well, at least you will start out looking ladylike.' Offering Otis some more of the refreshing tea, Emily said, 'You wouldn't have liked those new models at all, would you? I can scarcely see you, stepping out as you do on Southsea front, in those narrow skirts.'

51

'Goodness no! They are so perfectly *you*, Ma.'

'Do you think so?' She smiled at the thought of all those tissue-lined boxes already on the van for delivery to The Grand.

Emily Hewetson was not really concerned for Otis's immature opinion, but she did want somebody to whom she could talk of the six new gowns she had ordered. Six! She laughed lightly. 'Heaven alone knows what your father will say.' And oh, the trays of Madeira and sponge fingers they would have sent to their room over the next week or so.

'He would never say a thing to you about your clothes. I don't think he would mind if you had bought the jackets Madame showed you as well.'

'Ah, my dear, that is where you are mistaken. When you have a husband you will know what I mean. The wife of a prosperous lawyer may go a little over her dress allowance if her husband feels flattered by having his wife looking rather better than his colleagues' – clients have no confidence in a man who has a dowdy wife – but to go too far over at one time is to appear spendthrift.'

'Pa would never deny you a couple of jackets – they were terribly pretty on you.'

'They were, weren't they? Horribly expensive. I did love them. But I shall have them, never fear. And your pa will feel all the better that he thought of buying them himself – as a surprise. You know your pa and surprises.'

Otis did. It had apparently been his idea to surprise her by the trip to London for the new clothes. 'But he will not know about them.'

'Oh, be sure he will know, Otis. He will know that Madame had thought only of me when she ordered, and that I refused them, reluctant to be profligate with the money the poor man works so hard for.'

Otis smiled a falsely compliant smile at her mother whilst she said to herself, I shall never, never be like you, Ma. You may as well have a bowl of trifle for brains the little use they get.

PUBLIC MEETING

'A woman understands not philosophy, but the making of a dumpling. Stick to socks and avoid sociology, and look after your husband . . .'

Ladies! This advice was given to women in Portsmouth Town Hall recently by Mr Victor Grayson.

The combined societies advocating both female and universal suffrage meet in unity tonight to put the varying arguments for
DEMOCRACY AND JUSTICE

Mr Frederick Pethick-Lawrence
Miss Blanche Ruby Bice
Portsmouth Town Hall, 7.30 P.M.
Admission Free. Collection.

Jack Moth did his very best to show concern for his mother in the way that his father would have done, though he did think that his father, having been so careless as to do this to his mother, might have – this year at least – come away from London for a couple of weeks. It was never admitted, but the whole family knew very well that George Moth hated not being at work and that some particularly difficult investigation would always come up only days before they were due to leave.

One day, Jack thought to himself, one day I shall tell him just what I think.

It was now the Tuesday when Victoria Ormorod had said that she would be attending a public meeting in the town hall. He had carried out a survey of the hall and the roads leading to it so that he might loiter with the intent of seeing her when she arrived.

When he had asked his mother if she would be happy for him to go out that evening, he had discovered that it was one of Nancy's free evenings.

'No, I shall not ask her to change her evening off, Jack. To servants, free time is part of their wages. I would not go to my servants for a loan of money, neither shall I ask Nancy for a loan of her evening. Particularly as you have free time for the entire day.'

'It's a pity that Father doesn't give you a bit more of his time. I sometimes wonder whether he wouldn't rather live at Scotland Yard and visit us occasionally.'

'Jack! Your father does the kind of work that knows no hours.'

'My father does the kind of work that absorbs him so that he does not know that we exist.'

When Anne Moth looked down at the little jacket she was embroidering, Jack was at once contrite. 'Oh, Ma, I'm a beast. It is only that . . .' he paused, wondering whether he should tell his mother the whole story of how he fell in love and was likely to lose the lovely Victoria Ormorod if he did not go to the town hall tonight. He knew that she would be touched by the tenderness of it.

He related his romantic story. '. . . And I may never see her again after tonight.'

'You will probably fall in love many times, Jack, before you discover your true love.'

'How many times did you fall in love before you met Pa?' He, of course, knew the answer, having heard their story related often.

'*Touché*, my dear. But holiday romances usually have such short roots that they do not transplant well to everyday marriage.'

'Goodness, Ma, I am not thinking of marriage.' Which was not true: he had thought of marriage to Victoria Ormorod very many times lately.

'As it happens, Mr Martin Hewetson has kindly said that

he will come here this evening to discuss something with me. Esther will be here, and Nancy will be back by ten, so go along to your meeting.'

He gave her the kind of hug a young man gives his mother as compensation for having got his own way by playing on her maternal love. Having received many such hugs, Anne Moth smiled at her tall, handsome son and said, 'Get along with you, and take your cupboard love with you. And what is this meeting all about?'

'Blessed if I know. A Mr Pethick-Lawrence is speaking, that's all that I know.'

She looked up sharply. 'Frederick Pethick-Lawrence? Then it must be a Suffrage meeting. He once spoke at a Fabian meeting I attended. A good speaker, he was very persuasive.'

With that, everything about Victoria Ormorod fell into place. She was – she had to be of course – a supporter of female suffrage.

'Enjoy your evening, my dear, it will do you no harm to listen to what Mr Pethick-Lawrence has to say.'

Now, as Jack haunted the entrance to the town hall, and saw the posters announcing Mr Pethick-Lawrence, he understood Victoria Ormorod's manner – the way she had approached him at the fountain, her firm handshake, and the off-hand way she paid the luncheon bill. And she had said to him: 'You may not enjoy the meeting.' But he would. He really had nothing against women having a voice.

By the great trek of people making for the town hall, it was obviously a very important meeting. It was no wonder Victoria wanted to be here: it seemed that every young woman in every surrounding parish had come out in the summer sunshine. Many wore sashes of purple, green and white; others red, green and white. Some came in little groups carrying banners indicating 'WSPU', 'NUWSS', 'WOMEN'S CO-OPERATIVE GUILD', 'UNION OF WOMEN

TEACHERS', 'UNION OF WOMEN WORKERS'. There were Women's Freedom Leagues, Church Leagues and National Leagues, Conservative Women, Temperance Women, Liberal and Independent Labour Women.

Which, Jack Moth wondered, might Victoria Ormorod support? Or could it be that she supported the Women's Anti-Suffrage League and had come in opposition to all these? No, no, that did not fit at all.

At the entrance, young women were thrusting handbills and literature into people's hands. Accepting one, he smiled down at its distributor, who wore a white hat trimmed with red and green and an armband showing that she was an 'Official Steward'.

'Nancy!'

'Oh, Lord! Master Jack. Whatever are you doing . . . ? I never took you to be interested.' A shadow crossed her face. 'I hope you aren't an "anti" and come to beat us all up.'

Had a servant spoken so familiarly to any of his Cambridge friends, she might well have been sharply rebuked, but Jack Clermont Moth had inherited much of his mother's attitude to the pecking order. 'I'm not an anything. Somebody asked me to come along. I didn't even know that it was a Votes for Women meeting. More to the point, I never took you to be interested.'

'Oh yes. I'm interested in the whole lot of it. I don't know all that much yet, but I have a friend who is teaching me. I do love the rousing feeling you get at meetings like this. It is food and drink to me.'

Jack saw the shine in her eyes, transforming her from the rather undistinguished servant who went determinedly about her work, to a bright, enthusiastic young woman in a white hat.

'You look very nice tonight, Nancy.'

'Thank you, Master Jack. I hope you enjoy the meeting.'

'I understand Mr Pethick-Lawrence is a fine speaker.'

'They're both good speakers. They say the two of them fair turns your belly over – pardon the expression.'

The crowds were thickening and he found it difficult to check every face that passed them. But he felt sure that he would be able to pick out her statuesque figure and copper hair.

Nancy continued thrusting literature into people's hands. 'Was you supposed to meet your friends here, Master Jack? It an't going to be easy, and if you wait too long you won't get a seat.'

By seven twenty-five the hall was full.

'Tell you what, Master Jack, if you want to you can come round the side with me where I'm going to get the collecting bags ready. You can get a good view of the audience from there, so you might be able to pick out your friends.'

The meeting got under way. And from his elevated position Jack systematically scanned the rows and rows of faces. He had got about half-way when Mr Pethick-Lawrence began speaking but, urgent as he was to discover Victoria, Jack found his search disturbed by a growing interest in the speech, and when the speaker talked of 'wealthy women who own houses and land, employ servants and run the complex economy of a household and are yet debarred, merely because of their sex, from having any say, by way of a vote in the political life which is so vital to her interests', Jack's thoughts were drawn to his mother. Was he mistaken, or had she looked eager when she had said that she had heard Mr Pethick-Lawrence speak?

Frederick Pethick-Lawrence's speech received such tumultuous applause that it drowned the jeers of the 'Antis'. In spite of his desire to continue scanning the hall, Jack joined in. Nancy, who had come to stand by Jack, thwacked her hands together rapturously. 'Isn't he fine? Isn't he a fine speaker, Master Jack?' And he agreed that it was a truly passionate speech.

57

'Passion? You'll hear passion now. Blanche Ruby Bice is next. Come down with me into the aisle and listen.'

Realizing the impossibility of finding Victoria Ormorod in this great crowd, he went with Nancy who guided him to stand by other official stewards from where he continued to let his eyes roam over the heads of the large audience.

The buzzing and rustling suddenly ceased, and he followed the direction of all other eyes towards Miss Blanche Ruby Bice. Dressed in a white suit, her abundant copper-coloured hair bulging from under a plain, flat hat, Blanche Ruby Bice moved to the podium. The striking woman in white who had hushed the audience without a word was, without doubt, his own Victoria Ormorod.

Whilst he had been waiting in the street, she must have entered through a private entrance with the rest of the platform. And whilst he had been facing the audience and scanning their faces, she had been looking down upon them from the platform. Whilst he had looked for Victoria Ormorod, she had become the apparently heroic orator, Blanche Ruby Bice.

When she reached the podium it was obvious that, whatever the posters said, this was Miss Bice's meeting. It was a woman's cause and she was a woman. And what a woman. Jack Moth's entire body felt singed by her presence and excited by the prolonged applause of the audience before she had even opened her mouth.

She did not begin speaking immediately but, without excuse or apology, she withdrew the pin and removed her hat, unwound a long filmy scarf, and flicked off her gloves finger by finger. All this she did so slowly and with such deliberation that for one fleeting moment Jack wondered where it would stop, and saw ahead where she pop, pop, popped the buttons at the neck of her blouse, unfastened her cuffs . . .

Having held the audience like an accomplished actress, she held up her bare hands in fists. At even the most rumbustious meeting of a Cambridge debating society, Jack Moth had never heard the whoops, whistles and applause that greeted her opening sentence.

'Ladies and gentlemen, *I* am ready to fight for justice. Are you?'

Smiling, confident, she waited until the noise subsided into silence, then she leaned forward over the podium, resting on her forearms. Informal. Friendly. Smiling. Her eyes crinkling at the corners as they had crinkled at Jack over the tin-topped table on the pier.

'This voting business that we have come together in Portsmouth to talk of this evening; this act that is so sacred, so important to the future peace of this country, so vital to the well-being of any democracy . . .' She paused for a second, held up her hand and changed the tone of her voice to brusqueness. 'I do not exaggerate, for I sincerely believe that the vote is all of these things. But . . .'

Now all puzzlement '. . . there are men (very many men) who would have us believe that it is only *their* sex which is capable of rational thought, only *their* sex which has the necessary grasp of fundamental politics to decide upon who shall govern us, only their *superior* sex which is capable of philosophic thought.'

'Quite right!' The response of that anonymous male voice did not raise the laughter it must have anticipated – it raised only angry hissing. Victoria/Ruby Bice held up her hand.

'Ah, the gentleman says "Quite right". Perhaps he is one who believes that our great novelist, George Eliot, ought to be at home making dumplings whilst her butler is thinking philosophical thoughts about how he may use his vote.' The gales of derisive laughter must surely have made the heckler wish that he had never opened his mouth.

Jack leaned forward, wishing that he was as close to this goddess of a woman as he had been when sitting opposite her on South Parade Pier.

'Does he also say "Quite right" when asked about

convicts who have the right to vote? (I mean of course *male* convicts). Does he say "Quite right" when questioned about lunatics (*male* lunatics) having a perfect right to vote? And does he say that it is right that a *white slaver* and a *drunkard* should have more say in the government of this country than any woman in the land?'

If Victoria Ormorod knew anything, it was obvious that she knew how to use the passion and the tension that she had built up.

'And so, whilst the convicts, lunatics and drunken white slavers of this country are voting, what of our women? What kind of women are we – we dumpling makers – who do *not* have a say in our own destiny?'

As she spoke, she used her hands constantly – long, large hands that bent backwards at the knuckles like a ballet dancer's – and Jack could not but help remember the practical way those hands had dampened the towel and picked the streak of seagull lime from his sleeve. Had that really happened? Had she really teased him about laundering her towel, and had he sat tête-à-tête with her eating sandwiches and fruit?

She continued, 'A woman may be a nurse, and not have the vote. A woman may be a doctor, and not have the vote. A woman may be a mayor, a teacher, a skilled worker or factory labourer, and not have the vote.'

She paused briefly; the silence was so charged with the tension she had built up that it seemed possible that it would arc like electricity. Her voice, quiet now, penetrated to the furthermost corners of the large, silent hall. 'And a woman may be a *mother*, she may be the help, guide and be the greatest influence in the life of any man. It is she who will teach him most about morality, to know what is right and what is wrong; it is she who will teach him to be honest and honourable . . .' Again she paused, seeming to let her gaze search out every eye for a response. Then her voice came out powerfully, passionately. 'But she is not . . .' she pointed her two forefingers like pistols '*not* to be trusted to have any say in the making of the very laws by which she must live. *She may not*', again the pistols, '*have the vote.*'

The audience loved it. Loved the way she used her hands, small gestures; used her eyes, raising her brows; sometimes putting her forefinger to her mouth in a manner of contemplation before making her point, a gesture Jack Moth recognized.

Her speech lasted twenty minutes, although Jack Moth had no real idea of time whilst his eyes were fixed on Victoria. When the official expressions of thanks were being made, Nancy tapped his arm, saying, 'I'll have to go and pass my collecting bag around. What did you think, Master Jack? Wasn't she splendid?'

'Very.'

Something in his tone made Nancy look twice at him. Well, she thought, our young Master Jack's had his eyes opened tonight. 'Perhaps if you wouldn't mind, I should be obliged if you wasn't to tell the mistress.'

'I'm sure that my mother would not have the slightest objection.'

'It's not so much that, sir, it's that, if you believe in something like this, there don't hardly seem a word that passes between people, in the normal way of talk, without it don't have some bearing on your beliefs. And there's times when it can be real uncomfortable for both parties, if you see what I mean. I've always found it best to keep my work and my politics separate.'

'I was hoping you would tell me the arguments. I really am an ignoramus on the subject.'

'Well, Master Jack, there isn't a single argument that's worth hearing *against* women getting the vote, and Miss Bice has told you the reasons *for*.' And off she went to pass her collecting bags out.

Having hung about at the beginning of the evening like an errand boy waiting for a scullery maid, when Jack left the hall he allowed himself to be quickly carried away by the stream of people. He might easily have made his way to the back exit from which the speakers were bound to leave, but he felt odd, his thoughts at sixes and sevens, and certainly not adequate to come face to face with the woman who had swooped into Portsmouth Town Hall.

The ten-minute walk to Garden Cottage, Southsea, took him half an hour. He did not know how to think of himself now. When he left the house he had been in love with an ideal woman. Now . . . ? He supposed that he was still in love all right, but with whom . . . with what? He had guessed her to be – now he cringed at the very idea – he had guessed her to be a singer or perhaps an actress.

What had she thought of him? His eagerness. The boyish way he had obeyed her rules about laundering the towel. His foolish banter. God, let the pavement swallow me up! She must have been quite amused. Whilst young Jack Moth had been making a fool of himself, Miss Victoria Ormorod had been in on her own secret that she was in reality Miss Blanche Ruby Bice who was – as was now plain to Jack Moth the ignoramus – a renowned and adored public speaker.

'Did you enjoy Mr Pethick-Lawrence, Jack?' his mother asked.

'Oh . . . yes. He was very stimulating . . . very.'

Anne Moth had not been a wife and mother for twenty-odd years not to know when a member of her family was put out. Wisely, she thought, say nothing, it will come out when it's ready. 'Why don't you have a nice glass of port, Jack . . . and you can pour me one.' He did not notice that his mother's cheeks were already flushed and there were empty glasses on the tray. And he had entirely forgotten that Mr Martin Hewetson had paid her a visit that evening; about what, it never occurred to Jack to enquire.

When Nancy returned she was not wearing her hat or armband and she looked at Mister Jack with nothing that suggested that they had seen one another since tea that afternoon.

Grand Hotel,
Southsea

Messrs Hewetson, Hewetson, Batt & Hewetson,
Solicitors
High Holborn,
London

Dear Hew,
I shall be back in the office on Monday, as arranged. Southsea is pleasant enough, but one longs for something to do, some purpose to the day.

A small bit of good fortune, in that Mrs George Moth (before marriage the Hon. Anne Clermont – the Clermonts being, as you will surely know, Wessex's foremost family) has asked H, H, B & H to handle a matter concerning her will which is (at present) in the hands of Asners of Mayfair.

No purpose in writing this, except that I have too much time on my hands, and I thought that you might like to know that we have a Clermont as a client. I explained the complications, but Mrs Moth was adamant that she wished me to draw up a document on the spot. Of this more when I return.

Yours, Martin

Martin Hewetson had been surprised at the change in Mrs Moth that had taken place since he had seen her last. At Bognor Regis they had been only nodding acquaintances but he remembered clearly that she had been a petite, energetic and vivacious woman appearing to be much too young to have a grown son.

On the evening of his visit, as he had sat across from her in Garden Cottage, he was shocked at the change. Quite apart from the usual changes brought about by her condition, she was swollen and heavy-looking, with deep indentations on her fingers where rings had had to be removed, a moon face and puffy eyes. He had asked after her health and she replied that she was her usual fit self. He saw her reply for what it was. She did not wish to discuss her health.

He had often thought that it was a bit unfair that women had to undergo these discomforts and ravages to their lovely bodies in order to perform a natural function like repro-ducing. He would like to have a son, but he did understand Em's lack of enthusiasm for the act from which they both gained such enjoyment when it occurred. Prevention was hardly mentioned even in the privacy of one's bedroom, but Martin had firm opinions on the subject, even though he had not aired them since he was engaged in a debate at university: the sooner the adult population is able to view the sexual act openly and discuss it frankly without whispers and blushes, the sooner research into the regula-tion of pregnancies will come about, and we shall see an end to barefoot and unwanted urchins in the mean streets, and to couples performing unnatural forms of copulation for the sake of limiting the size of family. He had sounded pompous, but had been sincere. He supposed that Em knew what was what, but she was as loath to speak of it as of any other bodily function.

He had never known how, at the age of twenty, he had gained such knowledge or had formed these views, but he had done so and he had never altered, even though he had married a lovely and desirable woman. Thus, on Em's say-so, they were to remain without any son to whom he could hand on Hewetson's. If Otis had been a boy, what a thriving practice they would have.

The daughter Esther had come in and had, he had been glad to observe, been polite and concerned for their comfort. 'May I get you something?'

'Mr Hewetson looks like a port man – am I right, Mr Hewetson? I'm afraid that it is our servant's evening off, and the place is too small for more than one.'

'Nevertheless, ma'am, it is charming.'

'It is, isn't it? Bring a tray and glasses, Esther, and then either go into the garden or read in your room. I have a little private business to which Mr Hewetson has kindly agreed to attend.'

The girl had brought the tray, plumped her mother's cushions, kissed her spontaneously and left the room. Either she had grown up, or it was as he supposed – that the episode at Bognor had been a storm in a teacup. She did not look at all the kind of girl who would get up to any nonsense.

'I compliment you upon your daughter, Mrs Moth, she would seem to have a very sweet nature.'

'It is about Esther that I wish to speak to you.'

She had paused for long seconds before she went on. 'I'm sorry . . . I was trying to find the best words . . . I have a small property which was part of my inheritance from my mother. Putting it simply, I wish to make this over to Esther. I dare say that people who know that I am a Clermont will always suppose that I brought wealth to my marriage; but that is not the case – a certain amount of good solid stock and a little property, that is all. In my family, everything seems to end up in the hands of the males. I have always been somewhat rebellious – I suspect that part of George's attraction for me was that my father forbade me to marry him.' She smiled briefly, a smile that Martin Hewetson did not understand. 'I trust that such confidences are not embarrassing to you?'

'Madam, I should be a poor lawyer if I could not listen to my clients with understanding.'

'I read you correctly then, at Bognor.'

He raised his eyebrows, surprised that she had even remembered him.

'Well then, about Esther. I have one or two properties which my mother bequeathed to me – she had three daughters, she provided a little for each of us. And so I wish to provide for Esther. My will has been settled for years – my husband of course inherits. The Clermonts have provided for Jack, as they provided for his education at Winchester College. Jack, with all his advantages, has not the faintest idea of what he will do when he eventually comes down. Esther, however, has known for years what she wishes to do. She will teach.'

'Ah . . .'

With a look, Anne Moth invited him to explain that 'Ah'.

'Otis too. For the last couple of years, she has been a perfect bore on the subject of Teacher Training College.'

'I am glad: there is such a lack of opportunity for intelligent women in the professions generally, that good women teachers are vital. My impression of Otis is that she is a very bright girl who would never be content to have her hair dressed and wait for a prospective husband.'

Smiling wryly. 'Mrs Hewetson would not care to hear that.'

'Children seldom fulfil our ambitions for them. Now, the property. At the moment it is let off in rented rooms. It is nothing grand, but it has income. Esther will need assistance during the years of her training, and if something should happen so that I am not able to provide for her, then I do not want her to be at a financial disadvantage; neither should I wish the Clermonts to feel that they are obliged to support her. If she owns this little property, then she will be totally independent and able to withstand pressure.'

She had handed him three letters already prepared prior to his visit. One was for himself, one for Esther Moth, the third for a Ninian Moth.

'I am not morbid, nor am I proposing to leave the world yet, Mr Hewetson, but one must always be prepared for our Maker playing tricks on us and calling us in at a moment's notice.' She had smiled.

'God forbid that He should call you, ma'am, when you have this new child to live for.'

'I intend doing my best to give my baby son a fond mother.'

'A son?'

'Oh yes, I am as certain of that as I was that Jack would be a boy and Esther a girl.'

'Three children, ma'am. They are most fortunate. I have never wanted Otis to be an only child.'

Again she smiled her enigmatic smile. 'There is time yet, Mr Hewetson, is there not?'

The turn of their conversation made him hot. He would have loved to have poured out to her and confessed to the passion, the plugs of sponge, the self-abuse and longings for another child, the frantic moods of Em when she believed herself to be pregnant again. But such an open confession to another human being – particularly one of the other gender – was impossible and he felt not one bit hopeful that things would be different in his own, nor yet even Otis's lifetime. What fools we are, he thought.

Instead, he had asked, looking at one of the letters, 'Ninian Moth?'

She had delicately patted her mound. 'This is he. In the event of my death, that letter is for my son as yet unborn. George and I have already agreed on names. Instructions in the unlikely event of this being a girl are contained in my letter to you.'

As he took his leave of her, he said, 'Now that you have dealt with the necessity, ma'am, all talk of death can cease. I shall draw up the papers and bring them down here to you within the week. You will have your child, provide for your daughter and live to be a hundred.'

On returning to The Grand, he would have liked to relate to Em the gist of their tantalizing conversation, but its frank trend, no less than professional ethics, forbade it.

Maximilian Hewetson – known almost universally as Hew – was, at twenty-five, a junior partner, the last of the names in the Hewetson, Hewetson, Batt and Hewetson partnership – and Martin's half-brother. He was a very good-looking man with a fashionable narrow face, dark eyes and hair. He was clean-shaven, except for a beautifully-sculpted moustache that flicked up at the ends – as did both his mouth and his eyebrows, all of which gave his face a look of permanent good-humour. And this is what he was: a good-humoured, good-looking man. He was also good fun, which is exactly what a niece wants in an uncle. He was, too, a bachelor. A bachelor in a good London law practice, with a decent income and very nice rooms in which he entertained very well.

Emily Hewetson's afternoon-tea friends said that it was time that he settled down. They probably did not know why they thought this, except that they did not like decent bachelors to go to waste. Much safer to have the junior partner out of 'rooms', married, respectably housed. A young man skating around London single was not the thing in a lawyer.

Otis, naturally, thought marriage would be the worst possible fate for her dear Uncle Hewey. Competition in the form of his wife would not exactly be Otis's choice for herself either.

When he stepped off the train at Portsmouth Station, Otis was glad that she had asked Esther and Jack to come with her to welcome her Uncle Hew. He leapt lightly down and, whilst resting a sociable hand on a porter's shoulder and giving instructions as to his bag, waved his curly-brimmed bowler at Otis.

She was wearing her new womanly clothes of broderie anglaise petticoats under a plain-fronted celandine-coloured skirt with folds at the back that swayed and swished as she walked; from its wide waistband burst a frosty white, high-collared blouse whose dozens of narrow vertical tucks gave it the shape of the body within. Her shiny hair swooped upwards and backwards to be caught and pinned in a bunch of curls. The flattering style, given her by her mother's Southsea man, was topped by a flat hat with yellow ribbons. Boaters were *de rigueur* for all seaside promenaders.

When she had first appeared in her new role as young woman, she had obviously created an effect on Jack, for his gaze had followed her every move, which made her feel extraordinarily powerful. She did not exactly want him to fall down on bended knee and swear everlasting love for her, but she did like it that she had captured his attention. She had flirted with him; he had responded.

If Esther is right and he is in love, then he isn't exactly faithful.

Now Max Hewetson was feeding her new-found delight

in capturing his adult interest. Holding her at arm's length, whilst she mocked herself with a twist of her parasol, he said, 'Just look at you. One thing's for sure, I shall no longer call you "Dumpling". You are a lady . . . nay, a *woman*.'

'Uncle Hew! Not in company.'

As Maximilian Hewetson's eyes said when they lingered upon Esther: And *what* company! What absolutely splendid, ravishing company.

Esther Moth, dressed in similar style to Otis but with a blue and white striped skirt, her fair curls bunched high under the brim of her boater, looked back into Max Hewetson's eyes as though she was quite a woman of the world.

His voice said, 'Well, how delightful . . . the famous Moths. We meet at last. I have heard so much about you from Otis.'

Jack Moth was gentlemanly, as befitted a Cambridge man who had been abroad. But he was not effete like many of his colleagues: Inspector Moth had seen to that. Jack was to Max Hewetson as he was to very many people, an intriguing mixture of the two social cultures of his parents. Not that anyone could have put a finger on that being the reason for his likeableness: it was that he had the best of both worlds but was unaware of it.

Otis said, 'Ma says I may take you off to the seafront at once. Pa says that he will talk shop with you later.'

'Splendid! What is the plan? Nothing too strenuous: I mean to keep you two dancing till dawn.'

Esther Moth laughed. 'Mr Hewetson, you do not know Southsea. The Assembly Rooms do not stay open so late.'

'Well then, we must start early and dance every dance. Now then, whither do we wander?'

Esther and Otis exchanged glances, leaving Jack to speak up as they moved out into the busy road. 'If it is not too much of a bore, we thought we would take some refreshment on the leisure pier at Southsea.'

'The sea, mademoiselles, yes, the sea. I had wondered whether you might want to show me something fearful such as the very house where Charles Dickens was born, or the house where the Earl of Leicester fell to his death, or poor old Conan the Doyle's surgery in which he was forced to give birth to Holmes and Watson in order to pay the rent . . . mind you, I should not mind looking at the latter, but this is a morning to breathe the ozone.'

Esther, who had heard a great deal from Otis of the famous Uncle Hewie, had expected more – or, perhaps, less, for she thought him rather too jolly for so good-looking a man. Esther liked handsome men but preferred that they be serious and intellectual.

That was Jack's trouble too, he was far too jokey. Truly, it was impertinence on the part of men to think that women are entertained only if they are lighthearted and talk of inconsequential matters.

Esther had ideas, theories, beliefs that she would have liked to test out against men, but she hardly knew any men – Jack was so often away and in the vacations refused to be serious because he had enough of that kind of thing in term-time. Her father was always too tired or was going somewhere. Her schoolfriends' brothers, whom she met from time to time, expected her to listen and be amused by them. Her uncles and cousins she seldom saw, since they mixed with a very different level of society from that of the Moth branch of the Clermont family.

The sea is flat, and as glittery as bathroom glass newly cleaned with vinegar. Short waves, edged with white ostrich plumes, uncurl and roll along the shingle shore like ringlets let loose from their pins.

Saturday morning and the hotels facing the sea are busy with cabs and porters and departing guests. Resort visitors on longer vacations stroll – as do these four – apparently aimlessly, eastward and westward, back and forth along the promenade between the two piers.

71

The morning is of the kind that English travellers like to set in the aspic of memory to take with them when setting forth down the Solent to go abroad – calm, sun-bathed and clear. Glittering windows, bright stone and well-painted façades, the hotels and apartments border the town with their pillared entrances, iron-railed gardens and window boxes, iron balconies and iron-framed canopies.

Set out before the hotels is the open common, the Rock Gardens, and Ladies Mile gardens. Here a vast army of invisible men, in coarse shirts, thick trousers and waist-coats, bend their backs to clip straight edges to the gardens, they razor its grass, dead-head flowers, feed, mulch and rake its borders to a profusion of foliage, bloom and scent.

Sloping away from this controlled environment is the seashore, which, except for the twin pier and a couple of rickety wooden jetties, is middling wild. Here, young ladies with full skirts and nipped waists walk uncertainly on shifting shingle, occasionally clutching their young man's arm for support, whilst their married sisters, and mothers with full bosoms and stay-boned waists, walk the flat promenade. The predominating colours of the women's clothes are those of the sweetpeas and annual summer plants blooming in the town parks.

The men here see themselves as gentlemen; and retired sea captains see themselves as gentlemen of rank, their naval titles being cherished and aired daily, lest anyone think that these are merely old men wearing peaked caps and blazers. With great frequency these retired officers, who still ache to issue orders, soon take 'JP' to their name. What would the Portsmouth Bench do without its retired naval officers to clap offenders in irons?

Children with broad hats and healthy faces patter around the sedately moving adults. Little girls dare the waves to touch their boots and squeal at a spot of foam; small boys hurl back into the sea large stones that have taken a millennium to be eased out of the water and up the beach.

But we are talking only of Southsea, and only of the promenade, and only of the people with enough leisure and income to spend their Saturday mornings with nothing more to do than to wait for Saturday afternoon.

In Nancy Dickenson's part of town, whose shoreline is a continuation of that of Southsea, things are different.

There. The air smells of fish, tar and oil, of unwashed clothes on unclean bodies. Peeling doors and shopfronts, market stalls, noisy taverns and grimy bars. A smell of fish and staleness. Cobbled streets, dankness and water. Poor houses, street runnels. Dogs on the loose. Strings of monotone washing strung across yards. Sailors briskly coming ashore, sailors lurching aboard, sailors making business with prostitutes. Alleyways, yards, narrowness. Rickety wooden structures that strangers can never fathom. Occasional splash of colour from a potted geranium in deep shadows. Back-yards that smell of fish and beer, urine and vomit. Even in the sunshine, walls greened from dripping gutters are damp.

There the sea has no shingle to push around for, before the waves can unfurl, the swell hits the man-made piers, wharves, landing-stages and docks, and slaps itself against these barriers, churning its soggy cargo of fish-gut, rotten vegetables, rotten fruit and, occasionally, a rotten human. There the sea is apparently not even middling wild, but when the tide runs it runs deep and fast in the undertow, surging and swirling and sucking its way in and out of the narrow channel.

There the children go mostly barefoot and often bare-arsed. They are thinner than average and shorter. Already many work the Saturday market, pushing carts, holding horses still, shouting wares and minding stalls whilst the holder goes to the tavern or the cockle-stall; and many young girls are at their machines in the stay or shirt factories.

Close to the Harbour Station, where the two worlds

73

meet, the shoreline is a stinking sludge of oil and sewage and mud. Into this ooze at low tide, near-naked children leap to retrieve coins flipped by passers-by. The mud-larks are popular entertainment. As far as anyone knows, few children have come to harm here. Good healthy mud . . . certainly good, healthy pickings.

On Saturdays, Nancy does not get time off. She is at Garden Cottage pressing out the creases where she has altered the waist of her mistress's gown, and pressing in the pleats of the minutely tucked bodice of Miss Esther's dress and stiffening Master Jack's collars to spring-coils.

So, she is not with the people she knows best, the crowd of girls and women released from the stay-making factory who, fuelled by the prospect of not having to get up in the morning, are hurrying and laughing to wash their faces and arms and feet and put on their best skirts and hats and go about in groups.

At least the single women are.

The married ones who have put in six and a half days bent over a sewing machine in the crowded factory, look forward to a day at the sink beating dirt out of clothes, a bit of a gossip over the clothes-line, an evening in a bar with a glass of stout, and a night on their backs with their hard-handed men.

To anyone outside this community and outside its time, dockland is not a gentle place. Girls become drudges too soon, boys become cheap labour. But they have taste-buds that respond to beer and cockles and sweetness of any kind. They have ears that love the old squeeze-boxes played in bars, and street-organs trundling the streets. They have nostrils through which they are tantalized into wanting hot pies and hair-oil and flowery scent. And they have nerve endings as sensitive to the touch as any lady and gentleman who have tempted one another in bed with Madeira and sponge fingers.

It is from those docklands, where she has been meeting

some of her most ardent admirers at their factory gates, to Speakers' Corner on the promenade at Southsea, where she is to address equally loyal but better-off members of the NUWSS, that Victoria Ormorod is striding like a youth.

THE AUDITORIUM OF THE THEATRE ROYAL, PORTSMOUTH, IN 1900.

Aunt Flora, I have arrived safely, but have not yet seen Martin. Otis sends you her love. She looks much more her age now that Em has got her up a bit. (Pleases you, eh?) Am taking luncheon al fresco on the Pleasure Pier. Southsea appears to be a most affable town, with much to do. Within a mile or two of where I now sit is the Isle of Wight, all green and mysterious. Yours,
Maximilian Hewetson

Jack, pleased to have male company, was on tenterhooks and feeling a bit of a cad as he watched Max Hewetson leisurely writing his local view cards.

It had been Jack's scheme that they come here, and to achieve his ends he had been forced to use subterfuge, for had Esther known why he wanted to come, she would have teased him in a very childish way. His trick had been to let Esther and Otis believe that it had been their own idea to eat here, and it had worked, for Otis had sworn them to secrecy about the true reason for coming this far from The Grand Hotel. 'We cannot help it if we happen upon a meeting, and if it happens that we are caught up in the march by accident, then Pa cannot say anything, but if he believes that it is a scheme, then he may well try to chain me to the wall again.'

Jack felt caddish, because they were here not in order that Otis's uncle could take in the sea air, but so that Jack Moth could once again see Victoria Ormorod in the flesh and hear her as Blanche Ruby Bice making an open-air speech at Speakers' Corner. He knew that there was some bad feeling between Victoria's faction, the NUWSS, and the militant

Pankhurst followers, the WSPU, to say nothing of the Anti factions. The Pankhurst faction worked to get publicity and notoriety, to get the police and press involved, to get arrested, to get reported, to go to prison.

Jack Moth knew all this and, now that it had come to the hour, foresaw the possibility of another fiasco involving Otis as when, in showing off to Otis, he had capsized the dinghy. Then as now, Otis's exuberant enthusiasm for new experience had carried the scheme along.

'Heavens, Jack, we only wish to hear the lady speak. Don't you consider it part of one's education to listen and debate issues? Surely you do? I have heard that at university there is a great deal of debate going on.'

Jack thought that Esther, in her sly way, was amusing herself looking on to see whether anything might happen. Now, second thoughts. Father had said that he might come down next week – Jack would be mortified to be accused of not caring for the women whilst Father was sweating away in London.

Too late! Max Hewetson had heard the band and seen the tops of the banners as the parade, flanked by police constables, made its way past the Rock Gardens to Speakers' Corner.

'I say! Is that a carnival? Shall we go and look?'

He noticed that the two girls again glanced at one another, and wondered whether this parade was the reason for the rather over-long walk they had brought him on to eat a few indifferent sandwiches and a slice of rather good apple pie.

When they reached Speakers' Corner a large crowd had already gathered.

'Heaven save us,' said Max Hewetson, 'it's Mrs Pankhurst's Lot. Who wants to hear their twaddle?' Jack Moth's neck reddened and stiffened and looked ready to crow. Oh, Lord! thought the older man, been and ruffled some feathers. Has the young cock fallen for the twaddle, or for some campaigning young lady?

Following the direction of Jack's gaze, Max Hewetson had no doubt. Not a girl, but a full-blown woman. Certainly the lad had taste, even though she might prove wasted on so young a graduate. 'Who's the pretty copper-nob?' he asked.

'I believe that she's called Blanche Ruby Bice, and I believe that she is to make a speech on the conditions of work in the local shirt-making factories.'

'Ah . . . so *that's* Ruby Bice. Of course I have heard of "Miss White, Red and Green" – isn't that how her name is made? Who has not heard of her? But I have never seen her in the flesh, so to speak.' And very nice flesh too: his gaze taking in the detail of Victoria's figure and face. 'I've heard it said that she is a French aristocrat. But I say . . . look at that hair . . . Russian princess, no less.'

'From her looks, that may well be true,' said Jack Moth, placated by the warmth of his acquaintance's admiration. 'How do you come to know of her? Until this week, I had never heard of Ruby Bice.'

'She makes speeches. That's how she gets known. In London, she can fill any hall to capacity, so I've heard.'

'Does she go to prison?'

'No, no. The trouble-makers are Mrs Pankhurst's Lot. Apparently our Miss Ruby is a bit of a pacifist. I should like to know what she would do if a man grabbed her by the waist – she'd soon become a warrior lady then.'

'I don't see that that is the same thing at all, if you don't mind me saying so.'

'Not at all, old man.'

'Well then, any lady fights for her honour, no matter what.'

'But pacifism means peacefulness, and not peacefulness when it suits,' said Max Hewetson with the condescension of a Sunday-school teacher, or perhaps with the sweet reason of a lawyer.

'I believe you are mistaken. I can see that a woman may be

77

pacific in her beliefs yet not eschew entering a fight . . . as in fighting for a just cause. Your argument fails because you equate passivity with pacifism.'

A banner pole carried horizontally caught the two debaters behind the knees. 'And if you two ignoramuses don't shut up, you'll get a demonstration of the difference.' The interrupter of Jack and Max was a small woman wearing the mauve, green and white of 'Mrs Pankhurst's Lot'. 'If you want to hold your own meeting, go some-where else, though if you ask me, you'd do better to listen to the speaker.'

Jack was more than willing to stand and look at the woman who was still Victoria Ormorod as he had known her during those days when he had fallen secretly in love. She was dressed in the plainest of clothes, a full-sleeved white voile blouse across which rested a band of white, green and red which swelled and fell over the contours of her figure, and rose and dipped with her every breath; a creamy white skirt with the same plain front and swaying back as at the last meeting, and the ubiquitous white flat straw hat, around which was bound a ribbon of white, green and red.

Jack Moth's heart cracked, for it suddenly occurred to him that such a creature could not possibly have remained in an unmarried state. She did not wear a ring, but that did not signify, he had heard that suffragettes often went ringless. Then he remembered that he had undertaken to be responsible for Esther and Otis. 'Where are the girls?' he whispered to Max Hewetson.

'They have wormed their way to the front.'

'Lord! They shouldn't be there.'

'Oh come, Jack, there will be no trouble today – the sun is shining.'

'Sssh! Sssh!' Hissed all around them.

'You stop here, old fellow, and I shall fetch them back.' He disappeared into the crowd.

Suddenly the crowd cheered, and he was lost. Victoria Ormorod stepped up on to the banana-box platform. He did not care that she was Ruby Bice, he did not mind what she said, yet, almost against his inclination he was drawn to listen.

She smiled in a most friendly way at the crowd, and at some policemen. 'Gentlemen, the day is so hot that we shall not take it amiss if you remove your helmets and loosen your collars.'

Some wag called, 'Or we could do it for you.' The crowd laughed, and Victoria Ormorod shook her head at them in disapproval.

'No, no, ladies, the NUWSS is a peaceful movement, concerned to better the lot of working-class women, which we cannot do if we are languishing in gaol.'

A woman shouted, 'They take no notice of our cause if we are not destructive.' Supported by some cheers by members of Mrs Pankhurst's Lot.

Jack would have liked to leap to her defence and tell them to be quiet, that he had not come here to listen to them, but to the great Ruby Bice. Oh Lord, how the name clashed with her personality. She was Victoria Ormorod.

'. . . and only today, I was in a factory where girls work from eight in the morning till eight at night for less than half of the agreed rate, and there are girls, of sixteen or seventeen years of age, who work for as little as one and sixpence a week.'

The crowd drew in its scandalized breath.

'Yes, ladies and gentlemen, in your own town. One and sixpence! Less than the price of a six-inch pudding basin (which, for those among us who may not be *au fait* with such domestic matters, costs one and ninepence). And do you know what these girls are producing . . . for less than the cost of a six-inch pudding basin?' Her eyes alighted on Jack and held his gaze. 'They are producing items of uniform for the Royal Navy.'

Her eyes still held Jack's, but only Jack knew that; to the rest of the crowd she was addressing each of them. She said to him, 'If our English officers knew of the conditions under which their uniforms are made, I am sure that they would never wear them.'

Jack nodded, indicating how fiercely he agreed.

'Thirteen shillings and sixpence is the agreed Board of Trade rate for an eighteen-year-old girl performing this very best kind of tailoring.' Her eyes returned to Jack. 'And we intend to put an end to such injustices as these.'

A man at the front of the crowd called in a hectoring voice, 'What you going to do, dot the factory manager one with your parasol?' He was either a brave man or an idiot of the first water to ridicule the idol before her own crowd.

Jack thought him a fool, but wonderful Victoria Ormorod was not put out in the slightest by him. She smiled at him, and then at the audience. 'Poor gentleman, he still believes it necessary to use violence to achieve one's ends. Now, if you will allow me, sir, I will continue my story of my visit to the tailoring sweat-shops of Portsmouth. There will be plenty of time for questions later if you wish.'

He would not give up. 'Would you say you were a pacifist, then?'

From the university debating society, Jack had learned the technique of heckling speakers to throw them off balance. It seemed obvious that this was the man's purpose.

'Yes, sir, I *would* say that I am a pacifist, an ardent one. I believe in settling any dispute by peaceful means.'

'Right, so that if your meeting was to be spoilt by some person who kept interrupting, you would not lose your temper.'

'I hardly promise that, I have a very fine temper. However, what I do believe is that the world has had its fill of aggression. Our only fight is for the minds of our masters. Our army is the common people, our ammunition, words.'

80

'You got plenty of them, all right.'

The audience, most of whom had come solely to listen to their adored Ruby Bice, were becoming restless. There were a few angry shouts to throw him out. Victoria dowsed those sparks with laughter when, indicating the wide expanse of sea, she said, 'We can hardly throw him out . . . can we?'

'You never answered my first question . . .'

'Which was – would I, ah . . . , "dot" a man with my parasol? In a word, no.'

A clear and angry voice rang out, 'But I would!' And a celandine-coloured parasol clouted the man across the head, sending his hat spinning underfoot and the man crashing down.

Jack recognized both voice and weapon.

It was the parasol which had been with them all morning. He had held it, retrieved it, hooked it on table edges and twice saved it from loss. The parasol was, unmistakably, the one covered in the same fabric as the skirt that was cut to sway provocatively.

His heart sank as police dived into the little mêlée with relish, where they were then attacked themselves. He tried to push forward, but the crowd closed in and so barred his way. Anxiously, he skirted around and reached the front, where he saw Max talking to a policeman with the same comradeliness as he had used on the porter. But it didn't work. The constable, firmly gripping Otis's arm, marched her to where a sergeant and a contingent of constables waited beside a police van.

His father would no more believe that he was blameless of the consequences of this incident than of the episode at Bognor.

The birthday celebration dinner – and Otis's entry into the world of assembly-room dances – was not at all as had been planned.

If there is one thing at which the English middle-classes excel, it is 'putting a good face on things'. Had it not been for Max making light of the incident, Emily Hewetson would have made her excuses to Mrs Moth and dismissed the whole idea. But Martin Hewetson had said, 'Don't let us be too hasty, Em, not just now we have got a Clermont on our books.'

'For goodness' sake, Martin!' she snapped. 'You sound like a grocer.'

He had shut up, knowing that Max could twist her round his little finger.

'But *twice*, Max, first at Bognor and now here. That young man has no sense of responsibility. You are not going to tell me that he didn't know what happens when there are suffragettes about.'

'Be fair, Em, Jack Moth was no more to blame than I.'

'He must have known that there are often scuffles there on Saturday afternoons . . . you could not be expected to know that.'

'It was a quiet enough meeting, and most of this talk about mayhem is got up by the newspapers.'

'So, what you are saying is that the meeting was quiet but Otis created a disturbance . . . is that what you are intimating, Max?'

'Dear Em, not at all. The man was being an utter bore – we have free speech in this country and he would heckle. I think Otis was quite splendid dotting him one over the head.'

'Max! How can you, a partner in Hewetson, Hewetson, Batt and Hewetson, sit there drinking tea and say such a thing?'

'Look, my dear, what is done is done and no harm has come to anyone. If you are going to fret about it, then you will have worry lines by the time you are forty.'

Max knew her age well enough, and he knew too that damage to her complexion would concern her quite as much as damage to Hewetson Batt's reputation.

'If you take my advice, Em, then you will let me give Otis and her friend their dinner and dance, and everyone will behave as though nothing untoward happened.'

'We must say *something*, if only to show that young man . . .'

'Em, Em. If you will go on about Jack Moth, then I shall think that you are having a sly dig at myself, for I was standing close by Otis and Esther.'

'But you were not to know.'

'It is no good you making excuses for me, Emily. I should have insisted that we all move on very quickly, instead of which we idled there looking for a bit of entertainment.'

'Entertainment! Really, those women should all be locked up.'

'I'm sure that would please them no end.' He grinned at her and she succumbed as she always did, and agreed that they should have their social evening and try to enjoy it.

'I don't know what young girls of today are coming to. Otis is so irresponsible. I don't know what will become of her if these women get their way and are given the vote. Things like the running of the country must be left to men who understand these things. Can you imagine Otis having a say in governing the Empire?'

Martin, who had kept his head down, knowing that his half-brother had a way with Em in a state, said defensively, 'What you say then, Em, is that the terrible Jack Moth is more suited to governing the Empire than say – yourself, for example.'

Such a comment was unfair in a family wrangle, so she ignored it.

'I shouldn't worry, Em,' Max said. 'It won't happen. And in any case, you women have enough to do with families and servants – and sorting out dolts like me.' He smiled engagingly at her.

Before he left her sitting-room, he broached the subject, as he had promised Otis and Martin that he would. It was a gamble whether this was the best moment, but he thought he knew his sister-in-law well enough. 'I'll tell you what I would do, Em, if Otis were my daughter. I would get her doing something that was so time-consuming that she had no time for idle hands, and so well regulated that there was always someone on the look-out for her welfare.'

Emily Hewetson cocked an eyebrow at him quizzically.

'I suppose you have come to plead her case for applying to Stockwell College. I dare say she has put you up to it, or Martin. Probably both.'

'Well, not specifically Stockwell — but that is one possibility: there are other good colleges teaching degree courses. And she certainly wants to do it. That's half the battle, isn't it?'

'But Max, Otis a *teacher*. Do you really wish to see your niece teaching sums in some grubby little school?'

'No, Em. But I should not mind seeing my niece as head of one of these splendid Girls' Trust Schools.'

'And never marry! There is no question of both of course.'

'Of course Otis will marry. But she does have this bee in her bonnet about education, so why not let her see what it is like? Sign her up, but make a pact with her that she cannot withdraw on a whim. She may well hate it after a month, but make her stay there. Let Martin draw up a document if you like — that will show her how serious you are.'

'Three years. She will be twenty when it's over.'

'Right. A much easier age for a rumbustious young lady like our Miss Otis.'

Fully aware that he had charmed her into it, she agreed that Otis should apply for a place at Stockwell College.

Before dinner, the Hewetsons assembled in a small lounge to await the arrival of their guests, and turn their good face to the world. Otis knew that she was again being tested and on sufferance. It was not too difficult for her to appear sedate, for the experience of the afternoon had been quite chastening.

Nothing much had happened, except for being grabbed and hauled before a police sergeant. Uncle Max had dealt with the situation, saying that the heckler had been exceedingly unpleasant over many minutes, and that his young niece had been understandably annoyed at such disrespect.

It had not been pleasant, having a uniformed police sergeant in full view of passers-by wag a finger and tell her that it was quite within his power to handcuff her, put her in the Maria, haul her off to the cells and threaten to lock her up until her case was heard. A power he adjusted slightly once he had read Max's Hewetson, Hewetson, Batt & Hewetson, Attorneys-at-Law card. 'I'm giving you a caution then. And if you'll take my advice, young lady, you'll steer well clear of that. there lot. They're trouble wherever they go.'

Otis's instinct was to contradict him by telling him that he was quite wrong, it was she who had made the trouble, the wonderful Miss Ruby Bice had not for a second let the man's rudeness and taunts ruffle her – but she chose discretion.

If it had not been for the fact that from experience Otis knew that things always got back to parents, she would have told them nothing of what had happened. As it was, Uncle Max had related it as a funny story in which Otis appeared as the victim of a gross mistake and ended up being ticked off for it. They had not fallen for it entirely: there had been a lot said by both parents, and the Bognor incident had been mentioned. Otis appeared chastened before them, endeavouring to use Ruby Bice's technique of not arguing, rising above a desire to answer back.

Her mother had suggested that she wear a pretty new pink creation sent down from London, but when Otis arrived in the public sitting-room, she was dressed in a cream skirt, not intended for evening wear, and a white bodice with large sleeves. Emily Hewetson forbore to say anything, her own highly complicated creation of tucks, flounces, lace and piping being greatly to her satisfaction. Otis forbore to ask whether her mother knew that the girls who had sewn it may have earned not enough to buy a six-inch pudding basin.

The surprises of the day were by no means over, for when the Moths arrived, there, tenderly assisting his wife, was Inspector Moth.

Otis, having on the last occasion seen him only as Esther's formidable father, was surprised to discover that he had metamorphosed into an older edition of Jack, and for the first time saw that a man did not necessarily lose his handsomeness or attractiveness when he became older than twenty-five. And she had been gratified when he had boldly and slowly let his gaze take in her own transformation. He had smiled and bowed over her hand. 'I trust that this beautiful young woman does not change back into a barefoot urchin at the stroke of midnight?'

Otis would have been furious had anyone suggested that she had learned much from observing Emily being pro-vocative to attractive men, but she smiled and held his gaze and his fingers a second or two longer than was proper – as Emily would.

Emily Hewetson had quite forgotten what a handsome man the inspector was and, as she had on that other occasion when she had met him, thought: He really must have been a man any impressionable young girl might easily have run away with. He took her hand, making it look very pale and delicate in his enormous one, and bent low and kissed it with a very old-fashioned courtesy.

'Ma'am,' he said, 'I must ask your pardon for coming unexpectedly when your kind invitation was already declined on my behalf. But I could not miss my little girl's birthday celebration, and I have only minutes ago arrived from London.'

How Emily's rose-buds tingled at the pressure of his warm lips, the outlines of which were not entirely smoothly shaven.

'My dear Inspector, you have no need to apologize, this is entirely a family occasion. We are pleased to have the opportunity of renewing the acquaintance. Your family must be delighted to have you with them again.'

'A flying visit only, ma'am.'

Anne Moth, her eyes slitted with smiling, said, 'He came down especially for me.'

She and Mrs Moth greeted one another with the sweet politeness of two mothers who know that their children have been up to something and each hope that it is proved that they are not the one to be found wanting as a parent. 'Mrs Moth, you are blooming. The ozone in Southsea must be of a very high quality.'

Emily Hewetson had forgotten that she was cross with Jack Moth when he said in a low voice, '*Mea culpa*, does the lovely lady forgive me?' and allowed herself to be as charmed by him again as she had been on her visit to Garden Cottage. For all their faults, this family was indeed a very interesting one, to say nothing of their extreme personableness.

After dinner, Mrs Moth, pleading that she felt a little disturbed, no doubt because of the excitement of George coming and the heat of the night, decided to sit on the terrace where she would get the sea breezes. She insisted that George have at least a turn or two in the Assembly Rooms. Martin Hewetson insisted that he too would prefer sea breezes and an opportunity of sitting with Mrs Moth.

Otis and Esther told one another how wonderful it was that, after expecting to be in disgrace for what had happened earlier, they were having the best party ever, with their two families behaving like old friends.

Neither of the girls had previously attended what was to them a glittering celebration. Last year Esther had attended a police officers' occasion, but it had been stuffy and no one had had any style. Here, where the high society of Southsea, the Royal Navy, and the Royal Marines had come to dance, the men wore immaculate formal dress or dress-uniform and the women had fashionable gowns with swooping *décolletage*.

That she had not much inside her own prettily swathed and flounced bodice had not, until tonight, concerned her very much. Otis was fortunate, her bosom was already as full as a woman's and strained against the white voile of her plain blouse. Well, thought Esther, perhaps this is all I am going to get. Perhaps she would be like her mother and only have any bosom to speak of when she was in that condition. Well, that wasn't so bad, Esther quite liked babies. She felt vaguely sad. Until, that is, just as they were all walking through to the terrace, her father appeared with a young man whose back he slapped in hearty pleasure.

'Anne, Anne, you will never guess who it is that I have discovered. In barracks in Southsea, but enjoying a spot of leave right here at The Grand.'

Mrs Moth was sure that she never would guess, nor spoil George's delight by doing so.

'My life-saver! The young man who dragged me from the Thames when I was unconscious and bleeding from the wound dealt me by that villain.' Turning the young man so as to include Emily Hewetson and the girls in his pleasure. 'And only just in time.'

Emily responded as required. 'Goodness! How dreadful.'

George Moth laughed loudly. 'Why, ma'am? That he was in time?' Again he slapped the young man's shoulder.

'I know who you are,' said Esther, 'you are Pa's famous Lieutenant Blood.'

The Lieutenant's eyes alighted upon the pretty, fairy-like creature with pale golden hair and delicate figure, a porcelain doll of a girl he could have swept up in his arms and run away with.

It was the dearest of all love stories. Love at first sight.

To the nine people present at the moment when the young man took Esther Moth's hand and said, 'Lieutenant Bindon Blood, at your service, Miss Moth,' there was, for ever after, a fleeting moment of strangeness whenever the noun 'blood' – proper or common – was uttered; for Anne Moth said a quiet, 'Oh, George!', and looked with astonishment at her white satin shoes into which rivulets of scarlet were running.

Several hours later, a dedicated and concerned obstetrician said that, no matter what, there was nothing that could have been done. 'Mothers who are apparently perfectly healthy, die in childbirth. We do not know why.'

What was done to Anne Moth in order to try to save her was not childbirth. But, in the face of the tragedy and grief of her death, to say so might be thought of as pedantic and cruel.

Inspector Moth had the weakly, premature child christened Ninian within an hour of its birth. A name he did not like, but which was a Clermont name and one which Anne had wanted. When Esther first saw the tiny creature she felt as heartsore for it as she had for a motherless kitten she had once reared on milk given by dropper. Not only heartsore but as protective of it as though it were her own child. Because of the kitten, she had called her shrivelled little brother 'Kitt'. No one, except Esther, expected the baby to survive; but it did.

Part II

Dear Ma & Pa. This is no artist's fancy, it is a truly heavenly place. As much as I shall enjoy returning to Stockwell and my studies, I long for this holiday never to end. I am glad that I did not go to Berlin with the other girls, for springtime here is truly beautiful. I believe that I have found my spiritual home. Shall be returning to London on the noon train Sat. Father dear, if you would meet me with the trap and take my things round to the college, I shall be for ever grateful. Lovingly, Otis

The Otis Hewetson who sat in purple shadow, resting her back against a tree overlooking a valley flooded with spring sunlight, was a serene and more ladylike Otis than the one who had flung herself in gratitude at her father when he had agreed that she might attend Stockwell Teacher Training College. She had done so well in the entrance exam that she had been accepted into the college months before the usual age, and had proved to be an exceptional student.

Martin was proud at the way his daughter was turning out. But not so Emily. What mother wished to confess to a clever daughter? Particularly a daughter who professed ambition. 'It is not as though she is a plain girl, I am sure that there is not a bachelor in London who would not be eager to secure a wife with Otis's looks. But she appears not particularly interested in young men.'

Which showed how little mothers can know their

93

daughters. What Otis was not particularly interested in was the type of eligible bachelor in front of whom Emily was inclined to dangle Otis as bait.

The sun rammed a rod of gold down through the tree where Otis sat, and lit a gleam in her hair. Lively hair which attested to good health and frequent washing in natural herbs: natural herbs and Bach flower remedies being essential to the well-being of young women of her set. Although during term-time her fine complexion lost some of its colour, now that she had been a few days on this bicycling tour, she was blooming and slim-waisted. Ever since that time three years ago when she had copied Victoria Ormorod's cream and white style, Otis had seldom worn any colour. Today she had on a divided skirt and a full-sleeved blouse suitable for bicycling.

She was not alone on this hillside.

Esther Moth too was enjoying what was for her the first break away from home in three years. She gazed blankly at the far distant range.

Otis laid a hand on Esther's hard clenched one.

Esther breathed out heavily. 'It is the anniversary that is always so hard to deal with, I dread its coming. It will be three years this year . . . People keep saying that time heals, but how much time? It goes away sometimes, I can go for days and not think of her; or if I do it is not miserably; but then comes a day when I wake up in the morning and it is as though she died only yesterday, and I hear her say, "Oh, George" – you remember how she did? It is my clearest memory of her . . . looking down at her shoes, it obscures all my nicer memories of her. "Oh George," she said and there was all that blood in her shoes.'

'I wish that I could say "I understand", but I don't . . . I have no idea what it must be like for you. Nobody that I have known, with your mother's exception, has died. Isn't that extraordinary?'

'There are times when I wonder whether I grieve for her

94

or for myself. And there are other times when I feel so angry that I could smash anything to hand. The waste! How could anyone think that there is love in a God who wastes a gentle, kind person?'

'Perhaps, when Kitt grows up, and you can see the whole picture, there will be some kind of answer to that.'

'Otis! What balderdash.'

Otis nodded resignedly, and put her arm about Esther's small shoulders. 'Of course it is. It was a cruel and heartless death. But it is just that I wish to say something that will make you feel better.'

Esther leaned into the circle of her friend's arm. 'You are like her. Pacific, kind, and will do and say anything to make things better. Not like me. Alas, poor Esther, who cannot ever have a birthday without remembering how her mother died having a child wrenched from her. I'm vinegar-sharp and angry. I prod people who have sores so that they will be as miserable as I.'

'Nonsense! You are unhappy today because for a moment when you awoke you had forgotten that your mother was dead. Anyone would be unhappy with such memories as you have. You are entitled to be vinegary on occasions. If you may not, then who may be? I can be sharp enough when the mood takes me, yet I have been given a life of love and pleasure.'

'I had looked forward so much to this holiday with you, and what do I do but spoil it.'

'One crotchety outburst won't spoil a fortnight in this lovely scenery.'

'I wish that we could spend more time together.'

Otis did not respond. Although she had not shown it to Esther, she had been angry when she had heard that Esther had given up her place at college to bring up her baby brother.

Emily Hewetson had said that she was shocked at Otis's reaction.

95

'Otis, it is the girl's duty. Who else is there to care for the child?'

'Why any more Esther's duty than the baby's own father, or Jack's for that matter? Jack has already had his chance, he has been to university.'

'There are times when I think you say foolish and outrageous things to shock and provoke. How could a man care for a tiny baby?'

'In the same way as Esther – by learning how.'

Emily, perceiving the seriousness with which Otis took her argument, felt afraid and had grown shrill. 'Well then, I suppose that in your world we should see young men pushing perambulators in Kensington Gardens, whilst young women, no doubt in top hats and morning dress, go to the City.'

'I do not see why we should not go to the City, but oh, Ma, what woman would be seen dead in such a silly form of dress?'

Emily had felt like crying. 'Because of nature, Otis. That is why they should not. Because Esther Moth's place in the world is to marry, bear babies and rear them; not Jack Moth's, not Inspector Moth's . . . but Esther's!'

'Kitt is not Esther's baby.'

'The child is her *brother*!'

'He is Inspector Moth's *son*.'

'She is a woman and so has a natural duty to the child.'

'If *she* had impregnated Mrs Moth then I might have agreed with you.'

Emily had been so shocked that she had pointed to the door and told Otis to go to her room and wait for her father to deal with her. But Otis had made a joke of it saying, 'Oh, Ma, there's nobody like you.' And having hugged her, rushed away to a lecture.

Now Otis said, 'I would love it if you would be included in more of our evenings . . . you know that we do have a rare old time of it on occasion. And you have other friendships. You must get out more than you do. Kitt doesn't need you one hundred per cent of the time. Why don't you ask your father to spend more time at home?'

'What friendships?'

'Well, Bindon Blood for one, isn't he a constant visitor?' Esther flushed and frowned but did not reply.

Otis drew a few lines in her journal and handed it to Esther. The sketch depicted a glowering cartoon likeness of Esther Moth, and the quote, 'Oh what's the matter with 'Melia Jane, She's perfectly well and she hasn't a pain, And it's lovely rice pudding for dinner again.'

For seconds Esther stared at Otis's cartoon drawing, then her mouth twitched and she smiled, almost against her will. 'Otis Hewetson! Why will you never allow anyone to have a serious wallow in self-pity?'

'A wallow's all right, but I don't think that I should stand by and watch you drown in it.'

Esther took Otis's hand and rubbed it gently against her own cheek and, using the silly language they used as girls, said, 'Yer a bit of orl right, gel.'

'Gerron ya soff fing.' The affection in which Otis held Esther showed in her eyes. As always she tried to mask the anger, pity and guilt she also felt. She pitied Esther as she would have pitied any young woman who had set her heart on serious education and had been thwarted. The guilt was almost second-nature, for Otis had developed a keen aware-ness of the many privileges she enjoyed because she had been born to them. She now mixed with a group of bright young women who regularly inspected their consciences and took a very different view of society from that of their mamas.

They had discussed the iniquity of Esther's situation and come to the conclusion that Esther had capitulated too easily. Inspector Moth, who never let his personal life interfere with his duty, was able to uphold that code only because he had a young and vulnerable unmarried daughter, whose duty it was, he considered, to step into her mother's shoes. What was more important than to keep the wheels of the Moth domestic life oiled and running? – certainly not two or three years of study in a female college.

He had blackmailed her with her love for him and her mother and her duty to the helpless Kitt. As Esther had related it, he had obviously packaged it very well, but as Otis saw him he was unfair and selfish.

'I hardly like to ask you to give it up, Esther,' he had said. 'I know how much you had set your heart on this studying business, my dear, but I could never give my full attention to my own serious duties knowing that some employed woman was running my household. Lord, it is difficult enough coping with the loss of Anne without the worry of wondering what I should find when I return home each day.' His eyes had been wet. Esther could scarcely bear her own tears, but his were terrible to her.

How much more heavy to bear was his loss of a wife than Esther's loss of a mother.

Jack had made an honest attempt on Esther's behalf. 'Father, it seems to me that the codicil drawn up by Mr Hewetson at Southsea was Mother's way of saying that whatever happened she wanted Esther to be free to follow her chosen career.'

'That, Jack, is something we shall never know. I must say that I find the entire business extraordinary. That your mother, who had a perfectly sensible will drawn up years ago, should suddenly, whilst on holiday and without consulting her husband, call in a solicitor of brief acquaintance and have him make those somewhat hole-in-the-corner arrangements . . . Well, it beats me. And if Esther feels strongly that her own ambitions must come before the welfare of the family, well then, come first they must.'

'Hole-in-the-corner, Father? How can you say that!'

'I do not mean that it was an underhand act in *that* sense, but I cannot see why she went to Martin Hewetson rather than wait to see her own solicitor.'

'I don't like to say it, Father, but wouldn't that have been rather too late?'

Esther, panicking at the prospect of yet further rents in the fabric of their family life, said, 'It's all right, Jack. I appreciate what Mother did in securing a little independence for me, but I would prefer to forget all about college and be at home to look after Father and Kitt.'

'And the income from the property can be invested so that when Esther finds herself a husband, she will have a tidy nest-egg of her own.'

When Otis heard that Esther was giving up her place at Stockwell, she rushed to see her own father and exploded, 'She can't, Pa! She absolutely cannot. You must go and see Inspector Moth and tell him that Mrs Moth wanted Esther to go to college. Why else should she call you in like that? She must have thought she might die, mustn't she? And she wanted to make Esther secure because she knew what would happen to Esther if she had to rely on her father for support.'

'Otis, Otis. You do fly off in all directions. I have seen Inspector Moth and told him everything that went on between myself and his wife, and if Inspector Moth is satisfied that he is carrying out his wife's wishes, then who are we strangers to say otherwise?'

She had tried to get Max Hewetson to do something for Esther. 'Oh, be blowed about stuffy old ethics, Uncle Hewey. Esther needs somebody to defend her, she's in no fit state to decide anything, she needs support. She longs to go to college, Mrs Moth knew that and wanted to ensure that nothing would stop it. Why can't somebody speak up for Mrs Moth? After all, it was her property and she wanted Esther to have it so that she could be independent. And now she is not.'

'Otis, my dear. There are times, when you are in full voice, that I believe that women might make very good advocates – never mind the truth of it, show us the passion.

99

For all we know, this gift to her daughter might well have been made in a moment of sentiment. Had she lived, it might well have been revoked upon her return to London.'

'Uncle Hewey! You know that's not true. But if you will not tell him, then I shall.'

Having known his niece and her flouncing little tantrums from the day she was born, Max Hewetson said, 'That's right, Otis, you tell him what's what.' Never, of course, dreaming that she would.

The overwhelming atmosphere and smell of the Police Court where, upon enquiring for Inspector Moth at his office, Otis had been directed, had not deterred her. When after many enquiries she had at last seen his imposing figure striding towards her, she had momentarily been put out at her own audacity, but remembering how Jack, when they were all at Bognor Regis, had confessed that he had ceased being afraid of his father once he had seen him in his combinations, Otis soon reduced the revered detective to human proportions.

She had forgotten how large and overbearing he was. And how handsome. He had taken her hand and paid her a compliment on her appearance as though they were meeting in the foyer of The Grand Hotel, and suggested that, as she said the matter was private, they go to his office in Scotland Yard, which was close by.

Determined not to have her resolve weakened by his manner, she began her speech as soon as they were in his office. 'I know that it is impertinent for me to have come to you, and I know that my father would be furious with me if he knew that I had, but I know that I am right to do so.'

'In that case, perhaps you should not be hasty. Wait.' And he had gone from the room and reappeared with a bottle and two glasses.

'Finest port in the country.' Without enquiring as to her tastes, he handed her a glass.

She looked at it suspiciously. 'This is not port wine – it's not red.'

'I assure you that it is. Taste.'

She did. 'It *is* port.' And sipped again appreciatively.

'Now that is what I like to see, a young lady who can recognize a fine white port when she tastes one.' And he had refilled her glass.

But she saw what he was attempting to do, and put her glass down firmly.

'Inspector Moth. You will not perhaps like a woman who speaks her mind, but that is what I am going to do. I do so because Mrs Moth was always a kind and understanding lady, and Esther is very dear to me.'

He smiled encouragingly, leaned back, raised his feet on an open drawer and listened.

'Ever since I have known Esther we have talked of going to college. We even dreamed of the possibility of in the future starting a small school of our own. I know that Esther had told her mother of her plans, and she said that Mrs Moth had said that it was a splendid idea and that we should never let anything stand in the way of our youthful ambitions.'

His eyes not leaving her for a second, Inspector Moth rocked himself in his captain's chair and nodded as though in agreement. Feeling that she was attaining her object by reasoned and civilized presentation, she accepted a little more of the white port wine.

'I take it,' he said, 'that you think that Esther should not be at home attending to womanly duties, but should be joining you at your establishment for "young ladies with a purpose in life" – isn't that the phrase?'

' "Women". Not "Ladies", we do not wish "*Ladies*" upon ourselves. "Women of purpose".'

'And you believe that what my daughter has chosen to do has no purpose?'

'I did not say that, I believe that care of children and teaching them is the foundation of a better society. I know that Esther wants very much to go to training college, and I believe that Mrs Moth wished her to. And I believe further that if you do not let Esther have the education she really wants, then you will not be carrying out Mrs Moth's wishes.'

'I see.' He had nodded as though he had never before considered the point. 'And how have you come to these conclusions?'

'I can see no other reason why Mrs Moth would have consulted my father and have him make provision for Esther. And from talking with Esther I know that she has always longed to continue her education.'

'This was before she decided *against* becoming a purposeful woman.' His eyes crinkled slightly and his lips were raised at the corners.

'Mr Moth, if you think that you can intimidate me with ridicule, then you do not know me very well.'

'Miss Hewetson, you are an extraordinarily attractive young woman and I would never dream of either intimidating or ridiculing any attractive young woman, particularly one with such nerve.'

'Nerve?'

'Yes, miss. George Moth is a man to be reckoned with, didn't you know? Hardened criminals and murderers think twice when they have to face Inspector Moth, prostitutes quail and police sergeants jump.'

'Perhaps their jumpiness has more to do with their consciences than with yourself. If you believe that your rank in the police force intimidates me, then you are wrong. As far as I am concerned, you are my best friend's father.'

He raised his eyebrows and made a gesture that suggested that he gave her that point.

'Miss Hewetson, you had me fooled, and there's not many who have done that. On the few occasions when I have come across you I took you for an inconsequential, scatter-brained, over-indulged bit of a girl. But I look at you

102

now . . .' He had paused whilst his eyes took in her face and figure. 'And I see a young woman to be reckoned with.'

Otis had felt both strong and weak. The weakness she put down to the unexpected potency of the port; the strength she acknowledged was pride in having done the right thing in confronting a man as important as Inspector Moth in the defence of her friend.

'Thank you. But you don't get round me with flattery. Are you going to let Esther go to college?'

'Esther is free to do whatever she chooses.'

'You know that she is not. A misguided sense of duty to you and to her baby brother prevents her from doing what she wants for herself and to which she has a right.'

'Would such sense of duty prevent you, Otis?'

The use of her first name was natural, but sounded unexpectedly intimate.

As he had done a minute ago to her, it was she who now paused and looked at him as if for the first time. Although he was over forty and as old as her father, he was extraordinarily attractive. The same straight, wide brows as Jack, but with the bushier eyebrows of a mature man, the same mouth whose line was deceptively shaped in a smile, the same strong, straight nose and firm jaw, but where Jack's physiognomy was fine, the father's was fleshier and more solid. It was, Otis thought, the face of an intelligent man who had seen and heard everything good and bad in human nature, and she saw in that moment how it had been that Anne Moth had found herself so self-satisfied in a pregnancy at the age of almost forty.

What must it be like to be physically loved by such a man? Or by any man for that matter.

'No, it would not prevent *me* – any more than it would yourself, or Jack, or my Uncle Hew or my own father. You would not dream of expecting Jack to forgo his education, you should not expect it of Esther.'

Having said what she had come to say, she rose and held

out her hand. 'Thank you for seeing me, Inspector Moth. I should be grateful if you would not complain of me to my father – it would upset my mother if she thought I was tramping round London on such errands.' She raised her eyebrows questioningly.

He nodded. 'Provided that you too are discreet.'

Suddenly, with one hand low on her back and the other about her shoulders, he quickly drew her into a close position where he was bending over her. His mouth was firm upon hers. She could smell the Police Court upon his clothes, his own warm, masculine sweat, the lavender shaving soap upon his skin. Firmly he pushed open her lips and made contact with her tongue.

She had never seriously kissed or been kissed before, yet she knew instinctively how to respond. His mouth was moist and warm, and the sandpaper roughness of his chin rasped her own. Briefly his large hands moved over her body and she did not want to move from them. It was a long and passionate kiss, an adult kiss, a kiss that set the wheels and pistons of Otis's womanhood into motion. She could not tell whether it lasted seconds or minutes, but she did not draw away, instead, after the first puzzling moment, she allowed herself the full experience so that, at last, it was he who drew slowly away with a look of surprise in his eyes.

'Well, well? Goodbye, Miss Hewetson, and thank you.'

Oh, the anger later. By that kiss, which she had been giddy enough to return, he had effectively spiked her guns. He had kissed with such . . . ? On her way back she had no words to describe it . . . such *contact*. She guessed that he knew well enough that she would never go running to her father. To tell her mother was out of the question. Ma would expect such a violator to be thrown out of the police force. She would forbid Otis to see Esther and Jack, and declare that she was not safe to be allowed out alone – particularly unsafe to allow her to keep her place at Stockwell College. Certainly she could not tell Esther, who in any case would hardly believe that her father was a man to embrace young girls only months after his wife's death. Otis knew what her own reaction would be if someone accused Pa of such an action. She could perhaps tell Jack, but for what reason? It had not been a violation, had she not responded?

She could imagine how smug he would look. *What has she complained of, Jack? That I did not go further? That she did not lean more heavily against me? Ask why she did not cry out, why she did not run from the office when there was help only feet away. Ask her how her mouth came to mould itself to mine and how her tongue came to curl around mine.*

And now, three years on, when she imagined how Esther's mind was shrivelling as her own expanded, she felt that her own participation on that day was partly to blame for Esther's situation. Had she behaved like any normal young girl, and been shocked and complained at once, she might even have used the incident as a form of blackmail; then Esther might have gone from her father's house and taken her place at Stockwell with Otis. As it was, she concluded from images sent to her in dreams that she had in a moment of aberration confused the inspector with Jack.

Now as the two young women shared fruit and mineral water and sank into an hour of quiet enjoyment of the splendid views, Otis reflected how, in the course of these last three years, they had both changed. Esther had grown quite sober and accountable, Otis, if anything, more assertive and hungry for experience than on the day she entered Stockwell.

That first day. It had been so thrilling.

'Esther? Do you know the first thing that I did when I arrived at Stockwell?'

Esther, absorbed in making a water-colour sketch, shook her head absently.

'I wrote you a postcard.'

'Mmm. Oh yes, I still have it. Chichester cathedral, I

believe. You wanted it for your collection. Remind me sometime and I will give it to you.'

'Gloucester cathedral.'

'Mmm.'

They drifted into the mood of the unusually warm spring day. Esther's water-colour was drying too quickly; Otis's pencil fell from her hand.

VIEW OF GLOUCESTER CATHEDRAL

Esther, Briefly. New Address: Stockwell College, Stockwell Road, London SW. I hope you will not think v. badly of me for not writing before. I did think it was awfully kind of you to tk all that trble in measuring things in my rm. Curtains lvly. Many thanks. Write sn. O.H. (Hppnd to hv. card by me frm last hol – how dull but plse save for colln.)

Although it had been September, Otis remembered that it had been a day much like this, unseasonably as warm as July. She had said to herself that this was perhaps the most significant day of her life. Certainly the most significant so far. She remembered having been glad that she had decided on her dull red and rust woven skirt and white blouse rather than her favourite white and cream. In the midst of sensible colours and peasant-like weaves like her own, that would have appeared too outrageous for a newcomer. Freshlings were easy to pick out, being the girls who did not call out or fling themselves into one another's arms, or fall into a delighted hug of reunion.

On arrival she had deposited her belongings in her college lodgings, met no one, and was panicked into thinking she had got something wrong, only to find that living so close she had arrived eagerly early. In the main assembly rooms of the college proper, having read every notice in sight, she sat on an outside wall in the sunshine and watched her future colleagues arrive.

A three-year course. Three years of reading, listening to lectures, discussing and acquiring knowledge. The shiver that went through her was almost erotic. The first stage in making reality of her dream was here.

This is Stockwell. The college that has been almost on her doorstep since she was born. It could have been built here with Otis Hewetson in mind. A college in which women were acceptable. Had she set her heart on reading for a law degree, then she would have been in for a battle with the establishment that would never have been won. As it was, she had determined that she would be a teacher. Not just a teacher. She had closed her eyes at the late summer sun and drifted on, to a day when she received a sealed scroll, to a day when she took rooms in some poor area of London where there was a need of good teachers, to a day when she stood in her first classroom, to when her first pupil passed the entrance exam to a new Oxford or Cambridge women's college that would be created for daughters of the poor, to the day when she was Miss Otis Hewetson MA, to a day when she stood before an assembly of uniformed girls and addressed them as their new Head.

'I say.' The voice that aroused her day-dreams was soft and timid. 'I'm awfully sorry to bother you.'

Otis opened her eyes to see a young woman of her own age, eyebrows raised and eyes wide as a startled rabbit's.

'I'm new. I've just arrived. I'm awfully sorry but I don't know where to go. Could you . . . ?'

'I'm new too.'

'I say, are you really? You looked so confident dozing there in the sun that I was sure that you must be in your final year . . .'

'Thank heaven,' Otis said. 'I thought that I must look such a rank beginner that everyone would notice me quivering. I believe that we are masses too early. Come and sit with me.'

'Are we allowed?'

'I don't know, but I doubt if we shall be sent to the Head for it.'

The girl laughed. 'No, I suppose we shan't. It is going to take some getting used to . . . you know, being responsible.'

'I'm Otis Hewetson. How d'you do?'

'Catherine Campbell . . . I'm pleased to meet you. I saw your name – Otis . . . easily remembered – we are in the same place of residence. You are next to my friend who can't get here until tomorrow.'

'You have a friend starting at the same time?'

'Oh yes, we always planned to keep together.'

Otis thought of Esther, caught in the web of duty that had been spun for her and from which she would not attempt to escape.

It had been in an attempt to try to revive something of the old Esther that Otis had arranged this Easter bicycling holiday in the Trossachs. This time, though, she did not attempt interviewing Inspector Moth, but wrote him a polite letter asking that he persuade Esther to accompany her on this tour. Equally politely, he had replied that he was pleased for his daughter to spend a few weeks in such healthful pursuits. Not only had he engaged a temporary housekeeper, he had also ordered a new bicycle for Esther, and hoped that the two friends would enjoy themselves and return to London invigorated.

As they pedalled their way back towards their lodgings at the end of that day, Esther Moth felt more at ease than she had done in ages.

No one at home ever wanted to talk of her mother. Her father immersed himself in his work and went from the house, often for days at a time. No one could say that he neglected the physical needs of his family: he had engaged a nursemaid for Kitt and was never mean with the money with which Esther kept house. But he disliked talk of Anne, telling Esther when she put flowers before her mother's portrait on her birthday that she must not be sentimental, or, as when she told little Kitt stories about her own childhood, that she must not dwell upon the past.

Jack was seriously studying law and, whilst he would occasionally mention their mother, he rarely had time to listen to Esther who did not wish her memory of her mother to become dry and shrivelled. So that these Trossach days with Otis, who didn't think her morbid or maudlin if she talked about her mother, were like water to her parched memory.

As on several occasions over the last week, talk of the past turned to talk of the future, when Otis yet again tried to get Esther to talk about her forthcoming marriage to Bindon Blood, the lieutenant – now captain – who had fallen in love with Esther that fateful night in Southsea.

Everyone had agreed that the young officer had been wonderful on that occasion in the way he had taken command of the situation.

He had given orders to hotel staff to clear the room and close it off to the public, and had himself run to fetch a doctor he knew of who lived in the vicinity. All through the night he had sat with Esther and Jack in an ante-room in the nursing home whilst their father had waited to see whether the flickering flame of Anne Moth's life would burn. It was the handsome young lieutenant too who had had a carriage standing at the ready to carry the forlorn family back to Garden Cottage and had helped Nancy Dickenson see to their physical needs.

Anne Moth's frail baby had had to be cared for in the nursing home for six weeks, during which time Esther and Jack continued to stay on in Garden Cottage with Nancy in attendance.

Lieutenant Blood, being in barracks at Southsea, continued to be of great comfort and assistance to them. Inspector Moth showed his gratitude by welcoming the officer to his home whenever he was in London which, once

Esther had returned home with baby Kitt, was as often as Captain Blood could manage.

Having once saved George Moth's life, as well as being a tower of strength in time of crisis, the obliging and kindly officer, having no immediate family of his own, found a place in that of the Moths.

If Esther Moth did not love the dark-haired, olive-complexioned, serious young officer quite as much as he loved her, she certainly loved him, and was endlessly grateful for the concern he showed for them all in their time of crisis. How could she have done otherwise than accept him when he had produced a diamond and opal ring?

Now, in a few months' time, in the summer of 1914, she would be married to him.

But to Otis Hewetson it all seemed to be such a waste of a girl who would have made such a good professional woman. Heaven knew, the world was short enough of them. Even so, she took a great interest in her friend's forthcoming career as a wife.

'But won't you ever have a home of your own?'

'Windsor Villa is my own home.'

'You know what I mean, you and Bindon, together, alone.'

'Perhaps one day, when Kitt is a schoolboy. But with a house the size of Windsor Villa, we shall virtually have our own apartment within it. If we took a place of our own, it would have to be close to the barracks or there would be little point, and if I were to take Kitt, then he would miss Father and Jack. As it is, Bindon can be in London in a couple of hours, Jack and Father need not be put about by having some strange woman house-keep for them, and Kitt can grow up in Windsor Villa as Jack and I did. Mother loved living close to the Heath, she would have wanted Kitt to grow up there. And Bindon prefers a London house anyway.'

And what about Esther? Otis longed to say. Does Esther

want to continue as mistress of Windsor Villa, as house-keeper to Inspector Moth, as foster-mother to Kitt and Jack? Doesn't she want to be a bride in a home of her own choice, unencumbered by ready-made domestic responsibilities? But Otis did not say any such thing, suspecting that it would be heartless to force her own boat-rocking philosophies about independence upon Esther. Esther seemed able to cope better with the status quo. And in any case, Esther's selflessness often made Otis feel self-centred, and guilty because of it.

'So long as you don't forget that you were once Esther Moth,' was all that Otis allowed herself to say.

'But I shall not be. I shall be Mrs Major Blood.'

'Esther! A major?'

Esther flushed and smiled as though it was she who was to be promoted. 'We believe so, and in time for the wedding.'

The road became steep so they dismounted and pushed their heavy iron bicycles along. It was late in the afternoon, but the sun was quite hot for the time of year, and dust rose at every footstep; a bank on the north side was green and gave off the fresh smell of moss. Had one of her Stockwell College friends been with her, then Otis would have said something about the air being flavoured with pepper and salt, and they would have contradicted, and each given their own interpretation of the smell of the air in which pollen, dust and moss mingled. But, because Esther had joined the domestic ranks, such a comment would have seemed too self-consciously *outré*.

Of all the friends, and she had gained many during her time at Stockwell, she still retained her greatest affection for Esther. There were times when they did not see one another for weeks, yet as soon as Otis was in Esther's company she could relax. This holiday in particular had done much to forge their already strong bonds.

'Stop, Esther.' Spontaneously, Otis dropped her bicycle, put her arms about her friend's slim shoulders, and kissed

111

her fiercely on both cheeks. 'Why have I never told you that you are my very favourite person. I think that if I were Bindon Blood then I should want to marry you.'

Colour suffused Esther's neck and she held herself a little away from her friend's embrace. 'Otis! What on earth do you mean? You are not . . . I mean, you are not an . . . unnatural woman?'

Now, holding her friend at arm's length, Otis smiled. 'Would it change things between us if I were? Several of my Stockwell friends are.'

'Of course it would, but I am sure that you are not. You are not, are you? Otis, don't play the fool with me. You did not mean *that*, did you?'

'No, dearest Miss Moth, for my sins I am fixed on the male of the species, although when I see my women friends in the company of their women partners, I am a little envious of the ease of their lives. But as for you and me . . . what I mean is that you are sweet and kind and self-sacrificing and you never think of yourself and I am afraid that when you are set up with Bindon, then I shall never see Esther Moth again. What I mean is that you are such a very *nice* person and that I feel that I must tell you. Why are we all so afraid of owning up to our feelings about those we love best. I wonder if any man at all deserves you – and yet you plan to give yourself to four of the brutes.'

'That is no hardship – for I love them all. And shame on you, Otis. How can you say that little Kitt is a brute?'

Retrieving her machine, Otis smiled fondly at the thought of the featherweight, stick-armed little boy, whose serious application to puzzles and games delighted her on the occasions when Esther had brought him to visit in Otis's room.

'True, for the present Kitt is only an honorary brute – a kitty-brute.'

Not, she thought, a rogue like his father. And, as always when the image of George Moth flashed into her mind, her thighs became taut and a tremor ran over her breast. The times she had wished that it had been Jack Moth who had stooped over her, enveloped her in his long arms, Jack who had felt the outline of her figure, breathed heavily and forced her lips apart.

In these modern times she might have, as had some of her faster friends, taken a lover. Taken Jack Moth briefly until she had worked him out of her system. The recurring problem of the father had no solution unless and until something equally erotic obliterated the memory of that brief moment of mutual passion. As for Jack Moth, he was friendly on the few occasions when they met, but he still treated her in the brotherly way that he had always done.

Of course the one person with whom Otis wanted to talk of her entangled feelings was Esther, but of course she was one person with whom this was impossible.

Once Esther's normal good spirits had returned, the two friends talked and laughed their way through the rest of their holiday, and returned to London refreshed and as brown-skinned as hop-pickers – Esther to her wedding arrangements, and Otis to her final term and the world of professional women.

ANNOUNCEMENT OF DEATH

CLERMONT – MAJOR GENERAL SIR NORBERT CLERMONT,
LATE OF THE HUSSARS (THE RED BRUNSWICKERS).
SUDDENLY IN LONDON. PRIVATE BURIAL SERVICE IN
FAMILY CHAPEL.
REQUEST NO FLORAL TRIBUTES

Although Jack Moth – as did Otis and her women friends, and as did many modern young men in universities and colleges – earnestly discussed politics and world affairs, he did not, in that same spring of 1914, foresee his own future, except in wig and gown, swishing dramatically through the Inns of Court in London.

Although in 1911, whilst menaced by no power, Germany had greatly increased her army by the adoption of an Army Act, followed by further acts in 1912 and 1913, Jack Moth had no idea that these measures meant anything more personal to him than did Sinn Fein and the Irish problem. In 1914, Jack Moth was not alone in assuming that such machinations of certain rogue governments were a matter for other governments rather than for individuals.

Although Russia worked at the construction of military railways and armament factories; although Belgium secretly adopted compulsory measures, and France lengthened the period of its own military service and deployed its navy in the Mediterranean, and although British naval strength was now concentrated in the North Sea where Germany's navy was massed, it did not occur to Jack Moth that the ominously drawn forces of the Great Powers of Europe were to have any effect upon his personal life. There was talk of war, but war was fought by professional soldiers. His future brother-in-law, Bindon Blood, would probably see active service, but Jack Moth's destiny was as a great advocate. Not yet, of course, he was still only in his early twenties, but that was his plan and ambition.

Somewhere entwined in his plan for the future was Victoria Ormorod. When he envisaged the distinguished Mr Justice Moth, he saw him accompanied by the noble profile of the judge's copperheaded lady.

During the last three years, during which time he had seldom seen her, and then only by attending her meetings and taking her somewhere for supper or tea, his youthful head-over-heels love had been changed to a kind of warm devotion. Had he been asked to put into words what his feelings were for Victoria, he would probably have found it impossible. Only that they were always present: not disturbing, nor intrusive to his studies, but he was alive to her, aware of her presence on this planet at this time. Above all, he had the notion that she was, like himself, marking time till the appropriate moment when their lives should merge. He was in no position to ask anything of her yet.

Back in 1911, on the evening following Anne Moth's death, having read an announcement of it in a Portsmouth paper, Victoria had written Jack a letter of condolence, which she went out to deliver personally a short while before she was due to catch a train to leave the town. As she approached the cottage, Jack Moth had come through the gate. He had looked so haggard and distraught that she would have had the earth swallow her up rather than intrude upon his grief. Suddenly, her note as she held it out to him had felt pathetic and formal.

'I am so sorry,' she said.

'Thank you. I'm not yet really aware that it has happened.'

'I read of it in the paper, I thought . . . I just wanted . . .' She relinquished the note, 'I wanted you to know what my thoughts are . . . I hope that you will not think it trite.'

'Thank you, that is very kind.' He looked directly into her eyes, and tears that had already been close to the surface brimmed and spilled over. Touchingly, the tall and broad, handsome young man made no attempt to dash away his tears, but stood looking at her in the orange glow of the setting sun.

'I wish that there was something that I could do. One always feels so helpless in the face of someone else's misery.'

'You could walk with me. You do not have to talk, but I should be so glad of your company.'

So she walked with him. From Garden Cottage where they had been standing, all around the perimeter of the Common and then across it, past the fountain where she had loaned him her towel, along the darkening promenade and back again, past the brightly-lit glass dome of the Leisure

Pier where he had bought the comic postcards for his friends, then along the walled waterfront to the ancient Round Tower and to a little pebbled bay beneath the walls. Here, with their backs to the stone of the old fortifications, and by the light of street lanterns and an unclouded moon, they sat whilst the train on which Victoria Ormorod should have been travelling steamed out of Southsea Station.

Whilst they had walked they had scarcely spoken. Once or twice he had looked at her and when necessary had politely handed her through gates or around rough patches of the pathway. On the sheltered curve of beach where waves and wash from vessels going in and out of harbour rushed back and forth, he began to toss small stones at the white crest of each approaching wave, becoming more and more violent with each throw until, almost mechanically, he was hurling pebbles, as large as his own hand, with great ferocity. Suddenly he ceased, and stood with his arms hanging loose, breathing harshly.

Only then had she gone to him and taken his cold hand, sticky with salt from the pebbles, and drawn him back to sit on her shawl against the wall still warm from the day. There he had wept, and she had held his head against her breast until his racking sobs subsided. There, with her confident hand caressing his temple, he had felt his shock begin to ebb away. There he had at last raised his head and found that she had been willing to comfort him with kisses.

She had stayed with him, holding him close until the tide had turned and they had no option but to escape via the archway through which they had reached the little hidden bay.

Then she had walked with him until they were almost back to Garden Cottage, when she had kissed him briefly and said, 'I will go. I know that you can now be strong for your family', and had hurried off. He had never known that her luggage had awaited her at the station and that she had

116

had some difficulty in regaining a room for the night at the Beach Hotel.

When he returned to his studies, he began to take life more seriously. On the first occasion when he had sought her out, she had been formally polite to the point of remoteness. But to Jack the memory of that evening was a kind of icon stored in his memory. Whenever his mother came to mind, he touched the icon and was comforted.

Whilst he was still at Cambridge, he went to parties and functions with young women, visited some foreign bordels and had brief and unserious love-affairs with equally unserious young women whom he met from time to time whilst visiting one or other of the Clermonts. But their caresses and kisses were as watered milk to Cornish cream when compared to Victoria Ormorod.

The only other woman to come near to being Cornish cream was Otis Hewetson. He liked Otis: she had something of the forthrightness, and gave off the same air of confidence as Victoria, but she was as yet immature. Perhaps one day she would be cream, but so far it had not risen to the surface. It had been the confident maturity of Victoria Ormorod that had first attracted him and had gone on doing so to the extent that, with the exception of Otis, he scarcely found a flicker of interest in any woman who was not ten years older than himself.

As he dressed to go out, Jack Moth thought how strange the house felt without Esther. She was as small and fair and light as their mother had been, yet somehow her presence, like his ma's, appeared to fill the house. He listened to the water noises as the nurserymaid filled Kitt's bath, he heard Kitt's high shrieking laugh as she played chase to get him undressed. He wondered whether Father was in and concluded that he was not for, though he was heavier-handed, like Esther, one knew when he was in the house.

With Esther away, Bindon Blood was not likely to call. Come to think of it, he had not been up from Southsea for some time. Jack assumed that most military types would have their free time curtailed now that there was not only an Irish problem for the army to sort out, but a European one too.

He hummed as he knotted his tie, at the same time reading again the handbill announcing that the guest speaker at the next meeting of the Hampstead Fabians would be Blanche Ruby Bice. 'Non-members welcome.'

He heard the front door open and a heavy tread in the hallway that announced his father's return. Unusually early, for his father was seldom in the house at this time of day.

'Anybody there?'

Jack had never fathomed why his father should call out when he came in, for certainly Esther or one of the maids would hurry to greet him and take his hat and cane and hang up his overcoat. The temporary housekeeper could be heard dutifully enquiring about the requirements of the master's mealtime, then his springy step taking the stairs, as always, two at a time, as though he was not over forty years of age and not above fifteen stone in weight. Then the squeal of Kitt's excitement as he was surprised in his bath by his father.

Jack decided to go along to the nursery too, for he found great pleasure in playing with his pixie-like brother as he splashed with his boats and ducks.

'Look, Jack, look!' Kitt pointed to a tin seal which George Moth was winding up for him. The inspector, kneeling and with his shirtsleeves rolled up, placed the toy in the water where it whirred and paddled its way towards Kitt. Although he smiled at Kitt and again at his elder son, Jack thought that his father looked tired.

'A live seal? Lord save you, Kitt, just you watch he don't nip your bott,' Jack said, kneeling also – and in his newly-pressed trousers.

''Tisn't real, Jack. Look at him, isn't he splendid? Dada

got him from Hamley's.' 'Splendid' was, at the moment, Kitt's latest and most loved word.

The nurserymaid sat on a stool, moving only to add more warm water from time to time, and watched the two men – each well above six feet in height, and brown-haired, long-legged and broad-shouldered – as they joined in the watery games with her slight, blond-headed charge. When she read the lurid reports of the many murder investigations in which her employer was involved, she could hardly believe that the awesome Inspector Moth and little Kitt's Dada were the same man. Almost as strange was the knowledge that Kitt's Mama, whom she knew only from daguerreotypes and portraits of her, should be the mother of Master Jack. On the occasions when Miss Esther and Master Jack took Kitt out on to the Heath, anyone could believe that they were in fact the parents, for Kitt was very like his sister.

When there was no more hot water, the two men rose reluctantly from their knees and left the nurserymaid to put Kitt into his nightshirt. As they descended the stairs together, Jack looked down at his wet and crumpled trousers. 'Damn. I was going to wear these.'

For a second the father looked momentarily crestfallen. 'Out this evening then?'

'Yes, later.'

'Ah. Pity. For once I've got an evening at home.'

'I'm sorry, Father, but I'm expected.'

'Oh it's all right, all right. It is only that it is a long time since we talked, and I thought . . .'

Jack nodded, surprised, because they had seldom 'talked' in the way his father now inferred. The last time, as Jack recalled, was when he was about to come down from Cambridge and his father had asked him about his plans. Compared to some fellows' fathers, his own had been exceptionally non-interfering: he would give advice if asked, but rarely offered it gratuitously.

When Jack said that he proposed going in for law, his father had said, 'But not in my sort of game, I imagine.'

Surprised, because he had never thought of his father as being involved in 'The Law', Jack had replied that he meant the law proper, not police work. At which his father had merely raised a wry eyebrow and said, 'At least we shall be on the same side of it.' To which Jack had made the right reply by saying, 'I shouldn't like to be on the wrong side if I came up against you, Father.'

And when Jack had asked whether they could afford for him to continue his studies without any prospect of return for years, George Moth had said, 'What I have is mostly from your mother, Clermont money, and there's a deal more Clermont in you than there is in me, so why shouldn't you have some of it?'

They reached the landing of Jack's room. Jack stood back to allow his father to pass, but he did not do so. Sensing that his father did not want to go, he felt guilty at his own insistence. 'Well, excuse me then, Father, I must change.'

'Is it all right if I come in?'

'Heavens, yes . . . of course it's all right.'

While Jack changed, his father sat and watched him, sized him up, whilst Jack watched too, noticing small signs of some agitation, a thing his father rarely showed. 'If there is some Clermont in you, m'boy, I can't say that it shows. Pure-bred Moth those limbs and shoulders.'

Jack smiled at the note of pride in his father's tone. 'The only one of the three of us who is. Esther and Kitt take after Mother.'

'A pity the Force didn't win you, a young man with brains and education can go to the top these days.'

'Not whilst the best appointments are made by civil servants from men outside.'

George Moth did not reply, knowing that Jack was only quoting his own words. It was unlikely that George Moth's own rank would ever be much higher than superintendent.

'Never fear on that score, Jack, the Clermonts always look after their own.'

'Then why is it you never expect to hold high rank in the police force?'

'An intruder, Jack. Something that the society of hunt-ball families finds it hard to forgive. I persuaded your mother to marry outside her own circle – beneath it in their eyes – which was entirely unforgivable. This country is in the hands of a few families, which is why I shall never hold high rank in my career.'

'Then it's a wonder the Clermonts haven't cold-shouldered Esther and me.'

'You are a fact of their lives, lad. No matter what, you, Kitt and your sister are an entry in the Clermont family archives, you appear as branches on their family tree, you are of the blood. No matter what, your future is in bond with theirs.'

Many times since his mother had died, Jack had wanted to talk with his father about her family, but he would never open up. This evening, Jack felt, it was as though he had come home purposely to unburden himself of the Clermont family. Why else had he asked to come into Jack's room?

'I'm a Moth, Father. One has only to look at Grandfather Moth and Uncle Dick and Uncle Fred and Cousin Joe and then see me to know I'm no Clermont.'

'If your blood were to be spilled, lad, the Clermonts would expect it to run out blue. And they might well be right. I see your mother in you every day.'

Jack smiled inwardly and concentrated on re-arranging his hair. Every day? They could go for a week and not see one another. But his father had always had this sentimental streak in him. Jack had suspected long ago that this sentiment was part of the reason why his father could keep on and on searching doggedly for some man who had killed a girl with his fists. In his father's heart, Jack suspected, a young dead prostitute was a girl not very different from

121

Esther, except for the circumstances that put the one girl on the streets and kept the other within the bosom of her family. Jack was almost right, except that it was sensibility rather than sentimentality that he observed in his father.

Having made himself ready to go out, Jack turned and leaned against the wardrobe. 'I must go soon, Father, but I shan't be late back.'

George Moth nodded his understanding, but continued as though he had not heard. 'The Clermonts have always been a military family, Jack.'

Jack smiled. 'With all those portraits of red coats and gold braid at Mere, one can scarcely avoid that conclusion.'

'Do you like Mere?'

'It's fine for a holiday. I shouldn't like to live there. I'm a Londoner, Father. I should die of boredom if I had to spend longer than a month in Lyme Regis.'

'But what if you had no choice?'

'But I would have a choice. There is no law that can compel anyone to live where they don't wish to.'

'What if you were to inherit Mere?'

'*Inherit* it? How could I, when there are all the Clermont cousins?'

'But *you* are a Clermont cousin.' He paused and then plunged on, 'And I happen to know that you will inherit from Sir Norbert. Your mother has always known and so, naturally, have I known from her. I believe that is why she willed her own property to Esther.'

Father and son looked at one another for long seconds, George seeing genuine astonishment, his son seeing veracity. And something else – concern.

'Did your mother never hint?'

'No.'

'No need to snap off my head.'

'I'm sorry, Father. I didn't intend . . .'

'I dare say I should have chosen a better time, but we so seldom . . .'

'I know. It wouldn't have made much difference, it would have come as a shock to me whenever I discovered it. Are you sure?'

'I am sure. You don't seem delighted at the prospect.'

'I am not.'

'Most young men would be overjoyed to inherit a prosperous estate like Mere.'

'I am not most young men. How did you feel about inheriting from Ma?' Jack knew that he was entering what might well be a minefield, for his father had a very masculine pride and, as far as he knew, his father had never used a penny except to continue to pay the necessary fees to put himself into Law.

George Moth stood up and, with his hands thrust into his trousers pockets, walked to the window and stared down into the street below. Without turning he said, 'Belittled!' He pressed his forehead against the glass. 'I loved your mother, and she loved me. Had she not, then I should never have taken her away from those people – her people. They thought that I must be a fortune hunter – they don't seem able to comprehend a poor man who can love a rich woman and not want her wealth. But I never did, and still do not. If she had been a factory girl or a dairy-maid I should have wanted her. Wanted *her*. That was what they could not understand.'

Jack understood. He knew scarcely anything about Victoria Ormorod except that she was involved in protest and politics and that her world was as alien and distant from Jack Moth's as Anne Clermont's had been from George Moth's. And quite suddenly he knew that if he did not secure Victoria for himself now, then he might lose her. He took his topcoat from the wardrobe.

'You're going?' George Moth asked, as though he had not seen his son's earlier preparations.

'Yes.'

George Moth took a brush from the dressing-table and brushed his son's shoulders. 'Norbert Clermont is dead.'

For a brief moment they both seemed to stop breathing. 'Sir Norbert? Uncle Norbert?'

The father took a broad sweep of the brush from shoulder to hem of his son's coat. 'Discovered in St James's Park with a young guardsman. Both drunk. Arrested. Damn fool of a station sergeant – should have known better than to leave a sodomite unattended in a cell with anything he could tie about his neck – especially one with a title.' At last George Moth looked directly at his son.

The son removed from his father's hand the clothes-brush that had been working as though powered by a machine. 'Sir Norbert? A pervert?'

George Moth heaved a sigh and sank down on the bed, his large hands hanging loose between his heavy thighs. 'Yes, lad. Sir Norbert high-and-mighty Major-General Clermont when he's at home. Buggered a lower rank in a public place and couldn't face the music. Topped himself with his own braces.'

'Sir Norbert has committed suicide?'

'Yes, Jack, yes, the damned fool. St James's Park of *all* places. The man must have been an idiot! Half the London force knows already, the rest will know by tomorrow. It will be hushed up, of course. I dare say the word will go out that he was found dead of a heart attack in St James's Park. Your Clermont inheritance will be pure as the driven snow.'

'Clermont inheritance be damned! I want nothing to do with it.'

'I understand your feelings, m'boy, but if you'll take my advice then you will do nothing in haste. If there's one lesson I've learned in twenty years, it is never to jump in with both feet. Give yourself pause and think about the consequences.'

And, at that moment, he believed it.

'Get off then, lad. If I've made you late, I'm sorry. But you realize that I had no option but to say what I have said.'

'Of course, Father. I should have been mortified to have heard it from anyone but yourself. I dare say rumours will be flying. I don't believe that many of my colleagues know about my Clermont connection, but this is just the kind of thing that would bring it into the open.'

George Moth stood at the door and, with a diffidence that was rare in him, said, 'All those red coats, lad. When this war comes you will be expected to join the regiment.'

For a moment Jack looked as though he did not know what his father was talking about. 'An officer and a gentleman, eh?'

His father nodded.

'Thanks, but I'll leave all that kind of thing to Esther's beau. I'll stick to learning to cut and thrust with words and leave the sword stuff to them that likes it.'

Inspector Moth looked his son – who was now groomed and ready to go out – up and down. 'You've got a fine figure for a uniform, son.'

Jack laughed and gave his father a genial palm on his shoulder. 'And a fine head for that fur cap with the toggles, Father? I've also got a few more brains than to waste them fighting old battles over regimental dinners as my future brother-in-law does. If I was ever fool enough to go for a soldier, then it would be as a decent, common, foot-slogger.'

'Ha! Romantic nonsense. That's no Moth speaking. We've been the common foot-sloggers for too many generations to think there's much decent about life at the bottom.'

> *Miss Nancy Dickenson, 25 Spencer Road, Southsea.*
> *Nancy, My grandmother has died, and there are the usual arrangements to be attended to. If you will take the Hampstead meeting, I shall be for ever grateful. Victoria*

In the three years since Nancy Dickenson had been active in the suffragist movement, she had, as she would have put it 'come out of my old shell'. Although she was still a domestic worker, she was no longer the peripatetic cook-general she had been when she worked for the Moth family. By chance a bit of good luck had come her way in that when applying for another position she had been taken on by two sisters who lived in one of the newly-built villas on Southsea front, and these two sisters were deeply involved in what they called The Women's Cause.

The O'Reilly sisters were ginger-haired, independent and rebellious. They were the scourge of the city fathers, who could hardly dismiss them because they were not only of Southsea's social cream but were well-informed, articulate and, above all, wealthy ratepayers. Once the Misses O'Reilly had discovered that they had engaged a servant who was an adherent to their cause, they began a course of political grooming to which Nancy took as a duck to water.

They had been the organizers of the series of meetings at which Victoria Ormorod had, in her Blanche Ruby Bice persona, spoken three years ago at Southsea. The O'Reilly sisters were proud of their association with Victoria. She had been their 'find'. It was they who, having some years before heard her intelligently heckling a speaker against universal suffrage, had taken her in hand much in the way they later took Nancy Dickenson in hand. But with one difference, which was that, whilst Victoria insisted that she should have separate private and public faces – hence her alias – Nancy Dickenson traded on her own name which was already known in the docklands of Portsmouth where she did a great deal of speaking at factory gates and trade union meetings.

Nancy would never have the kind of aura that surrounded Blanche Ruby Bice, but she was a good plain speaker against the sweated stay-making factory-owners and uniform workshop conditions, and could always turn out a good local following in any protest or procession.

This was the first time that she had ever substituted as a speaker outside her home area.

When she saw that it was a Fabian meeting, Nancy had assumed she would be speaking to the converted and that this would be a small, earnest gathering of quiet socialists. But when she came out of the station, her eye was caught by the announcement of the meeting on a large, professionally-produced placard. Reading it was a young man whose profile was familiar. She inclined her head to see him better.

'Why, if it isn't Master Jack. An't I right?'

He looked at the smartly-dressed woman wearing a beautifully tailored fawn suit, georgette blouse with flowing scarf and a wide-brimmed hat, and frowned slightly as his memory flicked through faces. 'Nancy?'

She laughed. 'Of course it's Nancy. I haven't changed that much in three years, have I?'

She knew of course that she had changed, and felt a rush of pleasure at the knowledge that she looked every bit the handsome woman that her employers had made her. A lifetime of making something of herself with any bit of a thing that had come her way was good training, and now the scarcely outdated models pressed upon her by the Misses O'Reilly had given her a small wardrobe of elegant clothes.

She had a good, full-bosomed, wide-hipped, fashionable figure, which was firm from work and plain food. Although she was not beautiful, she had the same wide eyes and good teeth of her mother, and her father's poker-straight back. Not so outstanding and striking as Victoria Ormorod, but very presentable now that she had given up trying to efface herself.

Jack Moth, with a look of pleasant amusement, pumped her hand as he would have an old college chum's. 'Well, I'll be blowed. Nancy. Hampstead Station, of all the places to meet Nancy Dickenson.'

'You even remembered my name, Master Jack.'

'Of course I remember your name, you were extraordinarily kind to Ess and me in Southsea.'

'And how is Miss Esther and the master?'

'He is still the same. Esther is about to be married.'

'Married? I thought that she was going off to college. Dear Lord, how I envied her that. Fancy choosing to get married instead.'

He held her gaze earnestly and was still holding on to her hand as though he did not want to lose the link between them. She felt his hand tighten slightly.

'She is as good as married already, keeping house for me and Pa and looking after young Kitt. She might as well have the pleasure of a dashing soldier husband.'

'Baby Ninian?'

'Young Kitt . . . he's almost three. We started calling him Kitten for obvious reasons, and I don't believe anybody remembers that he's got a proper name.'

'That baby lived, I didn't hardly like to ask? He was so weak and frail when you took him home. Well there, that just shows you. I should never have thought it, him being so little and so early coming.'

128

'Do you ever come to London? Do you? You should come and see him. He's a splendid little chap. Life and soul of the house.'

'Well, I'll tell you something nobody knows as yet. I've been going with a bloke off and on for some time – from Bethnal Green – he wants us to get married . . . but I don't know.'

'He's a lucky man, Nancy. Do you still make those special bread-and-butter puddings?'

'Of course I do. And what about yourself?'

'Me? Oh I'm still waiting to become somebody. I did get my degree.' He mocked himself as he said, 'First Class Hons.'

'First Class, eh? Your ma would have been proud of you.'

'Yes, she would, wouldn't she? Now I'm studying for the Bar.'

'The Bar. That's quite high up in the law isn't it?'

She became slightly embarrassed when he did not answer immediately but stood looking intently at her. She could not have guessed from his expression that his pause was for the sudden thought: *Oh Nancy, why aren't there more people in the world like you? No airs and graces. No pretence. As straight and honest as they come.*

'Yes, I hope to be a barrister one day.'

'Well now, if that isn't a blooming good thing to be these days . . . I shall keep you in mind if I ever find myself in choky.'

She was torn between being on time for her meeting and not wanting to let him go without doing something – what, she did not know; he had said come and see Kitt. She saw him glance at the station clock.

She said, 'I don't want to appear rude, but I've got an appointment in half an hour and I don't yet know where to go.'

'So have I, Nancy, but I did want to ask you about yourself – what you are doing now.'

129

'Well, Master Jack, I'm still a domestic, but what I am doing tonight is this.' She pointed to the notice of the Fabian meeting. Part of her wanted to hurry to it and the rest wanted to stand and ask him about his family and how they had fared without Mrs Moth.

'Why, that is exactly where I am headed, Nancy. I know that hall, it's only a short walk, we can go together.' She felt him touch her elbow as though they had never been master and servant. There had always been *something* about that family. Of all the people she had worked for, they had been the only ones – until the O'Reilly sisters – who had ever treated her as though she was a person and not a bit of machinery they had hired for the season. He had even remembered her name – usually they didn't even remember your face.

She fell in alongside him, feeling strange – for it was seldom that she walked with a man alone, except when her own and Wally's free weekends coincided. These days, her life was filled with women. As well as Wally, she had quite a few men admirers, but these were the likes of widowed grocers, young butchers, postmen and deliverymen, most of whom would have been perfectly happy to have got her into their kitchen or bed, but did not want the company of a woman who read more of the daily paper than the sport and crime pages. And men who did read world affairs were often so earnest that they seemed to want to talk of nothing else except their own philosophy. Wally was just right, he could enjoy a union meeting or an evening at the music-hall equally.

'You are still doing your bit to get the vote, then? But all the way to Hampstead from Southsea? I assume you are still there.'

'Oh yes. I have a very good permanent position.'

'I thought you liked us holiday casuals.'

She smiled up at him from under her large brim. 'Fancy you remembered that. I thought it was time I settled down into something a bit more secure, only to find myself doing more and more of this sort of thing – speaking up for women. I've never been this far before. To tell you the truth, I feel real-ly nervous about it. I mean . . . I dare say you come along thinking you was – were going to hear Red Ruby.'

The swing of his step halted perceptibly, and she felt that when they heard of the change of speaker a good many people would feel a bit cheated. But there . . . she could only do her best.

'Isn't she . . . ?'

'Death in her family.' Nancy remembered the evening when she had first done something practical for the NUWSS and had acted as steward at the meeting. He had gone there looking for Victoria, and hadn't known that she was the platform speaker. She had suspected that he was mooning around after Victoria. She remembered too being herself half in love with him – Jolly Jack . . . That's just what he had been, jolly – until that terrible night when they had gone out to The Grand. All of them dressed to kill and so happy: dainty Miss Esther with a silver band on her pretty hair, the mistress, dainty too in spite of her condition, suddenly lively as a girl, the inspector down from London; the two big men in dress suits walking about that little cottage stooped because of the low beams, both of them hitting their heads on doorways until she had pinned hanging paper fans as warnings.

'And are you . . . ? Do you mean to say that you are taking Victoria's place?'

Nancy nodded, noting that he knew her as Victoria and not Ruby Bice.

'You have become a public speaker? You talk to people like these hot-head socialists.'

'The Fabians?' She looked amusedly up at him. 'At least you can rely on them not to throw tomatoes at you. They come as a very polite set, proper ladies and gentlemen to

131

anybody who's been shouted down by a crowd of Pompey "dockies".'

He stopped and turned to her. 'Nancy, you give me hope yet. I, the future great barrister, still tremble at the thought of opening my mouth before half a dozen law men and court officials, and yet you will face a crowd of dockyard workers. Miss Dickenson, I salute you.'

She felt his firm, warm lips upon her bare hand and could have fallen for him. A future barrister. She wondered whether she would be able to speak at all knowing that he was to be in the audience.

As Nancy suspected it would be, the hall was full. Red Ruby Bice was always a crowd-puller.

Victoria had apparently been very excited about this invitation. Miss Nora had said that the Hampstead intellectuals were the power behind the socialists' throne and that the audience might contain anybody from Nancy's own favourite, Bernard Shaw, and H.G. Wells the writer, whom she knew from when he worked in Southsea, to any of the Labour MPs. They were all likely to be found visiting Hampstead.

From her place behind a plush, cloth-covered table, on which was an artistic bowl of flowers, Nancy Dickenson scanned the audience. Nobody looked at all as though he might be Mr Shaw, which was a blessing at least. Jack had said that he would sit at the back because of his height. Nancy hoped it was not because he would find it easier to slip away.

Then suddenly she saw the Chairman bow slightly in her direction and announce her name to polite applause. If she had learned anything from watching Victoria Ormorod at work on the speaker's rostrum, it was not to rush.

She did not use such drama as slowly removing her gloves; instead she stood and smiled and said, 'I'm Nancy Dickenson and I am a servant. A cook-general. I was up at

5.30 this morning and I wouldn't mind if you'd agree to me sitting down to talk to you this evening. I promise you'll not get any less from me. In fact, with the weight off my feet, you're likely to get more.'

The answer was a hum of amusement which clattered into applause.

'Thanks. I'll take that as a vote in favour of the resolution.'

Jack Moth, seated on the very back row, saw, from the incline of people's heads as they smiled at those seated next to them, that Nancy was not an amateur at this game. His heart had sunk at the news of Victoria's absence, but Nancy had raised his spirits. I've waited this long to tell Victoria my feelings for her, I suppose I can wait a bit longer.

'You know now that I'm a cook-general, and you can see that I'm a woman. I'm twenty-seven years of age and have been working one way and another since I was four. My father was a dockyard worker – that's a job so dodgy that a man never knows whether he'll get a day's work or no until the ganger's chosen his men for the day.

'My mother? Well, my mother wasn't anything – just my father's wife. If the docks system is a bad one, where a man gets his day's pay by a ganger choosing "You and you and you",' she pointed at random to men in the audience, 'then the system that got my mother her job for life is worse. A man says "You" ' – she now addressed the woman seated next to her on the platform – 'and that's it! You've got a job for life.' In the slight pause and on another level of thought, Nancy listened – not a sound. You've got them, Nancy. You've got them hooked and they want to hear the rest of the story.

And they did. These artistic and literary people were almost voyeuristic in their desire for insight into the lives of those on the dark side of humanity. *Hard Times* come to life for them.

'And that job is one that we tend to speak of in hallowed

133

tones. "Wife". "Wife". You ladies who have already got that title – when you are next alone, try it out. Say it over to yourself fifty times. Not now, not now, you've got to listen to the rest of the Dickenson story. Well, that job that my mother was picked for – being Alf Dickenson's wife – didn't have a great deal going for it. For a start there was no pay . . . I mean, even the poor little stay-makers I see every week get paid. Not a lot, but at least the factory-owner acknowledges that they're due something for their labour.'

Jack felt himself falling under the spell of this plain-spoken working-class woman who had cooked him meals and cleaned his room. First Victoria, then Otis and now Nancy. What extraordinary women their movement produced. Was it the cause that made the women, or the women the cause? Whichever way it was, the three of his acquaintances had developed a certain power that could not be ignored. And he suddenly saw that their cause was right.

One could perhaps account for Otis, even for Victoria with ancestors who were, according to her, self-confident women, but if a servant-girl, daughter of a poverty-stricken dock-worker, could rise from near illiteracy to where Nancy was now, what else were women capable of?

Watching Nancy spellbinding her audience, Jack Moth thought that he had discovered a profound truth. There were women who were not only the equal of men, but perhaps their superior. It was a sobering truth.

'As well as no pay, my mam – in her job of being Alf Dickenson's wife – got no time off . . . not a single hour in any week that she could claim as her own. And as for her working conditions . . . Well, when I was growing up we had a one-up and one-down with an outside tap shared by six houses and sanitary facilities that were cleaned by the tides twice a day. Her keep was pretty negligible and when things were bad, she was the one who went short.'

More than any other person in that audience, Jack Moth was riveted by Nancy's description of her family. She had lived with his own family, cooked for them, slept under the same roof and breathed the same air as them, and yet the only real fact that he knew was that she had been born in a poor part of the town.

Suddenly she laughed and wagged her head. 'Oh dear, I can almost hear some of you thinking, "What's this to do with Votes for Women?" "What has a day in the life of a dock-worker's wife to do with The Cause?" "Has she come to the wrong hall?" "Is she a mad woman?" Well, for sure I'm not mad, and if you'll bear with me we will get round to the business of votes.

'One of the things I used to ask myself when I was growing up was "Why did she do it? Why did she ever let herself in for the job of Alf Dickenson's wife?" And when I had thought it through, I didn't have a single, clear-cut answer.

'Women sometimes become wives because they fall in love, and often because they have a natural need to have children. We become wives sometimes because there is a promise of a roof over our heads when we're shown the door by our own families, or because we've got ourselves into "trouble" – and in my neck of the woods it might be because we've been raped on the way home from work. So we do a deal with a willing chap who's looking for somebody cheap to cook and clean for him.

'My mam? She fell in love with Alf Dickenson, and found out too late that the marriage bed was no bed of roses. But she had chosen it and she had to lie on it – as well as work in a factory to get a few shillings to keep the family going. In as many years he gave her more children than he'd got fingers on his hands, and he'd likely have started on his toes if he hadn't fallen into the water between the dock and the ship he was working on. It's all right, don't feel embarrassed about wanting to smile – there are times when I have to smile myself.'

The atmosphere in the hall was electric. It is doubtful

whether any Fabian guest-speaker had ever been so bold and honest.

'My father was a man brought up to use his fists – and he used them. On my mam and on all of us children. He was a drinker and, in a funny way as it turned out, it was no bad thing . . . because if he had not been drunk, then he wouldn't have fallen into the docks and my mam would have had half a dozen more children that she could not feed on his non-existent wages.'

Now she rose to her feet, placed her hands wide on the table, leaned slightly towards the audience and smiled upon them warmly. 'And now to the matter of the votes. Many years ago radical suffragists, like me, rejected the notion that women should strive for the vote "equally as accorded to men", because that would not enfranchise the majority of women.

'Mrs Pankhurst came upon the scene and urged something similar – "a property or householder's vote". Of course, from her point of view this wasn't at all a bad idea, because it would give her and her kind the power that she would deny her poorer sisters who are neither tax- nor ratepayers. In her desire to win this privilege for herself by any means, she urges her members to ignore all other social reforms and concentrate their attention on securing the vote for a small élite of women.

'Never mind the rest of us!

'I and other radical suffragists urge only total and universal suffrage. What use is a vote if women are not educated? What use is a vote if we have no rights in the work-place, if working mothers have no facilities for the care of their children. If this country is truly the fine, democratic nation that it holds itself to be, then women *must* have the vote. *All* women must have the vote. *Working* women must have the vote.'

Although she was now impassioned and articulate, she was forced to wait for the applause to die down.

Not noticing that – as always when she came to this part of her speech – tears were trickling down her cheeks, she held her hands palm outwards in an attitude of supplication.

'Alf Dickenson's wife must have the vote.'

Jack Moth found himself on his feet with both hands in the air, cheering her along with the rest of the audience. He was so moved that for the moment he had forgotten why he had come here.

> **HEREIN LIE THE MORTAL REMAINS OF CAROLINE**
> **1829–1914.**

Victoria Ormorod detested funerals. The one she had just left was worse than any. The macabre secrets of the graveyard had always disturbed her; now she shrank from the thought of her grandmother encased in pine, lowered into a pit and left to rot.

She tried to think of it, as her grandmother had said they should: None of you are to fret when you bury me. I had a good life. It will be just a box of old skin and bones that's been hanging about the place for seventy year and more. And until we can have our bodies set fire to nice and clean, then they must be buried for hygiene purposes. 'Hygiene purposes' lay behind the few rules she had for the running of the 'Home'.

I shan't be in there, never you fear, I shall be off somewhere interesting and where it don't rain too much – I don't reckon eternity will be much fun if they've got rain there.

Aunt Kate, Grandmother's ally for fifty years, had looked into the grave and said, 'That's the end of an era. The Old Lady was the last of her kind.'

In spite of her melancholy mood, Victoria smiled to herself: not only was Kate several years older than Grandmother, their era, the one when rural communities had been opened up and changed for ever, would not be ended until Aunt Kate died. But Victoria knew what Kate meant, that it had been her grandmother who had run things for forty years – things, meaning the benevolent (hygienic) lying-in home for village women and a shelter for children.

Although she must have been a young woman when she took charge of the place, in Victoria's memory her grandmother had always been the 'Old Lady'. Her temper as gingery as her hair had once been, the Old Lady had, with only a few exceptions, been fiercely against men and the maleness of the world; it was she who had fostered Victoria's inbred rebellious nature.

The name 'Caroline' which was inscribed there was the one given by her mother; her father's surname she abandoned, as her lover, the father of her three children, had abandoned her. *I don't want no man's name, not even the one I got from my father, no nothing from any man-jack of them.*

The funeral had, to Victoria, been a formality; she and her grandmother had taken leave of one another a month ago: 'I've seen this happen times enough to know that I've got about four or five weeks before the end, and I reckon that if you and me talked to each other for every minute of it we should still find we had something to say. I never had favourites, as you well know, Victoria, but if I did have, then you would be it. The main thing is, we said most things worth saying years ago.'

As Victoria walked back to the house with the aged and arthritic Aunt Kate silently limping beside her, she wondered about her own future. Am I as strong as Kate and Grandmother were at my age? She has always told me that I am – and I could be whilst she was there reminding me.

Perhaps, like that of Pinocchio's cricket, Grandmother's voice would always be in her ear. What a comfort if that were true: Lord sakes, Vicky, don't be such a wet week in a

139

thunder-storm. When you know what you say is the honest truth, you must not be afraid to say so.

And on that last occasion when, even though the Old Lady was dying, her voice had been tetchy and strong: 'Victoria, war is a man's thing. Look at it this way, there don't seem no good reason why men was given bigger and stronger bodies than ourselves (for I tell you, there hasn't ever been a job known that a woman didn't have her own way of doing as good as they. Women have done it all, from the killing of beasts to the chopping down of trees and the building of anything from a boat to a cottage). But there it is, men have got this strength and for some reason they think that they have got to throw it around . . . they have to size up to one another, take things from one another, show everybody who is master. Perhaps it's inbred in male humans just like charging and goring is inbred in some beef bulls, but that don't mean that women just have to sit back and let them do it, we have to show them how to live peaceable and we have to try to change things. Lord above, how unfair and unjust that is. We carry them, birth them, have our bodies turned all way out to get them – 'tis women's sons as much as men's that go away to fight and get killed and hurt, and we don't even have a say in it.'

The straggling line of mourners wends its way through the old churchyard. Kate pulls back to rest on a tombstone, Victoria sits beside her. The lichen-encrusted stone is warm and the grass that covers the graves is long and seeding, neglected these days as is the very fabric of the village. Kate and the Old Lady had known the village before the last of its young blood leached away into the industrial towns. They had seen the old mansion turned into a brewery and the downs slashed open to insert railway lines.

Except for skylarks, birds, which do not in any case do much singing in July, are silenced by the growing heat, but bees make up for it as they constantly visit the scabious and cornflowers that have infiltrated from the surrounding fields.

Springing from one grave is a briar, and Victoria wonders whether it was planted as a memento. From others grows cranesbill, and in dust-dry patches along the paths red pimpernel lies flat open to the sun. Two ancient yews whose root spreads are equal to their huge canopies must be infiltrating the subsided graves. This is the oldest part of the graveyard, where the stone tomb of a long-dead squire had been one of the first to encroach, with its granite marker, upon centuries of unnamed graves.

The Old Lady's grave will not have an identity.

I want you to lay me there in the old way, without any old cross or marker. Anybody who cares tuppence for me will know where my bones are, and the others can bide curious.

There are thousands of spring bulbs at home. Victoria thinks that she will bring some here and cover her grandmother's grave with them: perhaps that is as good an end as any of us deserves, to feed roses and yew trees and spring bulbs.

'She left me some money, Aunt Kate.'

'I know she did, Vicky. It is so you can keep on do-en your work to get us the vote.'

'Yes, but what sort of a midwife will I be if I keep spending weeks at a time away from here. I always feel guilty when I go away and leave the others to make up for me.'

'If it was any of them that had the gift of the gab like you, then it'd be them that she would 'a left the money to. It an't as though it's personal money is it? It's money for a purpose, so don't you let me hear no more of that sort of talk. Guilty! Whoever heard the like? There's plenty of midwives about, but not women with the gift of the gab.'

'When I go this time, it will be different. There is talk about an international campaign for peace, and they want me to help with the organization and running. It will mean being away from home for quite a long spell. Perhaps longer than my time in Sicily.' That name, spoken in the dry heat and the hot smell of dry grass and dust of the simmering graveyard, brought for a brief moment to one of the windows of her mind a tall, broad young man with heavy black hair and a handsome profile. Tankredi. And now, Jack Moth. Victoria Ormorod, always attracted by unsuitable men.

'I know that, Vicky. I shall miss you. You always been like one of my own. The Old Lady and me shared our children and our grandchildren. I always took to you because you was like me, always one for books. I don't think nobody except you realized how hungered I was for books when my eyes went. When you read to me it was like they all come to life.'

'Cathy?' Victoria's spirits, sprung with a quick laugh, rose.

'Ah, you was a sight that day, standen up on Ole Winchester Hill callen "Heathcliff, Heathcliff" clear across the valley to young Derry Carter. You was a couple of young tearaways.'

'Derry Carter.' Natural child of the Lord only knew who, he had somehow come under the Old Lady's care. 'Lord above, I haven't thought of him for years.'

'He volunteered for the war, on his own accord. A course, you can't blame him, there's nothing much round here 'cept the brewery, and they only wants girls because they'm cheap – brings they here in a wagon from Blackbrook town.' She gazes up at a sky that is to her a misty haze of cerulean blue, the same colour as her own old eyes. 'I always did like the old Cathy but what happened was never right – they all treated that young Heathcliff so bad . . .'

Victoria squeezed Kate's arm and helped her to her feet. A decade ago she had used up her three score years and ten: it could not be long before she too was buried here.

It was a midday of one of the last days of July, so they walked slowly in the pre-noon heat. The horsy smell of ox-eye daisies mixed with that of drying grass recently scythed hung dustily around them. The comforting village sounds of barking dogs, the whirring and clattering beer-bottling plant, the clang of a milk churn being rolled, a lowing cow, all came to attack Victoria in her throat and tear-ducts – she could hardly bear the thought that once again she would be leaving it all.

Again she and the old aunt had fallen into silence. Inevitably Victoria's memories of her grandmother flitted about her mind, as random as a flight of bats. As soon as the Old Lady had read of the assassination of the Archduke, she had said that nothing could now stop the whole of Europe going to war: 'Now listen to me, Victoria, you got to face it. If you women start talking peace just when the country got the smell of fighting in its nostrils, you won't be very popular, because if there's one thing that raises the English to dangerous stupidity, then it's a whiff of war. But you know and I know that war is a sin and a crime against the people that are sent to fight in them. "Thou shalt not kill." That's an order as plain as plain, and "Thou shalt not kill" can't be twisted to mean anything else. We are supposed to be Christian – why good Lord, girl, labouring people should be gathering in the streets at the very idea of putting swords and shot into other ordinary labouring people. My mother and father were rebels in a great cause. Did I ever tell you?'

She had, many times. And how they had lived in exile because they had stood against bad conditions and bad laws. And before them, down the ages, other rebels. A family history designed to produce a woman like Victoria who was prepared to be one of a tiny minority to speak out against the coming war.

'I have a few pound put by. Some of it came from my mother. It would have pleased her to know that you had inherited her nature. She knew well enough herself that women can never do anything unless they can live independent. The Pankhurst women can only go about the country because they've got the means – and so must you have.'

At Kate's pace they reached the lych-gate from where Victoria looked back at a scene that was at once both universal and unique. The world over, there were small village churches surrounded by fertile fields and, closer to their walls, by generations of people who tilled those fields, yet nowhere else on earth was there another place like this one, where lay those who had gone into the creating of Victoria Ormorod.

Something extraordinarily sad touched her and in the shade of the lych-gate she shivered.

'You must have got cold hanging about so slow with me.'

'No, no, it was just a goose running over my grave.'

'Let's say that it was a good fairy touched your shoulder.'

1914

Standing rigid before the cheval mirror in her bedroom, Esther Moth, having sent away Kitt's nurserymaid who had been helping her to dress, watched her head being wreathed in stephanotis and orange blossom by Otis Hewetson who was already dressed for the wedding.

Otis groaned. 'I shall never last the day in all this boning: it has been ages since my waist was so confined, I shall probably faint.'

Esther made a mock fierce face. 'You just try stealing the limelight with a trick like that.'

Otis stood away to view the head-dress and its short lace veil. 'I say, Esther, you are the very picture of a virgin fairy. So beautiful.' From behind she put her arms about her friend, taking care to avoid crushing the white georgette and tulle bridal gown. 'I don't think that Bindon will have the courage to violate such an image of purity.'

'Otis! You say the most outrageous things these days. I think that the women you mix with must be very saucy.'

Otis smiled. 'But such bland sauce, you may be sure, Esther. We are ladylike in the extreme, for who would be likely to put their children in our care if we were not?'

'Ladylike! When half of you go about uncorseted and the other half smoke tobacco.'

'And the other half have love-affairs, and the other half envy them.'

Otis smoothed her temporarily nipped-in waist and

thrust-out bosom. 'Not uncorseted – merely unboned. You really should try, give your poor figure a little freedom.'

'You will become saggy.'

'On the contrary. Without stay-bones, one's muscles hold one's figure in the correct position.'

Esther lifted the veil to cover her face and picked up a posy of flowers with trailing ribbons and surveyed the finished picture. 'Well, I should not like to go about like that.'

'I dare say that Bindon would not mind, though. Have you never thought how devastating it must be for a lover to press his loved one to him, only to feel a parcel encased in whalebone. I think that it must be rather like taking a mouthful of Dover sole only to discover that it is not filleted.'

'Heavens, Otis, if it is not for the men that we lace ourselves in, then why do it?'

'Ah, ha! Why indeed? Think about that some time when you are not so preoccupied.'

Now they both looked in the mirror at the reflection of a bride.

Otis knelt at her friend's feet and adjusted the folds of her skirt. 'Jesting aside, Esther, I have never seen a more perfect bride. Are you ready?'

'Yes, tell Father that I am ready, if you will, but I should like a few minutes to myself.'

Occasionally during the past month, since the preparations for Esther's marriage had been nearing completion, Otis had encountered George Moth. He had behaved with such charm and respect that, had it not been for the fact that she had occasionally caught a particular look in his eyes, she might have wondered whether the episode in his office had been her imagination.

She had also encountered Jack, and on each occasion her

heart had leapt as though a wonderful surprise had been sprung upon her. She could not get over the fact that in the three years since the Southsea holiday, they had gone from being boy and girl and had become man and woman. Jack's attitude towards Otis was almost that of two equals. He behaved as though he greatly respected her, and in fact said as much.

She tried to understand herself and her interest in both Jack Moth and his father, but came to no conclusion except that she must simply have a penchant for tall, broad men – much in the way that she had a penchant for common oysters: my salivary glands respond to sight and thought of the shellfish, other of my glands respond to this particular type of man.

Today she was to spend many hours in the company of both men.

Jack Moth and the groom were to leave for the church from the army officers' club at which they had stopped overnight in the company of several of Major Blood's fellow officers, who were to form an arch of ceremonial swords for the man and wife.

George Moth waited alone in the morning room of Windsor Villa with a glass of whisky in one hand and cigar in the other. He was in formal dress which is best suited to men with long legs and broad shoulders. His tailed, cut-away coat was hanging on a chair. When Otis Hewetson came in he rose, hastily put on his coat, and bent briefly at the waist in a bow. 'Charming, most charming.'

'Charming' was an acceptable compliment, but George Moth would have liked to have used a much stronger language such as communicated his true emotions. That time when he had incautiously kissed her he had let his moment of arousal get a little out of hand. What had stimulated him was that, although she had only been a girl, she had not been afraid of him. Until then, only Anne, of all the many women he had encountered in his life, had felt sufficiently unintimidated by him to stand up to him.

'Esther is ready,' said Otis. 'She thinks I should leave now, she will be down in about fifteen minutes. She wished to be on her own and would like you to go up to her when it is time.'

'You should not leave for another ten minutes. Will you sit down?' With a questioning expression, he indicated a tantalus.

'Thank you, no, but I should like a little white wine with mineral water.'

He smiled and jammed his cigar between his teeth. He quizzed the bottles. 'Malvern, Perrier or Nocera Umbra?'

'The Malvern, please.'

He handed her the prettily cut crystal glass. 'Nice, safe little drink.'

She glanced at him, indicating that she knew he was making an allusion to the last drink she had accepted from him. She accepted the glass and took a drink from it. 'Thank you, that is beautifully chilled.'

'I dare say you think that I should apologize for my behaviour at the time of the white port?'

'After almost three years? I believe that I should have insisted before now had I expected that. I was full of myself and college and was probably very pert at the time.'

Yes . . . full of herself, and so much like Anne at twenty.

'That's as well, for an apology suggests regret, and I have no regrets.' He looked her up and down. Nothing else about her was at all like Anne. The mature Otis was tall, full-figured and brilliantly coloured in cheeks, lips, and eyes. The bridal attendant's dress was of a deep rose shade, and feminine in silhouette, the gathered skirt being hitched at the sides so that glimpsed inches of her calves were revealed as she moved. He thought: She must certainly outshine her mother these days. Again he felt desire rise in him. God forgive me, she's twenty-five years younger than I am. She is Esther's age.

'The shade of that dress suits you very well. You have flair. Few women with your hair colour would have chosen to wear dark pink. You really are an extraordinarily disturbing young woman.'

He watched her response carefully. An experienced interrogator and decipherer of clues, he read no signs that she was troubled, rather, she was intrigued and not displeased.

She said, ' "Young Woman" used in that tone smacks very much of my mother when she intends "Young Hussy".'

'I think that your mother does not know you very well if she refers to you in such terms. I never intended "hussy" – it is a word that indicates a want of intelligence, an attribute I know that you do not lack.'

Raising her eyebrows in acknowledgement, she looked pointedly at the clock.

George Moth knew that almost everybody would be assembled at the church by now, but he wanted to indulge himself for just a few more minutes. Where's the harm? Esther will not be the first bride to arrive late.

'It is still too early. You should not leave until eleven fifteen. The church is not far.' Lifting the lids of two boxes of cigarettes he offered them, saying, ' "Hibiscus" and Virginia. Do you use them?'

'No.'

'I am glad to hear it.'

She gave him a purse-lipped, wry smile. 'I prefer a cigar . . .'

Is she trying to crack the whip at me, put me in my place?

'. . . but on my allowance I can afford only *Vevey Sans*.'

George Moth wrinkled his nose.

'We are not all detective-inspectors who can smoke *Mil Maravillas*.'

149

If she was trying to pull him down a peg, George Moth knew that she had the ability to do so with style, for there were few women who would know that the '*Aguila de Oro*' band he had removed from his cigar indicated that – at £25 a hundred – it was one of the most expensive cigars money could buy. There were even fewer women who could detect it only from its fragrance.

'High days and holidays – my only indulgence.' He indicated a brass-bound wooden humidor. 'You are welcome . . .'

She laughed and waved her refusal of his offer. 'I thought that you did not approve of a woman who uses tobacco.'

'I may approve of the woman and not her use of tobacco.'

'I should have liked to try one of your *Mil Maravillas* but I really must leave now; my mama taught me that it is not polite to keep people waiting.'

He bowed to the inevitable. 'The fault is mine.'

'Would you mind?' She nodded at the cigar he was smoking and, without waiting for his permission, took it from his fingers. As he would have himself, she rolled it between her fingers, feeling the condition of the leaf, smelt it gently, then placed her lips around it and, with her head tilted back and half-closed eyes, drew in a mouthful of the aromatic smoke, holding it in her open mouth before expelling it gently.

George Moth had been enjoying cigars for twenty years, yet in all that time he had never known that there could be such sensuality associated with the intake of a mouthful of smoke. He could not take his eyes off the moist, red circle of her lips as it contracted about the cigar and relaxed as she blew a ring. Before it dispersed, he reached for it and caught it between a finger and thumb, not taking his eyes from hers as he did so.

When Anne Moth had carpeted Windsor Villa, she had chosen expensive, close-tufted Wilton which entirely deadened any footfall.

Esther, framed in the doorway, said steadily, 'Is it not time that you were at the church, Otis?'

1914

Major and Mrs Blood, in Southsea for its romantic associations, had taken a suite overlooking the sea in a modern hotel.

'I'm sorry it is cut short, my darling girl.' Bindon Blood stretched across the table and kissed his pretty wife on her temple.

Bindon and Esther were taking tea al fresco on the balcony of their suite under a green-lined canvas awning. A constant stream of people, soaking up ozone and sun, walked the promenade below. In other circumstances, Esther Blood could not have brought herself to encircle her bridegroom's neck in full view of anyone who chanced to look up, but this place had, for her, taken on the feeling that it was enchanted, and so rendered them invisible to any inquisitive stare. If she had had any self-doubts as to her motives in marrying the man who had courted her faithfully until she had agreed, those doubts were now settled.

Poor Otis, she believes that she has the best prize in her books and discussions.

The wedding night which, had she taken notice of her mother's closest friend she might have expected to be rather less than romantic, had instead been a glorious revelation, nothing akin to the biological account in a textbook, nor the imagined 'tupping' that she and Otis had once giggled about. Perhaps it was that she could still remember overhearing her mother telling that friend, 'Had you responded to Theo, instead of rejecting him, then your wedding night might have been as satisfactory as my own. After all, it is the most natural event in the world, is it not?'

Esther too had found that the act which her ma's poor friend had found to be so peculiar was entirely natural and satisfactory and wonderful. Bindon was gentle and understanding, and as practised in love as one would expect a soldier to be – even though she did not want to know how that came about – and Esther was unafraid and responsive.

The consequence of so satisfactory a wedding night was that they had spent much of their time in Southsea repeating the experience. If Eros had scored a gold on Bindon Blood three years previously, he now released a full quiver of darts at Esther and scored with them all.

Each time the handsome soldier looked at his wife's daintiness and fragility, he wanted to carry her back yet again into their rooms. I am so lucky! he told himself a hundred times.

'Darling Ess, I can hardly bear going back to barracks. The thought of the company of the fellows . . . I want to be with you. I want it to be the two of us, alone in a house of our own, the key turned in the lock . . .' He pulled her down on to his knee and kissed her gently. Until now, although he had never realized it, he had been a lonely man, as he had been a lonely child in his solitary-living grandfather's house. Lonely in the midst of battalions of men, lonely in the mess, even lonely saluting an acknowledgement at the end of a solo played in public.

'I really can't see why the army should need a band playing in a war.'

He hugged her for her naïvety and felt himself becoming aroused at the softness and lightness of her body.

How can I go to fight a war just now?

'I am not only a bandsman. Bandsmen are trained soldiers first and musicians second. I know how to handle firearms almost as well as I do a musical instrument.'

He felt her stiffen slightly beneath his caresses. She

slipped away from him and went to lean over the balcony railings. Watching her, he again wondered whether he could ask her to come to live in this town. Until now, until he had experienced these almost overwhelming surges of passion for her, he had said that he would be happy to live in Windsor Villa. True, he did love London. Compared to the dull gentility of Southsea, and the routine of the barracks, London was a continuous adventure. But he no longer wanted that adventure, he wanted his wife close at hand. When he was in barracks he wanted to know that when he came off duty her soft comfort was awaiting him.

He went and stood beside her. The tide was receding. He liked to watch these waters which were unique with their twice-daily surge that came swirling in between the one stony beach here and another on the Isle of Wight four miles across the water. He encircled her with his arm, wondering whether she would think him lustful if he let her know that he wanted her now, only hours after an episode at lunchtime. Her very fragility and paleness made him a beast in comparison.

But by tomorrow, or the next day, who knew what orders he would be obeying, for which part of the country he might be *en route*?

He peered over the railings upon which were supported boxes of lushly blooming geraniums, the odour of which the two of them would probably remember with affection for the rest of their lives. 'What's new in the state of Denmark?'

'Could you bear having Kitt live with us?'

'Why do you ask? I thought that was the plan, that that was the reason for us living in your father's house . . . so that you could continue to mother Kitt.'

'I mean bring Kitt down here. Rent a house in one of those pretty little lanes . . .'

'Darling Ess! Do you think it possible? I thought it essential that Kitt is not disturbed until he reaches school age.'

She turned, put her arms about his waist and pressed herself to him. 'If he is with me, then it cannot be much of a disturbance. And think how he would thrive in this wonderful air. In any event, the disturbance to me, if I can only be with you when you have time to travel to London, is too dire to contemplate.'

This time it was the wife who led the husband back inside.

Part III

1914

Greywell Villa in Stormont Street, Clapham, was immaculately decorated without and within. Its interior was lofty and light from long windows which had pretty lace pulled into their corners and much of its furniture, which was of the same period as the house, was proudly stamped 'Gillow'. Plainly Greywell was the home of a professional man who had secured a steady flow of fees over a long period. Its shrubberies burgeoned and its small lawns invited no boots to indent their surface. Controlled roses and clematis, pyracantha and vitis softened its red-brick walls, and the only way that herbaceous plants in the borders lost their heads was by dead-head pruners, as flowers for the house were delivered twice a week.

It was in Greywell, set in the desirable area of Lavender Hill, that Emily and Martin had spent more than twenty years of married life with few unpleasantnesses. Only two of real seriousness: the first was when Otis had got it into her head that she wished to go to college and read for a teaching degree; the second, also brought about by Otis of course, was when she had been to college and wished to put into practice what she had learned.

There were times when Emily Hewetson felt that the lot of a mother with a headstrong daughter who had an indulgent father was almost too much to bear.

'Had I not been a good mother, Max, then her behaviour would at the least be understandable.'

'Em, my dear, I think that you have done marvellously. It

is probably in her nature, your excellent upbringing of Otis can have nothing to do with it.'

'She has made some very peculiar acquaintances and picked up some strange notions since she was at Stockwell.' Emily gazed disdainfully at her forkful of salad, 'One thing I will say, *I* was against her going in the first place.' No names no pack-drill, her expression said. 'I do not know how Inspector Moth managed it, but *his* daughter was persuaded from taking up her college place . . . and now look at her, married to a most likeable army officer. A musician, too; such a civilized and sociable way of soldiering.'

'You attended the wedding then?'

'Extremely civil of the man. He had us seated with some of the Clermont members of the family. It was quite a small affair, but almost quality. Quite lavish – faultless in fact. I must admit that I was surprised at the taste shown. I should have wanted something a touch more striking in a gown for Otis, but she was a very dainty kind of a bride. Otis could carry off something far more elaborate. Quite expensive though.'

'You enjoyed it then, Em?'

'I did, I did. A strange mix of the simple and the lavish. I found it interesting; as I observed to Martin, quite as one might have expected from such a strange mix as the bride's parents were. The groom had practically no one except his fellow officers.'

'Another slice of beef, Hew?' asked Martin Hewetson, keeping his head below the parapet.

'Is that not absolutely typical of Martin? Here I am with my nerves in shreds for our daughter, and he continues slicing beef.'

'We may as well be replete if we are to worry, my dear.'

Emily Hewetson chewed the tender fillet as though it was a poorly cooked servant's cut.

'You must not fret because the young Moth girl beat Otis down the aisle, Em.'

'Oh Max, how you do reduce everything. I am not at all fretting that she reached the age of twenty and no young man has seriously courted her. I would not *dare* fret or I should be soon informed that we mothers turn romance into a marriage market. Market! What a term. I know that these are modern times and that young women are receiving education, and wish to spend more time outside the home than was thought proper in my young days, but the fact remains that marriage, home and family are central to a woman's life. The fact also remains that all mothers feel more at ease in their minds when a daughter is settled.'

She had insisted that Martin bring Max home for lunch so that they might decide how best to tackle the problem of Otis's latest decision. Emily had honestly believed that, once the Stockwell College business was over and it was out of Otis's system and the girls dispersed, Otis would return home and settle down.

'I really did expect that you would be more co-operative, Max. Martin has always been far too indulgent, and she has gone beyond an age when I can say anything that she will heed.'

'Then you may be sure that she will take not the slightest notice of me, Em.' Which was not strictly true for, of the three of them, it was to her Uncle Hewey's views that Otis Hewetson was most likely to listen. Max Hewetson, however, involved as he might be in Greywell, did not wish to become embroiled in the discussion that had been going on in his brother's household recently. 'Might I have some more of that beef, Martin?'

Emily breathed in heavily, raising by two inches the flounces which emphasized her bosom.

The effect of this was lost in the rattle and rustle caused by Otis rushing into the dining-room and sitting at table still wearing her hat.

'I am sorry to be late. But the buses are so full at present. There are soldiers everywhere.'

'Otis, if you like to remove your hat before you eat, and

161

not behave as though you were a visitor to your home, I should feel better able to digest my food.' Had the men not been present, Emily might have suggested that her daughter might like to hold herself together with a proper corset, but she knew that that battle was as good as lost. She had the feeling too that this new battle, in which she had hoped to enlist the aid of Max, was about to be lost also.

'No time, Ma. I have to go out again almost at once.'

'Otis, no! You have not settled for a single minute since you left college. I believe that you are avoiding us.'

'Of course I am not, Ma. Why on earth should I do that?'

'You know very well. I asked Max here hoping that you might listen to sense.'

'Now Em, don't you go bringing me into it.'

Emily Hewetson looked as though she felt like hitting the traitor.

'Right, Uncle Hewey. And don't go bringing me into it either. You have had your say, Ma. You have made it very clear that you do not approve of my taking a teaching post in Islington.'

'Islington! Do you hear that, Max?'

'And Pa has had his say – he would prefer that I teach in a pleasant, fee-paying girls' school. And now Uncle Hewey has had his say, which is that he does not want to be brought into it.'

She helped herself to a tomato and beetroot and ate quickly.

'And you are determined to leave us and go off to live in some squalid little rented rooms?'

Otis put down her knife and fork and rested her hands in her lap and turned to her mother in an attitude of conciliation. 'I have no intention of leaving you and Pa,' she said gently. 'I shall come here frequently I hope. I should like to keep my room and have some of my things here as I did whilst I was at Stockwell. But I do want to live as part of the community whose children I shall be teaching.'

'I really do not know how this has all come about.' Emily closed her eyes and gave herself a shuddering shake. 'You have been obstinate about my going to inspect these rooms, and I did believe that you would not go so far. Now, however, I insist that your father takes a hand. Martin, it is up to you.'

'Uncle Hewey came yesterday. You approve, don't you, Uncle Hewey?'

Emily Hewetson burnt a look at the viper who had been calmly eating her roast beef at her own lunch table. 'You have been there? And you said nothing? Max!' She was deeply hurt and Max would suffer for it later.

Looking faintly uncomfortable, but putting a face on it, Max Hewetson said, 'I kept my word to Otis that I would not. Really, Martin,' (though his eyes were fixed upon Emily) 'the rooms are perfectly clean and respectable. There are no trees in the streets and no gardens, I will give you that, but it is not at all badly kept up. She might have done very much worse.' Now he looked at Otis who stared innocently back at him. 'It will be very convenient for her living over a little restaurant. I sampled the food myself, it was excellent, I assure you.'

'Over a restaurant! Martin, you must do something.'

'Very well, Em, I will go and inspect the rooms.'

At which Otis smiled inwardly. As with her Uncle Hewey, so she had always been able to twist her pa around her little finger. Her rooms were secure.

Martin Hewetson very much disliked finding himself in the situation where his two women were in disagreement. He had never yet found a satisfactory way of dealing with it. What tended to happen was that, unless forced to do so, he offered no comment until he was alone with each of them, then he would sympathize with each argument, and at the same time would diplomatically try to ease in a bit of the opposing viewpoint.

'Neither I nor your father will be able to rest easy in our beds whilst you are living in the midst of those people.'

Otis opened her mouth to defend 'those people', but her father spoke first. 'Em, my dear. I think that we have to admit defeat on this. We have lost the case. And we really ought to give Otis credit for her common sense and trust her.'

But Emily was not in a mood to concede anything.

Otis folded her napkin and had arisen before Max Hewetson could give assistance. 'Yes, Pa, I am afraid that you have lost the case. No matter what. All that I need is my letter of confirmation.' It was not often that Otis's expression was so determined but, when it was, it was easy to see how much of her mother's forceful character she had inherited. 'Not that I admit that there was any case to answer. I am now a trained teacher and I believe that I shall be a very good one. Where are trained teachers most needed? We are needed where the children are poorest and most deprived. Now I ask you, Uncle Hewey, what use are the bad teachers to those children? And if I am to teach them, then I must know about them. Can you imagine how impossible that would be if I were to live here and only visit on a daily basis? How patronizing that would be: Miss Lavender Hill condescending to teach London's poor children.'

Whatever retort Emily Hewetson might have made was interrupted by one of the maids bringing the midday post to the master. This he sorted, handing one to Otis. 'Shouldn't you say that this was the one you have been waiting for?' With the name and address facing, he handed Otis a long envelope.

'I have been accepted! Oh! I cannot believe it.'

Otis felt that having stopped breathing she would never start again. 'Look, Ma. Look, Uncle Hew. "Miss Otis Hewetson BA." There! BA. Did you ever think that you would see that, Pa?'

'No, my dear, I never did. Well perhaps in this last year . . .' and he thought how, if she had been a son, she would now have been coming into the practice.

Max Hewetson, using a suitably avuncular voice, told her that she had been a very clever girl and that he intended buying her a bracelet inscribed with her name and qualification. He thought how fast things were changing and how difficult life would be for a man married to one of these new women.

London's poor! Oh, how Emily Hewetson ached to arrange a wedding such as their friends had not seen in twenty years.

1914

Jack Moth had not wished to visit his inheritance, Mere Manor, but Esther had persuaded him that, whether he liked it or not, he had certain duties and responsibilities. And, having persuaded him that he must at least visit the place and talk to the estate manager and staff, and as Bindon had been ordered away on a seven-day firearms course, she volunteered to accompany her brother.

'Have you thought about the staff, Jack? It is not their fault that Sir Norbert left the place in your care.'

'Nor is it my fault that Sir Norbert was irresponsible enough not to consult the person he nominated to run the damn place. He should have found out at least that I am not only not a fit person, but am not in the slightest interested in country estates and farms.'

'I doubt if it would occur to any benefactor that his heir would be upset at having a country estate wished upon him.'

'Then it should have occurred to him. It is a Clermont way of trying to claim me. Whatever I become in life, I want to have become it by my own efforts. I will not have my life interfered with by the Clermonts. They have to learn that they cannot buy everybody.'

'I should have thought they learned that when Mother and Father married in spite of them.'

In the end Esther had persuaded him, and the outcome was that they were now dining on an express train as it steamed through the West Country towards Lyme Regis.

'Oh Jack, come on, cheer up.' His sister poked him in the ribs as she used to when he was in a mood with his mathematics and flung his books across the room. 'Are you sure that your objection is not to do with the fact that Sir Norbert turned out to be not the kind of person a man can be proud to inherit from? Not a little afraid of what people might think?'

'Ess!' Jack almost blushed at what his sister was suggesting. Married woman or not, he was taken aback both that she knew of Sir Norbert's secret life and that she referred to it openly.

'Being a married woman has gone to your head. You have come out with some very shocking things recently.'

'Oh, how stuffy you are growing. You are in grave danger of becoming a lawyer. Mentioning perversion to my own brother is hardly shocking, there is no one to overhear us. It would be quite understandable if you were perturbed that people might wonder whether you had inherited Mere for some special reason to do with him.'

'Oh Ess, do give over. How much do you think that people know? I mean, the whole matter was hushed up and nobody mentioned anything at the funeral or the reading of the will. Lord, Esther, how comes it that you know? I mean, dammit, it is not the kind of thing young women usually know about.'

She raised her eyebrows. 'Don't you mean that it is not the kind of thing that young men like to *believe* that young women know about? I think that I knew about him before I was old enough to know that he was perverted. You remember how he used to take us all down to the lake and how he would always be ready with a towel for the older cousins – not the girls. Girls get to sense such things when they are still quite little; so that when a man like Sir Norbert takes no interest in them, they see at once that he is not the same as other men around them. He never made much fuss of any of us girl cousins, or bought us any of the expensive surprises he did you boys.'

To Jack, Bindon was stodgy and a stuffed shirt with no imagination, yet somehow he had been the catalyst for change in his sister. A cliché it is true, but she had blossomed. Yet to Jack he was the same unimaginative army officer who had courted her faithfully for three years.

'Marriage suits you, Ess. I shouldn't have believed it.'

'You have just said that it has gone to my head.' Unexpectedly, she blushed. 'I think that I am very lucky to have found someone like Bindon. I only wish that he was not a soldier. I am afraid for him going off to fight.'

Jack put his large hand over her tiny one. 'Bindon will be all right, Ess. I ask you, what general is going to send the drums and trumpets into battle?'

Appreciating his attempt to comfort her by joking, she smiled. 'He says that he is a soldier first and a musician second.'

'Perhaps they will keep him in a safe place and only bring him out to sound the bugles when there is a victory.'

'Oh Jack, aren't wars the most terrible things? I never thought about it before. Until recently wars and battles took place in history lessons and Shakespeare plays. When I was young, I never thought of there being actual people involved, but simply Roundheads and Cavaliers, Picts and Scots. Suddenly, wars are fought by men called Bindon, and Alexander and Philip and Robert and Jack.'

He was about to say something about that when she said, 'I have to tell someone. I am going to . . . I am expecting a child.' She was visibly delighted.

'Ess! So *soon?*'

'What is that supposed to mean?'

'Dearest Ess, it means nothing except that I am surprised and delighted. I had not expected to become an uncle so soon. You will be the best of mothers.'

She pressed his hand and smiled affectionately. ' "Uncle Jack". How does that sound? I have written to tell Bindon.'

'Well, he will be pleased.'

'I know. We had planned to take a house in Southsea and suggest to father that we take Kitt with us. But I suppose that he will not return to Southsea until the war is over.'

'Father must take responsibility for Kitt now. He has relied upon you for too long. I think that you and Bindon should still consider taking a place on your own. If you stay on at Windsor Villa, it is inevitable that you will still be responsible for Kitt.'

'But I want to be close to Bindon when he returns.'

'Do you know where his regiment will be based when it returns?'

'No. Though he has heard unofficially that it is to be moved to Salisbury.'

'That would be about two hours' train journey to London, and another half-hour to get to Hampstead.'

'Yes, not really much difference from the time it takes him to get from Southsea to London.'

He smiled and clasped her two hands between his own. 'And scarcely different from the journey we're on now. Salisbury to Exeter and five minutes in the trap to Mere.'

'Jack!'

'Why not?'

'Leave London?'

'Yes, have your child at Mere, Ess. Take the place as your home, put the mark of normality on the place, the mark of the Moths.'

1914

Otis Hewetson looked around her rented rooms with satisfaction. For this area of London they were quite luxurious; as well as having a living-room with a dresser and a minute iron range, it had a separate small bedroom. Her landlady had shown her how to get the range going, although as yet Otis did not know much about how to prepare food. In answer to her mother's questions about how on earth she was to survive, Otis had given the assurance that, as her rooms were above a small restaurant, she would eat out. Barker's Pie Shop, which 'restaurant' Otis never mentioned by name, sold baked potatoes and peas, in addition to a variety of meat or fruit pies. It had four small tables for diners at the rear. This facility, known by Lou the proprietor as The Parlour, might truthfully be described as a restaurant.

It was a Saturday and the first day in her own accommodation.

As she smoothed the counterpane Otis tentatively, gently, sniffed the air and smelt lavender bags, Mansion polish and the all-pervading aroma of the baked pies and potatoes from below. From Greywell to Market Street would have been a culture change that even Otis, with her determination to succeed, might, at one time, have found difficult, but the three years in accommodation with several of her sister students from Stockwell College had knocked the corners off her. There she learned to make toast and muffins and brew tea, to light a fire, clean a room and see to her own linen, all without the aid of the servants to which she had been accustomed since birth. Now, the smell of the clean room was her own achievement. She felt that she could survive in the world perfectly well without paid help.

I have earned myself a supper. She went downstairs and along the passage that led into Lou Barker's shop.

'Settled in then, duck?' Lou Barker was the same age as Emily Hewetson and looked old enough to be Otis's grandmother. Under her old-fashioned cook's cap her hair was grey, but few people ever saw the hair, for she was in her working clothes to get the oven going at five o'clock, and still in them when washing down the tiles of The Parlour at eleven. In the six hours when she was not working in the shop she lived the rest of her life.

'Yes, it looks a real treat, Lou.' Nowadays, in addition to the English of the class into which she was born, Otis spoke two other dialects – the plain schoolteacherish pronunciation of the classroom, and slightly bent vowels when in Lou's or local shops. 'I'm famished. I don't mind what it is so long as it's food.'

Lou soon carried a plate of steaming meat pie and potatoes into The Parlour. 'There y'are, dearie, get yer ribs round that. I'll bring you some tea when it's stewed a bit longer.'

Otis had to admit to herself that it was perhaps the way that tea was served in her adopted country that she found most difficult to like. Strong Indian blends, stewed until they were dark and bitter, then made rusty red with sweet condensed milk. The sweeter the tea, the sweeter the giver. Sweetness was the great sign of affection here. In good times food was lavishly sprinkled with it. On Saturday nights children were taken to the market and bought bags of sugar fish and humbugs. Otis was still shocked at the profligacy of parents who could not afford shoes in which to send children to school but blew sixpence on boiled sugar and saw it gone in an evening.

Lou put down a tray laden with teapot, cup and saucer and an opened tin of Fussells, Unfit For Babies, milk with a spoon standing in it. 'You can help yourself to milk, I got plenty. You sit there as long as you like; there won't be anybody in till the pubs turn out.'

The pie was good. Even so, she did for once momentarily long for one of the Hewetson's Saturday evening, leisurely meals of light foods and iced puddings, with some of Pa's phonograph music, shared with Uncle Hewey, or perhaps a client of Pa's who might be interesting.

As she ate she thought of Esther and wondered whether she was well. Since the wedding, everything had conspired to keep them from one another. She knew from a letter about the pregnancy and about the possibility of her going to live in Lyme Regis and about Bindon being in France. It seemed ages since she had even remembered to wonder whether he might be safe.

From time to time as she ate at the little table for two, the shop bell rang, a bit of banter or gossip was exchanged and the bell rang again. Lou came in, took away the empty plate and brought in a slice of apple pie.

'Goodness, Lou, I shall soon become much too plump if I continue taking my meals down here.'

Lou smoothed down her own round bosom and hips. 'Tell me one man who likes bones? A bit of flesh is what they likes. "Cushions without feathers" my dear old Alby used to say skinny women was. You eat in Lou's and you'll get yourself a feller in no time.'

'I can't have a fellow, Lou, teachers aren't allowed to be married.'

Lou laughed. 'I never said nothing about getting married.'

The bell rang again and Lou went into the shop part. A deep voice percolated through to Otis. A man asking Lou questions, in a voice that Otis thought familiar. A school governor or education official? At last she gave in to her curiosity and leaned to one side so that she could see into the shop where, looking back in her direction was six foot three inches of Detective-Inspector George Moth.

Raising his eyebrows in surprise, he turned to Lou Barker. 'I thought you said you had had no customers this afternoon.'

'That lady's not a customer in the regular way. She lives here.'

'Lives *here?*' Interest and perhaps amusement flickered in his face and went out. Turning to Lou, he said, 'I still think that I should talk to the lady.'

Otis felt confused.

Lou said to the inspector, 'You just wait here whilst I clear away and I'll bring you a drink of tea in.' To Otis she said confidentially, 'He's after that chap that was lassooing girls round their throats. His name's Moth,' she laughed, 'not as you'd think so to look at him, would you? He's been down this way a couple of times before this. He's a plain-cloves copper but he's not a bad chap once you get to know him. We had some trouble one time with a slasher. Old Moth copped him as soon as he was brought in on the job. Now he's asking questions about . . .'

'Thank you, Lou. I can do my own investigation.' To Otis he said with an absolutely straight face, 'Inspector George Moth of New Scotland Yard, miss. I'd just like to ask you one or two questions.' In a tone too low for Lou to hear above the clatter of her baking pans, he said as he sat down in the chair facing her, 'The first being: Do my eyes deceive me?'

'Of course not. This is where I live and work.'

173

'Well I'm damned! I beg your pardon, but when Esther said that you had gone to teach in a school and were living away from home, I imagined that you must be with one of those establishments like the one our Kitt will be attending soon – all shiny little boots and sailor suits in a pretty house with a green in front.' He looked around the tiny room with its folding card tables, folding camping chairs and flaring gas lamp.

'How is Kitt?'

'Kitt? Oh he's fine. I miss him of course, but he's much better off in the country.'

'Kitt in the country?'

'With Esther. Didn't you know that she has gone to live at Mere – the place Jack inherited from his uncle?'

'Yes I did, but not about Kitt. The last time I received any news from her was to tell me about her expected child.'

'I understood that she had written to you recently.'

'Most of my letters go home, and I haven't been back for a few weeks. I really must make the effort to go there.'

Pushing back his chair he said in a louder voice, 'Well thank you, miss. I'll let you finish your tea.' And lower, 'If I waited just along by the archway, would you walk with me for a few minutes? I should like to talk with you but don't want to queer your pitch with Lou. Rozzers are not favourites in this area.'

It did not take her very long to say, 'Very well. In say fifteen minutes?'

George Moth left, and Otis went back upstairs where she took off the everyday skirt and blouse in which she had been working, washed her face and hands and changed into a plain two-piece costume and a coat. Then she let herself out by the side door. Before she put the key into her pocket, she looked at it, smiled and squeezed it with pleasure. *Independence!*

She arrived at the archway and found no one. As she hesitated about what to do, an arm was slipped through hers

174

and the bulky figure of George Moth was suddenly at her side.

'I thought that it was only Sherlock Holmes who could melt into his surroundings.'

'You are as easy to confuse as Dr Watson.'

'Are you on duty?' she asked.

He looked at his watch. 'I suppose I am, but in my line of work there are no fixed hours. I am following a certain line of questioning on my own. It is the way that I often work.'

'Why did you ask me to come out?'

He looked down at her. 'I don't really know, except that I was surprised to find that you were Lou Barker's tenant and Lou doesn't know that you know me, and habit makes me keep that bit of information to myself.'

'Why shouldn't Lou know?'

'No reason . . . it wouldn't matter, but I assumed from your disguise that you too are hoping to dissolve into the background.'

'It is not a disguise, but I don't want the children I teach or their parents to be put off because they think that I'm different from them.'

'Otis . . . you *are* different from them. You cannot be otherwise with parents like yours, education like yours, background like yours.'

'I am surprised to hear you say that.'

'Why should you be?'

'Because you married a lady who . . .'

'Ah. You think that she dissolved into the background of the class she married into. She thought so too.'

'It seemed to me that she did from what I saw of her. She was not at all superior and snobbish as people of old families are. At least, the ones I have met have been.'

He guided her through alleyways and down lanes that were new to her until they came to an open space with some grass and trees and a few wooden seats.

'Will you sit for a few minutes? It isn't closing time in the parks for an hour yet.'

They sat.

'Anne was a Clermont when I met her, she was a Clermont when she died. Part of why I loved her was that difference from me and mine, and I believe that it was the same for her. Neither of us changed. We could not, and neither can you.'

Otis gave him a non-committal shrug of her shoulders.

'You recognized my *Aguila de Oro* cigars, you must have noticed the portraits on the walls of Windsor Villa . . . and the Sèvres plates, the Florence glasswear? My wife had a romantic notion that she rejected the Clermont values for the sake of love. What happened was that she brought those ways with her into our home. Of course, she could do no other. She had always taken her tea from fine china cups, so she thought nothing of it, and when she bought me a present of cigars, then of course they were the brand that her father had smoked.' He turned to look at her and laughed. 'And I am a weak enough vessel not to resist.'

'I hope that you aren't implying that you think I shall fail in my attempt to take on a similar identity to that of the people I live among? I shall not.'

He stretched out his long, solid legs and rested his arms along the back of the seat in an attitude of relaxation. Although he was not touching her, she felt the warmth of his body, remembered how it had felt to be enveloped by it, and stiffened her back away from chance of contact.

'Have you ever gone hungry?' he asked.

'I could manage if that were ever my misfortune.'

'Supposing that you were penniless and had a starving child, or you were married to a man who gave you no money but who would beat you if there was nothing on the table . . . could you creep down in the night and steal a pie from Lou?'

'I think that you make the same mistake of many of our class in thinking that poverty equals dishonesty.'

'Did I suggest that? I merely asked whether you could do it.'

'The answer is "no" then, because I know how long and hard Lou works. In the circumstances you suggest, I would probably beg or borrow something.'

'Lou would do it.'

'Steal?'

'Yes.'

'I don't believe it.'

'That is because you have never had a starving child or been beaten by your man.'

'And to become initiated into this class I must have such experiences?'

'You will never become one of them, Otis.'

'If I do not, then I shall never become the teacher that I want to be.'

His fingers tentatively touched her upper arm. 'Teaching is too arid an occupation for such an exotic creature as you are. You should always be dressed in strange pink colours and long drop ear-rings as you were at Esther's wedding. You do not suit plain grey flannel and rooms above pie shops.'

Her breath halted and her thighs contracted.

At that moment she felt a desire – to experience every muscle of his torso, every sinew of his legs, every hair on his body. The image of her virginal counterpane as she had left it teased her. I have only to offer to make tea for him and I could have the experience. *The* experience. The one we all talked about at Stockwell but few of us had.

If only he were Jack, I would do it.

She leapt to her feet. 'I am sorry that you do not like my suit, Inspector Moth, I was rather pleased with it. I really must get back, I have so much to do.'

'Don't be so touchy, Otis.'

'I am not at all touchy. But I do have work to prepare.'

'I will walk with you then.'

'There is no need.' She held out her hand. 'I enjoyed our walk. I am sorry that I have been no help in your investigations.'

'There is no need. My enquiries are into a crime that . . .'

'Other women in this area do not get police protection – I do not wish any privilege.'

'Nevertheless, I shall walk with you. The women in this area do walk out with men you know. So stop being prickly and walk nicely.'

Otis did not carry the protest any further, but walked with a formal space between them. When they reached the dim archway, he halted and held her elbow. 'I very much want to kiss you, Otis, but I should not take any such advantage of you as I did before.'

'I am sorry, that was a mistake, I was carried away. I had some notion of wanting to comfort you.'

'Otis! I am an old hand at tweaking out the truth, and I have experience of women. You responded to me as though you wanted nothing more than to be taken.'

'To be *taken?* Oh no.'

'Very well, if you say so. Then let me kiss you now?'

'I . . . No. What would you say if it were my father asking Esther for a kiss?'

'I should say that it was so entirely unsuitable as to be wrong. But you, Otis, are a creature with no age, you are Botticelli's *Venus*, and have stepped into the world as a fully-formed woman. And in your presence a man is not aware of being a grandfather or a schoolboy, he is both youth and maturity.'

Not for the first time, Otis Hewetson understood why it was that Anne Moth had been so taken by this enigma. She did not know how to respond to so romantic a speech from a man who aroused her physically when in reality she wanted his son.

'I forgot to ask . . . how is Jack?'

Presumably accepting her rejection of him, he walked on

178

with her towards Lou Barker's shop. 'Jack? Well, I believe that Jack is thinking of answering the call to arms. He has been given several white feathers.'

'Oh poor Jack. That is a terrible practice.'

'And poor England if young men like Jack do not volunteer.'

'You surely cannot want him in the army?'

'Of course I don't, but the army is in dire need of healthy young men, which is what Jack is . . . he is needed. Like yourself, he has been infected by the desire to become anonymous. He says that when he joins he will go as a common foot-soldier.'

'I believe that our common foot-soldiers are being wasted. I cannot bear to think of Jack being used so uselessly.'

Now they were back in streets that were familiar to Otis. She held out her hand once more. 'This time I shall go on alone. Please give Jack my regards. I will go home tomorrow to collect my letters and then write to Esther.'

He shook her hand and bowed briefly. 'Thank you for your company. My investigations in this district are by no means ended; we shall perhaps see one another again.'

As she walked away he said, 'Otis.' She paused but did not turn around. 'How many of your schoolchildren have parents who have letters awaiting them in some large villa in Clapham? How many of them receive any letters at all?'

Still without turning she raised her hand and said, '*Touché.*'

1914

Dear Wally. The circumstances with the Miss O'Reillys have
changed. They have gone 'pro' this war and are thick with Mrs
Pankhurst's Lot. They would like me with them, but you know that
is impossible. The only employment I can find is hotel work. Miss
Althea thinks that I should be a munitionette and was annoyed
when I pointed out that it was the munitions that helped one lot of
working men kill another lot of working men. They have not given
me notice, but the atmosphere is not good.

*You have asked me plenty of times and I think that I should like
to 'try my luck' in London. I took the bull by the horns and will be
on the train that gets into Waterloo at six o'clock tomorrow. I
remembered it was your early turn so wondered if you could meet me
and help me find digs. If not, don't worry, I can find my own way
about. Yours, Nancy*

In some ways, although she had not agreed with them,
Nancy understood her employers' change of mind. Having
been for so long in the vanguard of local campaigning, their
arguments had become as familiar as their faces, so that
people had stopped listening. Nancy too felt that, whilst she
could always gather a loyal factory crowd around her, she
was preaching to the converted: they liked to hear somebody protesting about the government, about working
conditions, about 'Them'. But soon after she had replaced
Victoria as speaker at Hampstead, Nancy had felt the urge
to get away.

Now she was away and living in Bethnal Green. Wally,
who was a tram driver, had got her a job as a conductress.

He was, as Nancy often gave him credit for, a real decent sort of a bloke, and he knew everyone in the area worth knowing. Thus he had been able to find Nancy some comfortable lodgings in Bethnal Green, and thus a few weeks later he had known a seaman who had a nice little engagement ring at half shop price.

Nancy settled down in London as though born there. Wally wangled it so that she could do her training on his tram and Nancy had never expected to be so happy. Although he spent a lot of time on union work, Nancy did not mind. She had plenty to occupy her. She discovered also that because of his union activities he knew scores of people in the area and had dozens of friends.

'I got just the job for you, Nance.' And she would find herself helping with some fly-posting. Or, 'The WSP is short of helpers. I said you wouldn't mind helping out. You don't, do you, Nance?' Nor did she mind. If she had once thought of herself as a rebel in her home town, now, in the presence of anarchists and communists, she found her beliefs to be fairly commonplace. Soon, however, she found herself giving her time to a cause that gave her back the feeling that she was in the vanguard of radical ideas – she was drawn into a group which was dedicated to providing birth control knowledge to ordinary people.

War, for Major Blood, had started on the week following his honeymoon when he received orders to join a party taking horses to France. Surprised, never having had anything to do with horses except by way of leisure, he nevertheless travelled to Southampton where he discovered that not only was he to join a party, he was to take charge. With the bit of luck that every officer needs to get by, the sergeant was an old Sweat who had experienced worse than horses being in the charge of a bandsman.

Amazingly in all the confusion of an army on the move, reservists were eventually allocated to companies, horses laagered, and wagons hooked into transporters. The enforcement of censorship was surprisingly easy, for nobody knew anything except where they were at any given moment. Bindon spoke to Esther by telephone. 'I'm afraid that I can't say where I am, but listen.' He held the instrument out of the window where it picked up the screams of seagulls and ships' hooters. In the excitement of his preparations to embark, it had not occurred to him that his new bride might not be equally aroused. 'You're not weeping, Esther?'

'Of course I am weeping, Bindon. What woman would not weep when she hears the sounds of an army leaving home.'

'Oh, my dear.' He was genuinely shocked. 'You must not worry on my account. They've given me a company of horses to command.'

And she had giggled. 'Horses?' A little strained, but it was better than the tears.

The rumour was that their destination was Rouen, as part of the first British Expeditionary Force – it turned out to be true. The sheds where both horses and men were assembled were rank and hot and had scarcely cooled by evening when the last of the men left them to board the transporting vessel. As an officer, Bindon Blood had been allocated space in a minute cabin which was even more stifling than the sheds had been. He dumped his bags and went up on deck and sat with, but apart from, a group of NCOs who had apparently served together everywhere from South Africa to India. He knew no one. In his previous existence as a bachelor he would have taken out his pipe and listened to the stories of the NCOs, but as a husband just back from a honeymoon with the most exquisite bride in the world, he could have wept for himself.

Had it not been for some anarchist student taking a pot shot at some Archduke in some godforsaken Austrian town, then he and Esther might have lived an enchanted existence. He might even have resigned his commission. He would probably have been welcomed into any orchestra in London.

Suddenly, the grinding and bumping at the quayside ceased, the air freshened, and they were at sea on their way to fight a war.

To fight a war!

Above all else, Bindon vowed, I shall go back to Esther whole.

The NCOs accepted a fill from the major's tobacco pouch and they all sat through the next hours as the vessel ploughed its way towards the war zone. The first excitement was when a pilot boarded; then land was sighted, which Bindon was able to identify for the NCOs as Le Havre, then Quillebeuf, and slowly along the Seine to Rouen.

At Rouen, Bindon was able to transfer his command of horses into the hands of a cavalry officer who, for some reason, was aboard the same vessel as Bindon, but not in charge of horses. No one questioned the strange ways of the army; they were used to them.

His stay in Rouen was about a fortnight, during which time he was attached to a company of mixed Regulars and Reservists. The Reservists, poor devils, were despised by many of the time-serving men. Yet, as Bindon reasoned, they're as much in France as the rest of us, and worse off than we are by not knowing the ropes and dodges.

And then they marched.

Full packs, rations, ammunition, entrenching tools, maps and handbooks.

And then they entrained for God only knew where.

Here and there a cup of coffee and a roll at a railway station – this being France there was not a sign nor scent of a fragrant cup of tea.

And then they marched again towards the land of flat fields and dykes.

The roads were clogged with marching men and convoys of lorries. At first the sight of townspeople and villagers cheering and waving tricolours lifted the spirits of the men, but after twenty such accolades it was necessary for NCOs to prod a bit of a return waving and cheering from the footsore soldiers.

It had taken twenty days of marching, sleeping in woods, sitting in peaceful, newly-cut cornfields, eating bully-beef and biscuits, brewing tea and waving. The closer they got to the Belgian border, the more dispirited and antagonistic-looking the peasants appeared. It was hot, extremely hot. The men were ordered to dig in. That order counter-manded. Then the first order reinstated. There was, as with everything else, so it seemed, a shortage of picks and shovels, so that men sweated and swore as they attacked the rock-hard ground with their light entrenching tools. It was almost as light relief that they saw in the distance a German reconnaissance aircraft.

And then came the first sound of guns.

They were in the war.

The odour that pervaded the classroom was one that Otis would remember for as long as she lived. It was the smell of unwashed little children in unlaundered clothes. It wasn't all that unpleasant – rather like a face-flannel that had been left rolled up and soapy, plus the fustiness of the interior of an old cake tin – but it was pervasive. The corridors and cloakrooms smelt of Lysol and the row of lavatories across the playground smelt of themselves. Two of these were kept locked for the use of teachers, but it was only *in extremis* that a teacher unlocked one of those doors. Otis wondered how one managed when it was the time of their Eve's Curse – prudently wearing one's linen strips or pads a day or so before the expected event appeared to be the answer.

The school did not boast a Principal, but each division – Boys one side of the divide, and Girls on the other – had a Head. There was a third Head, Miss Mason, who managed the Mixed Infants, and it was to Miss Mason that Otis answered.

The Mixed Infants had been assembled in one room for the purpose of worshipping God. The twenty or so new intake children who were in Otis's own charge were in a bewildered little group around her. As the six- and seven-year-olds sang stodgily, fidgety, gasping breaths at the end of lines, Otis looked over the source of her ambition and the material that would fuel her driving force from here on.

Little bundles of ill-fitting, ill-assorted clothes covered by large, coarse aprons.

'All fings bright and beautiful, All creachures great and small . . .'

Few had socks, very few had boots that fitted or were in a state of repair. Some boys had near-shaven heads. Most of the girls had their hair tied back with string, though here and there was a bit of ribbon. There, on their first encounter with the rest of the Mixed Infants, they stood as though planted, overwhelmed and afraid, perhaps on account of something dire they had heard from an older brother about what big children did to you at school.

'He gave us eyes to see them, and lips that we might tell . . .'

Otis, apprehensive too at the responsibility of it all, longed for the assembly to be over so that she might return to feeding the minds of these small, underfed, rough-skinned, rickety children. Here was the most basic clay of humanity that one could find, and it was going to be hers to mould and make into decent vessels and, with luck, perhaps form an occasional small work of art.

'How Great is God Almighty, Who has made all fings well.'

This was Kitt's first train ride. Because military movements disrupted civilian travel, it took Esther, Kitt and Nursey hours and hours to get from London to Exeter, but with a cat-nap here and a picnic there, Kitt took the journey like a seasoned traveller. Esther was proud of him, kneeling solemnly at the window, asking sensible questions such as why had the fields turned to red once they were steaming through the West Country, and was that the sea or a wide river as they slowed down at the estuary. He was petted by ladies and given joeys or sixpences by gentlemen. Although he had been told that he would not see Dada so often when they got down to Mere, all in all, Kitt thought that going down to Mere was a splendid adventure.

Two of Windsor Villa's longest-serving members of staff – Mrs Clipper the cook and Ernest, who had no designated title except Mr Clipper, but was a most excellent general handyman and better than anybody in an emergency – had gone on ahead to Lyme Regis. Only Nursey travelled with Esther. She hoped against hope that the Windsor Villa couple did not fall out with those few domestics still remaining at Mere.

Ernest, widely grinning, was waiting with a trap at the station. Esther breathed a mental sigh of relief. Ernest had never been able to disguise his emotional state, glowering when put out at the master's occasional attempts at pruning, grinning when sharing a smoke with him in the greenhouse, weeping silently at the death of the family dog. Ernest was grinning. He talked all the way from the station to the very steps of Mere Meldrum, commenting on the virtues of the place as though Esther knew nothing of it and might be a purchaser.

'Lord, Miss Esther, this 'ere air down here is as good as a florin tonic. Like Mrs Clipper says she can't think of nowhere better for you and the Little Master. Mind you, as you can see, there's a bit of uppin' and downin' as far as the streets of Lyme's concerned, but like Mrs Clipper says, who wants to go gallivanting round the town when there's such grounds and views over the sea from your very doorstep. And do you know that bit they call The Cobb? Well, they say that it was writ up in some story where a lady fell down some steps and is quite famous. Well, our place is right above there and looks right down on it.'

Mrs Clipper, nowhere near as garrulous as her spouse, took a moment from her domain to assure the missis that it was every cook's dream below stairs, and not to be fooled into thinking that the local girls was simple because they spoke slow because it was just their way.

Jack had been right. It was a place in which a woman might wait in peace and tranquillity for the birth of her baby. So that by the time George Moth came to visit his children at Christmas, he saw not only that his daughter was the very image of a madonna, but that she had turned a soulless antiques museum into a comfortable and homely place in which she, Kitt, and the entire domestic staff were as settled and pleased with themselves as they could be.

When he watched her calmly rocking, her hands holding her small mounded belly, a faint secret smile upon her mouth, he knew why she had worked with such enthusiasm to create this atmosphere of security and comfort.

'It will be our first home. Mine and Bindon's and baby's . . . and Kitt's too I hope.'

George Moth wondered how much news of the war on the Western Front reached this idyllic spot, for certainly

189

during his stay there he saw no newspapers with their ever-lengthening lists of casualties; and the letters from his son-in-law which Esther insisted that he read were as were all letters from that place, cheerful and non-committal.

1914

My dearest Wife, Of course, I have always known that men are men the world over, knowing the same emotions. The last thing we want is to kill one another. We trusted them and they trusted us. No treaties, no signatures, nothing but the goodwill of ordinary men, a cask of beer and a plum pudding. In exchange for a picture of his Gilda, I gave a photograph of you. Neither of us could speak the language of the other, but in his great muddy boots and winter great-coat, he pirouetted and pointed at you. I told him 'Esther' and he nodded. The word he used means fairylike, or dainty. He mimed the query 'Children?'. I held my hands over my belly, and we both wept and shook our heads at the mindlessness of what we were doing to one another to gain a few yards of foreign mud. I send you Gilda so that when you read of atrocities, you will for a moment question whether it might be propaganda. Both sides use this means of building up hatred and nationalistic emotions. When we take prisoners, they are in a state of terror because they expect us to commit the most cruel acts. That is not to say that neither side is capable of barbarity . . .

Christmas morning and it was all quiet on the Front.

When the fog lifted it revealed the shocking sight of some unarmed enemy soldiers standing above their parapet waving.

No one had rescinded the order to shoot, and because of a suspicion that there might be fraternization on Christmas Day, Headquarters had sent down an order specifically forbidding it.

'Don't shoot!' The voice carried easily across the short

distance between the two lines. 'Don't shoot, we have beer for you.'

A kind of tremor ran through the British line when a cask was hoisted and rolled into no man's land. There were men out there. Ordinary blokes like yourself who wanted to stand you a round of drinks on Christmas morning.

A grey uniformed soldier pushed the cask further into no man's land. A German officer followed and stood open-handed facing his enemy lines. For moments no one knew what to do. This was the first time that the Tommys had seen grey uniforms worn smartly; they were more used to the sight of them bloody and fragmented, and mud-soaked and rat-gnawed, or worn by slouch-shouldered dejected prisoners-of-war; but here was a Boche officer's uniform standing open-handed offering a cask of beer.

The first move by the British was when an officer climbed up and walked the equal distance and faced the German. 'Please, take the beer. It is good beer.'

The British officer nodded. 'Thank you. We have something for you. Your English is good.'

'Thank you. I was in England one time for a year. I have in Winchester a cousin by marriage.'

'I have never been to Germany, I hear your lakes are impressive.'

'You should come there.'

'Tell you the truth, old son, I've been working my ass off trying to do just that.'

The men of both sides wondered what their officers could have said to one another to have caused such an outburst of laughter.

Men on both sides emerged unarmed and cautious, slowly at first and then with longer strides, until grey and khaki intermingled. A German soldier appeared with a tray containing glasses and beer in bottles which was poured for the officers.

'Today, we do not shoot one another. *Ja?*'

A British officer raised his glass. 'Against our orders, old son, but *ja*, today we do not shoot one another.'

A presentation of a Christmas pudding was made to the Germans, and after the men exchanged regimental badges or photographs of their families or girlfriends, the two sides withdrew across the frost-hard ground to their own sides for a silent night that was eerie in its peacefulness. Following the incident, Bindon Blood longed to write and tell Esther of the emotions he experienced and the way he spent Christmas night in contemplation.

At eight o'clock on Boxing Morning his reverie was interrupted by three pistol shots. The two sides exchanged greetings daubed on a flag. The answering three shots fired into the air was the signal to start up the killing once more.

1915

BLOOD. *To Esther Clermont Blood (née Moth), wife of Major Bindon Hubert Blood, on 4 May, a daughter, Stephanie Anne, at Mere Manor, Devon.*

NOTHING is to be written on this side except the date and signature of the sender. Sentences not required may be erased. *If anything else is added the postcard will be destroyed.* (Postage must be prepaid on any letter or postcard addressed to the sender of this card.)

I am quite well. ~~I have been admitted into hospital~~
~~{sick~~   } ~~and am going on well~~
~~{wounded~~   } ~~and hope to be discharged soon.~~
~~I am being sent down to the base~~ ....
    I have received your letter dated ..... *April*
~~I have received your telegram dated~~ ....
~~I have received your parcel dated~~ ....
Letter follows at first opportunity .... ~~I have~~
~~received no letter from you.~~ ....
Signature only. *B. Blood. Maj.* .... Date. *May. 1915*

During the month in which Esther laboured to produce her daughter and observe the lying-in and resting required by ladies of Mrs Blood's social class, 60,000 men were killed or maimed.

1915

Otis Hewetson looked at her class of 'babies'. They had spent a year in her care and, as far as anyone could tell, had come to no harm. Without exception they had learned the alphabet by heart, and most could read and write a few simple cat-sat-on-the-mat sentences, and add together single numbers. There had been crises such as when 'dip' touched these babies' families.

'Please Miss, our Timmy went and died last night.'

And not only Timmy. Diphtheria and whooping cough had taken two of Miss Hewetson's Mixed Infants. Prevention of all ills was by sprinkling Lysol on the floors, iodine tablets to suck and purple fluid at the drinking tap. Otis walked slowly between the rows of little battered desks, straightening a chalk here, a slate there. Wilfie had lost hearing in one ear from a mastoid; it had been necessary to move him closer to the front of the class. At the front too were Elsie and Danny, the twins who had got charity spectacles for their sty-rimmed eyes. Kathleen's Dad had been killed, Rose's father had been gassed and Edward's had lost a leg. Head-lice had been rife and treated with a glutinous paste, then impetigo and scabies had a turn at the babies' skin. There were times when Otis thought that schools could do a lot worse than to start each day with hot baths instead of hymns. But it was a Church of England school where Cleanliness played second fiddle to Godliness.

She stopped behind Maggie Harris's desk. Her slate was empty. 'Hurry along with it, Maggie.' The child jumped to life and blushed. She had started school knowing her alphabet, how to count to one hundred and could recite as many nursery rhymes as Otis herself. Since May, Maggie had become a 'difficult' child: not disruptive, but given to forgetting her lessons and sitting staring into space.

At Stockwell College she had been told: The children of the poor will always have difficulties, a good teacher never allows herself to become personally involved in them. She must endeavour to ignore the home lives and concentrate on providing within the classroom an ambience in which the child may take in its lessons.

A good teacher should try to be aware of what events within the child's family might affect its classroom performance, but she must never be tempted to go beyond this.

How could a teacher ignore what it was that changed a child from the brightest in the class to a dullard? No, Maggie was not a dullard, her brightness was still there.

As soon as she had heard, Otis had ignored the Advice to a Good Teacher and involved herself in the home life of a Poor Child and, by going to ask her father's advice, had involved him also.

'It does sound as though this is an unfortunate case, Otis, and I am sure that if it were up to me I should never behave in so callous a way. A month's imprisonment is exceedingly harsh for a first offence.'

'Pa! *Any* term of imprisonment in this case would have been exceedingly harsh. Mrs Harris ought never to have been arrested.'

'She broke the law, the Defence of the Realm is a serious matter.'

'But Father, the Defence of the Realm Act was surely never intended to crush women like Mrs Harris. She is a decent and hardworking woman. Do you know the wording of the offence with which she's charged?'

'You told me, my dear – of being an "Unworthy Woman". But she *was* in a garrison town, there *was* a

196

curfew for servicemen's wives and the commander *was* perfectly within his rights to bring her before a court-martial.'

'For goodness' sake, Pa, the woman was visiting her injured husband's relatives.'

'The arresting officers were not to know that when she was out after curfew hours.'

Otis had thrown up her hands then. 'Curfew hours, Pa! This is England, she has a husband in France and a family of children. They have court-martialled her, withdrawn her dependants' allowance.'

'I understand how you feel, my dear, but you will soon discover that the kind of people with whom you have chosen to ally yourself fall into one bit of trouble after another.'

'Then it is they who need lawyers and solicitors isn't it? and not *our* sort of people.'

'Perhaps in an ideal world. Until then.'

But he had done something. He had spoken to a local solicitor in the town where Mrs Harris had been imprisoned and she had been released after serving only ten days. But those ten days had damaged little Maggie.

This was Otis's last day with these children, when they came back from the Summer Break they would start in Standard II where her only contact with them would be ''ullo Miss' as they rushed past her in the street. Maggie would be transferred into the care of Miss Trethowen, who might not believe that this child was as bright as bright and had come from a family where she had been taught her letters before she was five.

For a moment Otis let her hand rest on the child's shoulder.

A good teacher never allows herself . . .

'Very well, children. You may put away your slates.'

The last day of term ended traditionally with the children reciting their work and the teacher reading an uplifting story. Otis had thought that these little Mixed Infants would not gain much from the recommended Kingsley's *Water Babies* or the moralistic Aesop's fables.

'That was done very nicely, children.'

The Good Teacher will always praise work well done.

'Go to the green cupboard, Maggie, and carefully carry to my table the brown box.' Anything in a box will excite a six-year-old.

It has been found that a class of four streams will compete to their advantage. Rewards by way of ticks and paper stars on a chart will urge young children to compete on an individual basis.

They craned their necks as Otis opened the box. 'We must be very quiet about this, so that we shall not disturb Miss Trethowen's class because they are still working.'

She was sure that a box of Lou's individual apple-pies specially baked with no spice and plentiful sugar were a much more satisfying reward than competitive paper stars.

'Remember, this treat is a secret between us, a special reward for being such good children.'

If anyone walked in or the Head discovered the little party, Otis was sure to be on the carpet, but it was worth the chance of being found out, and she had an excuse ready.

I am sorry, Miss Verilees, but I thought it might be an object lesson in a few table manners.

When Miss Trethowen came in later to claim Otis's children of the poor for her register of next term's six-year-olds, all that remained was the faint aroma of apple and an indefinable collective giggling mood which she put down to end-of-term silliness.

1915

NOTHING is to be written on this side except the date and signature of the sender. Sentences not required may be erased. *If anything else is added the postcard will be destroyed.* (Postage must be prepaid on any letter or postcard addressed to the sender of this card.)

~~I am quite well.~~ I have been admitted into hospital
~~{sick~~   } and am going on well
{wounded   } ~~and hope to be discharged soon~~.
    I am being sent down to the base ....
    ~~I have received your letter dated~~ ....
    ~~I have received your telegram dated~~ ....
    ~~I have received your parcel dated~~ ....
Letter follows at first opportunity ....✓.........I have
received no letter from you....✓...........
Signature only..B. Blood. Maj........ Date..June 1915

Bindon Blood had been in the army for most of his adult life. A family tradition of music and soldiering had taken him along the same career path as three preceding generations of Bloods and, like them, he had loved the life where orderly men paraded in orderly patterns to orderly music. Until the extraordinary event of falling in love, life was predictable. His schooling and music tuition had been regular and uninterrupted, his entry into his father's regiment assumed, his promotion assured. He had always been a fine musician and a competent officer.

Now he was a fighting man, who carried sidearms, but very little ammunition. Ammunition was in desperately short supply. Now he was no longer a musician but a soldier living day to chaotic day in a place they called Passchendaele. Now, every vestige of military order was gone. Men were potted at and went down like grouse on 4 August. Food was whatever was available. Big guns were restricted to firing only a few rounds a day. There were not enough rifles to go round so that men went into battle with picks and shovels, arming themselves when they could from the dead and injured. For the first winter months of the war, on that front, it had been mud and cold and mud and frustration and mud and dead men.

According to Headquarters' statistics, he too should have been dead, for he had spent months being moved around the battlefields and had gone much beyond his officially calculated life-expectancy. But he knew something that 'they' did not know, he now knew that he was one of the chance statistics. If statistics proved that eight out of every ten men were killed within a month of arriving at the Front, they proved equally that two out of ten were not killed. From this belief he helped himself to the fact that there would eventually be a statistic which showed that a certain percentage of men would go home unscathed. Now, Bindon Blood was assured that he was to be of their number.

He was aware that he had many mad thoughts these days *but it's my madness that keeps me sane*. He chuckled to himself and began in his head another rambling, endless letter. *Darling Ess*, he withdrew to the only place where there was no chaos, *you have no cause to worry about me, I feel that my life is charmed. There is a magic bubble into which I can slip whenever I wish. In here there are green fields and trees, a yellow bordered sea, white cottages and red cows, for this is how I remember Lyme. There is a woman who slowly walks in those fields, or along the strand. I see the reason that she walks slow. It was a soldier who gave her the tell-tale silhouette that she holds as she walks. He who gave her that ever-swelling mound of love. Do you remember, Ess? Do you remember the sun and the sound of the waves? Do you remember the breakfasts and the rush to straighten the tumbled bed? Do you remember how she tried to muffle her cries of passion. Their laughter? His ecstatic happiness? This woman who walks so stately in the field . . . she is the woman who has given the soldier his charmed life, and it is she who will soon give life to the soldier's child. Oh, darling Ess, I can hardly bear it that you must have the child and I shall not be close by . . .*

He cuffed away some tears . . . how easily they came now that he had learned the knack. It was a perfect spring day. The town that had been prosperous in the Middle Ages was now inhabited by about only 20,000 inhabitants who lived by the beets and corn that their land yielded. So far, they had tried to ignore the battles that were fought around their flat country-side. Bindon Blood sat with his back against warm stone and rested, passing the time till his men would be ready to transport canisters of food to the battle-zone.

Even though publicly weeping, he was invisible to passers-by. Another piece of khaki like thousands more – Canadian, Pathan, Indian Army, British, Baluchi, Sikh – all anonymous pieces of khaki. Bindon Blood thought briefly of the times when he had been anything but anonymous; when, standing alone on a raised podium, he had performed solo; and when as a young officer in full dress uniform picked out by a spotlight he had played the Last Post before the King. Except at their wedding, Esther had never seen him in his splendour; gleaming buttons and insignia, plumed cap, braided jacket. He took out a tobacco-tin and papers. She did not know that he had taken to smoking. It hardly seemed to matter now, that his breathing might be impaired for the playing of wind instruments. His newly-discovered satisfaction from nicotine outweighed that consideration, the comfort of nicotine was here and now and the burning end of a cigarette could finish off a dozen lice.

With smoke curling over his face from a meanly-filled cigarette, he leaned his head against his recently-issued gas-mask bag and closed his eyes to the sun and wrote to his brother-in-law, *I wonder whether you will answer Kitchener's call for volunteers, Jack? I know almost nothing of military strategy, but even I must know more than those who are commanding us. I believe that they cannot understand that an entirely different set of rules must apply now that we are not using cavalry, otherwise they would not sit in England planning battles that cannot be won no matter how many tons of bodies they ship out here. We desperately need supplies, Jack, and armaments . . . not men, especially not untrained barbers, clerks and waiters who took the shilling in a moment of patriotic fervour . . .*

The first shells fell late morning.

It was Saturday, market day, and the town was busy. Bindon Blood, returning to reality, saw the same looks of bewilderment and terror on the faces of townspeople as he had seen on those of his own men, and they must have seen upon his, when they first experienced being targeted by an unseen enemy who fired at them from a great distance. Soon the market-place was cleared as the people ran into the town's cellars.

By midday guns were pounding continuously. By early afternoon, when there was a lull, there was turmoil on the roads leading westward from town, as a tide of refugees laden with possessions streamed out against the oncoming horse-drawn limbers of Bindon and his transporters.

By five o'clock walls were crumbling and towers crashing. The town was dying in a cloud of dust.

On the first light breeze of evening there wafted in from the north a heavy yellow cloud. It descended like a fog, catching men in the throat, burning their eyes and retching their guts. When men had no masks to protect themselves, they soaked any piece of cloth with water, urine, slops of tea, and held it across their faces. Horses with eyes streaming and rolling shrieked and broke out, crazed with panic. Foot-soldiers with blinded, burning eyes, staggered across the flat fields.

Behind the yellow cloud, with bayonets fixed and peering through the goggles of their grotesque rubber masks, came the German infantry.

Four miles of the line collapsed, heavy guns were abandoned as blinded, wounded and choking troops were loaded on to any vehicle which would serve as an ambulance. Ahead of the advancing enemy, Bindon Blood, his charmed life protected by his lucky gas-mask, organized the limbers of the gun-carriages, on which earlier the food canisters had been transported, to transport men to dressing-stations or shelter behind the lines.

Later, he remembered thinking: Providence issued gas masks alphabetically. My lungs are saved. I shall stop smoking. I shall play for Esther and the child at a great military tattoo, with the spotlight upon me. Esther will say, Listen, Baby, listen to your papa playing.

The soaked sack which was over the head of his horse served to make the creature rear and struggle to break loose. Bindon held tightly to the leather leading strap which he had twisted about his fist. The horse rose on its back legs, knocked Bindon flying, and leapt forwards, pulling a wheel of the limber across Bindon's ankle, crushing it into the road. He heard the scream before he blacked out, but did not know that it was himself. As he lay there with the remnants of gas swirling about him, his mask was ripped from his face by a retching soldier who could not believe his good luck at this find.

When Major Blood came to an agonized consciousness and in a pool of vomit, the remnants of his last thoughts before the horse reared were still with him.

Listen, Baby . . .
Listen to the strange music your papa's breath makes.

1916

In London, at Speakers' Corner in Hyde Park, Victoria Ormorod, with other members of the League for Peace, is in her usual Sunday morning place, arguing the case against continuing the war.

'. . . and a multitude of men uselessly lost. I was at The Hague congress where women of every nation supported the notion that in the twentieth century governments must give up the notion that disputes are settled by brute force. It is honourable to work for peace.'

A young woman, standing in the crowd that is gathered around the stool Victoria stands upon, raises her fist triumphantly. 'And so it is honourable for Our Boys to die for their country.' She receives cheers from some supporters. Later in the day the woman will be speaking, whipping up a jingoistic frenzy; then it will be the turn of Victoria and her friends to give this heckler as rough a time. Hecklers are the stone on which wits are sharpened.

Victoria is not thrown off-stride, but raises her voice above the cheers for the interrupter. 'This lady says that it is honourable for them to die for their country. Those *men* – I will not abuse them by addressing them as "boys" with such false sentimentality – it is true were no age at all. It is true also that they were the sons and husbands of women who had no right to vote. When it came to electing the government who decided that this country should go to war, no woman and scarcely any of those young men who have died had any say in it – the very people who have most to lose have the least power.' She pauses as a male voice cuts in singing, 'Here we go, Here we go, Here we go again . . .'

As she waits, her eyes slide over the crowd until she sees, standing at the back, the tall figure of Jack Moth. It is a while since she has seen him, and she hopes that he will not go before she can speak to him.

The singing man's regular cronies at Speakers' Corner take their lead from him and join in. Victoria rolls her eyes heavenwards, indicating that this is an old joke, but she will humour them. When they have finished, they move off to perform before another gathering further along in Hyde Park.

She continues, trying, at the same time as keeping a hold on her crowd, to keep Jack in view. Ever since the night when she sat and comforted him after his mother's death, her memory has kept insisting that experience upon her. 'The names of men in those shocking and ever-growing lists of the casualties of Flanders have not died for *their* country, they did not die for Canada, or India, or Wales, or Ireland, or Scotland, or England . . .'

The woman interrupts again, 'No! They have died for gallant little Belgium.'

Victoria turns on her. 'No! No! The young men in Flanders are dying for the pride and honour of incompetent generals, and for war-loving people like you. You tolerate 60,000 casualties in a few weeks rather than tolerate what you think of as defeat. I am not a general or a politician, I am a midwife – yet even I can see what the war lords could not or *would* not see – that it would have been sensible to withdraw from the Salient, to abandon Ypres and re-form a stronger line beyond the canal.'

For the moment the crowd has fallen silent. Jack is looking directly at her, and she wonders whether he has come purposely to see her.

'If we are not to continue pouring the very best of our young men down the barrels of the German guns, there is only one course open to us, and that course is to negotiate for peace.'

For a moment the Sunday morning crowd listens, but soon closes its ears to the unthinkable. Peace? Just when its blood is up, the whip raised and the fox in sight? No matter what, the crowd wants nothing except to lash out – even though it might lose its limbs in the attempt.

The British public does not want to hear the words 'negotiated peace', and these are at the heart of Victoria Ormorod's message.

The woman and her friends will go out with their white feathers, and join in the singing: '*We don't want to lose you, but we think you ought to go, Your King and your Country they need you so . . .*'

Young men, filled with nationalistic fervour, will listen to the whine of shells and the thunder of guns, believing that they hear bugles and drums.

There is an excitement in the air that comes when a country that has been spoiling for a fight is in the throes of fighting it. The crowd, whose attention Victoria has had for thirty minutes, knows how much blood is being spilled; it sees itself as part of a Nation in Mourning, and so wants no part of a negotiated peace – it wants vengeance.

When Victoria's supporters hand out leaflets these are rolled into balls and shied at the members of the League for Peace.

Victoria has not been home for weeks. Her way of life has for years been almost nomadic, a few days here helping to set up a local organization, a few days there speaking at rallies and meetings, sleeping wherever a supporter of the cause had room to spare. Her cause now was peace as well as suffrage.

Within the circle of supporters of the League, it was easy to believe that there was urgent and growing support, and it is true that their numbers grew steadily from the parents and relatives of soldiers. Young men who had been blithe-spirited youths when they were shipped to France, but who had come back on leave changed; or been sent home injured, withdrawn and racked, not speaking of what it was that filled the night-time with nightmares. Or had not come back at all.

There were, too, many Quakers and other religious sects whose pacifist beliefs pushed them into speaking out against the continuance of the war. And some who believed that there were no circumstances in which they could go armed with the intention of killing another human being.

As Jack Moth watched Victoria Ormorod, he felt the same thrill of attraction that he had felt that balmy summer in Southsea before the war. He wanted her. Had wanted her since their first meeting. He longed for her fine body, longed to sit quietly with her, to sit and talk with her, to sit and listen. As he listened now, he resented the passion she expended on the crowd.

He watched the crowd with disgust. A man of about Jack's own age was gathering up leaflets and compressing them into a hard ball. As he aimed, Jack snatched the ball from him, caught his collar, jerked him back and spun him around so that he was facing into Jack's broad chest. 'Exactly what were you going to do?'

'They're damned traitors the lot of them. She should be locked up.'

'Because she speaks her mind? I should have thought you would be for that.'

'They are all in the pay of the Germans.'

'You are not only ignorant, you are contemptible with it.' And so saying, Jack Moth stuffed the paper ball into the man's breast pocket and slapped it hard, twirling him away as he did so.

'Excuse me.' The girl who addressed him was beautifully and expensively dressed, link-armed with another girl equally well got up. 'I just wanted to say how brave of you

207

that was.' She reached up as though to embrace him, and as she did so her companion deftly slipped a white flight feather into his lapel. In a second they had gone.

'Oh Jack, what a rotten thing.'

He had not noticed Victoria until she was standing before him. She reached up to remove the obnoxious badge of cowardice. 'No, Victoria, leave it. It is just a feather.'

'They are spreading so much awfulness, these women. To them it is a bit of entertainment to fill their bored lives. Who are they to tell one man to go out and kill another man?'

Smiling, he laid a hand across her lips. The soft feel of them was an aphrodisiac. 'I have been listening to that argument for thirty minutes.'

'I saw you. I hoped that you would wait.'

'May I walk with you?'

'I am free until this evening.'

'Lunch?'

'So long as it is somewhere cheap . . . the V and A?'

'Tramcar or walk?'

'Oh, I prefer a walk every time.'

They had walked along the autumn pavements of London, the air smelling more of leaves than of the more usual combustion-engine fumes and horse-droppings. They were warmly polite and friendly to each other, Jack asking questions about her work, but not saying much about his own life. From time to time, as he turned sideways to speak, he let his gaze rest upon the movements of her body as she strode along, swinging her arms.

'I am still a country girl,' she said when he laughingly feigned breathlessness. 'I cannot trit-trot as city women do.' Her figure was firm and beautiful, and he remembered again his surprise, when she had put her arms about him at Southsea, to discover warm softness instead of the whale-bone and steel hooks that shaped most female forms. He felt a great desire to smooth his hand over her round hip and cup his hand beneath the curve of her breast.

When they reached the Victoria and Albert Museum, the smell of hot food from the gentlemen's grill in the Poynter Room made them realize how hungry they were, so they ordered a grill.

Victoria pushed her coat back from her shoulders and looked around her with satisfaction. 'Isn't this *the* most wonderful room to come in to from the old, drab world? I always feel when I come here that I could have my appetite assuaged by the light and colour.'

Jack smiled at her. 'Shall I cancel our order then?'

'No, let's be greedy and have the food as well as the room.'

The Gamble Room in which they sat being polite to one another was indeed a satisfying room, highly decorated mainly in white, warm orange, blue and gold. Skirting around their sudden, unexpected intimacy, Jack, pointing to a frieze, said, 'Do you agree?'

She craned her neck to decipher the letters of a highly decorative alphabet. 'It runs off. I can read . . . "There is nothing better for man than that he should eat and drink . . ." and then it runs off.'

' "There is nothing better for man than that he should eat and drink and that he should make his soul enjoy good in his labour." Ecclesiastes, 2.'

'Goodness, I am impressed.'

'Gleanings of a child too smart for its own good.'

Victoria threw back her head and laughed. 'Oh, how well I know that child.'

When their food arrived, Jack, looking at a fairly meagre portion, said, 'Is this sufficient that we shall make our souls enjoy good in our labour?'

'It is not a bit of good asking *me*, I eat only to enjoy good in my person.' She pointed to the frieze with the handle of her fork. ' "There is nothing better for *man* than that *he*

209

should eat and drink and that *he* should make *his* soul enjoy good in *his* labour." That is a perfect example of the invisibility of women in our society. All messages are addressed to the man.'

'Dear Victoria, do you carry your soap-box everywhere?'

She smiled, quite unabashed. 'I have never used a soap-box – much too insubstantial. Bottle-crates are the thing. There, now I have had my say, tell me of the recent life and times of Jack Moth.'

'Since we last met, I have become a qualified and fully paid-up member of the legal profession.'

'That is wonderful news. I dare say your father and sister are very proud of you.'

When he had told him, his father had said: 'Well then, that's one up for the Moths, the first lawyer this family has ever known.'

He had not congratulated, or complimented. Jack knew that he had done extremely well to have been taken into a practice so soon. Junior though he might be, it was an achievement, and he would have liked his father to have acknowledged it. Jack knew that had he asked: 'Aren't you pleased, Father?' his father would have looked puzzled and said: 'Pleased? Why do you need to ask? You know that I am pleased, what else should I be?'

'Oh yes, I believe that he is. But I think that he would have preferred it if I had joined the police force.'

He watched her eating. Her lips were full and red, her white teeth grew slightly forward at the front of her upper jaw and peeped from her mouth, often giving her expression a slightly surprised look. He liked the way she bit honestly into her food. She did not toy or fiddle with what she was eating.

He imagined that this was how she would be with physical love. When she was hungry, she would accept and enjoy fulfilment. How amazingly wonderful if that were true. He heard such tales of failed marriages. Of husbands

210

who were shocked into celibacy to discover that the angelic creatures they imagined they had married had proved to have carnal appetites. And wives who had been trained from girlhood to expect nothing except that men were born to lustfulness and fornication, and had discovered that it was indeed the truth.

Today, beneath a wide hat, she wore her heavy copper-coloured hair piled on the crown of her head. All around her hairline the new hair curled and twisted and gave her head a delightfully opulent look. It suddenly occurred to him that this room – with its exotic columns of white and dark orange, its warm, tan-coloured frieze and floor tiles, the fresh luminescence of its wall panels and the beautiful north light coming in through the bluely decorated figured glass of the arched windows – was, if such a thing was not wildly fanciful, a Victoria Ormorod of a room. Exotic, striking, unforgettable. And as he had been drawn back to the room again and again since he was a young boy, so he felt drawn by this enigmatic woman.

She must know that I am examining her. Any other woman would blush and fuss and be coy. He wondered now, as he had done on other occasions, why he felt a slight tingle of apprehension in her company. He longed for her, was sure that what he felt was love, so why did he have that little niggle of unsuredness? Had she not been the splendid Victoria Ormorod, he would have flirted with her.

'Victoria. It wasn't chance that brought me to Hyde Park this morning. I came looking for you.'

'Well, and so you found me.'

'Marry me, Victoria.' He had known that this was what he wanted to say; and now it was said, inelegantly blurted out. 'I want nothing more in the world than that you be Jack Moth's wife.'

'Oh Jack!' She reached out and laid a hand upon his. Her green eyes looked at him straight on, and then, as their truth-seeking gaze penetrated him, he suddenly realized that those tingles of apprehension she caused him were because she brought to mind a tutor he once had as a young boy. The man had been kindness and understanding itself, and in character so straight that little Jack was never able to hide anything bad on his conscience and had always confessed without pressure.

'And . . .' He took her hand in both of his. 'And I have to tell you so that you will not think that I have deceived you. I have . . . Oh, Victoria, I am sorry . . . no, not sorry, that is the wrong word, but I wish that my conscience did not lead me to do it.'

She seemed to look right into him; when she spoke it was with a wry chuckle deep in her throat. 'Aren't consciences the very devil, Jack? Mine leads me to stand up in public and harangue passers-by, and I guess that yours has led you to enlist.'

Again he remembered his boyhood tutor: 'I say this to you more in sadness than anger, young Moth.'

I can't take her on. He thought that she was like a client who, in the interest of truth, refuses to plead 'Not Guilty', even though that plea is the way the game is played to get a hearing.

'Yes . . . Yes, it is true, how did you guess?' The Gamble Room was now almost full. China and cutlery clattered and people's voices hummed. Occasionally the musky smell of the gallery wafted in to mingle with the aroma of tea and grilled food. She bent forward slightly so as not to raise her voice above the level of background noise.

'I can think of nothing else that you would feel it necessary to confess to me.'

'I am not a poor man, Victoria. I recently inherited a house from an uncle. My sister lives there, but it would be yours if anything were to happen to me.'

'Jack, Jack. Is this what war does to people? You ask me to marry you in one breath, and in the next you tell me of the arrangement for widowhood. Come, let us go outside.'

212

They walked out into Exhibition Road, across Kensington Road, through the Alexandra Gate and on towards the Round Pond where they sat and watched small boys guiding model boats with hooks, and small boys watching them.

'Sundays are changing, Jack. Would you have been allowed to sail a boat on a Sunday?'

'It was a serious proposal of marriage, Victoria.'

'I know that, and I do not know what to say to you. I can give you none of the conventional replies.'

'A simple "Yes" would do.'

'I am sorry, Jack. I like you very much. I have since the first time I set eyes upon you.'

'You surely don't think that the difference in our ages . . . ?' He thought of Esther and Bindon, Esther being years his junior, and yet their marriage was as solid as could be. They were deeply in love. When they had returned from their honeymoon, he had envied them their evident ecstasy. He longed for the same between himself and Victoria.

'No, no.' She squeezed his arm in emphasis. 'Age is an irrelevance. If you were fifty and I eighteen, it would still be an irrelevance.'

'And the opposite age difference?'

'It would still be only a matter for ourselves. I shall not marry, Jack. I made up my mind to that when I chose my own name – I knew that I would never change it. We women have few enough rights as it is, even fewer rights within marriage. In law, a wife has little except the right to be got out of debt by her husband – she has not even the right to her own body.'

'But these husbands are not me. I adore you, Victoria. And I adore your body so much that I should respect it to the nth degree.'

'My dearest, Jack, of course you would. I like the kind of man that you are, but I should make you no sort of a wife. In the first place, I have my work in the movement which I shall never give up until men have equality with one another and women have equality with men. But within the law as it now stands . . .' She broke off and laughed her free, deep-throated laugh. 'Goodness! Listen to the Ruby Bice coming out in me. I had quite forgot I was talking to a fully paid-up member of the legal profession.'

He faced her. 'Marry me. Forget Ruby Bice and become Victoria Moth.'

She touched his cheek affectionately. 'Would you care to become Jack Ormorod?'

He smiled at the notion. 'Change my name to yours?'

'More than that. I mean would you give up entirely who you have been for twenty-odd years? Would you marry me and become Mister Victoria Ormorod, so that you have no status except what is given you by virtue of being married? Would you care not to be Jack Moth any more, but Mrs Victoria Ormorod's husband?'

He leaned a little away from her, not understanding her expression. 'Are you serious?'

Wryly smiling, she shook her head. 'No, dear Jack. I wouldn't ask a man to be subjugated to such an extent. Equally, neither shall I. My grandmother taught me the skill of midwifery and left me a little money in order that I should not need to rely on a man to provide for me. I shall never marry.'

'How can you be so sure? You may well fall so much in love that . . .'

Unheedful of the Sunday afternoon promenaders in Kensington Gardens, she pulled Jack Moth's head down to her own level and kissed him on the lips as expressively as she had done when he was a youth.

'Jack Moth. I quite fell for you when we met at Southsea, but on that last night you were in too much of a state of anguish for me to be able to tell you.' She held on to his hand tightly. 'You have no idea of the nervous energy that is required to keep people with my convictions going. We're harassed by police, we're lonely and the world is hostile to us. I wouldn't inflict myself upon you. If you want me, be content to have me as I am, separate and independent.'

For a while he was silent, then he said, 'I have only a short time before I must report to my unit. Will you come to Dorset with me?'

'To Dorset?'

'Mere, the house that was left to me, it is on the outskirts of Lyme Regis.'

'I . . . Yes, all right, I have not had a break from campaigning for months. I am sure the group will agree to my going.'

'My niece is to be christened, you could meet my family.'

The awful feather that the woman had stuck in his lapel that morning had been there ever since. Now he removed it and was about to throw it in the gutter when she stopped him. 'No, give it to me as a token.'

He threaded the quill end through a buttonhole of her bodice. 'A token of what?'

She considered. 'Of the many kinds of love that people can experience.'

Mere Manor, Meldrum, Nr Lyme Regis

Dear Otis,

It was good to hear from you. This is a very beautiful place, but it can be quite lonely. Of course I have Baby and Bindon, but no one to talk with. I do keep bright and smiling for them, but there are moments when I should simply like to 'let go' and have a good moan. I am sure that the mothers of 'your' children would be disgusted with such a whimperish creature. Truly, I am not, and if you were to come I vow that I should not spend the time close to your ear. I have so wanted to talk with you about things that cannot be said in a letter, and look forward to hearing more about your classroom experiences.

My true purpose in writing this letter is to remind you that you once promised to become one of Baby's godmothers. The christening is to be at Easter. Jack and a distant cousin of Bindon's are to be the other godparents. Easter is a good time to come to Lyme, for it is particularly beautiful at this time of year.

Your affectionate friend,
Esther Blood

Provided Otis did not appear at Greywell in her sensible working dress and shoes, her mother was not so inclined these days to take up the cause of Otis's ringless fingers. If she appeared in something stylish and wearing long earrings and a little of the expensive perfume with which Emily kept her daughter amply supplied, then Otis was deemed to be in the marriage market. For a number of reasons, Otis still had most of her mail addressed to Stormont Road. She was pleased to notice Esther's handwriting on one of the envelopes.

In the conservatory warmed by strong spring sunshine, Emily poured tea for her daughter. 'You will go of course, Otis. I saw reference to Mere Manor in a magazine recently – just architecture, of course, not the family.'

'With Jack not there, then there really isn't a Mere family.'

'Quite. Have you seen anything of Jack Moth recently?'

'Mother! Stop Mrs Benneting. Jack Moth is not at all interested in me.'

Emily Hewetson's wits were at their most sharp when it came to the prospect of coupling her daughter with some eligible male, so she noticed that Otis did not say: Stop it. *I* am not at all interested in Jack Moth. Well, there was hope still. If only Otis were living at home, then Jack Moth might easily have been invited to dinner at Greywell. As it was, all that Emily could do was to encourage and hope that a long weekend on a lovely estate like Mere might work wonders.

'You have been looking quite peaked, it would put my mind at ease if you were to accept the Bloods' invitation and take a few days breathing the clean air of Lyme.'

Esther looked forward to the weekend. Otis had said that she would be able to get there. Their friendship might have got off to a rickety start after Bognor, but it had endured. Both young women had other friendships, but this one was the one they each valued higher than the rest.

Esther felt that this was not the time for Jack to invite an outsider, but it was Jack's home and Jack was very dear to her. She knew that he had been interested in the woman since the year that their mother died, but he had seldom mentioned her except in passing or to say that he had heard her speak at some meeting, and now here he was saying that he had invited her to spend Easter.

George Moth looked forward to the weekend. Quite apart from his desire to see Esther and Kitt, he had the notion that if he saw Otis and Esther with their girlish heads together as they used to do before Esther married and Otis went to college, then he might be able to get her in a more acceptable perspective. Whenever he pushed a ring of cigar smoke from his mouth with his tongue, his mind went to her with her hair swathed in satin and wearing that clinging rose-coloured gown and glittering ear-rings. There were times when he felt perturbed at his desire for a girl of his daughter's age, and there were times, when he was in Effee Tessalow's paid arms, that it seemed most natural for a virile man to want a youthful woman. And there were times when he realized that he was a grandfather, and that he must be an old fool. The truth was that he found her self-possession stimulating and she fascinated him.

Jack was glad to be going to Mere, because he wanted Victoria to be with Ess and Bindon, Kitt and his father, to enjoy Mere in the hope that she would be won over by the idea of becoming part of the Moth family.

Victoria wondered how she had ever been tempted to accept Jack Moth's invitation. Easter was always a time when crowds gathered in London parks, and Ruby Red would be expected to be there, persuading the crowds, instead of spending time with an army volunteer. There was so much to do and so few people to do it that there was no room in her life for any more disastrous romantic interludes. After Tankredi . . . I promised myself, no involvement. Why am I never attracted to an easy man? Always such unsuitable liaisons.

Otis, even when her bags were packed and she was ready to leave for the station, was still not sure that it would not have been best for her to have made her excuses. Lately her rest had been disturbed by erotic dreams. She could deal with the eroticism but not with the upheaval she caused herself when she tried to analyse her own emotions. Often she longed for her old college coterie of modern young women who would soon discover the meaning of her dreams.

Helene would say, exaggerating her lisping French accent: La, theece eez easy, all that you need eez the tor . . . so? eh? of a young man.

Zena would say, 'Or of a young woman.' Linking her arms about Otis as she would do any of the coterie when she was in one of her half-playful seductive moods.

How simple it had all been then, talking up their emotions, their fantasies, their encounters and affairs. In their earnest discussion, usually about themselves, they would often account for their moods by blaming lack of physical fulfilment. Pleased with themselves that they had escaped their mamas and were modern enough young women to discuss such problems with dignity.

Well then, Helene would say to wind up their discussion, shall we all go away from Stockwell and find ourselves a beau wiz a diamond reeng? And then they would laugh at the very idea.

But, as Otis admitted to herself now, the problem of single women who did not have Zena's inclination to love women, was not an easy one to solve. *When taking a vacation in beautiful surroundings in the company of tall, broad men, the Good Teacher will always be on her guard.*

And on her guard she was when she followed her porter the length of the platform to look for a suitable seat on the Exeter train on which two tall, broad men were known to be travelling.

The compartments were already filling. Jack Moth, who had secured a compartment, greeted her warmly. She had not foreseen the presence of another woman. Clearly she was with Jack.

George Moth fetched magazines and saw to their bags with his usual charm and courtesy. Once they were settled into the journey, Otis and the Moths inevitably talked of Esther, and for a while Victoria was outside of their circle, though it appeared to Otis that she did not in the least mind but listened to their conversation with interest. Otis was preoccupied trying to place her. She did not recognize the woman's name, but was sure that she remembered having seen her before today.

'What is the baby to be named, Jack?' Victoria asked.

'Lord!' he answered, 'Ess never calls it anything except "Baby", do you know, Otis?'

'No, I don't know either. Perhaps she is to be christened "Baby".'

' "Baby Blood"! Strewth, poor little tadpole. Here's Father back from the smoker.' George Moth took his seat in the corner opposite Otis. 'Father, what is this baby to be called?'

'You will be ashamed of us, Inspector Moth,' Otis exclaimed. 'Three godparents on their way to a christening and none of us knows the baby's name.'

'Stephanie Anne, as far as I know,' said George Moth.

Victoria Ormorod, in a low, quiet voice, said, 'I am sorry, you are mistaken, I am not a godparent.'

220

'Ah . . . I am afraid I assumed . . . I am sure that your face is familiar to me, I thought that you were Bindon's . . . Perhaps we met at Esther's wedding?'

Jack, smiling at Victoria said, 'I'll tell you where, Otis, and when. Where, Southsea. When, the day you came out in your grown-up finery . . .'

And then she remembered. 'Of course!' She remembered Uncle Hewey and the parasol.

'Blanche Ruby Bice . . . you remember.'

'Lord! You so impressed me that for two years I copied your style of dress. I just hadn't connected . . .' Hadn't connected Jack with such a politically involved person.

Miss Ormorod smiled enigmatically and nodded.

George Moth knew that he was excluded from something and that he had obviously been excluded at the time. He turned over the pages of his newspaper with apparent absorption.

'Goodness, Miss Ormorod,' Otis said. 'How you fired my imagination that day.'

'It is what I try to do. I hope that it lasted longer than the day.'

'Well,' said Jack, 'she is as independent as yourself, I can tell you that.'

'I am glad to hear it,' Victoria said.

By tacit agreement, perhaps prompted by the inspector's restless pages, they began to talk of the passing scenery until they arrived at Exeter where Bindon was waiting for them with a motor-car.

It was not easy disguising their shock at the changes that Bindon's injuries had brought about in him. At his wedding he had been plump, smiling and erect in his dress uniform. His brown hair had been heavy and oiled, his complexion pink, his figure well-fed. Now, that same uniform would hang upon him as did his pale skin. His concave chest drew down his shoulders, and his limp hair was scattered with grey. Worst, were the bouts of a racking cough that left him weak and breathless. Each time he regained his breath he would say, 'I am sorry. I do apologize. It catches me so unaware that I . . .' And he would make an effort to appear his old self, acting the host, paying attention.

Esther was almost shrill with the excitement of showing off their baby. It was a wonderful baby, outshining any other for miles around. When Bindon was attacked by a fit of breathlessness, she would at once halt what she was doing and watch him intently but helplessly.

Little Kitt did not appear to have remembered Otis, but in no time at all took her on again as his friend when they all joined him for a run around on the grass before his bedtime.

Although Otis was outwardly unperturbed by the unexplained presence of Victoria Ormorod, she longed for an opportunity of questioning Esther about her. Explanations came about when the three women were seated in the shelter of an arbour watching the three men roust around with Kitt.

'It was very kind of you to let me join you this weekend, Mrs Blood. I thought that I should not come, as it was such a family occasion, but Jack wanted me to see Mere Meldrum.'

'Oh, do let's all use first names,' Esther said. 'It is not kind at all, we are pleased to have you. If Jack's friends cannot come here, then who can?' She almost let a look at Otis escape, but turned it away to Baby Stephanie at the last moment. 'Did you remember having seen Victoria before, Otis?'

Otis shook her head. 'Yes, but not the circumstances, until Jack reminded me. May I pick up Baby?'

The pretty little creature drew the eyes of all of them, and Otis was able to try to deal with the felling blow of jealousy without meeting anyone's eyes.

'Doesn't it all seem such an age ago? Here I am a wife and mother and you with your degree and a classroom of children.'

'You teach?' Victoria Ormorod sounded surprised. 'I am sorry, that sounded . . .'

'You mustn't let Otis's elegance fool you, she's more than a pretty dress and ear-rings,' said Esther. 'She has a London qualification.'

'And do you work in London?'

'Islington. I teach a class of five-year-olds.'

'Islington? What a small world. I shall be spending a great deal of time in that area. We have some premises on Green Lanes.'

Jiggling the baby and not meeting Victoria's eyes, Otis answered politely. 'I know Green Lanes, it is only minutes from where I live.'

'I had assumed that you were neighbours of . . .'

'The Moths? No, we have never been neighbours. My parents' home is close to Clapham Common, but I have rooms in Islington. I should never get to school on time if I had to come in from Lavender Hill each morning.'

'Perhaps I could persuade you to come and help out in our new bookshop.'

Otis hesitated, cautious of making any commitment, especially to a woman who caused her pangs of jealousy. 'I am quite busy.'

'I am sure you are. The life of a teacher is not the easy one it might appear. But a professional woman is exactly the kind we need in our new bookshop.'

Both women saw the expression of hurt that flashed across Esther's face. It vanished when Victoria said, 'This baby is so beautiful, she makes my heart leap just to look at her. May I hold her?'

The third godparent, Bindon's cousin, arrived. She was confident, pink and well-rounded, a female edition of Bindon's earlier self. After dinner that evening when the women were taking their coffee in the ferny orangery, she asked Esther, 'One doesn't like to ask, but when does the doctor think that Bindon will get back into the fray?'

Esther's shock was obvious. 'Get back, Maria? He can scarcely breathe and one foot is almost useless. You don't imagine that he is ever going to get well again, do you?'

'Well, I know he looks dicky at the moment, but we Bloods have always had good constitutions.'

'I believe it would take more than a good constitution to get over having one's lungs burnt by noxious gas,' Esther said. 'It is only because he was face down on the ground, and had been wearing a gas-mask during the worst of the attack, that he has any lungs at all.'

'Good care, plenty of rest, and this fresh coastal air – he will heal in no time. I was thrown once, in the field you know, broke both ankles, this left wrist and got a clout on the head. Doctor told my parents that it was lights out for me. D'you know, I was back in the saddle again before you could say Jack Robinson.'

The two other women saw that Esther was trying hard to be courteous to her guest. 'He doesn't sleep, he walks the house half the night. I don't want him to go back.'

'My dear, it is not a question of "want". This country *needs* every man-jack of us if we are to finish off the Hun.'

Otis, who thought that Esther looked as though she might burst into tears, said, 'But it is not every man-jack of *us* who gets shelled and gassed. It is the men who suffer that.'

Victoria, who had been sitting still and controlled, said quietly, 'The hurt to a German or an American is no different; the loss to their families is no different from ours. It's my opinion that nations must find a better way.'

Esther said, 'I hate all Germans for what they have done to Bindon.'

'And they must be put down,' said Maria.

'Why not instead hate the system that puts two sets of men at one another's throats. Why not put *it* down?' Victoria said. 'The hurt is going to go on and on unless somebody calls a halt.' She rose and excused herself to

Esther, 'I am sorry, I should not get on my apple-box under your roof. My throat is a little dry. Perhaps I should fetch a lozenge.'

After she had gone, the other three women sat in an awkward, chatter-filled silence which they were glad to have broken by the men coming to fetch them to play cards.

Otis lay awake, her brain afire, thinking especially of Victoria's comment about the hurt going on. It had never occurred to her that it was possible to call a halt to wars. The darkness and quiet beyond the pretty leaded casements felt strange after the night-time noises and street-lights she was used to. She had read the same page several times, but could not keep her mind on the thread of its meaning.

When she had gone to live above Lou Barker's she had at once become accustomed to the comforting late-night sounds from below her room. Now, she got out of bed and went to stand at the window. If there was any moon, it was hidden. Her mind would keep imagining Jack with every kind of battlefield injury.

Light flooded out on to the terrace from the ground-floor room where Bindon spent much of his days and nights since he had been convalescent. His cough cut through the house, the gas-light in her room hissed, water ran through the plumbing system and landing floorboards creaked. Alien, lonely sounds compared to the voices, traffic and Lou's metal pans.

She wished that she were back there where there was no wrecked soldier, back before she had felt the stab of jealousy about Victoria Ormorod taking precedence over herself in Jack's company; back where her vision of Esther was not of a strained and jumpy woman but of a pretty mother nursing her pretty baby; back to before she knew that Jack had enlisted in the army and was to report to camp after Easter, and to the time before Victoria had set her thinking about how unintelligent it was to settle disputes by killing young and healthy men.

It was long after midnight when Esther tapped quietly and came into Otis's room.

'I saw the light showing under your door . . . you don't mind?' She came in and sat down beside the gas-fire. 'I don't want that woman to be Baby's godmother, Otis.'

'You don't really have a choice, do you?'

She shook her head in acquiescence. 'I suppose I haven't. Bindon has no other family.'

'Don't worry. Jack and I will always see to it that Stephanie is kept on the straight and narrow.'

'Jack?' She snorted derisively. 'Don't you see the casualty lists?'

'Of course I do, but we must not be negative, we must be sure in our hearts that Jack's name will never be in the lists.'

Esther shook her head. 'Victoria is right. In the end they will all be gone. I do not want Jack to go, yet I want some revenge for what has happened to my bridegroom. I know that Jack wants that too. Did you know that it was when Jack saw what had happened to Bindon that he went immediately to the enlisting office?'

'No, I didn't know. That doesn't sound like Jack.'

'I wish now that I had not said that he should go. I could not bear it if he . . .'

Otis put her arms about the girlish shoulders of her friend, feeling almost guilty that she herself should be so robust, and at the same time feeling that she too could not bear it. 'Jack's a survivor, Esther, I feel it.'

'But Victoria is wrong, isn't she? We should not give up the war. Did you know that they call her Red Ruby in London?'

'She has so many names.'

'Do you think that Jack is in love with her?'

'Hasn't he said anything to you?' Otis asked.

'He has said nothing except that he hoped I would not

226

mind, but he had invited her to spend Easter at Mere. I shall ask him tomorrow.'

Otis made no comment, instead she asked, 'How are you, Esther? How have you coped? First Bindon going to France, and then your confinement followed so soon with the news of Bindon's injuries. You must have had an awfully hard time of it. I feel guilty that I have not been a better friend to you. But Dorset is so far . . .'

'The confinement was no problem – there was the lovely prize at the end of it.'

And your wedding-day prize was a man who looks now as though each breath might be his last. 'Bindon is going to be well again, then you and he and Baby will soon make up for lost time.'

'Is he? Will you guarantee it?'

'I'm sorry, it was a trite comment. I long to say something to comfort you. Or perhaps it is that I feel too fortunate in a world that's full of trouble.'

'Fortunate? Oh Otis, how can you say that when you have not a man to care for you, and you do not have a child of your own. I know that Bindon is sick, and in my worst moments I know that he may not live, but I *am* fortunate. I have had days of such happiness with him that you cannot begin to understand. Perhaps that is why he may be taken away from me. I have wondered whether each of us is allocated a certain sum of happiness and if we spend it all at once, then there is nothing for later. And we were *so* happy.'

'You will be happy again. And you must surely be happy when you look at your sweet little baby?'

'Babies are always dying.'

'Esther! I have never seen so bonny a child as Stephanie is. Where has this idea of doom come from?'

Esther made a moue and shrugged. 'It is why I did not want to have her christened yet. If I give her a name, she will become a person and . . . Oh, you don't know how stupid it will sound if I put it into words.'

'Say it.'

'I have it in my mind that whilst she is just "Baby", then God will not notice her. And I would not have had her christened now had it not been that Bindon wanted it. And I have thought that he wants to see her safely christened because he has some idea of tying up loose ends before he dies.'

'He's not going to die. You don't believe that, do you?'

'I don't know, perhaps I do. I believe that he has it fixed in his head. Do you know that there are tribes where a person may die simply from knowing that a curse is upon them. I believe that is how it is with Bindon and me.'

Easter Sunday dawned early with bright sun and clear skies. Victoria was dressed and taking a walk in the direction of some sparkling water she had seen from her room window. At home, she loved this time of year more than any other. Old habits die hard, and she could not resist going to where she thought there must be violets, and there were, the short sturdy variety with bluish stems and wonderful perfume, a few of which she picked and pinned to her blouse. There were hazel and willow catkins fully out and ready to release pollen, there was the scent of leaf-mould and crushed greenery that rose at every step, and there were wood-pigeons and a distant cuckoo.

The evocative scents and sounds caused a sudden desire to be at home to flare up within her. Recently, Peace League speakers had each been addressing as many as five open-air meetings a day, as well as helping to organize others. There had not been time to think about home or herself. Or how she came to be entangled in the fibres of this family. She had been attracted by Jack – was still attracted by him. She liked the way he turned up from time to time, standing handsome, head and shoulders above the crowd. And would have liked to make love with him, to have an unserious, uncommitted liaison – as with Tankredi, with his passions, his ideals . . . his arranged marriage. But she knew such affaires left painful heartbreak that took a long time to heal.

Jack Moth had volunteered to join the war, and soldiers going away had romantic notions of a wife at home. Cynically, Annie had said that it was not romance, but that men wanted to secure a woman for themselves so that no other man should have her, to tie her down with her own vows whilst he marched off singing to the nearest bordello. No, no, what was she thinking of coming here, playing at being part of their family? She didn't want another family, there was none better than the one she already had.

It was the violets that had led her to think clearly. They reminded her of home, and allowed her to think clearly: Why do I always choose such unsuitable men? She knew the answer to that. Because I am attracted by people like myself – the ones who don't conform.

She was at the lake-side before she realized that Otis Hewetson was there before her, seated on a fallen tree. They greeted one another politely. 'I shall not disturb you, Otis, but it was *such* a morning. I thought that if I was going to be indulgent and idle my time away, I should at least enjoy it to the full.'

'I shall not be disturbed,' Otis said. 'Share my patch of sun if you like.'

'I will.' Victoria sat down and hooked off her flat, canvas shoes. 'Did you sleep well?'

'I must confess I find the country at night too quiet by half. Don't you find that?'

'I was brought up in the country, my home is still there – although I don't get back very often at present. I was just thinking how I miss being there. The hedgerows will have lovely green buds that you never see in town because of the dust.'

Victoria caught the girl in a puzzled look: She thinks I'm fanciful.

'I never took you for a . . . I mean, I imagined that you must be a city woman through and through.'

'No. I am a bumpkin. I have straw in my hair. I am surprised that you should think that I'm not a rustic, I should have thought my complexion and the way I stride about would give me away.'

'It is nothing to do with your appearance . . . I think it must be that one thinks of suffragettes as coming from towns.'

'Goodness, what a misconception. That is the view of a city dweller.' She laughed lightly. 'You believe that only urban people have minds.'

'I don't know that I thought much about it at all. But you may be right, the only politicians that I have met have worn silk hats.'

Victoria liked this girl, she was intelligent and open and full of life and humour. 'A great deal of the impetus to change the old order has always come from the countryside, and when we bumpkins went to the industrial towns, we took our ideas and dreams with us. I come from a long line of farming women who were not content to put up with injustice and inequality.'

'I am such an ignoramus on such matters.'

'You should discover for yourself more of women's history. I mean our *true* history.'

'I think that I should like to. But where, how?'

'Not in history books. Those are written by men about men and for them. The advent of popular education and women teachers ought to have meant the teaching of a more truthful version of history, but that has still to come.' Victoria laughed, pleased that the girl did not shy away. She was already intrigued by having heard that such a flower of that class should have rooms in Islington.

'You will have to learn not to judge women by the standards that men have laid down to suit themselves. How well would they fare if they were judged by standards laid down by women?'

230

Otis chuckled. 'I fear they would be quite second-class. Do you know, I spent three years discussing every subject under the sun with my fellow students, but we never once came near to these ideas. I think it is a wonderful thing to think about.'

'In every sphere we are influenced by the masculine.'

'That is true. That is so true. The world might be a very different place.'

'That is something we shall never know. But that is no reason why we should not discover our own history and justify our own art and take back our own religion. It may be that we shall find that art and music has no gender bias, but we must test it. Don't you agree?'

'I do. I absolutely do.' Again she laughed, her cheeks flushed with pleasure. 'How amazing. How closed my mind has been. I can see the world changing before my eyes.'

'I warn you, if you follow on this line of questioning, you are likely to be ridiculed, if you begin to attack the sacred cows . . . or bulls.'

'I can imagine. My father, for instance, probably thinks that such things were laid down on the day of creation: such and such constitutes a great painting, such and such else constitutes great music, and for ever and ever, amen.' She frowned. 'But then, so does my mother.'

'Many women are afraid to question anything. Some are too comfortable, some too afraid, others do not even know that there is anything to be questioned.'

Victoria saw, as she had seen on other occasions, the beginnings of enlightenment dawn upon the girl's pretty face, and felt her own spirits lift. Well, something good might come from this weekend. Annie said that striking a spark of awareness in a woman was like fishing. You cast out the bait, hope for a bite and then, when you feel a twitch on the line, gently bring the catch in. Victoria disagreed, the analogy was too predatory. She preferred the description that was analogous to a seduction. And this is how it was with Otis Hewetson, who was love-starved for an identity. Victoria, journeying round the country to address meetings, met young women like her in mills, factories, offices and homes. All of them with the same gnawing hunger to have a place in history, in society, in the future.

'Well I doubt that the world will change, but perhaps you will begin to see that there is another viewpoint.' Victoria knew that, had it been Annie here, then she would have touched the girl, held her hands perhaps, or put an arm about her, but Victoria did not find that kind of contact very easy. 'I have a close friend, Annie, who loves to quote a book of quite some antiquity – "Adam is the product of nature . . . Eve the creation of God. Adam was admitted to the Paradise for the sole purpose that Eve might be created." '

Otis laughed delightedly. 'Oh, what a boost to female spirits. I must remember that. My pa will love to hear it. But you mentioned the bookshop . . .'

'Would you? Oh wonders! We have prayed to find someone who would give some time to work there on a Saturday. Could you do that?'

'Yes. I could give a day. I am doing my best to live close to my pupils. It is not easy. I am ashamed to say so, but until I went to college, I had no idea how the majority of people lived. I think the first time that I had any inkling that working people were not different, just poorer, was when you spoke to the crowd on Southsea front.'

'When the meeting broke up in chaos?'

Otis bowed her head low and put her face in her hands, her shaking shoulders puzzling Victoria, until she saw that the girl was shaking with laughter. 'I was the cause of the police breaking up your meeting.'

'The girl with the parasol?'

Otis's laughter rang out across the lake and was joined by

that of Victoria. 'I was taken to the Black Maria and given a real dressing down . . .'

George Moth, taking the morning air with his son, saw the two women and heard their laughter. The older man, endeavouring to restrain his interest at seeing the apparent abandon with which Otis threw back her head as she laughed, wished that he had been the one who had caused her to laugh.

'I've wanted to tell you, Father, but the opportunity has never been given till now . . . I have asked Victoria to marry me.'

George Moth forced his gaze away from the tableau of the lake and beautiful women. 'Yes . . . well, I had feared as much.'

'Feared?'

'Yes. I am aware who she is, you know – the Bice woman . . . Ruby Red.'

'Why didn't you say that you knew?'

'I might ask the same.'

'What Victoria is or does is her own affair. In any case, I wanted you all to meet her without prejudice.'

'Which we have done, though Ess knows of the alter ego. The lady of Speakers' Corner, international committees, women's societies, suffragist federations – all kinds of unsuitable movements.'

'She works entirely within the law, she has nothing to do with the Pankhurst people.'

'I know that – I know them all, it is my job to know them, keep an eye on them. She is still Ruby Red.'

'So you did not meet her without prejudice.'

'An experienced detective does not jump to conclusions.'

'So why mention Ruby Red?'

'You'll not get far in your profession if you are so naïve, my lad.'

Jack clenched his teeth, determined not to quarrel with his

233

father over this matter. If Victoria did eventually agree to become his wife, he did not want there to be bad family feeling about it. 'A lawyer is trained to believe in his client without prejudice.'

'The difference being that you are not proposing to take her on as your *client*.'

George Moth wanted to end this discussion, and walk to where he could test his resolution to fight his feelings for Otis Hewetson and replace them with something more suitably avuncular. But there were things that must be said. Jack was going off to training-camp within days, men did rash things at such times. He did not put it past Jack to make a sudden decision and purchase a Special Licence to marry the woman. Although he well knew that he must tread carefully, he jumped in with both feet. 'Do you realize that if there were to be some trouble with the anarchists, or the hint of a socialist uprising, she would be one of the first to be picked up?'

'Picked up? You mean, arrested?'

'Of course arrested. You don't suppose any government would let the likes of Red Ruby and her cohorts give aid and support to revolutionaries.'

'You cannot be serious.'

For months now, the whole country, with the aid of journalists, had been in a fever of spy scares and rumours. Perfectly innocent people with un-English names had been hounded by their erstwhile neighbours, and harmless aliens had been put into prison camps. In other circumstances, Inspector Moth might have confided the nature of his new responsibilities to his son earlier, but with Red Ruby in the picture, it was not a wise thing to do. And now he had blurted it out in a fit of emotion.

'I am very serious.'

'Do you believe that I shall not tell her?'

'She knows. Of course she knows. Every agitator knows that he treads a fine line between freedom of speech and sedition.'

'If Victoria is anything, she is a most loyal English-woman.'

'She's an *Internationalist*, Jack.'

'I have never heard her utter a seditious word and I have listened to her speak many times.'

'I know.'

Jack looked as shocked as he felt. 'You . . . *know?*'

'My best man has seen you on more than one occasion.'

'Has seen me? And has reported to you?'

'Not reported. I have always thought that it was a youthful rebellion and of no consequence.'

'And you could come home, sit at the breakfast table with me and never say that you have had a man spying on me? I cannot believe it.'

'Don't be so flamboyant, Jack, gathering information is not spying. And in any case this man shows me personal loyalty, he never entered your name on official reports. So, as far as I am concerned, it is not an official matter. I had hoped that it was a passing fancy, that you liked the idea of free love that these people express.'

'They do no such thing.' Jack blustered in his fury.

'It is part of their philosophy of the breaking down of order, but let that go now, it is the question of your idea that you and she should marry that is important. I have said nothing about your action in rejecting the Clermont traditional regiment – I understand that – I even think that I understand your action in refusing rank . . . I do not understand how you can imagine a woman with her beliefs would take on all this.' He indicated the acres, the woodlands, the stables and the lovely manor house. 'She's a dyed-in-the-wool rebel from a family who have taken pride in their rebellion. If you don't believe me, I'll show you the records: riot, imprisonment, transportation, going back generations.'

The two women were now walking towards them, slowly, obviously at ease, stopping here and there to pick a few spring flowers. Otis's head was bare and George Moth recalled the fresh smell of her hair when he had sat with her in the park, which led him to recall the feel of her lips and the tip of her tongue touching his.

'I thought I knew you, Father, but I am shattered. As I have been about your attention to Otis.' He felt bitter and wanted to lash out, to wound his father. 'Leave Otis alone, you are too old and corrupt for such a sweet girl.'

His father drew breath to protest but Jack stopped him. 'You give yourself away every time you look at her. You are pathetic. Isn't it enough that you have a kept woman? Leave Otis alone.'

Now it was the father's turn to look taken aback.

As the women approached, they both tried to look relaxed and casual.

Jack said quietly, 'I shall make some excuse to Ess and go back to London soon after the christening. You may be right, in which case she will want nothing to do with this family, and she cannot be blamed for that. But if she will have me, then we shall be married at once.'

But he did not know that, under the tranquil atmosphere of Mere Meldrum, she had seen that her long-ago decision not to marry was not to be altered by a physical attraction for a man who struck a chord in her.

When Jack and Victoria parted, he looked less devastated than his protestations of passion might suggest. It was obvious to her that something had happened between himself and his father; she did not broach the reason. Also he was preoccupied with going to the training-camp.

When they parted, she kissed him lightly on the cheek. 'Thank you for taking me to Mere, it is beautiful. It has done me good to be away for a short while. I've been able to take an eagle-eye view of what is going on. There are things that I have to do. Perhaps it would be kind to say that I wish that things were different. But I can't, Jack. Marriage isn't for me.'

He held on to her hand, looking puzzled, as though wondering what on earth had been happening.

Her inclination was to hasten away, but that appeared too careless of his feelings. She said, 'Even if we had tried, it would have lasted only as long as we found excitement in one another's bodies.'

Once he had gone, she swung up the stairs to her lodgings with Annie.

'Well! You look like that cat that got the cream. Don't tell me you succumbed to the man who's gone for a soldier?'

'No, Annie dear, but I've found us a splendid woman for the bookshop.'

There was no telling where they were now. Rumour on the lower ranks had it that this was France, which, as far as they were concerned, was as good a general name as any to give territory which lay across the English Channel.

From Hampstead to training–camp on Salisbury Plain, from training–camp to a billet in a coal-mining village, from the village to the Front Line.

Until they embarked for France, time had been a slippery thing, slithering over anonymous days. But, once in the war zone, it set into spans of days at the Front and days behind the Lines.

Before that? For Jack, days of drill. Of inflamed muscles, blistered toes and heels, calloused soles. Night-times of oblivion. Arousal at first light with the rank odour in his nostrils of himself and other men whose tobacco and armpits were equally rank.

Drilled, paraded, sweated, hefted.

Elation, fulfilment, camaraderie and unreasoning dislike.

Enthusiasm, futility, acceptance.

238

Jack rammed a bayonet into the guts of sacks of sawdust and straw; aimed inaccurately at targets and learned to clean his rifle with the same pernickety care with which he tended his boots. He obeyed commands unquestioningly and submerged his ego.

The loyalty that developed was unique to the rag-tag raw group as it became unified and changed.

In the course of three weeks the amorphous parcel of ingredients that had made up John Clermont Moth were crushed into the mould of Private Moth which was quite unsuited to his old accent and manner. On the way to becoming Private Moth he learnt to roll a cigarette, to perform hitherto private ablutions without privacy, and to expect food to provide nothing but sustenance and exercise no satisfaction.

Like his fellow greenhorns, Private Moth learned to submit individuality for the betterment of the group wherein one laggard demeaned the unit and endangered its existence. And, like his fellows, he made friendships of a kind that might, in their previous existence, have taken years to become forged and enduring.

Over cobbled roads, the unit marched into a coal-mining village.

'Have you ever known the like of it? Take a man away from his own valleys, and put 'im down in another 'undreds of miles away.'

'Et's what et's all abowt, boye.'

Taff from the Rhonda and Farmer Giles from Norfolk. They had civilian names, and they had army numbers, but whilst they wore khaki they were, to their close companions, known only by the names that welded them to one another – Taff, Farmer Giles, Chalky, Ginge, Cully and Lofty. Except only briefly and on rare occasions, they kept them uninvolved with one another's domestic existence.

The shallow sentiment of a myth that called itself 'Hearth and Home' called its sacrificial young men by the name

'Tommy', but Tommy knew himself to be 'Taff', 'Farmer Giles' and 'Lofty'. Jack's family had never much used 'pet' names or names of endearment, but, having been given the name 'Lofty', he felt himself to be a more loyal member of their particular circle than he had ever felt as a member of his college teams and clubs.

As a youth, Jack had been on the Continent several times. He spoke French fluently and so, as well as being a wonder to his friends, he was useful during the long cross-country march. When it came to the price of a round of drinks in a town or a dozen eggs from a farmer, Lofty was their negotiator.

Two days before they marched to their encampment on the boundaries of the coal-mining village, they heard their first guns, a rumble that gave no greater surge of adrenalin than if it had been the sound of thunder which it resembled. A cheer went up and somebody played 'Onward Christian Soldiers' on a mouth-organ for the singing of a blasphemous version of the hymn.

It was probably the last cheer that this raw platoon was likely to give, for they were soon to be in terrain where orders were not heard clearly as on a parade-ground, neither would they carry as in clear Wiltshire air, but would be half-heard through machine-gun rattle and cut short by shrapnel.

Food-scraps not scavenged by dogs but by rats.

Blankets not shared by a few nibbling mice, but by lice that even with familiarity never ceased to cause disgust.

The plunge of a bayonet would not be into homely-smelling sawdust, nor its withdrawal accompanied by a hiss as it passed through straw. Here, beyond the mean houses, pit-tips and railway lines, would be snapping bones, stink, and slurping human viscera.

Here was the place to which Hearth and Home closed its mind.

Here was where few of those who got away would ever find the courage to speak of, but would never be rid of.

Here was where 'Tommy' ceased to exist.

'Men', 'Lower ranks', 'Casualties', 'Dead'.

But, thankfully billeted, Jack, like his companions Taff and Farmer Giles and the rest of their platoon, did not let his thoughts run further ahead than something hot inside him and his head down for a few hours' rest.

Wally Archer, as a single man of the right age, was one of the first to be called after Conscription was introduced.

He waited until he and Nancy had clocked off their late shift and were walking through the chill, January streets of Bethnal Green to tell her that he had received his papers. They were late because of the fog, a sodden, yellow cheesecloth that hung like curtains before their faces. The damp coalesced into drops on their uniforms and Nancy's hair, the chemicals from the gasworks and factory chimneys choked them, and the coal-smoke from domestic fires stung their eyes and throats.

'Gawd, Nance, nobody don't need to go to France tonight to get gassed, you can stop home and cop it.'

Because the sounds were deadened or distorted, cabs and other vehicles loomed suddenly upon them. Passers-by tumbled along, guided as well as they could manage it by railings and walls.

Wally's arm held Nancy Dickenson firmly as they made their way in the direction of Nancy's lodgings. 'I shan't go.'

'We could get married, Wally. It's only single men they're conscripting, isn't it?'

'If we get married, Nance, we'll do it because we want to. It'd be like a shotgun wedding. I shall go before the Tribunal.'

'I heard that they're making objectors go to France and collect bodies.'

'They'll have to carry me then, I don't want nothing to do with their bleedin' war, what's war got to do with people like us? Nothing! Our class hasn't never got nothing out of war except pain and death. Let them that wants a war fight it. Let some of them what's making millions out of munitions get out there with one of their own guns. Fat chance of that!'

'Then they'll put you in prison, won't they?'

'Not without a fight.'

'What about your mother?'

'Ma will be all right. If I was to join the army, she'd kill me before I even got there.'

Nancy smiled behind the scarf tied about her face. May Archer was a thin, brown-speckled, fierce little lady who would do anything for anybody so long as they didn't try to make a fuss about it. It was she, rather than his lighterman father, who had lit the fire of dissent in her only son. Yes, thought Nancy, May will be all right.

Wally knew that his activities as a union man and a leader in the bitter strike last May would not help him; he had even been on the front page of the *Herald*. A known follower of Marx, it was a chance for Them to get back at him.

The walk to Nancy's flat that usually took twenty minutes after any other late shift, had tonight taken them almost two hours. Usually Wally would go up with her for a cup of cocoa, and perhaps a pie or a plate of stew and a talk about his great passion, The Union, and then do the walk to where he lived with May.

Nancy let them in, and with exaggerated carefulness they mounted the stairs to her room.

There were people who would have wondered how on earth Nancy managed to live in such cramped space, but it was in a room not much bigger than this that most of the Dickenson family had slept. Being used to small quarters, Nancy knew exactly how to keep on top of things, so that it appeared always neat and clean. Most of the space was taken up by a single bed, a small table, and a cupboard which served also as a larder. A minute gas-fire beside a coin-in-the-slot meter and a primus stove were the only facilities.

An outside lavatory shared with other tenants was two flights down, and water needed to be carried from the ground floor. Routinely, Nancy carried her bits of rubbish down when she was leaving, and her water up when she returned.

Nancy pumped up the primus and put on the tin kettle, whilst Wally fed the meter, lit the gas-fire and laid their wrapped suppers on top to keep warm.

'It's this I shall miss as much as anything, Nance.'

'The good life never lasts. It comes and goes, but it never lasts.'

'Don't say that. You don't have to let them bleeders get us down. If they puts me in choky, it won't be for ever.' He put his arms round her waist and pulled her to him: she well-formed, he fleshless and wiry like May. They were almost the same height. 'We shall have good times like this again.'

She kissed him fondly. 'I love you, Wally Archer, you're the best man ever stepped foot in a pair of boots.'

'Now then, Nancy, you're only saying that because it's true.'

'I couldn't bear it if they were to put you in prison.'

'You'd bear it all right. And you must. I won't be the only one. There'll be other blokes like me and they're going to need help.'

'I don't know what I could do.'

'Plenty. You showed what you can do with your birth control.'

'Wally! You should call it Family Planning. You always have to call a spade a spade.'

He grinned at her. 'And a johnny a johnny.'

'Wally! I still don't find it too easy to say things out aloud.'

'I heard that you're damned good. Talks plain and don't make women feel embarrassed about it, is what I heard.'

'It's easier with the women. And I'm getting better at it.

The main thing is getting through to people so's they can help theirselves.'

She made a strong brew of tea and he laid out their pie, peas and mash, which they sat to eat on the one chair and a chintz-covered apple-box at the small table.

He pulled aside the net curtain that covered the window. On the other side of the glass, fog like dirty yellow plush pressed against it. 'I'd best make tracks. It's going to take me a time to get home.'

'Wally? It's a bad night. You don't have to go.'

He looked up at her from beneath his arched eyebrows and long curling lashes. 'You propositioning me, Nance?'

To hide her shyness, she collected the plates, put them in a bowl with a bar of soap and poured in water from the kettle. 'It seems awful you having to go out in this. You could have kipped down at the depot, if it hadn't been that you insisted on seeing me home.'

He took the kettle from her and kissed her long and firmly on the mouth. 'Lord help us, Nancy Dickenson, I thought you'd never ask.'

They stood face to face, enveloped in one another's arms. 'You haven't got room to talk, Wally Archer. I was beginning to think I should stop a virgin for ever.'

'You're a virgin, Nance? You ain't never had nothing?'

'Never.'

He hugged her hard. 'Lord, there's a turn up for the book.'

'I always thought I'd wait till the right man came along.' And if she was entirely truthful, she had always been afraid of finding herself with a baby and going down the slippery slope. But now she had the knowledge and the means to prevent that happening.

'And who is he then? This right man?'

'I don't know that I should tell you, might make you vain.'

He rasped her cheek with his day's growth of whiskers.

244

'Why not? It's something to be vain about when a gel tells you you're the Mister Right she waited twenty years to find.'

'Oh Wally, you are a nice, good man. Not only the right man, the best one as well.'

Before February was out, Wally's case had been heard by a tribunal consisting of men who were out of sympathy even with appellants whose pacifism sprang from religious conviction. It had no compassion at all for a man who, as the inquisitors told one another, was fighter enough when it came to leading a rabble of strikers, but had no belly to fight like a man for his King and Country.

He requested an appeal, but was turned down.

Walter Archer, known striker and agitator, had been a thorn in the flesh for too long so, with thirty other objectors, Wally was locked up in Reading gaol and later shipped to France.

> *Just a line. We have been warned today that we are now within the war zone. The military authorities have absolute power, and disobedience may be followed by very severe penalties, and possibly the death penalty, so I have dropped you a line in case they do not allow me to write after tomorrow. Do not be downhearted; if the worst comes to the worst many have died cheerfully for a worse cause.*

(Letter from Steward Beavis of Lower Edmonton to his parents the day before he was sentenced to death – later commuted to ten years' imprisonment. Wally Archer felt that he was in good company, being one of 16,000 men to 'object' to taking part in the war.)

On the Saturday following her return from Lyme Regis, Otis Hewetson, as she had promised Victoria, walked the short distance from her lodgings to the bookshop premises.

If Otis had visions of a shelved and neatly-rowed library, they were at once disabused. The bookshop consisted of a large room with a store-room-cum-office-cum-kitchen at the rear, and a dank but whitewashed and Lysolled closet in a dank and green yard. At some time a butcher's shop had existed on these premises, still evidenced by a steel track with hooks from which joints had once been displayed, and nicely-tiled but chilly walls decorated here and there with laughing pigs.

'Ah you've come, you've come.' Open-handed, Victoria Ormorod greeted her.

'Did you think that I would not?'

'Well, people do make promises . . . and intend keeping them at the time.'

'I am not like that.'

'Then you are a gem. Meet Annie.'

Annie was a pleasant-faced woman of about Victoria's age. She had brown hair that sprung free of its bun in frizzy curls. Her face appeared ordinary except for her brown, intelligent eyes. She kissed Otis on both cheeks, which caused her to start slightly at such familiarity from a complete stranger.

'We are pleased of your help.' She spoke with a northern accent and her voice, like Victoria's, had the forceful huskiness, when not in public use, of a seasoned speaker. 'We lot are allus kissin. It means nowt except that we are sisters.'

'I'm sorry, I didn't mean . . .'

'Aw, don't apologize. Took me a bit of gettin' used to, now I'm one of t'wost offenders.'

Otis took to Annie at once. 'I don't take offence at being welcomed like that.'

'Well, m'duck, that's enough about that. We've got trouble on our hands and you've come at t'right time. We've got a hop to organize.'

'Hop?'

'Aye, a dance to raise funds for the wives and kids of the COs.'

'They've started to call them Conchies in the playground. Those poor children, I wonder whether their fathers know how their action affects their children?'

'Aye, they know all right,' Annie said. 'And, make no mistake, it breaks their hearts.'

'The men are doing something perfectly legal in refusing to prolong this war,' Victoria said primly. 'The blame for the ill-treatment of their families should be laid at the door from whence it comes.'

'Perhaps so, but it is still the children in the playground who suffer.'

'Have you had trouble at your school?' Victoria asked.

'There have been a few incidents, not in the infants where I teach. But I know of a girl who has won a scholarship and the Headmistress is trying to have the award taken from the girl.'

'Ah, we know,' said Annie. 'The girl's dad was arrested and the *Gazette* plastered it all over newsagents' placards. Neighbours take it out on t'family. Easier than tekkin' it out on War Office if you've lost one of your own. But we have to stand up for what we believe. If we don't, then we're finished. It's hard for a man to stand up and be counted – harder if it's tekken out on his kids.'

248

Otis protested, 'But what about the child, she's the one to suffer?'

'But *not* at the hands of her dad,' Annie said. 'If *Gazette* hadn't done a smear on him, and the Headmistress weren't so vindictive, Minnie wouldn't have had a minute's suffering. Put blame where it belongs, Otis. You have to learn to think straight.'

'Come on, Annie,' Victoria said. 'If you don't stop being fierce, you'll frighten away the best volunteer we've had for months. And anyway, the girl's got a place in another grammar school.'

Annie held her head to one side apologetically as she gave Otis a brief hug. 'I know, I know. I'm sorry, lass, but I get that mad sometimes.'

Whilst this exchange had been going on, Annie and Victoria had been opening packages and sorting out leaflets and handbills.

Otis said, 'There is obviously more to the matter than one thinks, and it's not much good me standing around here spare. Tell me what to do.'

Victoria and Annie gave one another a satisfied glance, and Otis felt that she had passed some sort of test. What it was she did not know, but felt that the result must be that she was acceptable.

Victoria said, 'We thought if you would see to the bookshop this morning, it would leave Annie and me free to run around getting people together for tonight.'

Having explained briefly about the sales records and which were free leaflets and which not, Victoria and Annie left the shop in Otis's charge. 'You'll not be alone for long, Nancy will be coming in soon. And, by the way, if you can remember, here I am known as Ruby.'

'Is it all right if I read this stuff?'

'Lord!' Annie said with an infectious grin. 'The girl's a marvel, we'll have her on a soap-box in Finsbury Park afore long. And one thing more whilst I think of it. Nancy. Her chap's one of those who was imprisoned, she's heard that he's being sent to France, but nobody knows for sure. God knows what's happening to him, the rumour is that COs are being used to go out under fire to bring back dead and injured.'

They went, leaving Otis alone with the smiling pigs and piles of literature.

During her first fifteen minutes in charge of the shop, all of the callers were men and most of them appeared to be interested only in browsing and buying the *Herald*. Then a neat woman came in.

When Nancy had been told that a teacher named Otis Hewetson would be her helper this Saturday, she felt sure that there were not likely to be two with that name. As soon as she entered, she saw that she was not wrong: this woman was the girl who used to call at Garden Cottage a few years back.

'I'm Nancy.' Nancy had never been a one for all that kissing business between these women, so she shook hands firmly. 'I'll just put these out.' She knew from experience that some of the browsers of the political leaflets had been sent there by their women to get one of the 'Family Advice' leaflets. She knew also that in the first instance it was the men who came because the illustrations contained in the leaflets were reckoned to be a bit rude and could land her, and them, in court for obscene publications. The women would come in when the men had gone off to football.

She pinned up a notice saying 'Free Family Advice in private', and went back to where Otis was taking twopence for two broadsheets. 'What brings you here then?'

'I met Vic . . . Ruby, and she asked me. I live not far away.'

'Where do you live then?'

'In Market Street. It's close to the school. I'm a teacher.'

Market Street wasn't no Lavender Hill. And a teacher? In

her twenties and not married? Not what usually happened to quality like her, especially with her face and figure. Nancy's experience as a domestic worker led her to the conclusion that everything always came out in the end if you just waited. She'd get to know why Otis was living in Market Street. 'That must be a lovely job, teaching. No shift-work like in mine, out all hours, men with wandering hands who think the conductress is in the price of the tram ticket. Not that I'm complaining, it's a good job and the pay's better than domestic.'

'You're on the tramcars – a conductress?'

'Soon be a driver I hope, I've done the basics.'

'They are going to let you drive! That's really exciting.'

'That's if we can get the bosses to keep their promise. They're going to have to in the end. Soon there's going to be only old men and boys left, they're going to have to take on us women.'

With a pang, the danger that Wally was in leapt on her again as it did time and time again, and with that pang came another of anger. Wally was a straight-up-and-down man with true beliefs. The Tribunal had said that it was all a tale and he was nothing but a coward. If there was one thing Wally was not, it was cowardly. Any of his mates would tell you how he put himself in danger to save a copper from being trampled by a horse when the police had charged into the tram-men. And the time he had stopped a runaway horse still between the shafts and he was written up in the paper as a hero.

Wally had told the panel it wasn't their job to make any comments like that, and they had said they could say anything they liked to anarchist rabble-rousers. Nancy had only seen him once in prison, and then he had been shipped across the Channel.

There were times when she couldn't stand thinking about it. But getting angry didn't do anything. Like Victoria said, you should hold on to your anger and guide your energy into productive channels. They hoped to get a decent bit of money tonight; not only that, they were trying to set up another secret dormitory for men on the run, and to organize a second 'underground railway' to get men on the run away to America and Ireland.

It was a busy little shop, not only for its books and leaflets, but for the exchange of information and gossip. At two o'clock when the men were off to their pubs and football, things were quiet enough for Otis and Nancy to put up the 'Back in Fifteen Minutes' board. Otis made tea for them both and Nancy went out with a mug to her 'tame' copper and came back with two doughnuts from the baker. Otis Hewetson had looked a bit surprised at Nancy's friendliness to a policeman, but Nancy had said, 'He's one of ours.'

Otis's thoughts had at once gone to George Moth. Recently he had seemed to have reasons to be in Islington, and always somehow close enough to Lou Barker's shop for him to be 'just passing', usually when she was coming from school. Once or twice she had come in to find him sitting in Lou's drinking tea.

'Do you mean that he turns a blind eye?' She had not realized how hungry she had become; the tea and doughnut were blissful.

'He's a local bobby, the eldest child in a family of ten. He knows what poverty and too many children means. Thanks his lucky stars he's got out, and don't mean to have ten of his own. *And* he's been corrupted – took home a leaflet to his wife. Sometimes I ask him, How's the wife? And he says, Going along nicely on the Cream Sponge. That's what they call the Method.' She laughed for the first time and into Otis's mind came a vision of icy lemonade and the secret garden at the Moths' holiday cottage in Southsea.

'I know you, I'm sure. You are *that* Nancy, aren't you? You made us lemonade with cold well-water . . . in Southsea? Aren't you the same Nancy? Of course you are,

I can see. Why didn't I see it before? You don't remember me, do you? I was the girl who was always making a nuisance of myself at Garden Cottage. I haunted the place. It was so lovely there compared to The Grand. Don't you remember?'

'Of course I remember. I expect I look different without a cap and apron, I've been told how different domestics look out of uniform. I recognized you the minute I laid eyes on you. Even before I got here, I knew there couldn't be two Otis Hewetsons in London.'

'You didn't say.'

Wryly. 'People like me know not to ask questions when they find people in changed circumstances.'

'What circumstances?'

'I would have expected you to be married to some Honourable and living in one of the smart squares. I didn't know but what you was in some trouble, or maybe didn't want people round here to know you was from a posh family.'

'You're right, I don't want them to know that. I have found what I want to do, and I think that one day I may be very good at it. Don't laugh, but my ambition is to get a Master's degree and become Head of a school.'

'That's a fine ambition.'

'I have hardly told it to a soul.'

'But your mother . . . ? And your father, wasn't he a solicitor? What I remember of Mrs Hewetson is that she was the sort to go doolally if her daughter didn't find somebody pretty posh in the way of a husband. Whatever does she think of Market Street?'

'She has never seen it, and I hope never will. I feel safe there. I have a dear of a landlady who leaves me alone, never asks where I'm going, but she watches over me and would go for anyone who might harm me. I have wondered what Lou would do if my ma turned up on the doorstep and demanded to be let into my rooms.'

'You sound happy enough.'

'I am very satisfied with my life in Islington. If I go home for a weekend, I can hardly wait for it to be over. I have been here a while and now that Ma has seen that I have not been raped or sold to white slave traffickers, I believe that she has given up the battle.'

'Don't you believe it. A lady like her won't ever give up. Is she still as beautiful?'

'I suppose she is. Everyone says that she is one of London society's beauties, but it is hard for me to see anybody but Ma.'

'What about men friends? You're a very lovely girl, I should have thought . . .'

She was interrupted by a rattling door-handle. Their fifteen minutes' break was up.

'. . . that summer, I thought you was head over heels in love with Master Jack. You couldn't take your eyes off him.'

'He has recently enlisted in the army.'

Her hand stalled on the bolt. 'Never! Not another lovely man going to get flung into the bloodbath. God alive, we have got to do anything we can to try to get an end to it. My Wally and Jolly Jack gone together. It's like lights going out one by one, thousands and thousands of them lit for a moment and then snuffed just as they start to make a flame.'

> *. . . I know that this is not the way. I cannot think what else I can do . . . forgive me.*

Esther thought that Bindon seemed to be a little more his old self. Since Easter, he had more colour in his cheeks and he had stopped talking as though he was not long for this world, which was surely a sign that his depressed state was lifting. He had started taking Baby on his knee and even come to watch her being bathed. She had asked him whether he would care to have a spell in London, and he said that he would, and that they might have a night at the opera. Opera was one of his passions.

She wrote to her father '. . . *I feel that he has turned the corner. A month in London, with a bit of gaiety and colour, may just do the trick. When Jack came down to visit soon after Bindon returned to Mere on sick leave, Jack said that he felt like killing ten Germans for every soldier who was suffering as Bindon was suffering. I love Jack for doing this. I only pray that he will not be caught in the bombardment of some foreign village as Bindon was. If you do not mind, we shall travel as soon as we have seen to the domestic arrangements here. Dearest Father, how Kitt and I look forward to being with you again at dear Windsor Villa. Bindon asks me to send you his regards and Baby sends you a kiss.*'

On the first night of their return to London, Bindon was miraculously cured of the impotence that had affected him since that day months ago when he was sitting in that medieval town in Flanders, writing an imaginary letter to Esther. When shells had burst all around him, when his leg had been crushed, his gas-mask stolen from his face, and his lungs burnt by a whiff of toxic gas.

Although he did not know it then, his return to virility impregnated Esther. Esther knew. She lay on her back with her legs tightly together, her pelvis raised on her fists, helping the little tadpoles of the illustrations in Human Biology to swim onwards to the new baby who had been waiting there for months for its finishing touches.

She decided that they should remain in London for a few weeks longer than planned so that she could consult the doctor who had attended her when she was carrying Stephanie. Then they would all return to Mere – Esther, Bindon, Stephanie, Kitt and Baby. There she and Bindon would spend the seven waiting months caring for one another. She visualized them walking The Cobb, Bindon playing with Kitt, herself with her protruding figure that Bindon would proudly ignore on their walks but at night would eagerly include in his caresses; pushing Stephanie in her bassinet; then, later, Stephanie toddling along the promenade, or stumbling on the shore holding Nursey's hand, and herself wheeling the new baby in the sunshine.

What visions Bindon had of the future he did not relate to her. There can have been no sea, or fat babies, or talkative little boys, no sunshine. No sunshine.

For the second time in a few months, Bindon Blood was seared by a dreadful man-made chemical. If it was traditional that an officer and gentleman use his own weapon to end his life, then Bindon Blood perhaps did not see himself any longer in that role. When he swallowed the Lysol, it was at Wapping, a fair distance from the warmth and comfort of Windsor Villa.

The stevedores who discovered his body would have liked to see what the envelope in the corpse's pocket contained, but it was addressed to Inspector George Moth of New Scotland Yard. 'I know that I should not do this. Ask Esther to forgive me. Music is lost for ever and I can think of no other way to be rid of thoughts of decomposition and filthy corruption.'

George Moth knew, from his own experience of sudden and terrible death in the midst of renewed happiness, what havoc the grief and shock would wreak upon Esther's life. Looking at the suicide's distorted handwriting on Post Office purchased stationery, he felt crushed at the thought of having to face his daughter, who had said confidently that the worst was now over. He longed for the comfort of Anne's lovely body and soft upper-class voice.

As he often did, he went first for an hour or two's comfort with Effee Tessalow. Discreet and safe but with the low accent and voice of the music-hall girl she had been. He shrank from going home to Esther with his tragic news until he had talked to a woman and, as always, Effee was the woman.

```
┌─────────────────────────────────────────┐
│                                         │
│        NOTICE TO MEMBERS                │
│                                         │
│   THERE WILL BE A DANCE TONIGHT         │
│        FOR SPECIAL FUNDS.               │
│        MEMBERS ONLY.                    │
│                                         │
└─────────────────────────────────────────┘
```

Victoria was glad that Nancy had persuaded Otis Hewetson to come to the fund-raising dance that evening. It was one of the ways to get new people committed. If one had danced and had a bit of fun with a group of people, then it was easier to ask them to undertake some task.

Otis came early as she had said she would to help make sandwiches. There were terrible food shortages but somebody had managed to get a basket of eggs so there hung about the hall their sulphurous smell as they were boiled and shelled.

Victoria, who was slicing up loaves of bread, looked pleased as she greeted Otis. 'You did well today in the bookshop. Beautifully made-up account, we should have you for our treasurer.'

Otis smiled at the compliment. 'I was wondering about Nancy. Isn't it asking for trouble to sell those leaflets openly? It is against the law, isn't it?'

'Her leaflets? One diagram of a woman and a cross-section illustration of a male member? Hardly *The Decameron.*'

'But couldn't we be in trouble for being concerned with obscene literature?'

'Do you find it obscene?'

'Not at all. In fact, I thought it rather staid and clinical.'

'That is why we believe that an obscene publications' case would be unlikely to stand up in court. I hope that it doesn't worry you at all. We are not foolhardy, we have lawyers who support our cause and give us advice. But whatever the risk, poor people are as entitled to information as the rest.'

'Oh yes, I am in favour of that argument.'

'Then rest assured, it is worth any risk we take. Just think, if the poor have smaller families, where *will* Kitchener find his cannon fodder? Don't worry, Otis. Now you go through into the hall and enjoy yourself.'

A young man whom Otis had noticed a few times in Lou Barker's came in and handed Victoria a package.

'Ten. Good ones. Worth every penny. I've settled with him.' He winked at Victoria and smiled at Otis.

'Danny!' She snatched the package and slipped it into her apron pocket. 'You are too casual by half.' She frowned at him.

'Nonsense! It's only when you go about with slanty eyes that they suspect you of being an anarchist with a bomb under your cloak. And we are all comrades here, aren't we?'

'Be serious.'

'I will if you'll tell me who this is.'

'Otis, our new worker.'

His eyes crinkled as he smiled. 'When you said a teacher, I hedn't expected . . .'

'Danny Turner,' Victoria waved her breadknife at him. 'If you mention Otis's looks, I shall belay you.'

'Ruby! Heve y'ever heard me comment upon a female's beauty?'

'Yes, usually *before* you comment upon her worth.'

'Let me have that before you damage *my* good looks.' Which looks were of the devil-may-care handsomeness that Otis liked. He took the knife from Victoria. 'Miss Hewetson, I care not a fig that you are the most stunningly beautiful woman I ever set eyes on, I welcome you as a comrade in the cause.'

Otis liked him. He had a gaiety that was infectious.

Victoria patted her pocket. 'Well, I have to put these away, so you can take over my job and help Otis.'

'Yes, ma'am. Isn't she the sergeant-major, Otis?' He winked and the corners of his eyes crinkled.

'Somebody needs to keep you in line, Danny. Beware, Otis. He has a line of blarney that would charm an Irishman.'

'I've seen you in Lou Barker's shop.'

'You have? How did I not see you? I would have remembered.'

'I sometimes eat at the back of the shop: the bead curtain hides me.' He smiled, his features seeming to fall naturally so. 'I can't place your accent, it isn't quite . . . ?'

'Cockney, but I grew up in Australia – haven't been back here very long.'

He was broad and sturdy, obviously proud of his physique for, whenever she had seen him, she noticed that he always wore an open jacket and, instead of a conventional shirt, a garment rather like an under-vest with a bound neck. He had a soft complexion as delicate as a girl's, his hair was a jet-black mop of wild curls, his nose straight and shapely. His eyes were intelligent, but this was not the first thing one noticed about them: it was their colour – bright blue and fringed with long black lashes.

Like most young women whose eyes alighted on Danny Turner, once she had seen him, she was not likely to forget him.

Dropping his knife into a box, he took Otis's from her. 'Come and dance, this can wait.' And so saying he whisked her through and on to the rough boards of the hall floor. 'Can you Rag?'

Otis's eyes lit up. 'Can I? Can they play?'

'Can a duck swim? Have you heard of Kanute, King of the Keys?'

Otis shook her head.

'Then you haven't heard Ragtime.' He leaned across the piano and said something to the black player, who grinned, clicked his fingers against his thumbs, and ran his fingers fast across the keys and nodded to the three other musicians. A cheer went up from some of the young people gathered round the walls. The jerky music seemed to release a brake on Otis's movement as she tentatively flicked her heels out sideways. Her partner took her hands and at once they were in unison with each other and with the new rhythm.

Danny raised his eyebrows and grinned. 'You're good,' he said above the music.

'So are you,' she shouted back. 'Did you learn this in Australia?'

'Not likely. Picked it up on the boat coming home. Worked my passage as a waiter and learned from watching the toffs.'

From time to time they momentarily came in close contact, and Otis could feel that his body was hard and lithe and well-exercised. Once when he held her about the waist and said, 'Ah. Nice,' she frowned at him, at which he laughed, open-mouthed. Lord, what perfect teeth and a mouth as pink as a cat's. The music finished, and the young people who had been dancing groaned with disappointment.

'Come outside and cool off.'

Leaning against a tree at the side of the hall, Otis fanned herself with her handkerchief and laughed. 'I'm dead, absolutely dead.'

'You are out of condition. Too many of Lou's pies and not enough walking in the parks.'

'I know, my job, sitting for much of the day. I used to play Bumblepuppy to keep fit, but not for ages.'

He roared with laughter. 'Bumblepuppy? What's Bumblepuppy when it's at home?'

'A ball tied to a pole – you thwack it with a paddle.'

'Ah, top-drawer stuff like croquet. Requires a lawn the size of Hampstead Heath by the sound of it.'

Otis's face straightened and she did not reply. She hated to think that he was poking fun at her. She would never dream of ridiculing his peculiar accent.

Peering at her he said, 'I've put my foot in my mouth, heven't I?'

'I should go in. I came here to help.'

'Victoria won't mind. I've done a good deed today, I shall be the apple of her eye.'

He tucked a loose tendril of hair behind her ear. A gesture of familiarity that belied the fact that they had met less than half an hour ago.

'I am sorry. What did I say about top drawer that hit that particular nerve?'

'I cannot help my origins.'

'Of course you can't. No one says that you should try. Annie doesn't.'

'But Annie comes from the acceptable class.'

'Because she was a mill-girl? Don't be so idiotic, Annie's acceptable because she believes in what we do here.'

'And so do I.'

'Good. Then you are acceptable. I don't mind if you come from Mayfair, so long as you are one of us.'

'I am. I really am. It's only that sometimes I say things without thinking.' She paused.

He grinned. 'Like playing Bumblepuppy?'

The grin was infectious. 'Yes . . . Bumblepuppy.' Her shoulders moved with held-back laughter. 'Isn't it a ridiculous name for a game? I never even thought of it before.'

'No worse than Tic-tac-toe . . . and thet's played in the gutter, and I won't get huffy if you laugh.'

She held her head down, feeling somewhat ashamed of her previous petulance, but he raised it, holding her chin with finger and thumb.

'I take a chance that you tell on me to Ruby – she'll snap off the head of any man who doesn't appreciate a woman's mind more than he appreciates her face and figure – but I think that you are *the* most attractive woman I ever had the good fortune to see.'

Whether it was as Victoria had said that his blarney could charm the Irish, Otis felt lighthearted at his compliment. How much more enjoyable this rough and disorganized evening was compared to the highly stylish dances she attended in her other life where, instead of tea and egg sandwiches, wine-cup and water ices were served.

'I haven't enjoyed myself so much for a long time,' she said.

'They're a good lot.'

'I don't yet know much about the politics of it all, I'm afraid.'

'You don't need to. Only whether a thing's right or wrong, that's how I look at it. Good or bad, fair or unfair, people have always got a choice. It all comes down to doing the right thing.'

'You make it sound simple.'

'It is. If you take this war, it's just a case of asking yourself "right or wrong?" If your answer's "wrong" then you're agin it.'

'Don't you think that there is sometimes a "right" war?'

'I once heard somebody say that war is a bayonet, and at one end is a working man – and at the other end is a working man.'

'I suppose that's so.'

'It is – and I refuse to be the worker at either end.'

'Are you a conscientious objector?'

'Only in spirit. Because I've lived in Australia since I was a kid, there's no record of Danny Turner. I've got papers that say I'm a seaman.'

'Tell me about the men who are on the run.'

'They rely on us. People like Ruby and Annie, and you, I hope?'

Otis nodded, feeling herself being drawn steadily, willingly, into a world whose existence would have shocked her mother, who would have become hysterical at the knowledge that Otis was becoming involved. Simply by being there, she was committing herself. She had seen the handing over of some sort of illegally-obtained documents. Forgeries? Stolen? Certainly money had changed hands for them. What else went on here besides the handing out of subversive literature telling women how to limit their families; seditious tracts appealing to men 'Don't be a Soldier'? And the funds that this innocent 'hop' was raising, they were for the 'Underground'. And you, I hope?

'Yes. You can rely on me. But how can you be sure of that? I might report what goes on here, you don't know that I won't.'

'Of course we don't, but then who can be sure of anything? It's all a question of trust and judgement. We aren't fools. We check what it is possible to check. You have friends who are our enemies – well, one friend. Moth.'

Otis raised her eyebrows questioningly. 'Inspector Moth?'

'Superintendent. He's about to be elevated.' He grinned at her. 'We too have our spies. The police force has its dissidents.'

'So I've learned.'

'The Moth connection isn't important. Ruby knows them too, of course.'

'Well, thank you for that. So what is important?'

'Ruby's judgement and you choosing to leave the leafy suburbs and coming to live and work here. And I, for one, am glad that you did. Now come back and Rag with me some more.'

Back in the hall they were just taking their first steps to the music when the shout 'Rozzers!' went up. Danny at once let go of her hands and rushed over to a young man into whose jacket pocket he thrust some papers. At the moment when policemen burst in through both front and back entrances, truncheons raised as though prepared for attack, Danny Turner scrambled out through a window.

Danny's agility gave him a head start on the constable who gave chase. In the hall where several policemen were barricading the entrances, there was uproar. People shouting, a dog barking, a baby crying, little children wailing, and a crash of glass at the other end of the hall, where several other young men were scrambling through windows.

A police sergeant shouted for quiet and ordered all men to one end of the hall. Victoria and Annie remonstrated with him, asking for authority, which the sergeant declared he did not need, saying that they were searching for a conscripted man who had 'done a bunk'.

All of the men had papers that were in order, exempting them from Conscription registration. Nothing illegal having been proved, the raiders eventually retreated and the dance was given permission to resume. But the incident knocked the wind out of the sails that had carried the evening along with such enjoyment.

When the helpers were clearing up, Otis said, 'I don't understand what went on here.'

Victoria said. 'The men who've got an occupation that exempts them from Conscription hand over their exemption papers to men who have none.'

Understanding dawned on Otis. 'And the men who have legitimate papers create a diversion by escaping?'

'That's right,' Annie said. 'It's not against the law to run off. If they are caught they can't be charged with anything. All that the police can do is to give them notice to produce exemption documents within twenty-four hours – which of course they do. Would you like to see to it that Danny's papers are returned safe and sound?'

Otis did not at all mind. It confirmed her a member of the ardent and well-run organization.

> Greywell, Stormont Road, Clapham Common. London.
>
> *My Dear Otis,*
> *As a favour to me, please do try to be on time for Christmas Eve dinner, if not for my sake then for our guests'. When Max goes back from this leave, I want him to take with him a vision of what he is fighting for – home, family, tradition. We shall dine at nine P.M. sharp and I trust that you will give yourself time to bathe and change into the new gown I have had sent from Madame.*
> *Affectionately*
> *E.H.*

Emily Hewetson had gone to a great deal of trouble to prepare a traditional Christmas celebration – at least her domestics had gone to a great deal of trouble on her behalf, and Emily had herself done all of the persuading in Fortnum's provisions department as well as making up orders for the Army and Navy Stores.

She knew that Otis would not respond as she ought. Any normal daughter would clasp her hands and say how wonderful everything looked, and how had her mother managed to gather under one roof so many provisions and luxuries that were in short supply, and that the image of the great Christmas tree in the hall was what every soldier should carry in his heart.

But, Emily complained to herself, Otis had never been an easy child, had been positively difficult as a girl, and was now an impossible young woman.

267

'I tell you, Martin, no man is ever going to want her.'

'Em, you worry too much. Have you ever known a beautiful young woman, with Otis's expectations, to want for a husband?'

'I have never known a young woman like Otis. And what kind of husband? One of her rabble? Some coster-monger who eats eels on the street? I have kept well away from that part of her life, as you well know, but that does not mean that I am unaware of what she is up to. You have no idea of what has found its way under this roof. Even as I speak, in her room are pamphlets of instruction that I should blush for the servants to see. Lord, I can hardly bring myself to tell you.'

Martin frowned to please Em, but he was already aware of some of the activities which, though others of his ilk found nefarious, he did not. In his opinion Otis's idealism in wanting to educate the masses was worthy of the Hewetsons, who had always taken a liberal view in most matters. Surely only good could come if girls were well-educated and knew how to regulate the size of their families.

Awaiting the arrival of both Max and Otis, Emily and Martin Hewetson were arranging on the sideboard Christmas greetings cards and small sweetmeats and fruits. 'D'you know, Em, I think that at the moment we should be more concerned for Max's welfare than for Otis's. I'm afraid that there is something amiss.'

'With Max? I noticed nothing. He was edgy, it is true, but surely that is only to be expected in a man who has fought in battle.'

'I believe that he has had some terrible experiences.'

'I am sure that you are right, Martin. Killing people is not nice, and Max was never one for any sort of shooting party, as you well know. One thing though, his uniform does look so much better on him now that he has lost his tendency to podginess. I thought him very handsome.' She moved the silver-framed photograph of the military Max more centrally on the mantelpiece.

Martin needed someone in whom he could confide his fears about his young step-brother, but Em was not that person. But, he thought, who is?

Otis arrived well on time, followed by Max who looked fatigued, in spite of having been on leave. The dinner, the meals that followed next day and the little entertainments she had arranged, were a success, making Emily thoroughly pleased at being back once more as queen over such an elegant household.

Martin, as he watched his daughter over the two days of her visit, wondered at her chameleon-like ability to adapt to her surroundings. He had visited Islington on only a couple of occasions, but he had observed enough of her life to know that, in her plain clothes and un-elaborate hair style, she was a very different person. There she merged into the busy street-scape. Over Christmas at Greywell, though, she was everything that Em wished for in a daughter – with the exception that she would not rise to any bait when it came to eligible young men, and had once snapped too cruelly at her mother, 'What young men? There are none, they are under six feet of mud, or strewn about the pot-holes of the minefields. Or will you provide for me one like Uncle Hewey, shot to pieces in his mind?'

Fortunately Max had not been in the room, but it had brought into focus the fact that all was not well with his step-brother. Poor Em, she had seemed to deflate, with-draw; and he had seen her following Max with her eyes, smiling brightly at him when he caught her at it.

On Boxing Morning Otis and Max had gone walking, whilst Martin had taken Em to give thanks in St Paul's cathedral. In the afternoon Max had returned to his own residence to prepare for his return to his regiment. Over luncheon, Martin had noticed that there had been some kind of new rapport between Otis and Max: she had stopped calling him Uncle Hewey and he had seemed not so twitchy and, in place of his usual paternal patting and her pecking kisses, they had hugged in a very comradely way when they took their leave of one another.

After Em had gone up that night, it was Otis who proved to be the confidante Martin had been looking for.

'I tried to get Max to give it up, Pa, but I did not succeed.'

'Give up . . . ?'

'Fighting, killing, being killed, mentally breaking . . .'

Martin looked at the serious face of his lovely daughter. Looking back over the last few years, he marvelled at the changes that had turned a rumbustious girl, who had been kept in pigtails and tam-o'-shanter caps for too long, into this idealistic and passionate woman. And how imperceptibly that had happened. On what day had the line of her mouth changed? In which week had those small cracks appeared at the corners of her eyes? When had her chin risen and her jaw-line firmed? It was with Otis as it had been with Em, when one day he had noticed that her white hands were showing with the same brown markings of age as his own – the change had seemed to come suddenly. Logic said that they had not come overnight, but it had seemed so.

Em had an imperious air that others found intimidating, but Martin saw through it. Otis, on the other hand, was sometimes too approachable, too ameliorating. But on the evening of that Boxing Day when he sat in the unlighted room before the glowing hearth and a second, smaller, crystal-bedecked tree, Martin Hewetson felt a little in awe of his daughter whose year of majority had only just passed.

'You asked him not to return to the war?'

'Not merely asked – tried to persuade him.'

'Max would never do that.'

'The old Max, the dear old Uncle Hewey might not have done so, but he's changed. I believe that he was on the verge. If it had not been for his men, then I believe that he would have been persuaded.'

'But you were asking him to desert!'

'Of course I was.'

'But soldiers cannot simply walk away when they see fit.'

'It would put an end to them killing one another.'

'And have Great Britain overrun by the Hun? Otis!'

'Not if the common soldiers walked away also. Pa, isn't *anything* preferable to eighty-five thousand men being massacred in three months? A further thirty thousand in another month? Three thousand more in a single battle? And what if the worst did happen and we found ourselves under the rule of Germany? Didn't you used to love taking your holidays there? Aren't they clean, home-loving, well-disciplined people, according to you? Now they are the filthy Hun. Are you going to tell me that within a year or two of this war ending their businessmen and ours, their princes and ours, will not be hob-nobbing again? But poor old Tommy, he won't be able to hob-nob, will he?'

'Otis! That is spurious argument and you know it.'

She admitted it only to the extent that she gave him a short smile and a shrug of her shoulders.

'Your mother said something to the effect that killing is never nice . . .'

Otis burst in with a spurt of laughter. 'Killing not nice! Oh Ma! I can just hear her.'

'But what she was implying is that there are times when one must put aside finer feelings and do the other thing.'

'Such as human beings frying one another in gouts of burning oil? Or spraying acid on to the skin of one's fellow creatures? Or poisoning the air they breathe with lethal gas?'

'That is not what I meant at all.'

'But that is what it does mean to be in this war. That is what it means to Max.'

He rose, stirred the fire, added another log and lifted the port decanter as a question.

'Do you have white port, Pa?'

He smiled. 'I shall not enquire where an Islington teacher acquired such tastes. Yes, I keep some, but don't often offer it now that such things are in short supply. But I will gladly share my hoard with a daughter who has developed a taste for it. Shall I play us some music?'

He had recently persuaded himself that such a large room as this would benefit from a new Auxeto gramophone, and Em had had the pleasure of letting it be known, whispered into an ear or two, that the one hundred pounds laid out was not the half of it. He loved to find an appropriate moment to offer music.

'Lovely, and we shall sit and be cosy until midnight has struck, shall we?' She accepted the golden drink and tasted it appreciatively. It tasted of George Moth's mouth. I was a girl then. There are times now when I feel older than Pa. The music poured from the mahogany cabinet and drowned the nastiness into which Otis had been about to force her father's nose.

Cello and violin strains swirled around them like drifting mists, out of which loomed the scene that Max Hewetson had described to her that morning, and which was the nastiness that she had wanted her father to confront.

Otis had been relating what Victoria had told her about the international congress she had attended at The Hague.

'My dear child, you and your friends cannot win. The country has too much at stake to go in for a negotiated peace,' Max had said. 'Peace must now be fought for, it has all gone beyond the point where women meeting the King of Norway can influence matters. It will be a fight to the death now, no matter what.'

'Oh Uncle Hew, not more of the same. All these months – killing, killing, killing!'

'There have been too many corpses, Otis, for there to be anything else other than total defeat for the Germans.'

'Them and us, them and us, them and us. There are soldiers who want peace without fighting for it.'

'You are wrong, Otis. The men will not give in, to them anything but outright victory is unthinkable.'

'I believe they do. I meet them and listen to them. It is not the ordinary soldier who wants victory over a pile of bodies – he'll settle for simple peace. It is the jingoists and the leaders with terrible ideas of supremacy who want a fought-for victory.'

With a finger under her chin he raised Otis's face and looked into it. 'God preserve us, Otis, where did the laughing child go?'

'She went on a trip to Islington and ended up in a bookshop in the real world where she meets soldiers who have given up killing their own kind.'

'It is not a good place to be for a young woman with a conscience.'

'Dear Hewey, it is the *only* place for her to be.'

'So long as she is still here when I return and not languishing in gaol.'

'Don't go, Max. I know how to get you out of the country.'

Now he looked really shocked. 'Does that mean that you are involved in aiding deserters?'

'Deserters? That is your word. But yes, I intend doing what I can. I'll help conscientious objectors of any flavour – religious, political, registered, unregistered; any man who refuses to join in the shooting party.' She knew that this reference was an arrow that went straight home, for he had once told her how he had been ostracized at a weekend house-party for referring to a pheasant shoot as a fulfilment of blood-lust and refusing to take part.

'You are playing a serious game, Otis.'

'It's not a game, Max.'

'I am glad that you realize it. No matter that you are twenty and very pretty, the powers-that-be are in no mood to be mellow with their opposers.'

They had now reached open heath-land, where the wind whipped their faces.

'This walk is doing you good, Max. I thought that you would never get colour back in your face.'

They went to a seat where in summer one might sit beneath the great oak and look out across a green and pleasant land. Now, with the life-force withdrawn, the scene was straw-coloured, except for patches of white where the sun had not reached the hoar-frost. They sat with their warm, woollen coats buttoned around them, both aware that these two days at Greywell had been lived in never-never-land: Emily with her tree and trifles and roast beef, Martin with his thoughtful gifts and his loud orchestras coming from the mahogany box. Otis and Max playing the Hewetsons' family game as it had been played for twenty years, both feeling guilty for being part of it.

'Shall I tell you how they treat traitors and deserters out in France?'

Otis guessed that she knew that from what she had already learned at the bookshop, but felt that for the first time in her life she was going to be allowed to see inside her kindly, playful, jolly uncle.

'At one posting I was ordered to make arrangements for the reception of thirty or so prisoners disembarking from England. I thought this strange: why were prisoners being sent out of Great Britain? However, ours is not to reason why, et cetera, so I had the paperwork prepared and we duly received thirty-four men. It was not part of my duty to do so, but I went to look at them to see what sort of a bunch they were, ready for when orders came through about what to do with them.

'I suppose in telling you this, I am giving you ammunition for your league, fellowship or whatever it is, but what I found was extremely disturbing. I have no intention of describing the detail, but these men, many of whom had been in solitary confinement, had been fed only bread and water for God knows how long. The state of their clothing was pathetic! All of them had scars and contusions from beatings. All of them were under sentence of death.'

Otis nodded. 'And all were conscientious objectors, but

nevertheless destined for the front line of battle and no chance of escape.'

He turned to his niece and nodded his head. 'You really do know what is going on, don't you?'

'Yes. If it is the same group of men, then one of them had been going to marry one of the women at the bookshop.' She forbore to tell him the story of how close he had once come to Nancy that year when they holidayed in Southsea: those days had so little to do with these; those innocent people were as dead and gone as Mrs Moth.

'Take care, Otis.'

'It is not I who must do that. Why are you compelled to return to the fighting? I don't mean compelled by military orders, but I can sense that it is not because of the war that you feel that you must go.'

'It is because of the men. My own men, and those poor damned prisoners. My men . . . you say that soldiers do not wish to fight, well I tell you this, many of my own men would turn their rifles on me if I suggested that they stop fighting now. You may be right and they might have been tricked by the jingoism – I was myself – but now that they are in they have their comrades' deaths to avenge. They will go on facing machine-guns, treading on mines and firing at anything that moves.'

'And the Germans will do likewise and kill more comrades to be avenged and so on and so on. And when will it end? When there are no men left at all?'

'Soon. When the Germans surrender. In the meantime my men will go on fighting, defending their homes . . .'

'When what they are really defending are the homes of people like us, Max. Places such as Greywell.'

'And sentimental notions of decorated Christmas trees. In that regard what you say is true, very few of my men have anything much of their own worth fighting for.'

'I believe those are the first bitter words I ever heard you say, Uncle Hew.'

They had sat on quietly for some while, until their chilled feet had driven them to walk again, retracing their steps back to Greywell. When he took his leave of them, Emily wept.

Otis's thoughts drifted back into the room where her father was refilling her glass, where the fire glowed, the tree glittered, the music mesmerized.

Before she went up to her room, she related to her father what Max had told her of the brutalized prisoners. He said nothing, but had patted her hand as he used to do when she was little and had come to him for consolation after having tried Em's patience to the point of exasperation.

My Dear Otis. Now that I have seen with my own eyes generals, safely behind the lines, feasting in the French equivalent of Mere Meldrum, whilst their men were being slaughtered; now that I have delivered a despatch to a room in which they were planning, with unforgivable incompetence, the destruction of entire companies of men, whilst smoking cigars and drinking good French wine . . . I applaud every man who refuses to have anything to do with this war and every man and woman who will try to put an end to it . . . The theory is that a spit-and-polished soldier is an efficient one, and I suppose that there is something in that for one does feel degraded wallowing for days in one's own grime . . . We have taken a fair number of prisoners . . . Have you ever stood facing your own reflection and looked deep into your own eyes knowing that the eyes gazing back know you to your very depth, know things about you that you cannot bring yourself to admit? If you have done that then you know what it is like to engage the gaze of a man you have been trying to kill and who has been trying to kill you – neither one can bear the penetration for more than a few seconds . . . This is not the letter that you will receive, these are only random thoughts as I lie here and prepare to answer your welcome letter . . . What you will receive is a bland note that will pass censorship. Yours,
   Jack

Private 'Lofty' Moth sits and rubs his louse-bites gently. Up the line, old hands all have their own remedy for stopping the itching – spit, a dab of fresh urine, dandelion leaves. But where are any dandelion leaves?

Where, for that matter, is there any bit of green when

they are up the line? Any man in Jack's platoon would have surely chewed the very life out of a dandelion rather than rub it on the bites. Nothing comes up to scratching with broken fingernails.

They receive regular lectures on Personal Hygiene in which a captain warns against the many creatures that soldiers must become wary of outside the bounds of their home counties. Lice, fungus, women. At base camp he gives loud and emphatic lectures and invites questions. Few are ever asked. In the trenches, care of one's feet and louse-bitten skin are as important as food and drink. The Very Dangerous Women are not a problem this close to the enemy lines. Jack Moth claws all eight fingers into the hairline at the nape of his neck and shivers with satisfaction at that brief moment of self-abuse.

Jack has been removed to a 'cushy' part of the line, from where the two sides are well-entrenched and where any move by either side would lead to heavy losses for both. The British trenches are at least six feet and often more than seven feet deep, and at most a few hundred yards away from the enemy; in places as close as a few hundred feet. Somewhere, it was assumed, somebody had a plan of the trenches, but it must have appeared as a maze. Here and there where shells have landed the sides have been blown in and left in a state where earth, canvas, splintered wood and limbs are a compost heap around which new duckboards detour. But on the whole this sector is well-dug and well-maintained.

The platoon of which Jack is a member is on fatigue duty. During the day they curl up, helmet over face and hands in pockets against the vast army of fat rats, and sleep in a tunnel that serves the light railway and the trenches.

The sergeant arouses his men with a reluctant prod with the toe of his boot – reluctant because the sergeant, although his own youth is long past, knows what it is like to be young and tired. Once back in Blighty he is likely to be put on to recruit training duties. It will be no easier for him there to push boys, who might have been his sons, into some sort of fighting readiness, for he knows how short are the odds for them once they have crossed the water.

Jack arouses at once and shakes the heavily-sleeping figure next to him. 'Cully. Cully. Time for up.'

Private Cullington's fat, pink face grins up at Jack.

'I had a good sleep, Loft.'

'Good-o, Cully. Come on, let's fill our bottles.' Jack, who now as easily answers to Lofty as to his given name, chivvies his partner to the water tank. The choice of water is between that collected in shell-holes which might or might not contain long-dead soldiers and rats, or the tank which contains foul-tasting chloride of lime – the latter is marginally preferable.

'Last night for us up here, Loft.' Cully grins his childish, retarded grin and Jack winks his acknowledgement.

A few members of the platoon used the boy as the butt of their cruel jokes, others as a focus of their anger, but for the most part, like Jack, the men knew that now that the boy was in the army, no one would ever admit that a mistake had been made in passing Cully as fit, so he was theirs to protect as well as they were able. Which was not easy in the front line.

The night's equipment arrives and they unload. Tonight the bulk of it is reels of barbed wire for replacement. It is a job that they have done before. It means a silent journey over the top and into the shell-holed no man's land, and a silent placing of iron spikes and a silent playing out of the reels. It is about the only job that Cully is able to do without putting the entire platoon at risk. He treats it as something of a game: Cully's side must creep out in the dark, replace the wire and creep back again without the Germans finding out; going down flat and still if there is the slightest sound – a soldier's version of 'What's the time, Daddy Wolf?'

It is a short night, but they are back before dawn. The

only incident has been when somewhere in the blackness someone stumbled and was spiked with the vicious barbs, when the single curse 'Bugger!' caused a short rash of flares and a few rakings by a machine-gun from the German outpost.

They had been in the forward line for twelve days; last evening they dropped back. A short respite. A decent shave. Jack felt that he would have sold his soul for a full tub of hot water, a bar of carbolic soap and a rough towel. For the present, though, a wait in the queue and a good wash down under the sprays would be pleasant enough. A cycle of sixteen days. Twelve days divided between three fronts, and four days in the comparative safety of some village.

Coming up are the village days. For four days hundreds of soldiers, thankful that their number did not come up this time, will stay in and around a cow byre and a few sheds where there is hay to rest in and planks of wood for a table. The walls of this byre have been bombarded and the roof is not whole, but they are away from the trenches until tonight when, under cover of darkness, they will take supplies of ammunition and rolls of barbed wire up the line.

'Your turn to brew up, Loft.'

Jack takes a screw of tea-ration from each member of the squad of which he is a member. As a squad member of several months standing, he is one of the older hands. A few have been here longer; one of them is a captain. He has better quarters, better food, better odds of surviving than the men he commands, he knows how to keep his head down and look after number one. Another is the ageing sergeant, who never expected the men to do anything that he would not do himself, now kipped down with other sergeants: both were older hands than Jack Moth. Many – some boys, some almost of his father's age – are new and raw.

Jack dishes out the tea and passes round a tin of condensed milk. Dropping with fatigue, they drink without much of their normal exchange, and settle down in the straw for an hour before reveille.

Up the line they had an ear for where a shell would fall, and ducked automatically for those that would fall close at hand. But here they became jumpy. Old and new hands alike, they jerked their heads and played 'Statues' at the sound of any aircraft. They had been expecting a big German attack in the sector they were defending. But for now they could sluice down, parade, tend their feet and uniforms, eat hot food from the field kitchen and get in some sleep. Sufficient, uninterrupted sleep, that was the greatest deprivation up the line where, in the tunnel, although it was safe from the shelling, a thoroughfare for both men and rats, they slept in cat-naps.

In the early dawn, too much daylight comes in through the roof and the missing wall. Jack puts his cap over his face but, in spite of his fatigue, can only get into that state of half-sleep where the brain is afire. Where every image of grotesque horror, every moment of grief, every explosion of anger that has been pushed aside comes clawing its way to the surface.

He is not the only one who makes strange noises as he sweats and tosses in this state. He is not the only one to have seen a man come apart in mid-air; to have turned to shout something to a boy who did not shout back because shrapnel in the mouth had left him nothing with which to do so. Nor is he the only one who has gone into the attack with six friends, with whom he was drinking and eating in an estaminet on the last spell at base camp, and come out of it alone. They have all, except the very new members, become almost used to the sight of human viscera, brains, bone and decomposition; almost familiar with the sight of what they are often detailed to collect in groundsheets; almost hardened to the duty of recovering bits and pieces of their own khaki-uniformed company, indistinguishable, except for tatters of grey uniform, from the bits and pieces of young Germans.

The fact that they have become used to such sights does not lessen the impact upon the nerves, which are frayed to the point of breaking.

He rolls on his back, uncovers his eyes and looks through a hole in the roof at a patch of dawn-blue sky and thinks of Otis Hewetson.

Many times over the last months he has thought of her: How on earth could I have been such a fool? Since he had had time to think about it, he had become convinced that Victoria had known what his true feelings were. The kisses, the sudden passion to see her did not constitute his being in love with her any more than did her caresses of himself. She must have known that when she agreed to visit Mere Meldrum. Had she not shown an interest in himself, then he might have realized the truth of it sooner.

He sits up and feels in his haversack for pencil and letter-form. Otis had been the first to write, a friendly letter uncritical of his having volunteered to fight in the war she was against, and he had replied. Then she had written again, sending him chocolates and socks – absolutely the right items of comfort. Had she worked out for herself the most acceptable items? He liked to think that the chocolates at least were her own idea.

He would have liked to tell her that he had come to understand what she and Victoria were doing. But letters were censored.

The can of water over the makeshift fire is boiling again, so he rouses to brew himself more tea.

'Loft?' The pile of straw next to Jack moves and Cully's fat, pink face with skin like that of a child emerges.

Jack puts his fingers to his lips. 'Men're still asleep, Cully.'

Private Cullington shrinks down and makes a face like a small child who has been forgetful. 'Sorry, Loft.' He edges towards Jack and says softly in his unbroken voice, 'I was going to ask if you wanted a fag. I got some.'

'Thanks, Cully. Want some tea?' Jack shares his brew with the young simpleton soldier who pours in a stream of the thick, sweet milk and slurps awkwardly, as though he has not long learned to drink from a vessel.

'You ate all your chocolates yet, Loft?' His feigned innocence is as transparent as a child who knows that there is cake left but has been told that it would be greedy to ask for more.

Jack searches his pack for Otis's box and hands it to the boy soldier.

'You can finish them, Cully, they'll only get melted if I hang on to them.'

Private Cullington's grin is wet and loose, his mam had taught him his manners, perhaps realizing that some of his many defects might be forgiven if he knew how to be polite. 'Thanks, Loft. I'll give you some of mine if my mum sends any.'

'You've already given me some of your cigarettes, Cully – fair exchange.'

'I'll give you the rest if you like, Loft.'

'You hang on to them, or I might smoke the lot.'

'All right, then, I'll give you them one a day like my mam gives me prizes.' He giggled quietly. 'That's if you're good, Loft.'

Jack watched as the boy turned over the chocolates, pondering before selecting, and wondered, as he and other members of the platoon had wondered daily since Cullington joined them, whether the doctor who had been paid a decent fee to pass the boy as fit for active service, had actually *looked* at him, let alone medically examined him. For, although he was eighteen years old, and nearly as tall as Jack, Cully had a loose mouth, no beard, his sex organs had never fully developed, and he had the intellect and judgement of a child. In effect, that doctor had taken his fee to certify that an eight-year-old was fit to answer his Conscription call.

'Kit inspection soon, Cully. Get yours out and I'll look it over for you.'

The boy carefully stowed away the chocolate box and began to do as he was told. He was quite good at the routine business of army life – so long as he was told clearly what he had to do, then he would do it. What he could not do was to weigh up a situation and come to a conclusion. Worst of all was his sheer terror when under fire. Not, thought Jack, that any of us is any better, but at least we know enough not to put our heads above the parapet.

More than once it had occurred to Jack that what Cully needed was to get his hand above the rim of a trench when there was a hot-shot sniper about. A good Blighty wound. It had been done before – dangerously, for men had tried it and been charged with causing self-inflicted wounds, a charge that carried the death penalty. German snipers never gave up, but fired at tops of helmets, periscopes, waving hands or anything else that moved above the earthworks of the trenches. If a man's hand was too badly injured for him to thrust a bayonet and press a trigger, then he was no use at the Front. But Cully did not have the cunning to get away with any such deviousness, and in any case was too afraid of pain to do anything of that nature.

In one respect, however, Jack was envious of the slow-witted boy, and that was for his lack of imagination. When they were in the midst of a battle, the boy was terrified, but once the firing ceased he could easily return to his own world of calm bewilderment and submission. He would say: 'I'm glad that's all over.' And for him, until next time, it would be over. He could wet himself from fear, sponge and dry his uniform and forget it. He did not re-live the horror of the battlefield, nor did he appear to dream it. The wonder was that he had lasted so long.

Jack worried about what would happen to Cully if he himself were to catch a packet. Although there were others who felt it a damn shameful thing that the boy had ever been put in uniform, none would take him under their wing as Jack had done.

'You writing to your mam, Lofty?'

'I was going to write to the young lady who sent the chocolates, but don't know what to say.'

'Is she your girl?'

Jack drew deeply on the tattered cigarette Cully had given him. 'Not really, but I've known her since we were children.'

'Tell her the chocolates were the best I ever tasted. Tell her the strawberry ones are best but not the coffee. She won't mind, will she, you giving them to me?'

'She'd be quite pleased to know I shared them with a friend.'

'I'll bet she's nice.'

Jack smiled distantly. 'And she's very pretty.'

And I wish that I had not been such a fool as to have missed what was staring me in the face. Now that he was not only distant, but in hourly danger of never returning to England alive, he clearly saw that Victoria had come into his life at a time when he was youthful, of a romantic turn, and had nothing to do but be smitten by an older, exciting woman. Once smitten, it had only taken the evening of heightened emotion on the occasion when his mother had died for the excitement to turn to desire. From that night, he had continued to desire her and so assumed that he loved her.

When he had asked her to go down to Mere, he had, if he was honest, at the back of his mind a scene of seduction and some nights of requited lust. Even now, as he thought of her extreme desirability, he could easily have become aroused, but at this distance, and in these circumstances, he was able to distinguish between what he felt for Victoria and his growing longing for Otis.

My own dear Otis, If there is justice in the world, then you will tear up this letter and I shall get my just deserts. I believe that I

285

have been in love with you for years and was too blind and stupid to realize it. With Otis there was not only the carnal desire, there was too the assurance that he would want to be with her after the desire was satiated. *I can visualize Otis and Jack being elderly together . . .* He was not able to bring to mind such a picture of Victoria and Jack.

He put away the form and took out an envelope and fold of writing paper.

A bugle sounded. The day had begun. Parade. Inspection. Good, hot food with a bit of cooked meat instead of the ubiquitous bully-beef. Swedish exercises. A decent tea with hot soup and some of the good bread that the army somehow still managed to turn out. Preparation for the night run. And in between as many forty-winks as any man could catch on the wing.

In his knapsack, an unfinished letter.

My Dear Otis, In a few days we suspect that we shall be in the thick of it. Some of this will be censored. I must chance that because I want you to know that I love you, and have found you ever more in my mind. This is the first love-letter that I have ever written. What is in my head and my heart come out in words that look trite and will probably read as pedestrian. What I want to say to you can only be said with looks and responses, with kisses and caresses. Over here, our emotions become buried so deeply that one wonders at times whether, from the way we can perform actions such as using our own dead as stepping-stones through the mud, we feel anything at all. Yet at other times our feelings are so close to the surface that we can weep at the death of a dog . . .

Superintendent George Moth shuffled through the papers on his desk and took out the report of the raid on the radical bookshop. All such tactics were supposed to be cleared with his signature on a piece of paper before being put into action. He knew what he should do, which was to kick up a rumpus and haul the maverick inspector over the coals: quite apart from the insubordinate act, the raid had been a fiasco.

It was Saturday morning and he had no need to be in his office, but the alternative was to be at home where he would feel compelled to spend the day trying to do something to persuade Esther to snap out of her misery. He could hardly bear being near her, she made him feel helpless and hopeless. Somehow she had fallen back into her old role of keeping house but, whereas in the years before she married she had brought the breath of life to the house, she now smothered it with her alienating grief.

There seemed to be nothing that he could do. He had known instinctively how to deal with his own grief over Anne, work and work and, after a few weeks of painful celibacy, some urgent couplings with Effee Tessalow – ungentle because she was not Anne – until he found that he could go for a day without feeling the stab of self-pity and misery.

But Esther was not a man. Her whole life had been domestic and, until Bindon's wounding, had been happily so. Being a woman, she was unable to leave, as he had been able, the place from whence stemmed all the minutiae that fostered heart-ache.

George Moth had never been able to decide whether he was a good father to his children. He wished to be, he wished most desperately to be good now that Esther needed him. He had wished to be when Jack had gone off to war. It was that desire to make the lives of his children as bearable as he could that had prompted him to make the first move of reconciliation with Jack after their row at Mere and the subsequent silence between them. But Esther was not a man. George Moth would have known what to say to Jack in similar circumstances. He did not know what to say to his daughter. To enquire after her health sounded as though she was getting over a cold instead of the violent death of a mad husband.

For some reason he now found it more difficult to swamp himself with his work than he had that other time. Then, he had been a detective-inspector, always with a reason for tramping the streets, always with an interesting, suspicious death to deal with, a trail to follow, a hunt to be organized, an arrest and a case to be made. Now that he had risen to a superior rank, he was more desk-bound.

He had never understood why he had been selected for work in the Special Branch. Surely his superiors could not have known that his son had more than a passing acquaintance with one of the Listed Persons. Did they know now? George Moth doubted it, for whenever a report on the Islington nest came before him, the woman was referred to as Ruby Bice or Red Ruby.

And if they did uncover that piece of information? As he felt at the moment, he hardly cared whether they covered up their own inefficiency with a reprimand or blamed him for not giving notice of it and reduced his seniority.

He read the report again, seeing between the lines how that clever mob, two of which he had weekended with at Mere, had made the police raiding-party appear like a music-hall turn. He put the report into a folder and the folder into his private cabinet.

When he was ready he would speak unofficially with the inspector, tell him that he was a fool and that he might have jeopardized some more important surveillance of the department's. What he was doing, in fact, was to try to see that Otis did not come to anyone else's notice. The trouble was, in planting a young constable with local connections right in the path of the Islington nest, there was always the danger that the man's allegiance might topple over into his home camp. After all, a good many men in the ranks of the police had little reason to be loyal to the Force. Their wages put them on the poverty line, their hours were long and unsocial and the work often harrowing, boring or dangerous. But, as like himself, there were always idealistic young men ready to believe that it would all soon change.

He had tried to persuade Esther to have Otis visit her, thinking that he might get some guidance then about how to handle Esther's grave situation. For grave it was and worrying to live with one's daughter and see her slowly starving – emotionally and physically. But Esther had seemed to loathe the idea. 'Not *Otis Hewetson*. She is so . . . ? When I saw her at the interment she was so . . . so *full*. I'm sorry Father, but not now.'

George Moth guessed that he knew what Esther meant. Otis *was* 'full' – of life, of ideas, of passion, of enthusiasm. And her body was as wholesome as her mind. She had looked splendid. Her bright hair and healthy complexion had glowed against her long jet ear-rings and the black velour of her hat. Her voluptuous body had looked healthy and softly taut beneath the silk of her jacket and skirt. Dreadful as the occasion had been, George Moth had kept looking at her, finding her figure a haven for his strained eyes. He had wanted nothing more than to turn his back from the awful, awesome, hole-in-the-corner burial. Painful to him, and mercifully uncommented upon, was the contrast with that of that other soldier's ignoble suicide, when the ignoble Sir Norbert Clermont was interred in his own, consecrated, tomb. George Moth's heart had broken for his pathetic daughter.

He felt around at the back of a deep drawer, pulled out a bottle of malt whisky, stood it on his desk, thought better of it. If he went there at midday, then she might have returned to Lou Barker's.

```
┌─────────────────────────────────────────────────────┐
│                                                     │
│  HM MINISTRY OF WAR, WHITEHALL, LONDON.             │
│  THE MINISTER REGRETS TO INFORM (NEXT OF KIN)       │
│                                                     │
│  ...................................................│
│  OF ................................................│
│  THAT ..............................................│
│  WAS ...............................................│
│  ON ................................................│
│  THE REMAINS ARE/WILL BE/HAVE BEEN                  │
│                                                     │
│  ...................................................│
│                                                     │
└─────────────────────────────────────────────────────┘
```

Not wishing to be subjected to Lou Barker's quizzical gaze, George Moth went to the side entrance and quickly up the stairs that led to Otis Hewetson's door, but found her locking up. She was smartly dressed and carried an overnight bag.

'Oh! Superintendent Moth. I am sorry, I was just about to leave.' Her voice was thick and the rims of her eyes pink from crying.

'Oh.'

Otis saw that he was not merely a disappointed casual caller. Of all people to arrive at her doorstep and of all moments to arrive.

'I am on my way home. We have had bad news . . .' The lump in her throat stopped her and tears began flowing again.

'Here.' He took her key from her and reopened the door. 'You can't go like that. Come. Sit down. I shall make you some strong, sweet tea and then I shall find you a cab.' Picking up her case, he guided her inside. He deposited his hat and cane, and she sat on the edge of the bed and dabbed her eyes. Efficiently, he got out two cups and put the kettle on a gas-ring.

For the first time in years, Otis Hewetson felt glad to have someone to tell her what to do. Her first thoughts might have been: Of all people . . . But, of all people, he was one of the very few in front of whom she did not feel obliged to hide her feelings – Pa was one and Uncle Hewey was the other. She drew a letter from her bag and handed it to him.

'A note from my pa, you can read it – it's my Uncle Hewey . . .'

He did so, it was brief. Whilst he could not cope with Esther's distracted grief, he found it easy to gather Otis into his arms and tell her to cry it out, and that it was all right, and he would take care of her.

At the feel of his firm breast within the woollen cloth of his jacket, at the feel of his bodily warmth, his bristling side-whiskers against her cheek, at the smell of his cigar-smoke-permeated lapel, his lavender hair-oil and coal-tar soap, at the gentle touch of his lips against her neck as he rocked her comfortingly, she felt the flood-gates of her grief break and she sobbed into the starched white cotton of his shirt-front as he held her close.

'Poor Otis. What a damned thing. You were very close, weren't you?'

Recovering now, she blew her nose and mopped her tears. 'He was more than my uncle, he was my brother, my friend, and he was a second father. He loved me, he spoilt me, he could make me do things that my ma never could. Oh, George, I did love him, he was such *fun*. I just cannot imagine him as a corpse. He didn't want to go back, he thought it was so awful and unnecessary, but he had such loyalty to his men.'

George Moth smoothed away trails of her hair, and for a moment he was back again, smoothing back tendrils of Anne's fine blonde hair. He pressed Otis gently to him, she was warm and soft and vulnerable. For all her career, her independence, her conversion to radicalism, she was as feminine and womanly as Anne had been.

If only one could go back.

He would go back to that evening in 1910, when he and Anne had been getting ready to go out to see a play. How Anne had loved a play. She had lost a little weight and had asked him to retie the laces at the back of her corset. Looking over her shoulder whilst facing the mirror, he had glimpsed her small breasts, and she, having caught the look in his eye, had drawn him down to the llama-skin rug where she had given herself to him, he still wearing full evening dress. When he had got up again, they discovered that llama hairs were scattered over his black suit from shoulder to ankle. They had been late for the play because of the time it had taken them to pick off the hairs. All evening, each time they had caught one another's eye, they had exchanged smiles, felt smug and separate, they had been a couple. That was the time she had conceived Kitt. That was the time when the trigger of his heart-eating loneliness was depressed. That was the time Anne's doom was sealed ready for the bullet to be released in Southsea nine months later. How he missed her.

The kettle boiled furiously. He drew a few inches away. 'I will make your tea.' His voice came out unexpectedly thick. He coughed.

She shook her head. 'Not for a minute.'

He reached over and turned down the gas jet.

He was such a large, broad man that, as he bent over to lower her head to rest on the pillow, her entire field of vision encompassed only him. It was as though she was observing another person, seeing that the woman was in an emotional state, noticing that she was vulnerable to the strong man who was being caring and gentle with her. She observed too that the woman had wanted him, and had waited a long time for her full-blooded desire to be satisfied.

His face was close: she noticed that individual hairs in his whiskers were white, and there were small broken veins in his cheeks, but until now she had never noticed that his eyes were almost green. In herself she observed that uncontrollable glands were working overtime so that she had to swallow, she was aware of the raising of her breasts, the tightening of her thighs and the shortening of her breath.

She observed that Otis Hewetson wanted most desperately to be made love to and that, at that moment, it would not have mattered very much who the man was. That it was George Moth seemed somehow inevitable. If she was to make the journey from virginity to womanhood, then why not with him?

She pulled him to her and kissed him on the mouth. She felt his hands on her body, drawing off her clothes, felt the bed sag as he braced his weight on his arms, heard the soft, dull sound of him unbuttoning, felt a most luscious warmth of his flesh approaching her own.

With a sudden movement like an unsprung coil, she flicked herself away from him and rolled on to the floor. For a second she thought that he was about to descend upon her and take her anyway.

'No!'

For long moments neither of them moved, then she rose and pulled her clothes to rights. Slowly, in heavy silence, he turned away from her and did likewise. The room was humid with steam and the kettle rattled emptily. She turned off the gas-ring and automatically poured what water there was into the pot.

Facing him she said, 'I am sorry, George. I . . .'

'There are names for girls like you.'

The silence was heavy with suppressed emotions. He breathed heavily.

'I had no intention of playing the coquette.'

'Coquette! Have you any idea . . . ?'

He indicated that he would like to use her comb.

She fingered the teacups, not knowing what to do or say. She really had wanted him. No . . . she had really wanted the ultimate comfort of what she felt was a missing part of herself. To be joined with a man at that moment would have been to fit the last piece of a thousand-piece jigsaw puzzle. The satisfaction, the relief would be great. As great, perhaps, would be the regret after it was over, when the only remaining great experience would be death.

'Are you angry with me?'

He heaved a breath and slapped his knees. 'Angry? I don't know. I can't think. Yes. I'm angry.'

'I am sorry.'

'I wanted you. Most men would not have let you off so easily. They'd have finished what *you* started.'

'I'm sorry.'

'Don't keep saying so. You saved your honour,' he frowned. 'Isn't that it? Saved your honour from a lecherous old man?'

For long seconds she was silent. 'I did want you.'

He looked sharply at her, but she was not mocking him.

Suddenly the anger seemed to disappear from his voice. 'Old enough to be your father.'

'I don't see you like that.'

'Do you want me to go?'

'I feel a little awkward – you understand? I must go home.'

'I suppose that it is I who should be saying "sorry".' He picked up his hat and cane. 'I intended . . . I really only wanted to comfort you.' He shook his head. 'No, that's not true, at first I wanted that . . . then I desired you. Very much. I make no apologies for desiring you, only for taking advantage of the situation. You have everything, *everything* any man could wish to find in a woman. And I have wanted you for a long time.'

Absently, she poured tea into one of the cups. A kind of normality began returning. 'You have comforted me. I feel able to go home now and comfort my pa. He will be devastated, quite devastated. Hewey was years younger – like a son. I believe that I was crying for Pa's loss as much as for my own.' She sipped the tea: it tasted bitter but good. At last she let her eyes reach his and was surprised to see that he was unchanged. 'Why did you come?'

'It doesn't matter now. You have your own troubles. But I should be glad if you would come and visit Esther.'

Somehow they had agreed on this strange formality to cope with the situation: no matter that it might be ludicrous, it did work so long as they avoided looking at one another.

'Of course. I should have gone to see her before this, but I have so many commitments. I am trying to teach French to a few children – out of school hours. It is not the kind of thing that is popular around here, but I keep trying.'

He smiled to himself. French to little North London terrors? She really was so naïve, believing that she could change the world, change people by giving them what they didn't even know they wanted.

She said, 'If you want to have some of this tea . . . I have missed the buses that connect now, there is not another for forty-five minutes. Tell me about Esther, is she still badly grieving?'

When he had finished telling her how bereft she was, Otis saw how serious Esther's condition might become, but half an hour had passed and she had to leave. 'I shall come directly after this weekend. We must do something to get her out of this. I think for a start you should get a companion to live in. The nurse is not enough, Esther needs a capable older person. Someone who can stand in for her mother.'

'She would never agree.'

'I have an idea. I don't know if it would work out or whether she would . . .'

'Anything.'

'Ask Esther if she would like Nancy Dickenson to come and stay for a while. I think that she will agree, and I believe that I may be able to persuade Nancy to come.'

She refused his offer of a cab, so he carried her bag to the omnibus depot. When she boarded she kissed him lightly on the cheek and said, 'Forgive me. It would have been good. I hope that I shall not always fly away like that at the last moment. But – well, my career is vital to me. I will make sacrifices to protect it.'

The physician intended kindness.

'You must forget it, my dear Mrs Blood. Do not think of it as a baby, as a child. You lost a foetus which was unformed and but a few inches long. Spontaneous abortion is by no means uncommon. If you had gone full-term it may well have been born defective.'

Esther stared at him, her lips tight-drawn into an acquiescent smile. His words had no meaning: at least, what meaning they might have had was rejected by her own interpretation of what had happened to her.

Bindon was dead and she had been carrying inside her all that was left of him, a piece of his very tissue. That one time when he had loved her, he had given her the last of his life-force. Part of him had sought out the part that she carried and made it a whole being. Together they had made that tiny nucleus of the new baby. Of Tim! Bindon's son, Tim.

'Believe me, dear lady, you will recover more quickly if you will only make an effort. One understands the entirely beneficial grieving period for a husband, but it is not natural to grieve for something that was not yet a formed human . . .'

How could you know, you have never felt the struggle of the father's element to reach its destiny. I knew at the very moment that I had conceived; I felt the changes happen within hours. I knew that Tim was inside me. I felt his soul enter and knew his name was Tim. He was not a foetus, an unformed human.

The physician saw the smile and was glad that his words had persuaded this sad and tragic little lady to give up the unhealthy notion that she must grieve over a lump of tissue long ago disposed of by the nurse.

Esther said that she would follow his advice when he said that she should remain in her father's house with her little girl until she was returned to full health, then she might return to Mere: pick up the threads of her life once more.

But the threads of her life were not there to be picked up. They were destroyed, burnt away by Lysol, burnt in the domestic boiler. She was horror-stricken at the thought of ever returning to Mere, and London had become a most dreadful place in which Bindon's body lay in an ignominious grave. In an effort to steel herself to it, time and again she rehearsed in her mind the scene where she with Baby and Kitt and Nursey would arrive at the front door of Mere, mount the steps and enter. Each time the house is a chamber of desolation and emptiness. Every tuft of carpet, every dust mote is as much infused with Bindon as with his absence. She can never go back. Any more than she can remain here.

No one notices as they walk by, at least if they do they do not take much account of it as Esther, seated beside the water in Kensington Gardens, eats from a box of expensive chocolates. She has prepared well. There are twenty Floris cream-centred chocolates given to her by her father and twenty tablets of salicylic acid she bought on her way here. With each chocolate she eats a tablet. She eats her way through the entire box.

As she begins to lose consciousness, she thinks of Kitt and how sweet he had looked in his little overall ready for his first day at kindergarten. And Baby . . . *I should never have given her that name* . . .

It is warm in the sunshine of Kensington Gardens. Passers-by see a lady who has been indulging herself, perhaps secretly, with a box of cream-centre chocolates and then dozing beneath the trees. The box slips from her lap.

A soldier, on crutches and wearing hospital blue, picks up the box and tries to return it. When she does not respond, he places it upon the seat beside her and in doing so sees that she is clutching a chemist's box. He understands the signs, having thought of that avenue of escape himself not long ago. Quickly collecting the evidence of the aspirin box, he stops some passers-by and asks for assistance for the lady who appears to have suffered some kind of seizure.

Nancy Dickenson handed the official postcard back to May Archer.

'I think that's terrible. Not even an envelope?'

'No. Just as is. Walter Archer, Missing, believed killed. See, they crossed out "in action" – rubbing salt into the wounds. My poor Wally, he was a good boy and they treated him like shit just because he never wanted to kill nobody. When he called men Brothers or Comrades, he meant it. He never wanted to shoot none of them, yet there was some that come and chucked dog-muck at the windows and we had offal in the yard more 'n once. He'd say don't blame 'em for their ignorance, Mum, one day they'll see that I'm right.' She wiped her eyes. She had not cried over Wally, but her nose had run and her eyes had not been dry for all day.

'I know, May, it's what made me like him better than any man I met. But I'm not going to talk about him as though he's gone. It does say "believed" killed. We've got to hope.'

'I never set much store on hoping things would get better. I taught Wally that. If you want things to get better, I used to tell him, then you damn well got to get out there and do something about it. It's landed him in trouble a time or two, but it's the truth, Nance, isn't it?'

'It's the truth, May.'

'If it wasn't then I couldn't live with myself, because it was me bringing him up like that what made him get into unions and politics.'

'I'll let you take the credit for making such a good sort of man, but you don't take any blame for his conscience. He's a big grown-up man, and he makes up his own mind.'

'He do, Nance, don't he?'

'There you are, love, you said that as though he was still alive, which he just as likely is. You know your Wally.' She gave the scraggy old lady a brief hug.

'Right, Nance. I know my Wally, he just as likely will come turning up like a bad penny. I ain't counting on it, but you're right. I shan't give away his good boots or his coat or nothing like that.'

'Nor his books. He'll never forgive you if he got back and found you'd got rid of his books.'

The two women comforted one another, each keeping their end up for the other. They had both known enough death and disappointment in life to know not to let it drag you down.

'You'll come and see me when you start your new job. It's a long way away up Hampstead.'

'Of course I shall. It's not really far, a couple of twopenny tram rides.'

'I don't know why you want to go back into service. You're your own woman on the trams. I like to see that. It's one reason I took to you straight away.'

'I just feel that I've got to do it. It's like I'm the only one who can do the job. It's not like going back as I used to be. I knew the family years ago. The mother died in labour and now the daughter has lost one straight after her husband taking Lysol.'

'That's a terrible death. I once saw a woman who done that, she was a dreadful mess.'

'This one, the girl – well, woman she is now – she took something: aspirin I think it must have been.'

'I'm glad you ain't the sort to do nothing stupid like that, Nance. Money people never know how to stand up to things.'

'They don't usually get that much to stand up to, so they don't have as many lessons as you and me.'

'What she want you to do?'

'I don't know, just keep an eye on things according to what the father said. I don't even know the daughter wants me. I never hardly knew him in the old days, but the wife was the sweetest thing, and so was the daughter then. I'll have to be off now, May, she's coming out of the nursing home and the father wants me there when she comes.'

'Be a court case will there? Attempted suicide.'

'Father's a high-up in the police.'

'Oh well, 'nough said. He'll hush it up somehow.'

In Stormont Road, heavy plush curtains were drawn across the windows at the front of Greywell and an old-fashioned black-ribboned laurel wreath hung on the door as though a funeral was about to take place.

Emily Hewetson accepted her daughter's kiss and let her chafe her hands affectionately as she sat in the still, silent sitting-room where what Otis thought of as a kind of small shrine containing little mementoes of Max Hewetson had been set up on a table. A photogravure of Max in a wicker bassinet, taken with Martin; another of him holding the scroll of his law degree, and a third as an officer holding his cap in the crook of his arm. A medal ribbon, pocket watch, an army cap and swagger-stick, his own silver cigarette case engraved M.C.H., the silver and coral scent bottle which had been his present to Emily last Christmas, and the impressive thistle table decoration he had given to Martin and Emily as a wedding present – paid for on his mother's account because he was then still a boy.

Otis stood before the arrangement and picked up the photogravure of Max in uniform. 'Oh Ma, poor Max, are these his remains?' She heard Emily's sharp snort of irritation but did not turn. To Otis, none of this said anything at all about her uncle, about Hewey Hewetson. What it said was that a baby had been pushed in a bassinet, a stiff-backed and serious-looking young man had once worn cap and gown, and a stiff-backed and pompous-looking older man had been photographed wearing army uniform.

What would have befitted Otis's memory of her Uncle Hewey would have been the Tippoo Badminton set and the Bumblepuppy pole he had brought in and set up in the back garden one wonderful summer; the Flexible Flyer toboggan that could swish downhill on the grass of the Heath; the set of nursery-tale magic-lantern slides, or the boxed football game of 'Kick' which Ma had wanted to return to the Army and Navy Stores. But even as she thought of these and the many other surprises with which he had been bounding into the house for as long as she could remember – books, boxes of Little Mary wafers and petit-fours, tickets for plays, ideas for pleasant weekend expeditions – she saw that, without Hew's enthusiasm and sense of fun, those objects too would have lain there as lifeless as the swagger-stick and portraits.

'How is Pa taking it? Where is he?'

'He has gone to his office, and he is bearing up as one would expect. This same tragedy is visited upon many households at present. It is the supreme sacrifice for one's country.'

'Mother, I wish that you would not talk like that. It is cloying and insincere. *You* have made no sacrifice: it is Max who is dead.'

Emily Hewetson stiffened. 'Otis, I have put up with much over these last five years. I was against you going to that college, but your father saw no harm. I was shocked when you said that you were going to take a teaching post. I cannot even begin to tell you how it affected me when your father broke the news that he had agreed to your taking rooms in . . . in . . . of *all* places *that* part of London. Oh, but he *would* have it that all young ladies of the New Style were idealists and that they must have their opportunities. I have *never* held with his liberal way of thinking. And I have been proved right: it has been the ruination of you.'

'Oh Ma, please don't talk such silly and over-dramatic nonsense. I am not ruined.'

'Not ruined? When a daughter describes her own mother as silly?'

'If you will only think of it, Ma, you will realize that I have never said that you *were* those things – I said that you *talk* like that, you *say* them. You are like too many women, utterances pop out of your mouth without the slightest consideration. The drawn curtains, the wreath and black ribbons, this shrine to Max . . .'

Scornfully, 'It's not a shrine. All these things are tokens of respect because there can be no funeral.'

'Oh *Mother!* They are to impress the people whom you have probably invited for sherry after the memorial service.'

'Is that what you think?' Suddenly Emily Hewetson's composed face crumpled. Tears welled in her eyes, hung there glistening and then trickled into the dip of her eye-sockets where they were absorbed by the dabbing of her ylang-ylang scented handkerchief.

'Do you not know how to be womanly, Otis?'

At one and the same time, Otis wanted both to shake her mother and to comfort her. She *did* say silly and shallow things because it was expected, but she said them because to do so was in her nurturing and upbringing.

Otis suddenly thought of her maternal grandmother on the occasions when she had been taken to visit on her birthdays. Seated on a *chaise-longue* surrounded by her dozen children, helpless and cosseted, her life given to making as complicated a toilette as was possible before visiting or receiving other, equally cosseted, queen bees. A baby a year for twelve years and a lifetime of fittings, curling tongs, idle gossip and a husband who was seldom in the presence of his children except to oversee that they fitted the moulds of Empire Builder and Empire Builder's adornment.

Emily really had never stood a chance of being other than she was.

Otis realized that her own salvation had been a kindly father with liberal views and a carefree uncle who was close to her own age.

The sharp retort – And I have no intention of being womanly – that she had been about to make, disintegrated as she knelt down and put her arms about her mother's knees. 'I know that my tongue is too sharp, Ma. Things are out before I realize. I am sorry.'

She looked up to receive her mother's forgiveness and met Emily's unguarded gaze. It was snatched away at once, but for that second, Otis saw that her mother's grief was genuine and deep – much deeper and more affecting than one should expect for a brother-in-law. Otis, rising from her knees, went and sat beside her mother and, putting an arm about her neck, drew her on to her shoulder as though she herself was the mother comforting the child. Amazingly, Emily allowed herself to collapse, and she buried her face in her hands and sobbed silently.

'Oh, my poor, poor Ma. Hew . . .' She cut off what had almost slipped from her mouth about her mother and her uncle.

With that one glimpse into her mother's unshuttered mind, suddenly many things came clear. Grains of evidence, assembled from years of childhood observations, behaved like grains of silver nitrate under the action of developing fluid and an image came up.

Otis had been very young, and Max could not have been much out of boyhood, when she, awake but quiet in her nursery cot, had watched him unfasten Emily's hair and bury his face in it and Emily had twisted around and, holding his ears, had kissed him tenderly. Then at some other time she had seen him in his shirt-tails in Emily's boudoir, whereupon, seeing Otis watching from the landing that connected to the nursery, her mother had said that Uncle Max had a nasty boil that needed a plaster. Suddenly she remembered all the many other pats and strokes. One

Christmas, when they had all gone carol-singing, Otis had watched by the lantern-light Uncle Hewey's hand slowly sliding upwards under her ma's bodice. Otis guessed that they felt that they were safe enough flirting in the presence of a young child, and so they were – until the long processing of the photographic plate was completed by Emily's grief.

Emily guessed that she had given herself away to her clever daughter. What mattered? She had loved the boy, and not in the way she ought. The punishment for illicit love has always been that the lovers have no rights to public grief. She had loved him since he was little more than a schoolboy and she a newly-married young woman. She had always been too old for him, but he absolutely denied it, asking what difference the comparative ages of flesh and bone made when sensitivity was ageless.

He would touch her – she shivered at the thought: Do you feel that, Em? Which is your skin and which is mine? Which is the boy's and which the woman's? He was so *very* youthful and exuberant, yet with such an old head on those young shoulders. There had been times when it had seemed that their positions were reversed, that he was the responsible older one and she in giddy youth.

Their mild affair harmed no one. The one time when they had almost come to the point of burning their boats and turning the romance into an affaire, was when he had asked her to put a dressing on his back, and it had turned out not to be his back, but his thigh. Although he had still worn his underwear, she had seen that he was no longer a youth, but had abundant body hair and was fully masculine. How for a long minute she had had to restrain her own hands from reaching out to touch him. How fearful it had all been. Yet, how exhilarating. She had felt like an elegant courtesan in a French novel.

Otis said, 'He was the kind of man it would be difficult not to love, Ma. Everybody liked him.'

308

Without thinking, Emily's hand went to the locket that rested in the fold of georgette between her breasts.

Otis, guessing rightly that the locket contained not only Martin's portrait, but that of Max also, was surprised that she did not feel outrage for her pa, nor anger at those moments of deception. What was outrageous was Max's death.

'You don't *have* to go to the memorial service, Ma. It will be no end of an ordeal.'

The portcullis on their brief intimacy was lowered. 'I *do* have to, Otis. That is the difference between us. You do what pleases you, whilst I do my duty.'

At the memorial service held in the little Wren church in Piccadilly that had, according to Emily, been Max's favourite place to sit and ponder, Otis watched her mother behaving with perfect poise and graciousness to his friends and colleagues. When it came to the small reception at home, Otis did her duty as daughter of the house and then gathered her things and went quietly out to catch a bus, knowing that if Emily lived to be a hundred they would never again come as close as they had come that afternoon. It was the apogee of their friendship – from that point it could only fall away.

When Esther Blood opened her eyes after one of the particularly heavy and dreamless slumbers she experienced from time to time since her 'trouble', she was again puzzled about time and place. When this happened, she kept her eyes shut and sifted through what evidence she had to discover her present whereabouts. For a brief moment she had thought that she was in the little back room in the cottage at Southsea and that it was morning and she was being aroused by Nancy.

Then the whole span of the intervening years fell upon her and she uttered a small groan.

'You all right, ma'am?'

It *had* been Nancy Dickenson who had placed the cup of tea at her bedside. And then it came back to her that her father had persuaded her to promise that she would take on Nancy to help out whilst Esther was still suffering the effects of her trouble.

'Nancy?'

'Yes, Mrs Blood, ma'am. Nancy Dickenson turned up like a bad sixpence.'

Esther, who had taken a potion and fallen asleep fully-dressed, sat up and held out her hand. 'Welcome, Nancy.'

'Thank you, ma'am, I'm glad to be here, though I'm sorry you've had such trouble. Here, drink this tea, it's strong and sweet and it'll buck you up. I thought you might like to have a bit of a walk out . . . The master says you haven't done much walking of late.'

310

'No. My illness made my legs weak.' She took the tea and drank some of it.

'All the more reason to take a bit of exercise.'

'When did you come? I get a bit confused at times. I fell asleep and woke up to hear you in the room – I thought we were back at Southsea.'

'I've only been here half an hour or so, but there's no sense in hanging about doing nothing, so I thought I'd see what was what with you.'

'Well, that's nice of you, Nancy. Do you know where Kitt and Baby are?'

'The nanny has taken Stephanie out in her perambulator to meet Master Kitt from kindergarten. I haven't seen the little boy, but your baby is the very sweetest thing you ever saw. You are very fortunate to have her.'

Esther made no reply but concentrated upon drinking her tea. Nancy – starting as she meant to go on – sat on an upright chair beside the window that overlooked a very pleasant garden. She had made up her mind to bring the sad and broken Mrs Blood back from the brink where the apparent blessedness of oblivion had enticed her. Nancy, remembering the very nice sort of girl that she had been that summer at Garden Cottage, wanted nothing better than to make her want to live again.

'You've had a rough time, ma'am. What happened to you shouldn't happen to a dog.'

'You know about my husband?'

'Yes, and losing your baby . . . and the poor man. Life must have been so terrible for him to have gone like that, and terrible for you to have lost his child. I sometimes has to wonder what sort of a God it is that does such things to us.'

'Oh, Nancy, what a relief to hear someone acknowledge that. It is terrible to have your husband go mad, and it was a baby that I lost. I never imagined anything so terrible. And I do want to talk about them.'

The stones that had rested upon her chest for so long

moved a little, allowing her to inhale freely for the first time in a long time.

'Now, ma'am, if you'll tell me where you keep your stout walking shoes, we'll be off.'

And they were. Like a steam-roller, Nancy rolled over any of Esther's objections to venturing out. In a very short space of time they were walking in the park.

'If you want to hold my arm, that's all right, but it would be nice if we could keep going for half an hour. We'll have a rest then. Is there a little tea-house in this park?'

'A kind of kiosk that serves trays, somewhere through the rose-garden.'

'Right, that shall be our prize at the end, tea in the rose-garden.'

They walked steadily, and after the first five minutes Esther tucked her fingers into Nancy's elbow. Nancy, pulling the young, frail hand closer, held it firmly.

'Just now you said, "the poor man" – about my husband, about Bindon. People behave as though he was a criminal. The war did cruel things to him. They would not give him a Christian grave, you know.'

'Some people are bigoted and wouldn't know an injured creature from a sack of beans if it fell at their feet. What do they think, that a person takes their own life on a whim? People have got too much to live for on this world to want to give it up easy. It must be hard to do that, and needs some guts if you'll pardon the expression. There's too many laws made by people who don't know any better and they make criminals out of good people.'

Esther stopped walking and looked at her paid companion/keeper. 'Nancy, do you *really* think that? You're not just saying it to raise my spirits.'

'If you knew Nancy Dickenson a bit better, then you'd know that I don't just *say*. I might come out with some half-cocked things at times, but I don't never say anything I don't mean.'

'Oh Nancy! If only you knew how they all keep shutting me up when I want to say something . . . to explain. You do have to be brave, and a bit crazy, and it is so terrifying when you are doing it that it is only the craziness that keeps you going.'

'Well, ma'am, I can't say I ever felt that low. I've been very pulled down at times, but never quite that much.'

'Do you mind talking like this?'

'No, ma'am. Better out than in, if you ask me. I suppose nobody will let you talk about it.'

'Father, and the doctor and nurses, they say that it is morbid and that I should turn my thoughts to the nice things that there are in the world, and I can see that. I can see that Kitt is a nice, funny little boy and that Baby is pretty and delightful . . .' Her fingers were so tight that they were almost pinching as she held on to Nancy. 'But it is as though I cannot get through into the world where Kitt and Baby are living. Can you understand that?'

'Yes. I understand that very well, and it's my belief that the way to break through into their world is to get rid of what is tying you to the world where you try to eat a whole boxful of aspirin.'

Nancy felt her charge flinch and guessed that no one had said the thing outright.

'May we sit down please, Nancy?'

'Well, all right, but not for too long.'

'Nobody at all has mentioned the aspirin. They talked about somebody finding some "medication", but they speak now as though I ate a box of contaminated chocolates and it was that which made me ill. Yet they know and I know about the aspirin. Father, of course, cannot say anything because of his position, and my physician cannot admit to having colluded in covering up the facts. I don't know whether my father has paid him money or whether there is some other reason he has not reported my "illness".' She closed her eyes and turned her face in the direction of the

313

sun like a worshipper. 'Nancy, Nancy, you don't know the relief to be saying these things.'

Nancy smiled and thought of the way that she and Wally's mum had torn the world to shreds about the way they and Wally had been treated. Nancy had cried and May had comforted. May had railed against the world and Nancy had supported her. Nancy knew that she had a good few tears yet to shed over Wally, but she knew that at May Archer's she had a place in which she could shed them and in which she could get and give comfort.

'Come on, Miss Esther, let's see if we can get those legs of yours back in some sort of fit state to walk proper again.' She smiled. She wanted to hug the poor little love-hungry woman.

So why not hug? What were they but two women, each of whom had lost the man they had loved above all else and who had been loved in return. So Nancy Dickenson, in a brief but sincere clasp, gave Esther what she needed most at that moment, warm and spontaneous human contact. 'To the rose-garden, ma'am? I believe it won't be long before you are back on your feet again.'

'You are right, Nancy. I believe your walking cure is going to work.'

'Not "walking" cure, ma'am – "talking" cure. Let's you and me have a pact to be open with each other. You needn't worry that I shall step over the mark, I know better than that.'

'My husband's name was Bindon, do you think you could say it to me sometimes? If nobody ever says the name Bindon Blood, then it will be as though he never existed. Do you understand?'

'I understand. Have you still got some of his things? Maybe we could, I don't know, go over them sometimes. It's no bad thing to keep a jacket or pair of boots about in the place where they've always been.'

'What is left of Bindon's things are in Lyme. My father

314

gave away everything he had brought here; he said that it was morbid to want to keep things . . . but do you know, I notice so much the empty spaces his things have left.'

'If that's where his things are, then maybe we should go to Lyme once you are on your feet again.'

Esther smiled, something she had not done in a long time.

Victoria Ormorod stood in the bookshop and felt no usual lift of her spirits at the thought of what they had achieved in so short a time. Since Otis Hewetson had joined them, Victoria had had no need to give the running of the place a second thought. Nancy's work with local mothers had been taken over by Annie, who never used a euphemism to them where a four-letter word would do better. Danny Turner had got the underground escape route well-organized. What was there left that Victoria could legitimately say required her presence? The public speaking? Recently she had felt that she had said her piece so many times that the fire was going out of it. It was not that she had lost any of her conviction – rather, the need for a negotiated peace was confirmed daily in the long lists of Dead and Missing columns.

Recently too she had found herself thinking about Jack Moth, thinking and worrying about him. She had been right to reject his idea of marriage, yet her liking and the physical attraction that he held for her had deepened in his absence. She told herself that it was only just that. The old adage: Absence makes the heart grow fonder. She decided that she would write to him, but first she had to obtain his latest address.

Finding herself one morning in the vicinity of Scotland Yard, on the spur of the moment she went to enquire whether she could see Superintendent Moth. Local intelligence sources had informed her that there was now a large department devoting its energies to the suppression and confusion of the anti-war lobby, a situation that intrigued her no end.

Superintendent Moth himself opened the door to her.

'Miss Ormorod. To what do I owe . . . ?'

'Thank you for seeing me, I shall not take two minutes of your time, Superintendent.'

He had noticed it at Mere: she did not come into a room, she made an entrance, a foible that both irritated and intrigued him. It had never occurred to him that he too was given to making entrances and keeping centre stage. His height and broadness as well as his fine hair and good looks usually guaranteed this; but any man could be outshone by a woman with feminine beauty, erect carriage and presence. This time he did not mind, for there was something in her that he found stimulating. It was that same challenging thing that he found in Otis Hewetson.

Independent women. Strong. Arrogant. They had the presumption to try to change the established order to suit their own sex. Like Anne, they had set their faces against convention.

'I have more than two minutes.' He indicated a comfortable chair. 'Please sit down. It is my time of day to take a cup of tea. I have a man who makes a very good brew.'

She accepted, sitting very erect yet seemingly at ease.

'I came to ask after Jack.'

'Mercifully, he is still whole.'

'And to ask you for his present address.'

'Ah. You haven't got it?'

'No. Jack and I had decided against continuing our . . .' She baulked at any definition of what their relationship had been – she scarcely knew herself.

'Sons seldom confide in their fathers.'

A young constable brought in a tray with a teapot and two cups, poured and offered one to Victoria, which she accepted.

George Moth wrote down the address and brought it round to where Victoria was sitting. There he hooked his buttocks on to the edge of his desk and propped himself up on his long legs.

She now saw herself disadvantaged because she either had to look up at him or to keep her eyes level and allow her gaze to fall upon the trousered part of his torso, or to look down. She had wondered, before today, whether men who took this stance were showing thoughtlessness, aggression, subjection of the other party, or plain exhibitionism. She had to admit that if the latter, then Jack's father had a good figure to exhibit. Victoria Ormorod never let herself be bested when it came to the male showing who is master of the situation.

She arose so that, when standing, she was now in the dominant position: her closeness to him would have meant that he must extricate himself rather than simply move away. She handed him her cup and saucer so that he now had two. 'Thank you. You are right, the constable does know how to make a good brew of tea.' She stretched the fingers of the gloves she was holding and began to ease one on to her long-fingered hands. 'I wondered how Nancy is getting along. I know that she has given up her work to help in your household.'

'She is getting along very well indeed, she has done my daughter a world of good.'

'Your gain is our loss.'

'It will not be for ever.'

Because he showed no surprise that she should know Nancy, Victoria was now assured that he was *au fait* with the lives of the members of their group. But did he know that Otis was corresponding with Jack?

He swivelled round to place the two cups on his desk, but still did not attempt to move his position where his feet almost touched the hem of Victoria's skirt and where his eyes were almost level with hers.

There was a brief moment of solid silence, during which she observed at close range his healthy, ruddy complexion. In his forties Jack would look like this. His long legs would grow more solid and lose their litheness, the girth of his thighs would increase slightly at the same time as his flat abdomen would become rounded and his breasts pappy and flecked with white hairs. Momentarily she visualized the comfort there might be from having such a man in one's life in middle age. But Jack had wanted marriage. His profession was such that it would brook no scandal of an irregular liaison.

In that same pause, George Moth noticed that hidden here and there in that great, provocative bundle of dark, coppery hair were one or two creamy-white hairs. At the outer edges of her eyes were fine lines, and in the skin beneath her lower, heavily-lashed lids there was a suggestion of crêpiness. In his view nothing made a woman appear so vulnerable as the work of age upon her eyes. His gaze travelled down from her fine, straight nose, over her lips made fuller by the small exaggeration of her upper teeth, to her beautiful neck and to where her bosom swelled out beneath the white blouse and cream-coloured jacket. Feeling her eyes upon him he raised his own and encountered her direct gaze.

It was here in those brief moments of locked gaze that the two personalities clashed. Hers daring him to make one false move, his trying to force her to retreat.

Old adversaries.

On the female side, every wife who dared to stand up to her husband; every priestess who tried to steal back power; every bright girl who struck out against the tyranny of domesticity; every woman who, when religion became infiltrated by a harsh maleness, turned her back on it and returned to gentle witchery and older deities; every bride who secreted within her body a certain physick-soaked moss or sponge.

319

And opposing – every male who would prevent it happening; every priest and father and groom who was assured that he had a God-given right to supremacy.

Such women need strong men to dominate them.

It was the damned woman herself, with her assuredness and composure, who drew those thoughts from the dark part of his mind. He had a momentary vision of her, tousle-haired and heavy-lidded.

These men who have an air of assurance about them: Jack, George Moth . . . Tankredi.

The gaze unlocked and allowed their eyes to move to safety. Victoria, feeling that she had been holding her breath under water, drew in air. George Moth went to speak but found his voice-box momentarily cracked. He cleared his throat.

She moved away, freeing him to cross to the window where he appeared to be casually looking down. 'May I ask you something, Superintendent?'

'Of course.'

'Is it true that you are the head of the special department which deals with people like myself – members of the International League?'

She noticed his ears move and wanted to ask him whether he knew that this was a primitive ability that few people now had. Tell him that she too had that ability and that it denoted wariness. The ears relaxed.

'I don't know about people like yourself, Miss Ormorod, but I do have men under me whose work is to uphold the Defence of the Realm Act.'

'Oh dear, how disappointing.' She behaved as though fishing for a compliment. 'I had always considered myself to be some kind of disturbance.'

He turned, looked at her for a long moment, then said, 'Victoria, I may tell you that you are certainly considered to be that.'

'Thank you, Superintendent Moth. I should go. I have

signatures that must be collected for the Prime Minister.' She smiled provocatively. 'As I am sure you are aware.'

On her way to catch the tram she replayed the ending of the scene. If Victoria Ormorod knew anything, she knew the strengths and weakness of her adversaries, she had observed them at meetings and played them on long lines. As far as the set-up in North London was concerned, George Moth's strength was his power and authority; his weakness, she was convinced, was that he liked George Moth better than any other human being, and he liked to indulge him.

In regard to his sexual desires, he was probably like other dominating men she had known: he would always go after what was rare or taboo in his society, such as a woman of a much higher or much lower class, a black girl, a girl young enough to be his daughter or a woman old enough to be his mother, or a woman who was diametrically opposed to his views. He savoured a challenge.

She scrunched up the paper on which Jack Moth's address was written. It was a long time since a man had provoked her. For a good many months now she had been attracted only to strong women of her own kind . . . And to Jack Moth. But having seen beyond the police chief, beyond the father, and into George Moth the sensuous man, Victoria Ormorod realized the son was only the shadow whereas the man with forty years of experience of life was the substance.

From his window, George Moth watched her make her way into the street. He felt stimulated and pleased. He smiled. *She didn't come for Jack's address, she came to challenge me. She's a woman who is not alive if she doesn't have a challenge.* He had liked Otis Hewetson's brand of independent woman, but *this* woman . . . Otis faded beside her. But not Effee Tessalow. Recently he had spent more and more time at Effee's. She too was a woman who was not afraid of him, who challenged his authority by refusing to be dependent upon him and, although she said that he came first, she would not give up the other men who came discreetly into her rooms.

Jack Moth was recovering from a bullet-wound in the chest.

An inch or two one way, the bullet would have hit his heart and he would have made the Killed in Action list; an inch or two the other way and it would have been a simple flesh wound which, after attention at a dressing-station, would have enabled him to return at once to the fighting. As it was, the bullet nicked the left lobe of his lung, causing a 'Blighty' wound.

He had done the journey by railway to Le Havre in a state of nervous exhaustion and high fever, which was only slightly improved on the sickening crossing to Southampton. Because he spent the first fortnight of his confinement to a hospital in Essex in a state of almost constant delirium, visitors had been forbidden. George Moth had made the journey and forcefully got himself on to the wards, but he had soon seen that the medical staff were right: Jack was just recovering from an operation and was in no state to cope with anything except staying alive. Not only that, Jack had not recognized his father or known his own name or where he was.

George Moth was told in no uncertain terms that to give his son a chance of recovery he must stay away until the convalescent period. He had returned to London subdued and shaken. In the space of months he had seen two of his three children in a state close to death, and his son-in-law dead – all three youthful faces grown skeletal as a direct result of the war. On the train journey to visit his son he had sunk into himself, thinking how clean and simple, in comparison to the complex deaths caused by this war, was a passionate knife across the throat – the type of death that he used to investigate in the old days. One could do *something* about murder or rape; even if there was no satisfactory outcome, at least one was turning over stones. With a murder investigation he went out to look for the source of violence, but this national violence had come and sat upon his doorstep and he was helpless to do anything to turn it away.

Jack Moth knew that this stay in Lys House was only a brief respite, but for the present he was louse-free and not only slept in a bed, but in a bed with clean sheets. He knew that there was a gap in his memory. He could remember nothing of the late autumn of last year until the train journey to Le Havre.

'It is not an unusual phenomenon, Jack,' the doctor had said, 'A shock to the nervous system. The present theory is that the mind blots out those events with which it can't cope. It will all return when you are fighting fit. If not, then don't worry, it can't have been a pleasant experience having a bit of one's lung chipped away. Think of your loss of memory as a newly-formed scab – it will protect but irritate. You will probably have an overwhelming desire to worry it, but if you do and it breaks before the wound beneath is healed, then it will bleed painfully, perhaps become infected. If that happens, then it will have to heal all over again and perhaps leave you with a scar.' He had slapped Jack on the back. 'Don't pick it, old man, best not, the mind is a peculiar beast.'

The familiarity of the use of Jack's first name was because the MO had been at Cambridge with Jack and it was he who had thought that a Cambridge graduate and qualified lawyer would be happier convalescing among officers, even though his rank was only that of lance-corporal. And so, unbeknown to Jack, the Medical Officer had pulled strings so that Jack could be nursed in a convalescent home for army officers. It had not occurred to him that Jack preferred to serve in the ranks and had survived many months in the company of the lower orders.

Jack was now resting at Lys House in the depths of rural Hampshire.

Resting, but very jumpy. Every clang of a saucepan echoing up from the kitchens was a gas-attack warning being hammered on a shell case; farmers shooting raiding magpies and pigeons on nearby farms were surprise attacks by the Boche. Even the stillness could bring back to men like Jack, who were in a state of nervous exhaustion, the belief that they were still in the trenches and that the silence was the lull before the enemy stormed over the ridge. Often it was this latter state that caused Jack's loss of memory to make him unnerved. He began to wonder whether it could be something other than a sniper's bullet that had caused the blank weeks.

This was his second week of convalescence and, although his temperature was still high, Jack was now considered to be in a state of recovery and allowed a visitor. As he waited for his visitor to arrive, he walked through the grounds of the crumbling old mansion that had been brought into use as a recovery home.

It was the spring of 1917, and the contrast of this emerald green to that unending landscape of blackened tree-stumps, brown sucking mud and blood-tinged slime in which he had slithered and fought for the past months, was shocking. He wanted to weep with misery that he had only perhaps another few weeks of this peaceful place before he must return.

Like others shocked from their experience of the trenches, he was, as he thought of it, always in two minds. In his daytime mind he read books, wrote letters, talked to other patients and joked with nurses; but the night-time mind was the place where one man's nightmare scream would enter another man's nightmare causing him too to cry out, thus compounding the terror and confusion of both men.

On this spring morning, Jack is easy in his daytime mind, letting thoughts drift as thistledown drifts on a warm breeze. Even though he had the parks of London and more recently the acres of Mere Meldrum, Jack Moth has never been much of a man for thinking about trees and greenery generally. Now, with the sunlight coming through, he notices for the first time that newly unfurled beech leaves have a furry surface; he notices how perfect is the arrangement of a primrose springing from its fan of leaves; he sees wood anemones, lousewort and spurge; hears chiff-chaffs and house-martins; smells violets, crushed ferns and the clover-like leaves of wood sorrel. Of all these he can only put names to the violet, the primrose and the house-martin.

Though had there been poppies he could have named them. *Papaver rhoeas*. Except that I can't say it like Taff with his soft up and down voice.

Crouching in dug-outs and trenches, one discovered that the most unexpected of men had surprising funds of knowledge. Taff – as of course he would be – was a short-legged Welsh coal-miner and a botanist; or was he a botanist who dug coal? Taff and Lofty and . . . somebody? And Chalky and Nipper. And Farmer Giles – who had bowled for his county and could lob a stick bomb straight down the middle – and Leafy Green.

They were a group who had shared tobacco and horror, shared vermin and danger, shared Sergeant Trigg, Sub-Lieutenant Tree and Captain Bush.

There *was* somebody else, he was sure of it . . . who, who, who?

The confusion was one of the worst parts of this malfunction of his mind. The not knowing reality from nightmare, survivors from the dead. It was so debilitating to have to sift through the great mass of sludge that filled his mind to achieve one sure and solid nugget of reality.

He picked at the edge of the scab.

And . . . ? Nipper was a stockinger. I had never heard of a stockinger. How many Southerners know that making stockings is such skilled and well-paid work? Nipper was a geography fanatic: *Flanders is reclaimed bog-land, drained by ditches. Did you know that farmers here can be fined for not keeping up the trenches? Did you know that, Loft?* Looking out over the cratered and blasted landscape with its ditches gone, flooded again: that had caused some laughter.

At first sight of the poppies. Somebody had said that they had never seen such bright poppies. Somebody else said it was all the blood. Blood was a good fertilizer if you could get hold of it. Somebody said: These farmers are going to get rich when we've gone. Free fertilizer. As far as the eye could see the cratered fields had been scarlet.

He thinks of Mere for the first time in months, and wonders what he might sensibly do with the place. Poor Ess doesn't appear to want to return there, and who can blame her? Who would want to rattle round in a great place like that? Quite apart from it being full of memories for her.

He takes a beech leaf, rubs it between his hands, breathing the tangy smell into his lungs, imagining some healing power in the freshness.

Poor Ess. He longs to see her, but the letter he received from his father had said that since Bindon's death she had been under such a considerable strain that she had mis-carried a child. Poor Ess, he couldn't bear to think of all the misery that she had suffered. Perhaps he should ask his father to go ahead and sell Mere and offer Ess enough to buy herself a place of her own.

He wonders how his father would react to that; it must suit him very well to have someone there to be mother to Kitt. And whatever was going to happen to Kitt now? His father loved the child well enough, especially as he looked so much like their mother, but Jack remembers how careless George Moth could be with his children.

Out of sight, out of mind, it had been with himself and Ess. When he was immersed in a case that intrigued him, their father thought nothing of staying away from home for days, perhaps taking a few hours' sleep in the cells, a wash and shave at a barber's shop and out on the streets again, only returning home when his clothes smelt high, and carrying gifts for them all.

But in his absence, their mother had always been there. Was little Kitt to be disposed of to some paid woman until it was time to pack him off to boarding-school? Jack determines to speak with his father and try to get him to see that he must not treat Kitt as he had treated his older children.

Finding a weathered bench beneath a tree at the edge of the wood where it overlooks the rear terrace of the mansion, Jack Moth sits in the spring sunshine and thinks how wonderful it is to have only such sweetly domestic problems to think of.

From behind a net-curtained window, Otis Hewetson stands and looks out at the thin, close-cropped skeletal-faced man seated on a wooden bench, his face turned, like a scarlet pimpernel, directly to the sun. She knows that this is Jack, the doctor has said that it is, and she can see that the long legs stretched before him are long, as Jack's are long.

'He is not fully recovered, but don't worry, old Jack is a survivor.'

Otis frowned sceptically at him.

'Believe me, Miss Hewetson, they come down here looking like corpses, and in weeks they are fit and ready for action once more.'

'And mentally healthy?'

He raises his eyebrows, using the doctor-without-an-answer ploy, and sucks his tongue against his top teeth before he replies, 'I would say that few men who have been in the trenches are entirely . . .' He taps his forehead. 'I think in Jack's case it is nothing too serious. Nature's way of allowing the mind to recover.'

Otis's look penetrates, but he makes no comment.

'Well then?' The doctor rubs his hands together. 'Shall I have an orderly fetch Jack, or shall you go out?'

The few minutes facing into the sun with his eyes closed caused tears to form when he opened them, so that, for a moment, he had the impression of Otis as a shimmering mirage, then the tears overflowed, he saw that she was reality. He got up and went towards her, dragged down on one side by his healing wound.

'Otis. It really is you. I thought I must be day-dreaming.'

Covering her shock at his appearance, she smiled, genuinely pleased to see him, and stretched to kiss him on the cheek. Apart from that day in childhood when they had all floundered in the sea, she could not recall any time when they had touched one another. The slight rasp of his badly-shaven skin seemed to stay upon her lips. When he raised his hand to the place where she had kissed him, she wondered whether he realized that this was a new experience, or whether she had left that irritating cold moistness that some kisses seem to leave.

'Hullo, Jack. I'm sorry that I am not Esther, but the journey might be a bit much for her.'

He indicated that she might like to sit on the bench. His movements were frail and fussy, so unlike Jack Moth. He took her hands in his, the contrasting plumpness of hers making her feel almost embarrassed.

'Poor Ess. I keep thinking of her, is she really down?'

'I have seen really very little of her . . . my job, you know, we get so little free time. This is a mid-term break. Your father says that she is on the mend now. He told you that Nancy Dickenson is there?'

'He did, he did. I think that is wonderful. I hope they realize how fortunate they are. I once heard her speak at a public meeting, you know.'

They smiled at one another, but it was to cover awkwardness. Jack knew how he looked and imagined how she must feel seeing him thus. The ice must be broken: he had written to tell her that he loved her; he remembered that, but not whether she had replied, or even whether it had been sent.

Holding out his hands and turning them this way and that, then smoothing the hollows of his cheeks, he said, 'I shan't be like this for long.'

Earnestly, 'Of course you won't! The doctor says that you are making a remarkable recovery.'

'He told you about my . . . ?' He tapped his head.

'That you had a blank in your memory? He doesn't attach much importance to it.'

'I know. It's just that . . .' He searched around for the right words. 'It is that there must have been *something* if what he says is true. It is the not-knowing what it is. I am supposed not to try to recall it at present, but good Lord, Otis, how can I avoid trying to get back a missing piece of my mind – even though I know that I may have to look into the pit to find it?'

'Perhaps if you think of it as nature's way. It's said that women cope with the distress of giving birth by dismissing the memory of it at once. It does seem to be a very sensible thing to do, don't you think?'

'Perhaps so. Enough of me. Tell me about yourself.'

'Oh, very little to tell. Though I say so myself, I believe that I shall make a very good teacher. I even have five little children saying a few French phrases.'

'Really? French in infants' schools, that is forward looking.'

'It's a start at least. I sometimes wonder if I am right. A thing like that in a tightly-knit community can set a family apart.'

'You should keep on.'

'I shall. I believe that we shall all be the better for reading the literature of other countries untranslated, speaking one another's languages freely. Quite apart from my theory that all knowledge is valuable to the development of the human character.'

She turned to see that he was gazing inwardly, pulling his brows together, concentrating.

'Socks,' he said. 'I had some soft woollen socks. It's something about some socks.' He clenched her hand tightly with the effort of trying to remember.

'I sent you some.'

'You did?'

'Yes, perhaps it is those . . . ?'

'Fine, soft wool. Best quality army officers' socks.'

'I did send you some like that. I was told that all soldiers need good socks in the trenches.'

'Why did that suddenly come to me? Oh God! I wish that I could remember.'

'Don't try, Jack dear. I believe that when you are ready, everything will be put right.'

Healthy, confident and whole, his legs and large feet working like engines, the doctor, carrying a spectator's folding chair strode across the ancient, springy lawn.

Heartily, 'Jack, old son, you are already looking better for your visitor. If you go on like this, then we shall release you to complete your recovery at home.'

'At home?'

'I have a letter from your father suggesting it, but we shall see.'

With the arrival of the doctor upon the scene, Otis felt the delicate aura which had surrounded her and Jack fade in the intensity of his hand-rubbing heartiness. Perhaps she was not too sorry, for if she had been unsure of the wisdom of coming here, she was not reassured now that she was here. She felt that by seeing him so weakened and almost unmanly she was as vulnerable as he. If he had forgotten the socks and chocolates, then he had probably forgotten that he had declared his love for her. If, in their state of mutual vulnerability, he asked her, she would not find it easy to refuse to marry him. Not for love, but in an attempt at a recompense for being a young man who had been tricked by the contemptible war-mongers.

For half an hour they walked in the grounds of the old mansion until a nurse came looking for Jack to say that it was time to have his dressing changed and to spend an hour or two resting on the bed.

'You will come again soon, Otis?'

'Let us hope that you will be sent home.'

'A bit of a burden on the household, I should think.'

'They have Nancy Dickenson.'

'I thought that was a temporary arrangement.'

'That's the general idea, though I can't see Esther wanting to lose her now.'

'I should think not. I remember Nancy Dickenson, and she's not your average domestic, you know.'

'I know.'

'Do you see Victoria, Otis?'

'She is working harder than ever. The Peace League is to petition the Prime Minister.'

'And Victoria is in the midst of it all.'

'It is important.'

'I wish her luck of it.'

'It won't succeed.'

'I know. Honour must be satisfied.'

'Whose?'

Wearily lowering his eyes in a negative reply, he said, 'I think I would settle for peace at any price. It is the brass hats and the red tabs whose honour is at stake, they have the scent of Boche in their nostrils and they won't stop until they can wave his brush at the world.'

'Poor Jack.'

'Too many of our casualties . . . too many. Too many inept leaders who value men only when they are scarce – if

332

we were in unlimited supply they would willingly spend ten thousand of us to gain a few yards of bog-land. In fact they have done so.'

'*Déjà vu*. Max said something very like that on the leave before he died.'

'Max Hewetson was killed? I never knew. Poor Otis, you were very fond of him. Who is going to be left?'

He had red spots on his cheeks.

'I think you should go back. Shall I walk with you?'

He nodded absently.

In the large, wooden-floored hall of Lys House, Otis took both his hands to make her goodbyes, but he pulled her towards him and pressed her close and kissed her with as much force and passion as his weakened strength and bound ribs could manage.

A year ago and she would have wanted to respond – but now she was not certain.

'I will come and see you soon. Perhaps next weekend if you are not at home. Goodbye, Jack. I must go or I shall miss my train.'

On Petersfield Station she bought a book in which she could bury her head until they reached Waterloo.

But her mind wandered. Not for the first time she wondered whether it was as easy as it appeared for a woman like Annie who did not complicate her life with men, but had a preference for her own sex.

When I wanted Jack, he wanted Victoria and was not interested in me, and now that he says that he loves me, the tables are turned. George Moth treats me cheaply, and it arouses me . . . yet I could not sustain a real kiss with Jack.

Was Annie's appetite stimulated by the forbidden fruits? Or was it not as simple as that? Certainly Otis had never felt any desire for a feminine lover. But Danny Turner attracted her.

There was an aura of danger about Danny. Not quite bravado, but bravery. He pitted himself against the George

Moths and the Special Branch of the police, and came out winning. At least, he had done so far.

Without realizing what was happening, she had become enmeshed in the fabric of the Moth family. Too much had passed between herself and George Moth; too many complications attached to herself and Jack; she loved Esther like a sister and felt herself partly responsible for her welfare, and she had introduced Nancy into their household. It would be better to retreat from them, but there was too much that bound her to them to do that. And in any case she liked them.

And now she was committed to seeing Jack again. Not only that, he had said that he loved her. Undoubtedly he needed her just now. It would be too devastating to reject him outright.

It had already been arranged that next Saturday she was to go to York with Danny, accompanying him on one of his 'errands'.

He was involved in all sorts of covert activities to do with getting documents for men who were on the run from the military police. She knew that this 'errand' was by way of a test of the depth of her willingness to become involved in the 'Underground' system.

She would find a gentle excuse for not visiting Jack.

Musk Cottage, Denmead Road, Hambledon, Hants.

Dear Jack,
We hope you don't mind us calling you by your first name, but Arnold never had hardly any friends. When he was on leave he told us about you and we started to think about you as being Jack as that is what he always called you, excepting when he called you Lofty, and he was always on about you. It meant a lot to him having a friend, something he never had before. By rights he shouldn't have been in the army. Going about his work here with me and my husband to tell him how to go on he was always all right. There was things that he could do better than anybody because of his patience, as you will know from being with him. He was as honest as the day is long and loyal to a fault. He was not our own as I expect he said, but he was as dear as if he had been our own. More so than some, because we never had none of our own.
In a way I had already made up my mind to it that once they said he was fit for the army that he wouldn't never come back. We never saw how he could. His father would never let him have a shotgun nor anything like that. We knew what he was like. It was never right to take a boy like that.
We shall pray for you to be returned whole to your family. If there was ever a day when you was this way and felt that you could drop in we should be most grateful.
Yours truly,
Mr and Mrs Herbert Pearce

After being readdressed several times, the letter eventually reached Jack. By now he had left the hospital atmosphere of Lys and was convalescent in the more relaxed atmosphere of

Queen Alexandra's in London. Although not far away, he had not been permitted to rest in his own home; the War Office had received too many reports of men nursed at home being delayed in their return to fitness for active service by late nights and roistering.

In many ways Queen Alexandra's suited Jack. To have been at home with Ess who was still not herself, and his father, towards whom he still felt antagonism, would have been a strain. As it was he was allowed to receive visitors for bearable periods of time. It was only when he saw Kitt that he realized how much he had missed him.

Once, Esther had taken Kitt and Baby to stand with Nancy and wave at a distance. Baby was no longer a baby, and Kitt was a small, solemn schoolboy. To Jack, those changes were a measure of how much of his life had been wasted. Months and long months in a battle over a mile or two of cratered land. Who wanted it? And why? Young men on two sides of no man's land knew – the British sang it to the tune of 'Auld Lang Syne'.

> We're here because we're here because we're here because
>   we're here.
> We're here because we're here because we're here because
>   we're here.

Esther herself, pinch-mouthed, thin and aged by years, said that she was almost well and was thinking of going to Mere with Nancy and the children. Jack had thought it a good sign, especially as his antipathy to owning the property was retreating.

Otis seemed to be in fragrant full bloom, her step springy and her shining hair bouncing as, with her arms filled with flowers, she strode through the ward. She had been full of having her status upgraded and of an opportunity to teach in a senior school that she might be getting. 'I am torn, Jack. I know that the Head is a client of my pa's and I should not like to get the position because of that. But I can't tell you how much I want it. I should be the first female on the staff and I so much want to work towards my Master's degree.' He had thought she looked almost hungry to bite into that experience. The more unattainable she became, the more he wanted her. But if there was one thing that he had inherited from George Moth, it was a masculine pride that found rejection hard. Gently done though it was, he had already been rejected once, by Victoria.

Victoria visited him. Like Otis, full of life and purpose, she hurried up stairs and strode down long corridors, male eyes following her. The visit which might have been awkward was not. The war which had brought him here, injured and nerve-shattered, was not mentioned until the visiting time was almost over. She told him of her work with the League for Peace, and of some vague ideas about travelling in foreign countries. 'I don't know where, but I have a great desire to see as much of the world as I can – Africa, India, South America – there is so much, and I am already almost thirty.' She had wagged her head and laughed at herself, but he saw that she was serious.

And he saw more clearly now than when he had believed that he was in love with her that she was not a woman made for domesticity. 'You were made to be an explorer or a revolutionary, weren't you?'

Smiling, she had looked far off. 'Ah, if only you knew how many women are. I think that the best would be to explore science. If I had been fortunate enough to study at one of the great universities, that is what I should have done. To discover some new element, a new treatment for disease. My grandmother learned of the discovery of contamination through contact, directly from Semmelweis – it was he, you know, who discovered the link between unclean hands and childbed fever. How wonderful to know that you have done something so worthwhile. Oh Jack, why are we given so little time? What a niggardly creator to

337

stop us at three score years and ten. How mean to create us, give us minds and vision to form ideals, and then to chop us down before we have time to . . .' Suddenly she clasped both his hands and said earnestly, 'Don't go back there, Jack. The world cannot afford to throw away its human talent.'

She had fixed him with her intense gaze. 'When I was twenty, I saw the shocking sight of a man shot in the head and his actual brain matter going into the plough furrows. And I was not so much shocked at the sight of the injury as at the thought of the waste. I saw all his experience, all his schooling, his farming knowledge, everything he might have passed on to his children, running away. And I thought to myself, supposing he was about to make a discovery that would double a crop yield or clean an infested field. Hasn't something like that occurred to you?' She kissed him passionately, but on the cheek. 'Don't go back. You have so much better things to do for people than to help turn them into nourishment for Flanders' beet crops.'

His father had visited, but not alone. He had come with one of Jack's colleagues in the law practice. A desk-bound officer. The two young men had found little to say to one another. But at least a few more straws had been put in place in the repairing of the bridge between Jack and his father.

It might have been the constant stream of visitors bringing back some sense of normality to Jack, or that rest and decent food was healing him mentally and physically. Whatever it was that did it, Jack's memory began to return. At first only the name that he had been searching for during his weeks at Lys.

Cully!

And then the letter had arrived.

He had turned the letter over and over, then inspected the envelope for some revelation. *Pearce? Arnold Pearce?* He picked at the protecting scab. He looked up Hambledon in an atlas and was no wiser when he found that it was ten miles or so north of Southsea. He fidgeted to know why Arnold Pearce should not have been in the army and why his father had not allowed him to have guns. The letter, obviously written by someone unused to writing, and full of sincerity and pathos, was touching. The kind of thing that could, these days, bring him to the verge of tears. Damned tears! Damned, damned tears, like the blue hospital uniforms, were a constant reminder that he had ceased to be John Clermont Moth.

Then the memory of another letter, the form that men in the front line could fill in when it was impossible to write home. Jack had filled one in for Cully. Cully was not much good at writing. He had remembered signing it 'Arnie' and addressing it to . . . yes, Pearce.

It was almost with joy that he told his new MO that a piece of information had revealed itself.

Now, as he sat on the train and watched the town-scape of back-to-back terraces of Clapham become the semi-detached rows of Woking, then the landscape with country houses Liss, and then the downland farms where the engine got up steam and speed, Jack Moth almost wished the blessed black hole that had been in his memory would return, and wondered again what he could possibly say to the Pearces that could be of comfort. Yet he had to see them, not only because he owed them at least that, but he needed to see them so that he could face himself. He had failed Cully.

The last three weeks had been devastating. Beginning with Cully's name and ending on this train journey to Hambledon. No, not ending here: the Cully episode would never end. The best that Jack could hope for for himself was that he would be able to learn to live with the knowledge of Cully's death. For the first week after his memory returned, his physical condition had deteriorated from attacks of fever and terrorizing nightmares. It was worse than those nights in the early days of being in the front line, when he had been shocked and sickened at his first sight of eviscerated torsos, white splintered bone, and gouting arteries of men still living.

He had not been responsible for those horrors.

But Cully? He was responsible for Cully, all right. I should have fought for his discharge. He needed a lawyer to put his case. He needed somebody to speak up for him. Face the brass hats and prove that a mistake was made when Cully was certified fit.

Jack's conscience was a mad rat gnawing at the weak trap in which it was kept all day.

This was the first time that he had worn uniform since the holed and blood-soaked one had been removed from him by a nurse in a temporary hospital in France. It felt as stiff and uncomfortable as the one with which he had been issued on his first day in the army. When he had boarded a First Class carriage, the guard had said, Second and Third further along, and had been nonplussed when Jack ignored him and had taken a seat with a white linen head-cloth.

As the train sped past fields of ripening corn, the field-poppies inevitably send his mind back to the cratered fields across the Channel. Taff and Farmer Giles and some others were still there. Taff had written, the censorship lax so that Jack got a pretty fair picture of them. He had assumed that Jack's lung wound would be a 'cushy' one and that he would not be returning, but the doctor at Queen Alexandra's had said that in another few weeks he would be fighting fit. At least, according to Taff, they were having a quiet summer. Paris leave had been stopped and they were on the march. He described views between wooded banks of the Somme, their billets in some picturesque village, and the qualities of some good French beer. A natural story-teller, Taff. Jack missed the comradeship of that close group more than he had missed his own family.

Throughout his convalescence, he had given no thought to the future, his mind being so often preoccupied with the

340

dark hole in his memory. Now that it had been filled, he allowed himself to wonder what his future held. Not his immediate future, but that which it was bad luck to think about, the future in peacetime.

He left the train at Havant in the hope that there would be some kind of transport or something to hire to get him to Hambledon village, as he did not relish such a long walk. He found the concern of the porters and then the station-master embarrassing. They called him 'mate' and asked him about the war. There was nothing going Hambledon way, but they fixed him up with a ride on a strawberry-grower's cart.

At the pace of the old horse, Jack, sitting with the carter above hedge-height, was ambled along towards the Pearces'. The carter, glad of a bit of company, filled up on news that would be welcome in the Cricketer's Arms.

'You a relation of the Pearces then?'

Curbing his cultured voice as he had learned to do in the army, Jack said, 'No, but I served with their son.'

The carter wagged his head sadly. 'Bad thing. Floored Bert and Fanny it has.'

Non-committally, 'I dare say it has.'

'It was a carkin' crime taking him into the army. The whole village was up in arms. Well, Chrissy! I asts you, if things is so bad the army's got to take dafties like Young Arnie, then they must be bad. I mean, the lad was decent enough, but he couldn't help hisself when he got worked up.'

Most villagers in rural Hampshire are cagey with strangers – some will hardly give a townie the time of day, but there are the gabby ones, and not only was the carter gabby, he had had a good wet of Gale's ale quite early in the day. Using his court training, Jack nodded encouragingly and gently prompted him. He was thankful for this unexpected insight into the civilian Cully.

'The vicar wrote, you know. He told them that the boy hadn't never been normal and that he waddn't fit to be called

341

up. But they never took no notice. The trouble with Young Arnie was that he looked pretty normal, he waddn't mongol or anything. And you know how he was, willing and eager. Everybody liked him round here. I know he waddn't all there, but he was a nice enough lad, loved the cricket. But he never should a been a conscript.'

'You're right.'

'He wasn't never normal right from a baby.'

'Is that so?'

'You know how the Pearces came by him?' The carter was obviously relishing the chance to tell him.

'No, I've no idea. He never said, and I didn't ask.'

'I doubt he even thought of it. He never had the brain to spekalate. Some said it was a judgement of God, but if you ask me it was being shoved down a rabbit-hole.' He turned to Jack, satisfied that he had created an impression.

Jack raised his eyebrows encouragingly. 'Really?'

'His mother was summonsed and put in prison for it. Dilys Cullington – Dilly – sort of woman who'd stand up for any man for fourpence and lay down for a bob. I suppose she couldn't help it, she was left with half a dozen kids to bring up . . . Mind you, I'm not saying but what she wasn't a bit that way inclined . . . well, you know, some women are, an't they? Anyhow, she stood up for some bloke who left her with twins in her. For months she tried to say she waddn't, but she'd summit wrong with her guts – but you know how 'tis in a village, you can't keep nothing like that quiet, 'specially twins.'

'And Cully – Arnie – was one of the twins?'

'Ah. She went out on her own, birthed the babies herself and left them in the warren with all dirt and leaves covering them up. I suppose she hoped a fox'd come, she said in court she thought they was both dead inside her because they hadn't moved for a week. One was, but not Arnie.'

'What a terrible story.'

'Well, if it's true she thought they was dead, you got to ast

342

yourself why she went out there to birth them. But, there's worst things than that have happened in this here village.' He tapped the side of his nose.

'How was Arnie saved?'

'By old Bert Pearce. Out rabbiting with his dog, hears this cry, dog scrabbles the leaves and there was this here baby.'

'Good Lord, sounds like the Queen of Egypt finding Moses.'

The carter laughed. 'Ah. You don't know Bert Pearce?'

'No.'

'Well, old Bert an't no Queen of Egypt, as you'll see. Fanny's all right, though.' He nodded knowingly.

'And they kept him?'

'Ah. Bert and Fanny, been married five year, never had chick ner child. You wouldn't get away with it these days, but twenty year ago, nobody asked no questions, he'd a been a charge on the Parish. The vicar christened him and gave him back to Fanny and he was theirs. Vicar said he should keep his proper name, though if you asts me that waddn't a very Christian thing to do, seeing as how his mother was in prison for trying to kill him.'

They had now reached long neat fields planted with strawberries where lines of pickers were bending their backs and moving steadily along. An inn, a few straggling cottages, and a signpost to say that this was Hambledon, then more closely-built cottages.

'Here y'are then, lad. This is as far as I go. Bert Pearce's an't no more than a quarter of a mile.'

'I'm really grateful for you bringing me. What do I owe you?'

'Normally, I would of said a bob, but not to a serving man, nor to a chap that made friends with poor young Arnie.'

Jack was surprised to discover that Musk Cottage had one window converted to a shop window over which was a sign reading 'H. Pearce & Son. High Class Saddlers – Boots Repaired.' The door stood wide and he went in. Bert Pearce was indeed no Queen of Egypt. He was old, probably approaching sixty, brown and thin, and with skin as leather-looking and as tooled with lines as the finished saddles hanging from the low ceiling. He had a good face with large, well-lashed eyes that the girls had probably found attractive a few years back. Jack could only stand upright where there were no beams and no saddles. The man looked up over his half-glasses and then started.

'I'm sorry. I made you jump,' Jack said.

'No, only that I expected it was a customer.' He put down the pad and polish with which he had been burnishing the brass rings of a bridle. 'You're Jack aren't you? Jack Moth?'

Jack nodded.

'From your heighth. Arnie said that you was tall, they called you Lofty, an't that right?' He held out a thin brown hand, blued and powdery from the metal polish.

'I'm pleased to meet you, Mr Pearce.'

He looked down at his hand. 'I shall be in trouble with Mother, shaking your hand like that.'

His way of speaking, slow and ponderous, was exactly like Cully's. He had a nice smile and his own teeth.

'Mother!' He called into the passage. 'Come round the counter, lad.' He lifted the flap and, as Jack emerged, Fanny Pearce poked her head round the passageway door.

'What you want, Bert? I was just putting out the whites in the sun.'

'This is Jack, Mother.'

She clapped two small, plumpish hands over her mouth. 'Oh dear Lord, what a greeting.' She put up her arms and pulled Jack down so that she could kiss him and hug him. 'I can't tell you how much it means to me and Bert, you coming here.'

'I wanted to . . . very much.'

She squeezed his hand, her emotions on the verge of

spilling over. Probably in her forties, she was as pink and soft as Bert was brown and leathery. 'Fancy him not bringing you through the proper way through the front door.' She wagged her head, but from the way she said, 'You men!' it was obvious that genial chiding was part of her regular housewifely duties to keep the man of the house from back-sliding – and to show that she knew her own manners.

'Come through anyhow, if you don't mind.'

Ducking through doorways and under beams Jack followed her and Bert followed Jack.

The kitchen, where she sat Jack in the coolest spot beside the open door, was what one would expect from a pink housewife wearing a white apron. Whatever he had imagined Cully's parents to be, it was not the ill-assorted Pearces.

'I dare say you could do with a wet of summit.' Without waiting, Bert descended cellar stairs with a jug.

'You'll stop and eat with us?'

Jack nodded.

'A great lad like you wants feeding. If you don't mind me saying, your uniform's hanging on you. Are you sure you're better enough to be coming all the way out here?'

'I had a nice ride. A carter from the strawberry farms.'

'Dick Hanway. Hm. I'll bet there an't nothing you don't know about Hambledon now. Jack got a ride off Dick Hanway, Bert.'

'We wasn't expecting you or I'd have collected you.' Bert poured three mugs of golden beer.

'Home brew.' Bert drank his like a man used to quaffing well.

'It's very good,' Jack said.

Fanny said, 'I feel terrible not having anything special in.'

They were all skating around the reason for Jack's visit. But they all knew, so Jack left it to them to say what they wanted to when they were ready. Fanny laid out plentiful dishes of ham, cheese and pie and a cottage loaf on a board, and for the first time in weeks, Jack salivated at the smell and thought of food. Without ceremony, Fanny filled their plates.

'Mmm. This ham is so succulent.'

'Juicy?'

'Yes, yes, and beautifully smoked.'

'It was Arnold's favourite,' Bert Pearce said. 'He would have ate it at every meal if you'd have let him. Iddn't that a fact, Fan?'

Fanny Pearce nodded. 'Only my own cured though. Our own pig. Arnold could tell at once if it was somebody else's. He was cute like that, wasn't he, Bert?'

And so they gently put their toes into the quicksand of Cully's death.

'A course, Jack'd see a different side of Arnie from what we saw. Lads is always different when they're away from their mum and dad,' Bert said. 'I dare say your dad don't know the half you get up to, Jack, do he?'

'He gives me a long rope.'

'Best thing,' Fanny said. 'A course, we couldn't always do that with Arnold.'

'Of course not.'

'Apart from the fits though, he was pretty good,' Bert said.

'No he wasn't, Bert. We couldn't never have let him go like Mr Moth can let Jack go.' Explaining to Jack, 'It wasn't just the fits, he was never going to grow up to be a man.'

'He did go,' Bert said, with a fringe of anger around his words. 'He never had no choice.'

Fanny Pearce sighed, the white hills of her bosom heaving beneath her crossed hands. 'Yes, yes. It was like putting a boy of twelve into uniform.'

'Some people got a lot to answer for,' Bert said.

'But they'll not answer for it, Mr Pearce. The sort of people responsible for conscripting Cully don't ever get their just deserts, they are too remote from the harm they have caused. I say, do you mind if I call him Cully, it was his name in the army.'

'Oh no, we'd like it if you did. That's the side we never could see. It was terrible for us wondering how he was going to manage.'

'Actually, he managed very well. There were some things that he was extremely good at.'

'That's Bert's training.' A lone tear trickled from her eye; absently she took it on her forefinger and massaged it with her thumb. 'He always said he'd make something of him, didn't you, Bert?'

'I'd a made a saddler of him. Wait a minute, I'll show you.' Stopping in the act of refilling their mugs, he went through into the shop and came back with a small, gleaming saddle. 'Pony saddle. Made every stitch hisself.'

Jack took the object, ran his hands over the glossy leather and fingered the gleaming brass fittings. 'It's absolutely beautiful workmanship. I had no idea.' He felt the tooled ornate monogram and read out ' "A.H.P."?'

'He wanted us to get his name changed to Pearce.' Fanny hunched her shoulders. 'We always put it off. You do, don't you? You always think there's time. He made that about five year ago, there seemed to be all the time in the world.'

'I envy Cully his boyhood, being able to do something like this, living here.'

'You? With your looks and brains. 'Sides, you aren't going to tell me that you aren't used to better than this,' Fanny said. 'When you're not thinking about it you give yourself away in the way you speaks. You got a posh accent behind it all.'

'I envy the happy life he must have led with you. I was boarded.'

Fanny nodded at Bert. 'He was happy, wasn't he, Bert?'

'It was in his nature. He couldn't help hisself. He couldn't learn nothing much in the way of reading and writing, but

347

he could do things. And it didn't matter much if he didn't know his letters. He'd a made a damn good saddler.'

The shop doorbell jangled and Bert rose at once. 'You don't have to go back tonight do you, lad? We'd like you to stop over. Fanny's got to take stuff to Pompey tomorrow, so she could give you a ride down.'

Jack wanted to stay. Somehow, Cully, who was the source of his nightmares, had a presence here that might put them to rest.

Fanny said, 'He don't think – you men don't. You brought nothing with you, but there's all Arnold's stuff if you had a mind to spend the night.'

'I'd be pleased to. I really didn't know anything much about Cully and I should like to. He'd talk about his mum and dad, and the cricket team, but mostly he seemed to like to hear about what the rest of us did. And he liked to always be doing things: domestic things, like brewing up or making porridge.'

'Did he? That pleases me to hear that. I taught him that sort of thing. We was always worried about the day when he wouldn't have me and Bert, so we saw to it that he could manage on his own. And he mostly could. But he wasn't never fit to be in no army.'

'You are right, he was too young.'

The afternoon was restful. Jack wandered off around the village, plunging into woodlands and tramping around fields. Early in the evening he went to the local inn with Bert who said he wanted to introduce Jack as Young Arnie's friend. He played shove-ha'penny and table skittles and drank the local Gale's ale. They went to bed country hours, early so as to be up and about at dawn, Jack sleeping in Cully's room and in one of Cully's nightshirts. His scar, which had been mending, was painful, and his mind was afire with dark memories. Outside the open window nightjars called and nightingales piped, the scent of musk-roses and warm pig wafted in through the open window.

Still nobody had mentioned Cully's actual death. He puzzled about that. Fanny and Bert Pearce did not appear to show anything other than normal grief at Cully's death. Coming here, he had been apprehensive, not knowing what their reaction might be – anger, bitterness, shame even – certainly not this dignified coping with their loss. He began to wonder how much they knew.

Next morning they breakfasted on more of the ham, fried with eggs and thick bread. 'I've got to feed the animals before I load up. Do you want to come, or shall you bide there a bit, Jack?'

'Let me come.'

Leaning on the pig-sty fence, watching Fanny scratch the animal's back with a stick, Jack asked, 'Did you get a letter from the officer?'

She hesitated. 'No. You couldn't expect them to do that when there was so many getting killed. All we got was a form that said he was dead. Just his name and number filled in and the date and that he was dead. The same as thousands of families has been getting.'

No, Jack thought, not the same. Not many died as Cully had died.

'Nothing else?'

'Only a printed letter about his pay – he was getting it sent home. It's indoors there, still in his savings box. We shall have to do something with it, give it to the children's home perhaps. We don't hold with stone memorials or nothing like that. Let's just stop talking about it, shall we?'

'I'm sorry.'

'No, no. I didn't mean it like that. I don't particularly want to talk about the forms they sent and that.'

'You are a surprising lady, Fanny.'

'Why's that then?'

'Partly, I suppose, because I had a picture of you in my mind. Cully always referred to you as "my old mum". I never expected such a pretty lady.'

She smiled. 'And he called you "old Lofty", though I can't say there's much he didn't tell us about you. He thought the world of you. On his leaves he never stopped talking about you, I suppose because he couldn't write, he remembered every little detail to tell us. He never talked much about the fighting. What was he like? Bert can't stand to know about that side of it, but I want to know.'

'I don't think he realized the danger we were sometimes in.'

'That's what I thought. I once said to Bert that he'd either end up dead or with the VC. He was always the same. The kids would tease him into some dare that could a killed him, and he'd do it. Is that how he got killed?'

Now Jack was convinced that the Pearces did not know the circumstances of Cully's death. He had come here with some idea that he must provide them with an account that they could live with, but it was proving unnecessary. If anything, Fanny Pearce was the comforter.

He decided to lie to her.

'No. It could easily have been any of us. I was the reckless one. And got away with it. It doesn't seem just, does it?'

'If you're going to look for justice in this world, you'll need a strong magnifying glass.'

Musk Cottage garden was long and seemingly without a boundary. She took him to a small orchard, a row of bee skeps, a vegetable plot, from each of which she gathered produce and packed it into wicker baskets. She milked two goats, put the milk into long pans, and packed some cheeses into a hamper. 'It's the posh London shops that buy it. People round here don't eat goats' cheese. It fetches decent money. We tried to see to it that our bit of land was all put down to stuff that Arnold could manage and make a living by later on. Everything here's for feeding ourselves or selling.'

'Even the flowers?'

'Makes a few shillings in Havant.'

Jack shook his head and smiled at the practicality of it all, thinking of Mere and its acres and acres of grass and flower borders, of the fish in the lake that were not for eating, and the decorative crab-apples, cherry and plum trees that were grown for spring effect – unlike Musk Cottage's pruned and fruiting varieties, which were already becoming heavy with their commercial crops.

He helped her load up and said goodbye to Bert Pearce.

'Try to come again, lad. It's been balm to our hearts talking about Arnie.'

'I have to return to my unit quite soon. But when my next leave comes . . .'

'We want you to have this.'

By its shape and size Jack knew that this was Cully's apprentice-piece of saddlery. The easily-sprung tears that had made him feel so shamed and womanish at Lys House and Queen Alexandra's, seemed not unmanly here. Even so, he dashed his knuckles at his damp eyes. 'I'm sorry . . .'

'Nothing wrong with men's tears, Jack,' Fanny said. ''Tis a pity we didn't see a few more sometimes.'

He had expected the ride into Portsmouth to be by horse and cart, but Fanny drove a pointed-nosed little green van skilfully along the winding country roads. For the first three or four miles they were each within their own minds, then Fanny said, 'You're a bit tall for my little van.'

'I find it very comfortable.'

Taking her eyes from the road to look directly at him, she said, 'I'm glad. I love being in here, 'specially with the windows up and the engine off. Sometimes I stops along the lane just for the pleasure of being in here. I used to sing a lot on my way to Pompey, even talk to myself, have a good curse at things, say things I wouldn't want nobody else to hear. I cried my tears for Arnold in here.'

Jack looked around the little tin box on wheels. 'It is rather like the secret dens one had in childhood.'

'Can we pretend that's what it is? Exchange a few secrets . . . tell the truth a bit?'

'A confessional instead of a den?'

'Perhaps so. So, if it's not too impertinent, would you mind telling me how it is you're hiding yourself in private's uniform – by rights you should be an officer, shouldn't you?'

'No.'

'Tell me to mind my own business.'

'I'm not, as they say, officer material.'

'But you're officer class all right.'

'Some of my relations are inclined to be.'

'But not Jack.'

'That's right, not Lance-Corporal Moth.'

'Is it to do *them* down then? Or is it your dad?'

'My father? He's not concerned whether I'm a private or a general.'

'You're wrong. He minds all right. All fathers need their sons to shine. That's part of the reason why Bert wanted to give you the saddle. I doubt if he realizes it, but he wants somebody he respects to see that he had a son who could do something that not many could do.'

Fanny halted the van and put the engine in neutral gear whilst a slow herd of cows flopped and jostled its way along a narrow lane, rubbing their rough hides against the van, rolling their eyes at the windows. Jack hated the thought that the good done to him by these last cathartic twenty-four hours with the Pearces might be undone by a wrong word. Yet, not to be honest about himself was less than shrewd and intelligent Fanny deserved. Twice she had alluded to his accent or class. She knew that he hid behind his adopted accent, and rough table-manners. But then, why stop there, why not be honest with her about Cully's death also?

Compromising, he said, 'In civilian life, I am a lawyer. My father is a Scotland Yard detective, and my mother, who was a lady, is dead.'

352

'Ah,' Fanny said. 'I'm sorry about that.'

'It's six years since it happened.'

'And you want to blame your father?'

'Blame him? Of course not.'

'All right, have it your way.'

They sat silently for long moments, then Jack said, 'She had my little brother Kitt late in life, and she died giving birth.'

'And you don't blame your father?'

His gaze was withdrawn.

'Dear lad, 'twould be a very natural thing if you did. When our closest love dies, we all want to blame somebody for it. What we really want is to blame the person who has gone and died and took their love away from us, but we can't do that, can we? So sometimes we blames God, oftentimes we blames ourselves. I reckon you like to blame your father. The way you mentioned him over this last twenty-four hours, you had a strange sound of hate and love both in your voice.'

Jack felt uneasy and wished that they could drive on. Here he was pinned down for her scrutiny and comment.

She continued, 'I was that way with my mother. She was a drudge and I hated her for being it: yet the reason why she was a drudge was because she loved us and wanted to make life better for us. So I loved her too.'

'My father is a man of . . . I'm sorry, I don't know how else to say it . . .'

'This isn't the outside world remember?' She smiled. 'There's only the cheeses and the rhubarb in the back.'

'He's a man who can't keep away from women.'

'Truly?'

'I've known for years that he keeps a mistress.'

'And you don't have women?'

'I wouldn't if I had a wife and children.'

'Well then, I wish you a wife who will satisfy you.'

He flushed warmly, aware of her womanly presence, as

he had been since he first laid eyes upon her, feeling both bold and shy; in nature wanting to confess himself to her, in nurture trained not to do so.

'My mother was almost forty, and my father older.'

'And I wish you his same good fortune. Do you think that it is only young ones who has a licence to satisfy their bodies? Or that body-love is something that wears thin? Or that women grows cold with the years? Because if you do, you're in for a surprise. Instead of feeling bitter towards your father for his normal appetites, you should thank the Lord that you're his son and hope to take after him.'

Some long moments of silence.

'Was your mother happy about her condition?'

'Very.'

'Then thank the Lord double. Forty's no age at all in my eyes.'

A cowman slapped his hand on the van and shouted 'Right-o' as a signal that his herd had passed, making Jack jump and laugh nervously. He smiled at Fanny rather sheepishly. 'I thought it was the voice of God chiding me for talking to you like this.'

'Perhaps it is I talking to you He don't like. I'm afraid I do and say a good many things He an't too happy about.'

The cows were now well down the lane, but Fanny did not put the engine into driving gear, she gently patted Jack's hand with her fingers. 'Now I'll tell you something then. I'm forty-four years old, and I'm in the family way. Nobody knows excepting a woman I went to see in Portsmouth.'

'Doesn't Bert know?'

'No, you're the only one. I wanted to make sure. It would have been too cruel if I'd made a mistake, but sure enough, I'm four months gone with this child.' She settled her hands protectively over her convex abdomen in the way that his mother had done over Kitt.

'I used not to be able to bear seeing my mother do that. But with you it seems . . . well, a beautiful thing to do.'

''Tis not me, lad, 'tis maturity in you. You wasn't much more than a youth then, and town people are different about these things than we are. Arnold wouldn't have been shy of me.'

'He would have been a good nursemaid. Once, in Flanders, he took a dog under his wing. He was so gentle with that poor terrified creature.'

She gazed absently at where the cows were turning into a field. 'There's probably a lot you know about Arnold that I don't.'

It was one of those moments that had come and gone on other occasions over the last six years, a moment when he longed most desperately to have his mother back again, and for the first time he wondered how it must be for his father.

'I promised Bert that I would come to Hambledon again, and I shall. Certainly I shall come to see the new baby.'

'We ought to get going if you are to get back to London.' Opening the door, she unhooked the starting-handle.

Jack jumped out of the van and tried to take it from her, but she tried to hold on to it. 'Don't you ever do that again whilst you are carrying that child,' he said.

'Rubbish, I'm as strong as an ox. Anyway, who's going to do it if not me?'

He wrested the handle from her and engaged it, turned it. The engine fired and the handle kicked back. Rubbing his wrist, he said, 'You see? Think what could happen.' He held her firmly by her shoulders and looked down sternly into her pretty face. 'Fanny, I want you to promise me that you will never use this thing again. Get a horse and trap if you must do your own transporting, or better still get a carter to do it for you for the next months. Please, promise me.'

Drawing him to her she put her arms about his neck and kissed him warmly. 'You are the nicest, nicest of people, Jack, 'tis no wonder Arnold thought you was so grand. I am only sorry that your ma didn't live to see you a grown man. Very well then, I'll promise to get Dick Hanway to cart my stuff.'

The van started and they were soon going down the steep incline into Portsmouth, where Jack insisted upon getting a later train so that he could unload the van. On the station forecourt, he shook her hand warmly. She held on to it. 'I still have something else to say, Jack.' Her brow was drawn into the vee between her eyes. 'I know about Arnold, I wasn't going to say anything, but I've felt so close to you that I couldn't let you go without saying the truth. I know he wasn't killed through the war, and I believe he got himself into trouble.'

Jack felt the muscles of his stomach contract with apprehension. 'Oh God . . . no, Fanny.'

'I could tell from the form they sent that it wasn't the usual notice. Then I had a letter from a sergeant.'

'Trigg?'

'That's right, saying to the effect that although Arnold had not died in action, and that there had been a miscarriage of justice, that he had been a brave soldier. He asked me not to mention that he had written. It was a kindly letter from a nice man, so I burnt it.'

Jack clutched her hand between his two. Sergeant Trigg, Cully's other friend in the cells.

'Bert doesn't know?'

'About the letter? No. He was so cut up seeing the form, that he never read it properly – he thinks it was a normal notice about being killed in action.'

Jack opened his mouth to say something, but she put her fingers over it. 'No! I don't want to know anything else. I've had Sergeant Trigg's letter, and I've had this day with you. If two nice people took trouble over our Arnold, then that's all I want to know about it.'

Boldly he laid his hand briefly at the swelling from her waist. 'This is a very fortunate child.'

356

'Come for the christening.'

'If I make it back again.'

She kissed him. 'If you was my son, Jack Moth, I'd hide you in the attic and not let you go back to France at any price – which is what I should have done with Arnie.'

The plain-clothes detective leaned his elbow against the railings close to a street tea-bar, supped his tea and read his folded newspaper. He was good: looking like any street-lounger studying form for a sixpenny bet on the Ascot meeting, he waited for his man to emerge from the building opposite. It was dirty work even though it was in clean clothes. But he was a professional and so did not question his orders.

George Moth with his jacket, boots and collar off, leaned back against the brass bedhead, smoking a cigar and watched Effee's hair-brushing ritual. It had been her fair curling hair that had first caught his eye from his seat at the Alhambra, that and the fact that her height was not much more than five foot and her body so dainty that it looked as though it might break under the weight of the men to whom she sold her favours.

Through half-closed eyes and the smoke unwinding from the tip of his cigar, he saw her pointed elbows and slender neck, her narrow back and shoulders as they moved rhythmically beneath a silky oriental wrap which was peach-coloured embroidered with peach-blossom. He took his gaze to the long gilded mirror which reflected her pretty, serious face, lower to the curve of her throat, lower to where her wrap fell open revealing snatched glimpses of heavy breasts that would have been more likely on a much larger rib-cage.

There was a time when he had a husband's right to such

daintiness, such full breasts, such hair. Effee knew how to handle sensitively the exchange of money for her services, but she left him in no doubt that she did not belong to him. To an extent, by making her more financially secure since Anne died, George Moth had gradually persuaded her away from having a constant stream of men. Nowadays she took only a few 'regulars', mature men like himself, men she liked and chose to have.

The window to the room was small, and although it was midday, the sky was dark. Effee's reflection was softened and misted by the yellow light of an oil-lamp. Her room was not cluttered with frou-frou, scent bottles, cream jars and knick-knacks, as young women's rooms often are; her powder-bowl was porcelain and her few bottles cut-glass – not of the best but by no means tawdry or cheap. She owned a good wardrobe and dressing-table and some nicely upholstered chairs. In a curtained-off recess was a beauti- fully decorated set of large china basin, water-jug and chamber-pot.

The room had not always been so tastefully appointed, but had been changed slowly over the four or five years that George Moth had been coming here. He liked the room. He liked Effee. When he was here with her he could have an hour without any demands upon his mind, and here with Effee he could discard his responsibilities – to the Force, to the public, to his superiors, to his children and to his servants. In this nice little room he was responsible only to Effee who, until he had bought her furniture and paid her rent, had been anything from a soubrette in a comic act to an occasional singer, but mostly had been one of the Alhambra's many promenading women. He could have afforded to keep her entirely but she would never agree.

In this room he became a George Moth that his colleagues and family would scarcely have recognized. Kitt knew him, and Jack had seen him once, on that occasion when they played with the clockwork toy in Kitt's bath.

Outside, the storm that had been threatening broke with a bright flash of lightning and simultaneous clap of thunder. Effee jumped, but did not stop her rhythmic brushing.

The same . . . the same. Same fragility, same stalwart attitude. Anne had been afraid of thunderstorms, but would never reveal such a weakness except by those same little automatic reactions to a thunderclap. There had been a time when Effee had been afraid of him: no, not afraid, in awe.

George Moth was under no delusion, he had chosen Effee and paid her well because she looked like Anne. The similarity ended with the looks, which was why he seldom entered into a conversation with her until after she had earned her money – which she did very well.

Having completed the brushing, she arranged her hair so that it fell around her like a curtain of golden voile, and went to her lover.

'George. I don't like you to smoke in here.' Although her voice was soft, she mewed her vowels like a hungry cat. 'I wish you'd realize, it's where I live after you've gone home. I don't much like the smell and it hangs about my clothes and the furnishings and that.'

George Moth was taken aback. Effee had never been anything but complaisant, she would do anything to please him – like wearing the particular wrap he liked, and brushing her hair for ten minutes. He paid her to do these things, but even so she liked to please him. 'What if I say "No"?'

She caught the skin of her inner lip between her teeth, looked through the window, then returned her gaze to look him directly in the eyes. But she did not reply.

'I like my cigar.'

'I know you do.'

'Well then?'

She looked steadily at him, not aggressively, not defiantly. 'I wasn't asking you not to smoke cigars, I was asking you to respect my home.'

Suddenly he felt like a boy who has transgressed the rules of his mother's sitting-room: George! If you wish to behave like a hobbledehoy take yourself off to the yard.

And for twenty-five years it had been his job to search out the hobbledehoys who transgressed the rules of the City of London.

He removed the cigar from between his teeth and, holding it between finger and thumb, inspected its fine overlapping of leaf, its satisfying shape, its grey smouldering tip and dark moist end. He smiled wryly at her. 'All right, ma'am, you're mistress here.'

'I surely am, George.'

'Here you are then, take it and throw it away if it pleases you.'

'I will not! You're the one to do that.'

Genially, smiling at this new, confident development in Effee's manner, he rose from the bed and went to raise the window.

'Not out there, you wouldn't throw something from a window in your own house, would you?'

'That's true, Effee.'

Having disposed of the offending cigar in a covered dish, he sat on her dressing chair and encircled her in his arms. The rain was now loud and rattling against the window-panes, and the moist smell of the quenched heat and laid dust came in at the opening. The air that had earlier been charged was becoming refreshed. 'You've changed since the early days, Effee.'

'I know. It's been partly you but mostly me that's done it. I never liked being poor, and I wouldn't never have gone on the game if I hadn't of been.'

'Then I wouldn't have seen you at the Alhambra, and you wouldn't have brought me here.'

She pursed her lips. 'That's true.'

'And we wouldn't have had those good hours together.'

'That's true and all.'

Standing between his knees, her head was above his, so that he had to look up to catch her expression. Normally, the closeness of her wren-thin bones and satin-skinned breasts would have hastened and heightened his need for her, but this turn in her usual deference to him was somehow more deeply erotic than urgently lustful.

'You're very serious today.'

'I've decided to get out of the game, George.'

It was every prostitute's dream – to get out, or to become a madam. Very few of them achieved it, the pimps saw to that. He did not know what to say. He could not imagine what he would do if Effee were not here. He had been with her even whilst Anne was still alive. In the early days it had been as a result of sudden desire without preamble at times when Anne had been indisposed, when she was pregnant, or when he had been searching for days for some cut-throat or madman.

In more recent times, he had occasionally come to Effee when Otis Hewetson had aroused him like an urgent youth, and again when Victoria Ormorod had challenged him with her feminism and her sexuality; but often he came here to sit with his feet up, getting things off his chest.

In a queer sort of way, she was the most stable woman in his life. Effee was always here, nice-natured, good fun, a bit sentimental but not more so than Anne had been. If she came off the game it would mean back to the Alhambra again, the thought of which made him feel weary, spoilt as he was by Effee.

He never made believe that Effee was Anne, but she had Anne's same fragility as well as the other-worldliness that he had loved. Anne had come from a super-class and Effee from a sub-class. They were both equally mysterious and intriguing to George Moth. The women of his own kind were respectable, open and predictable; they accepted the established order; they had never rebelled against their place in the order of things. At least, they had not done so until the Victoria Ormorods and Sylvia Pankhursts had gone out on

362

to the streets and the Otis Hewetsons had eschewed their places in high society and done as they pleased.

'You aren't on the game, Effee. You can't say this is being on the game.' He hugged her playfully. 'I should say that you were a courtesan.'

She combed his hair with her fingers, drawing his head towards the cleft of her bosom. 'I do it for money, George.'

'Girls on the game have pimps and madams. They pick up their men and take anybody.' He allowed his head to sink against the silken wrap.

'I do it for money, George. You come when you want to buy something from me. If you want it over in five minutes then that's what you do, if you want two hours then you have them, if you want to make a fight of it, with me, then I fight you, don't I?'

'Stop it! That sounds sordid. You know it has never been like that.'

'Face it, George. Girls on the game let men use their bodies and get paid for it. I make *my* living letting men use my body. And I don't want to do it any longer. I've got money put aside and I've already been to see a little hat shop with rooms above. It's in Chiswick, and I reckon I shall be very comfortable there.'

'A hat shop!'

'Nothing wrong with hats. Everybody wears them. Women changes their hats with the seasons and the fashions. It's a good business to be in.'

'Wouldn't you rather have a husband and a few babies than be selling hats?'

'In time I might. I've got to meet somebody first. There's a nice class of person lives in Chiswick.'

'What about me?'

'You'll find another girl, Lord knows, there's plenty of us to choose from.'

'I didn't mean for this.' He kissed the nearest silky skin that presented itself.

He looked up at her and realized what he would lose. 'I meant what about me to marry? I'm a better class of person than your Chiswick men.'

She tensed and pulled back from him, covering herself with the peach-blossom wrap. 'There's times when your sense of humour isn't very funny.'

'I mean it, Effee. I think it's time I married again. I can't do without a woman about the place.'

'Well thank you very much! *You* want to get married, *you* can't do without somebody.'

'Dammit, Effee, I didn't mean it like that. Don't get so uppity.'

'I'm not uppity, but I do get a bit fed up at times with what *you* always want. And you coming and going as *you* please. You telling me about other women who winded you up. Did you ever think of anything *I* might want?'

'I thought you had what you wanted. This nice place, a bit of money to spend, come and go as you please.'

'Oh yes, and getting older. And wanting to get off the game . . .'

'And running a hat shop in Chiswick . . .'

'Don't laugh at me, George.'

'I'm not laughing. But *you* in a hat shop, steaming and re-blocking? Effee Tessalow ordering hatpins? I'm not laughing at you.'

And suddenly he was not. He saw how insubstantial his life would be without her. Even when he had flirted with the day-dream of Otis Hewetson, the dream had included a continuation of Effee Tessalow. Now that he looked at it, he had always taken it for granted that somewhere in the roots of his life would be Effee Tessalow for all time.

'When I say, it's time I married again, I mean it. I like the complete feeling of being part of something as basic and important as a marriage. Perhaps that is why I've always felt content in the Force, it is a bit the same. And I really *don't* like not having a woman about the house. It's true. A woman has a civilizing effect on a man like me. When Anne first died, I couldn't bear being there – you know that, wasn't I always here? And when Esther took Kitt off to Mere, the place wasn't fit to be called a home.'

'Well George, and what do you think it was like here when you left? I'm not bitching, there's plenty that'd like to be in my drawers. But I used to envy you going back to a place where everybody had a place of their own like pieces in a canteen of cutlery. Husband, wife, son, daughter, cook, housemaid, tweeny, scullery-maid, all in their proper slots. And I was what? A pie slice in a separate box of her own?'

'I thought you were happy.'

'I was, when you were here. Most of the time I was making do with my life between your visits. But I've had enough, George. I know you can't help it, but I fell for you years ago. So when you say, "Marry me" like that, out of the blue, you got to know who it is you're asking and why you're asking it.'

'Don't ask me to analyse it now, Effee. If I've hurt you, then I'll do what I can to make up for it.'

She sat down on his large lap, her face now almost level with his own. The hail had stopped and only soft droplet rain now fell. The sky lightened, wheels swished through puddles and rainwater rushed along gutters and down-pipes. 'It's a nice thought, but we couldn't even if we wanted. You're a rozzer, you've got children to think of; and you can give it any name you like, the fact is I've never earned a sou except on my back.'

'There's only Kitt now. Esther and Jack have done what they want to do with their lives. You'd be all right with Esther, and as soon as Jack comes out of the army, he is going to take a place of his own. I've been thinking for ages that I'd give up the Force. I don't like this new work I'm on. I've always been a detective, not a government spy.'

'Oh George, I never knew you was unhappy enough to pack your hand in.'

'People spying on people who are spying on people. That's no job for a proper copper.'

'George . . . when I get to Chiswick, you'll come and see me?'

The man with the racing paper was still waiting. He had got dampened by the hailstorm and had drunk too much of the stewed tea from the street-stall. There was something going on but he didn't quite know what. He provided pieces for the jigsaw that his superiors were making: only they ever saw the completed picture. He knew all about the super-intendent and the little piece of stuff he visited, but he could only hazard a guess as to why he had been instructed to report on his superior officer's movements. It was bad when one department was observing another. Nobody knew what was what and who was who any longer.

My Dear Otis,

Your astonishment will be no less than ours was when you hear that Father is to remarry. This has come entirely out of the blue and neither Jack nor I know the lady. Her name is Miss Frieda Tessalow. More than that we do not know. We have had a disastrous family luncheon where none of us seemed to know our place. Quite honestly I felt very sorry for the lady: imagine suddenly being catapulted into another woman's family.

I don't know how you will feel about this, and to be honest that is the reason why I am writing to you. I should not know how to say this to your face, but I had thought that you had warm feelings for my father. If you have not now, then I am sure that you once did have for, on the day of my wedding, I was standing in the hallway arranging my veil and heard what I should not have heard before I realized what it was. I was in a dilemma, as you will understand. I could hardly apologize; for what should I apologize? All that I can say is that from time to time I have hoped that one day we might have become something closer than friends. You did me the best of favours when you suggested that Nancy come to stay with me. I am very well recovered and we are preparing to go down to Lyme and open up Mere again. Please, please write to me there.

Lovingly as ever, Esther

PS: The marriage ceremony is to be a civil one with no guests. Thank the Lord for that! I don't know why I felt the need to write and say what I have written. I trust that you will understand.

Dressed in light-mourning lilac, and looking fresh and in her twenties again, Esther Blood trips lightly downstairs. Nancy Dickenson, wearing a duster coat in readiness for the journey, watches from the hallway and feels pleased at what she has achieved with Mrs Blood over the past weeks.

'All ready, Nancy?'

'Yes, ma'am. Nursey's got Stephanie running round the garden. Says it's going to tire her out so she will sleep on the train.'

'Well, the cab is waiting, so we may as well start. I will go and find Father and . . .' She now trips her way across the hallway to the breakfast-room. Father and . . . Esther cannot see a day when the superintendent's new wife will be anything except 'and . . .' Father had said she was to be Frieda to her and Jack, and Step-Mama to Kitt. But it was all so peculiar, so unnervingly sudden. Jack had been surprisingly sanguine about the whole thing.

'I don't know why we should be making such a to-do, Ess. If you think about it, it is a very sensible solution.'

'Why a solution when there isn't a problem?'

'I don't agree, Ess. Father looking upon you as the natural successor to Mother, and you allowing him to do so, *that* has been the problem.'

'I haven't minded.'

'Perhaps not. But I believe that you should have minded. You are still young: too young to be the widowed daughter, the housekeeper, Kitt's sister-stepmother. You must pick up the pieces and make a new life. The superintendent's new wife is here to stay whether we like it or not.'

At least there had been no great to-do about a wedding. The couple had gone to a Registrar and come quietly home to a family lunch. The lunch had not been easy. Between the time that George Moth had dropped the news into the lap of the family, and the installation of Effee a month after the day of the thunderstorm, he had tried to bring them together around the family table on two or three occasions.

Esther thought that it would have been better had he been more casual about it, allowing them to make their acquaintance over informal cups of tea or glasses of sherry. But no.

Father, with his usual confidence, had said that it was best for them all if they got over any initial difficulties over good roast beef. Jack had done it the first time, but subsequently had had some fine excuses as he was still convalescent at Queen Alexandra's and expecting at any time to be called before a medical board.

There had been a slight awkwardness about Nancy. She had always dined with Esther, and Esther wished her to be included in what she would refer to as the roast beef party. But Father had said that it was bad enough for Frieda – whom he sometimes called Effee – having to get to know the family without having Esther's companion there as well. But Esther had said that, come what may, Nancy was no longer a mere companion but a close friend, and must be included. Nancy, with her fine sixth sense, had asked Esther whether it would be all right if she went to visit Wally's mother at those times when the superintendent's new wife was dining. 'May gets very down sometimes, and you won't miss me for an hour or two.'

Without thinking, Esther had taken her usual place which was that which her mother had once occupied, and had organized the passing of the dishes. Effee/Frieda had been seated at the side, next to Father. Esther had flushed with embarrassment when she caught her father's eye. On the second occasion she had willingly given up the bottom of the table to its expected occupant, but then they had both felt awkward.

When Jack and Esther had compared notes, they had both said that the worst part was the uncanny likeness to their mother: they could momentarily be caught off-guard and find their minds flying back to earlier years. Surprisingly, Kitt took to her. If she did not know how to take the adult Moth children, then she knew how to talk easily to Kitt.

Steeling herself, Esther opened the breakfast-room door and was greeted by a fake of an old scene when her father, wearing his half-glasses and in his waistcoat, read the crime columns of the newspapers, and her mother, wearing a peignoir, wrote out domestic lists.

'Good morning, Father. Good morning . . .

'We're all set to go, Father.'

'Ah. There's a letter here for you – from Hewetson by the look of it. I think you might consider sticking to the man, he seems to have treated your affairs pretty efficiently.'

'I think I shall, Father.'

It was clear, by her nervous movements, that Effee could not decide whether she was in or out of this exchange. Esther smiled politely in her direction. Effee said, 'I hope that you have a good journey. It's quite a way.'

'At least this time Stephanie is old enough to be distracted or amused,' Esther replied.

George Moth said, 'And you won't have Kitt to worry about.'

'Oh, Kitt wasn't ever a worry. He's always been an entertainment on a journey.'

Effee knew from George that he and Esther had not seen eye to eye about the boy. She was reluctant to leave him in London, and he would not agree to him leaving the school in which he had settled.

George Moth stood up and kissed his daughter. 'Kitt will be still here when you return.'

'Just promise me that you will not do anything about boarding-school until I get back from Mere.'

'Boarding-school, George? For Kitt?' Sharply.

At the unexpectedness of her intervention, they both turned in Effee's direction.

'It's not settled, Effee,' he said.

'And it'd better not be, George, if you and me are going to stay friends.'

Here the fake 'Mother and Father at Breakfast' scene faded. Anne Moth would never have spoken as directly as this before the children. Esther saw the momentary cloud of irritation darken her father's face as he said, 'It's nothing for you to worry about, Effee.'

'Well, George, I beg to differ there. When I hear you mention Kitt and boarding-school in the same breath, it is something for me to worry about. I worry that you might be thinking of sending him to one. And if that is the case, then you will find me against you.'

'I tell you, nothing is settled.' He spoke to Effee but looked at Esther.

Effee said, 'I don't really want to interfere, Esther, but for better or worse I'm your father's wife now, and it's only natural that I should take an interest in his children. I know that it's you that's brought him up, and you brought him up really lovely, but it looks like me that's going to take over now, and I'm dead set against sending children away from people who loves them to live with people who don't.'

'Then we think the same . . .'

Effee smiled broadly. A smile nothing at all like Anne Moth's beatific smile.

'Well, that's a good start then, isn't it, George? Now all we've got to do is for me and you to think the same on this question of school.'

'There's time. Kitt's name has been down since he was a baby. There is no mad rush to decide one way or the other.'

'Oh yes there is, George. Esther is just off down to Dorset, and she won't rest happy unless she knows that she won't come back and find that you've parked Kitt with a lot of strangers.'

George Moth saw the image that he had had, of another frail and beautiful partner at the breakfast table and in the bed, disappearing. For years he had been buying her suitable furniture, suitable accessories, creating a mistress in the image of his wife, but during the hours, days and weeks that he had not been with her, she had still been Effee Tessalow; strong, independent Effee Tessalow.

He thought that he had suggested marriage on the spur of

the moment, but it may well have been that he had unconsciously been heading towards it for years. Otis Hewetson, Victoria Ormorod, and even Nancy Dickenson since she had taken charge of his problems, had all at one time or another fitted his image of George Moth's wife. But there she had been all those years. Effee loving him and Effee waiting for the snatched hours and occasional nights for him to love her.

'What is it that you want, Effee?'

'That you promise Esther that *we* are going to take over bringing up Kitt. He's going to live here and go to school close to home. It's not much to ask. Your parents gave you that sort of care, didn't they? The least you can do is give it to your own children. There's no question it's what Kitt wants. I'm sure it's what I want, for him. Isn't that what you want, Esther?'

'Yes . . . Frieda.'

'Well then, George?'

From the way her father smiled at his new wife, Esther knew that he loved her, and for a moment her body felt acutely starved of Bindon. She envied them and longed to be a partner in a marriage again.

'I don't see any objection to it, especially as I have decided to resign from the Force. I shall be more on hand than I was when you and Jack were young.'

The two women, superficially alike with their small, slight frames and clouds of fair hair, were taken aback; particularly Esther, who knew that her father's career was part of who he was. If he was not Superintendent Moth, then who was he? Mister Moth? She could not envisage that.

'You are going to resign, Father?'

'It is already under way. I have seen the chief constable. He has agreed that I should retire early.'

Effee said, 'Well, it's your life, George . . . I never was that keen on rozzers anyway.' She winked at him. Anne Moth had never winked in her life.

'What shall you do, Father?'

'I don't know yet. Effee and I will talk it over. Maybe we could sail round the world for a start.'

'Oh no we couldn't, George, we've got Kitt to think of. We couldn't go off and leave him.'

'Esther won't be at Mere for ever, will you, Ess?'

'That depends on a lot of things, Father. Now I must be going or Nursey will be in shreds with Stephanie. Goodbye then, Father.' She kissed him. 'Goodbye . . . Frieda.' She held out a hand for Effee to shake.

Effee stood up and unexpectedly kissed Esther on either cheek. 'Could you call me Effee? I was born Frieda, but I've been Effee that long . . .'

Esther felt the mantle of normality settling on her life. First Nancy, and now Effee Moth giving her hope that she could soon face the world alone.

'Goodbye for now, Effee.'

'I'll see nobody touches your rooms. We'll look forward to you coming back.'

From the front porch they waved at the departing cab, George Moth in his shirtsleeves and waistcoat and Effee in her peignoir – something Anne Moth would never have done.

16 Elton Court, Kensington High Street, Kensington, W

Dear Otis. This is my temporary address. Esther tells me that she has written to you, so you know the state of things in Denmark. I think that I shall be returning to the Front in a week or so and would like to meet you as a whole person rather than as lately as a withering vine in hospital blue. Perhaps you would like to go out to dinner with me? I rather favour somewhere as un-trenchlike as it is possible to get – the Dorchester? The Cavendish? Say Friday evening when I know that you will not have to go slaving in the salt-mines next day. Shall I collect you? Nine o'clock?

  Best Regs,
  Jack Moth

Friday evening at the Cavendish would be delightful, Jack. I think I should like to meet you there. Nine o'clock suits me very well. Otis.
PS. I should have started by saying 'Thank you for inviting me' – my social graces do not improve, do they?

In the gentlemen's cloakroom of the Cavendish, under the eye of a portrait of the Kaiser consigned there by the famous proprietress, Rosa Lewis – 'That's the only throne for old Willy' – Jack Moth ran a pocket comb through his hair before returning to the lobby to wait for Otis.

Had any of his trench friends seen him they would have been astonished at the contrast between the booted and putteed infantryman brewing tea with hot water from a gun-cooling system, and this tall, elegantly turned-out man in evening dress. However, Jack was unaware that these days the Cavendish was not the best place to appear in evening dress. As he waited where he could see the entrance, an inner door opened and an Aberdeen terrier raced out and attacked his ankles. Jack tried to fling him off, but he hung on tenaciously, yet still able to snarl and yelp as they went round and round together.

Onlookers gathered and some urged the dog on with, 'Attaboy, Kippy', 'Go f'r him, Kip', then, from the door through which the shaggy little animal had bounded, appeared a beautifully turned-out woman whose gaiety owed much to a little rouge and a lot of determination.

'Kippy! Come 'eah,' she commanded, and the dog unlatched his teeth but did not move far from Jack's heels.

'Well, sir?' Surprised, Jack saw that she was addressing not the dreadful little dog but himself.

'Well, madam?' Jack returned. 'Do I take it that this is your creature?'

'It is, young man, and so is this 'otel, and he is not no sort of creature, he's the renowned Kippy who's been trained by me to attack any man that comes to the Cavendish not wearing uniform.'

Jack was so taken aback by the woman's belligerent stare and her Cockney accent, that he did not for a moment know how to reply. However, into that moment dropped Otis's unmistakable voice at its most imperious.

'Then I suggest, Miss Lewis, that you post a notice, so that men who have had no opportunity of learning the new rules of your hotel because they have been a long time in hospital as a consequence of a much longer time in the trenches, are warned that they may be attacked by an animal with no discernment and fewer manners.'

For a long moment the two women faced one another, until the friend of kings and emperors was stared down by the Islington schoolmistress. The proprietress picked up her terrier and was about to say something when a man's voice intervened.

'Jack. Jack Moth, as I live and breathe.' A uniformed arm clasped him across the back. 'Well, just look at you. Who'd have thought it – we took you for a goner.' It was the doctor who had tended Jack through his convalescence.

Jack shook his hand warmly and indicated the dog. 'I just almost was.'

Ignoring the woman holding the dog, Jack turned to Otis. 'I'm so sorry the dog spoilt your entrance. You look superb. Let me introduce you . . .'

'Who could forget Miss Hewetson?' The officer shook her hand warmly. 'We met at Lys when she visited you.'

The proprietress of the Cavendish stepped forward and held out her hand to Jack. 'Kippy's ever so sorry and so am I. The young lady is right, he is indiscriminate and he must be taught better manners. Will you let the old Cavendish try to make it up? Best table, some bubbly, the latest music . . . ?'

Jack turned to Otis. 'I dare say you would prefer to go elsewhere, now that your evening is spoilt.'

'Of course I should not, Jack. I was particularly pleased when you suggested the Cavendish.'

'Right then,' said the woman, depositing the dog in the arms of a porter. 'I'll take you through meself.'

Having bidden farewell to the doctor, Otis and Jack followed the proprietress to a beautifully laid-up table not too close to the loud jazz band.

'Order anything that takes your fancy. Again, please accept my 'umble apologies, my dear boy, and you, miss.' She squeezed Jack's fingers, then, signalling to the head waiter and a wine waiter, she left them, ruffling the hair of the young men she passed, and giving them fond kisses.

Having ordered aperitifs, they were left alone. Jack laid a friendly hand upon Otis's.

'Lord, Jack,' she said grinning, 'we can't take us anywhere, can we?'

He met and held her eyes, enjoying the intimacy of their joint memories that went back to that first fiasco when they were children. 'You look wonderful. There's not a woman here can hold a candle to you. And your hair!'

Otis knew that she was dressed to turn heads. Although the dress that she had worn to Esther's wedding had then been very advanced with its glimpses of calf, nowadays many women wore mid-calf-length gowns like this one. A beautiful georgette creation with a wide-collared boat neck, huge gathered sleeves and panniers gathered from hip to knee, it was both modest in style yet daring in fabric. And her head was most outrageously cropped.

'Thank you, Jack. I really looked forward to putting on some glad-rags again. It's so much more fun when you spend most of your life in sensible clothes. I was in hot water with Pa about the hair – unfeminine – but at last I've done something to please my ma.' She smiled wryly. 'I don't believe you have ever noticed my appearance before.'

'The day your uncle came to Southsea, you wore a striped skirt and carried a matching parasol. At Esther's wedding you wore a strange pink dress that showed too much yet not enough of your calves. Beside the lake at Mere . . .' Ticking off on his fingers.

'All right, all right, you are more observant than I gave you credit for.'

'Let's dance.'

'Let's.'

It was said that the Cavendish jazz band could be heard outside even during an air-raid, but the noise didn't stop the urgent revellers from trying to talk above it.

After a couple of dances, Otis noticed that Jack's breathing was a bit laboured and perspiration showed around his top lip. 'Enough,' she said, making her own breathlessness the reason for returning to their table.

When they were seated he leaned across and said, 'I also remember what you wore when the dinghy capsized at Bognor.'

'Jack Moth, spare my blushes; but then none of us were exactly . . .'

He grinned, for a moment the old Jack. 'Dressed appropriate to the occasion, if you ask me.' He wagged his head. 'Oh Lord, how ashamed of you your mother was.'

Here at the Cavendish, no one would have suspected that the country was involved in one of the most terrible wars in history, or that there were shortages, rationing, hardship. The aroma of good food and fine wines pervaded the room. Linen and napery were stiff and immaculate, silver and crystal gleamed and glistened, flowers were everywhere, waiters, if somewhat greyer haired than in peacetime, were discreet and perfect in the practice of service. Above all, the officers and their companions were dressed to the kind of perfection that only maids, manservants and batmen could achieve.

'This is the life. What say you, Otis?'

'Not 'arf.' In a Cockney accent.

'You still do that very well.'

'I hope now without adolescent condescension. I now know the people who speak it. I'd be ashamed for them to see me here.'

'I understand. The war has taught me a few lessons in that direction. I have two really good friends: one is from the Welsh mining area, and the other is a Norfolk farm-hand.'

The look in her eyes went serious. 'What would they say to their corporal dining here?'

'They'd get a laugh out of him being attacked by a feather duster with teeth.'

'Didn't you know about Rosa Lewis?'

'I used to come here occasionally before the war. Her dubious past with royal lovers – goings-on in high places – made it a daring place to come to until one saw how very stodgy it all is.'

'You didn't know about her "war effort"?'

'No, it's ages since I came here.'

'She fairly rattles with jingoism, and your episode with the "renowned Kippy" isn't her first gaffe by far. She has white feathers with her wherever she goes, and she hands them out quite indiscriminately. If she makes a mistake then she tries to put it right by offering all the delights of the Cavendish, including the use of a nice clean tart for the night.'

He raised his eyebrows at her use of such a frank euphemism. 'Just as well I'm not partial to that particular course.'

Otis grinned. He was so easy to be with. How evil it was that some powerful war lord should see such young men as he as simply one of the parts of their killing devices. She guessed that he must have seen the cloud that was in her eyes when he looked up and met her gaze. She had noticed the same in his.

'Good Lord, Otis, what must you have thought when I suggested dining here?'

'I thought it your wry sense of humour.'

The waiter presented the dinner menu. 'Mrs Lewis insists that I point out to you the very best items. She is serving her famous quail pudding for special guests.'

'Otis, you shall choose if you care to.'

'I warn you, I love to eat well. You will probably have to wheel me home.' She smiled at him. 'You'll probably be ashamed to be seen eating with a woman who doesn't toy prettily with her food.'

'If you toyed, it wouldn't be mere prettiness.'

They were served with little pots of chicken-liver mousse and a chilled white Moselle. Rosa Lewis paused briefly at their table to see that their wine was a good one and that they had been offered her pudding. 'If you knew about the woman's jingoism, why did you not choose the Dorchester?'

'You know me, Jack, I seldom opt for the obvious choice.'

'Like this Moselle with the chicken? It is delightful. You shall choose again.'

After its jerky start, the evening began to slide along smoothly. The waiter said in a low voice that Mrs Lewis had suggested *Saint-Jacques et belons aux truffes* on a bed of julienne vegetables. 'Only for yourselves and the Ambassador, madame.'

'And,' suggested Otis archly when he had gone, 'his nice, clean tart for the night.'

She scarcely knew how to take the fond and indulgent look he gave her.

'You appear a lot improved since I last saw you. Are you better, Jack?'

His face clouded. 'Almost. I would have been entirely fit, except that I had a bit of infection. I've been before the medical board. They don't like men who make a slow recovery, it worries them that they may have to agree to a discharge. Let's not talk of that tonight.'

He looked thinner than the old Jack Moth, but more muscular and exceptionally handsome, his face sun-browned above his stiff white shirt-front. Certainly considerably less carefree now than five years ago, but better than when she had visited him last. His gaze was no longer open but, as Max Hewetson's had been, holding back, secret. Otis had seen that same look in the eyes of other soldiers she had met, both British and German captives, and each time she had done so it reaffirmed her conviction that this war was evil for the things men were being forced or encouraged to do to one another.

Recently Annie had contrived, through her network of friends in the right places, to get a few members of the League who spoke German, and of whom Otis had been one, into a prisoner-of-war encampment where they had talked informally to a number of Germans.

Although they had detected no real antipathy, they had been told by many of the German soldiers that their greatest fear had been capture, particularly by the British, who had the reputation of being perpetrators of the most appalling atrocities. Undoubtedly, as were British soldiers, they had been fed chilling tales by their superiors in order to produce fierce and fanatical fighters, but they said it had been impossible for them to fathom what was truth and what was propaganda. Certainly, they said, they had no cause for such fears now that they were in England.

Comparing notes later, the League members agreed that what was obviously true was that both sides believed the other capable of sadism. And perhaps there was some truth in it.

On both sides in this war, young men such as these here in the Cavendish who were dancing wildly and drinking heavily had, until it had been whipped up in them, no desire for militarism, yet had found themselves catapulted unprepared into the extreme barbarity of war – of shelling, bayoneting, bombing and gas attacks. And it had left them with that same look in their eyes as Max and Jack, where they constantly struggled against something unspeakable that was hiding behind a thin curtain ready to pounce.

In the midst of the urgent celebration, the eating, talking, singing and jazz-band music, Otis caught a vignette of Rosa Lewis seated at a table across the room. It was said that Mrs Lewis's favourites were officers of the Irish Guards. It was said that she always kept rooms available for the wives of any who were married. It was for this guards' regiment that several times every evening the band thumped out, 'It's a long way to Tipperary'. Now she was at a table pouring champagne for three young Irish Guards who looked barely twenty. One of them was unsteadily standing, singing along in a fine tenor voice, waving his cap to the beat of the song.

> Goodbye, Piccadilly,
> Farewell, Leicester Square,
> It's a long, long way to Tipperary,
> But my heart's right there.

Otis thought, She is doing the only thing she knows. Offering to feed them, then providing an hour of sexual satisfaction and a night of alcoholic black-out.

Was that what Jack wanted before he went back to France?

She forced her attention away from the young singer. 'Oh Jack, you have some grey hairs.' She fastened her mouth with her forefinger – an action that was like that of Victoria. 'You see, I have lost the art of civility.'

The lines at the corners of his eyes crinkled. Wasn't Otis Hewetson always so?

He watched her eating the potted chicken, then scallops and oysters, with obvious enjoyment, closing her eyes as she swallowed and humming small sounds of approval. 'I do so adore truffles.'

The elderly waiter allowed a small expression of approval to move his face when she selected *Truite en papillote* rather than the crayfish that was Jack's choice.

'I know a porter from Billingsgate and he brings me the most delectable crayfish every Friday,' Otis said.

'Except when there's an "R" in the month?'

She smiled at him, liking it that he approved of her, enjoying with him being drawn into the atmosphere of frivolity that prevailed in the place. 'Of course. My man is a specialist.'

When she chose duck with limes, he teased her. 'Is the Cavendish in competition with Smithfield too?'

'Lord, no. My man brings me only fish that I don't have to cook. I am not domesticated in the slightest, I'd have no idea how to cook a duck. If it were not for my good fortune to be living above Lou Barker's, then I should be reduced to living off bread and cheese.'

'And crayfish.'

'And cockles too. Have you eaten cockles? You should . . . and eel in jelly, we have that in the bookshop on Saturdays. Fish in batter. Wonderful food. I have tried to convert my mother to the cuisine of humbler Londoners, but she claps her hands over her ears at my delicacies whilst devouring *escargots* or frogs' legs.'

'The army's best delicacy is bully-beef and hard tack. There's a legend, and it may well be fact, that at least one soldier was saved from certain death, shielded from a bullet by a pack of hard-tack biscuits.'

Her face straightened and she reached out and rested her hand upon his clenched hand. 'Poor Jack.'

Before she could remove it, he took hold of her fingers and held them gently, moving his own in what seemed to be an absent-minded caress.

'No, not poor Jack, look where he is and who he is with. Poor Taff, poor Farmer Giles . . .'

His hand tightened on her fingers, gripping them strongly for a moment as though in spasm, then he brightened again.

When they had eaten perfect crème caramel and fresh figs, and their coffee had been brought, Jack asked if she minded if he smoked.

'If I were not to shame you absolutely, then I should ask for one myself.'

'There is something very satisfying to a man to see a woman relish good food. My mother enjoyed herself no end at a good dinner-table.'

'Such primitive acts, aren't they, providing and being provided with nourishment? I get something of the same pleasure seeing a man smoking, though I cannot believe that it is a wholesome habit.'

She watched him as he disbanded, pierced and lighted the green cigar. She supposed that his replication of George Moth's movements came from Jack watching his father perform them since he was a child. She had noticed on the occasions when she met parents of her children that it was not so much the features that made for family resemblance, but movements – perhaps a walk or the way of holding the head, something unconsciously copied – that gave the likeness of parent and child.

It being the most extraordinary event, she had expected him to mention his father's sudden marriage almost at once, but as the evening progressed he had said nothing. Now, watching his lips around the cigar, his mouth opening as he blew the smoke ceilingward, she felt that if he was not going to mention it, then she must.

'I had a letter from Esther . . . saying about your father.'

'I think she feels that she owes people an explanation for his behaviour. Which is how I feel also, I suppose, but there is none. My father is my father, he does as he pleases. I'm glad Ess has decided to stay in Lyme Regis for a while. The gossip will have died down after a month or so.'

'Is it so difficult that you can't talk to me?'

'Not difficult. A little wounding perhaps. And just a bit more proof that my father doesn't really see me and Ess as very important to him.'

'I'm sure you are wrong.'

'Why? We never have been very important to him. Always his work. He could spend weeks and move heaven and earth to bring a villain to justice, but not a single hour for a child being bullied at school.'

She felt a moment of anguish for the hurt child. 'It must have been a shock to you both. And what about Kitt, has he taken to a stepmother?'

'She's Kitt's favourite – and she is very good with him.'

'That's good. It would have been miserable for him otherwise. Esther was very non-committal.'

'You know Ess, not one to make dramatic statements.'

'Not like Otis. I think I should not be very controlled had it been my father who announced a stepmother out of the blue.'

'*Your* father is not a man who must always perform centre stage.'

Over recent months, George Moth's influence upon her desires and dreams had waned, but from time to time a memory of his overpowering largeness, his overt masculinity and her response to them could still cause her to feel disturbed. Upon learning from Esther's letter that he had married, she had felt a pang, but did not question whether it was of pique or regret. Not that she would have wanted to be George Moth's wife – or anyone's wife. She did not wish to be the guide and light to a family of children, but she longed to open the minds and broaden the horizons of classroomsful of them. She loved her work for those moments when she saw the excitement of understanding upon a child's face. Yet she had felt something when she read of his new wife; perhaps it was that Otis would have liked to know that she had been his first choice.

When they were ready to leave, Jack signalled to the waiter for his bill. The head waiter attended, saying that Mrs Lewis had had to go out, but she had left instructions to say that their bill had been settled by Kippy.

Otis felt reluctant to have the evening end. 'I have enjoyed myself enormously, Jack, and not only for the *truffes*. I shouldn't mind walking for a while.'

Eagerly, 'Oh let's. It is ages since I walked on a summer night, would you care to do that? I'd like to say goodbye to Piccadilly.'

The full anguish of his leaving hit her in the same way as when she and Max had sat together that last Christmas. He would go and she was as helpless as Rosa Lewis to do anything except administer superficial comfort. 'There are no lights after dark these days.'

'Of course. Everything seemed so normal in there that I forget the air-raids.'

He crooked his arm, and they walked. A surprising

number of other young couples were out too. 'Walking appears to be the fashion.'

'I walk all the time, every day. I sometimes wonder how it was that women such as my mother ever learned how to work their feet.'

By the time they had reached St James's Square, they had slowed to a dawdle. He stopped, gently halting her. 'Otis?'

During the course of the evening, she had decided that if what Jack wanted was that she be his nice clean tart for the night, then she would be that.

She looked up at him and for a moment she thought that he was going to kiss her. It was a balmy night, they had eaten splendidly, laughed, danced, and been easy in one another's company, and with the relaxed attitudes brought about by the war, it would not have been unthinkable to have exchanged kisses in the street.

Holding her shoulders, he drew her closer. 'Otis, you are the only one I can tell.' He paused. 'I have decided that I am not going back there.'

For a moment she thought that he meant that he was not returning to his father's house.

'Back where?'

'To France.'

'What are you .'. . ?'

The moment of silence seemed an age.

'What are you going to do?'

'I was thinking – of trying to get away. I have been thinking a lot about it, in the army one hears rumours all the time, tales about men who hopped on a ship and stowed away. Of course, one never hears the tales about those who are caught, but it ought not to be too difficult in the Port of London.'

Otis was stunned. Had Max Hewetson said, that last Christmas, that he was going on the run, then she would not have been surprised. She knew that he had seen through the veneer of duty to a conviction that what he was doing was wrong. But he would die rather than have others believe him to be a coward or a traitor – which was what he did. But Jack? Jack the volunteer who had gone to war to avenge his sister's tragedy? An hour ago, in the dining-room of the Cavendish, he had been the epitome of a young man enjoying the last days of home leave.

'Why are you telling me, Jack?'

'Before I last went up the line, I started a letter to you.'

They had walked twice around St James's Square and were now walking along Regent Street towards Piccadilly. The evening that had begun so lightheartedly was dying. Her mind was frantically considering the problems for Jack if he went as a 'runner'. So far she had been actively involved in the running of three men, and had been on the periphery in the organizing by Danny of several more. It was risky and fraught with distress. Men who did it were suddenly whisked out of the country with no farewell wave. A few took a wife or girlfriend to help in the subterfuge, but mostly the men left alone.

'What was in the letter?'

'A declaration of my love for you.'

'You mustn't, Jack.'

'You cannot order my love away, Otis. You can say that you don't feel the same for me, but there is nothing that you can do about what I feel for you.'

'I know . . . I know.'

'I do love you. I wish I hadn't been such a fool over Victoria.'

They had now reached Piccadilly, which was busy with late diners and theatre-goers. At a rank, Jack opened the door of a horse-drawn cab and handed her in.

'Where? Greywell?'

'No, to my own home.'

'Islington, then,' he told the cabbie.

Inside, they were quiet for a few minutes, sitting with space between them; then Jack moved close and put one hand on her shoulder, urging her to face him. 'I know that you have said that you intend following your career.'

'And so I shall.'

'Oh, modern women and their careers. There's no doing with them, is there? I love you, Otis, does that mean anything to you?'

'Of course it does. Of course. I simply don't know how to respond.'

'I had hoped that your response would be that you loved me.'

When she had watched him lighting the cigar she had wondered whether his mouth would feel like his father's, hard and insistent, but erotic and exciting. There was no doubt about it, she had enjoyed being kissed by George Moth and, when he had come within a breath of seducing her, she had liked the feel of his warm, heavy body.

When she stood outside herself, she could see that by society's standards she would be considered immoral. Her mother would be shocked beyond words and her father disillusioned, their friends shocked. A teacher! A woman who had young children in her charge to indulge her desires as though she were a man! A woman who had had all the advantages that birth into the wealthy, professional class could have, to admit to taking pleasure at the thought of being seduced by her friend's father, and recently making love with a man who, if found out, might be put to death as a traitor for aiding and abetting deserters. Yet, in her affair with Danny Turner she did not see herself, as others would, as a woman of easy virtue. Her conscience was as un-troubled as that of a pure but unsatisfied virgin.

Otis's body was young and healthy, she was a woman who could not be satisfied except by being made love to by a man. A man like Danny Turner who, like Otis, did not wish for any serious commitment from a lover. She believed that sexual desire was nature at work, and that rules which did not permit sexual fulfilment to a woman who taught children were asking to be broken. There seemed no logic in the rule that forbade married women to teach – one would have thought they would make the best teachers.

Her casual affair with Danny was perfect. He was as discreet in his activities as her occasional lover as he was with his missions with the men he smuggled out of the country. When he and Otis went together to get one of the men safely aboard his ship, they expiated their days of anxiety with mutual passion. Beginning strong and fierce with one another, and later relaxed and giving.

Now, complications. Jack Moth loved her. Had he, instead of saying 'I love you' said, 'I want to make love with you', she had already made up her mind to it. It would have been another kind of fulfilment. He had been her first awakening as a girl when she had seen him diving from the dinghy, lean and white-skinned, as pleased with his new-found virility as she had been of her burgeoning femininity. Had he said 'I love you' when she had seen him again that summer in Southsea, or at Mere, then she would have said, 'And I love you.' But now?

He said, 'I really did not intend to go any further than to let you know how I feel. One way or another I am about to go away, and I did not want to do so without at least letting you know how I feel about you – and now realize, how I have always felt.'

'Dear Jack, thank you. I have never had a man declare love for me – I feel overwhelmed.'

'Otis, I cannot believe that.'

'It is true. Jack, listen to me. If you are not going back to your unit, you'll need help.'

'I'll manage.'

'I can put you in touch . . .'

'I will not allow you to get involved.'

'I am already involved.' And she told him of her activities with the escapees.

When the cab drew into the kerb, holding his face

between her hands and guiding his mouth to hers in the dark of the cab, it was she who kissed him, her soft mouth parted. 'Until tomorrow then, Jack.'

'Very well.'

'It will be safer for you to get out, with the help I can get you.'

Father,
   A p.c. from Baby and me to say that we are enjoying the sea air of Lyme. Mere is looking most beautiful. Do bring Kitt and Effee to visit us quite soon, Esther

'Walk nicely, Baby.' Esther pulled on the safety-reins, halting the little girl who used the jingling breast strap to swing against, forcing Esther to lift her free of the cobbles of Lyme Regis's Broad Street.

'Swing-swing.' Baby twisted and swung in mid-air.

'Oh, Nancy, she should have been a boy, just look at the toes of her boots. Naughty Baby, if you don't walk like a little lady then we shall not have our treat.' Esther lowered the child gingerly so that her neat little white calf boots should not scrape the cobbles. Bribed by the reward of a cup of fruit juice and a biscuit taken in the open on the Marine Parade, little Stephanie walked sedately ahead of her mother and Nancy, who was guiding Baby's wicker baby-carriage – for which she was really rather too old, but which Esther did not like to leave at home on its own when they went on these outings.

'Perhaps you should let her run a bit, Mrs Blood, she can come to no harm once we are away from the roadways. I could take her down on to the sand.'

'I don't think so, Nancy. She's only three years of age, and yet such a wild little thing already, don't you think?'

'No, not wild, just full of curiosity and energy.'

'I should hate it if she became a hobbledehoy. The major loved femininity and daintiness.'

They turned the corner on to the Marine Parade. The tide was almost out, revealing the bay with its tawny sand and shingle sculpted into a scalloped edge by worn wooden groynes. To their left a green rolling horizon, to their right the long bare shoreline into which The Cobb hooked like a loving stone arm protecting bobbing fishing boats and dinghies anchored in its lee. Although it was well into September, the air was warm, and a balmy breeze carrying seashore smells rustled the skirts and hat-ribbons of the two women.

'Indian summer, Mrs Blood.'

'It seems to me that it has always been summer here.'

'I'm glad to hear you say that, miss.'

Nancy, who had been trying to find the right moment, saw that it was now. 'I thought that I'd stop out the rest of the summer, see you settled in . . .'

'Nancy, you're never going so soon.'

'It's not really "soon", I've been with you a fair time. And you're better, I can tell now that you've come home here.'

'It isn't my home, though. I'm really only my brother's tenant.'

'I can't see Master Jack down here away from things.'

'No, so he might not want to keep it on, in which case he'd want to sell up.'

'It's a lovely place. I quite fell for it.'

'Then stay with me, Nancy.'

'Oh miss, I'm no more the type for quiet coastal places than Master Jack.'

'But Southsea . . .'

'I belong in London, miss. Portsmouth and Southsea was

only where I was born and where I worked my first years. Since I went to London it seems to be my true home.'

'But what have you got to keep you there now . . . ?'

They had reached the little café which they had taken to visiting in the afternoons, and seated themselves on some folding chairs at an ironwork table. Stephanie, afraid that this wonderful treat might be taken from her, sat stiff-legged, diverted only by the bells of her harness, like the perfect little girl her mother wished her to be.

The relationship between the two women was no longer clear-cut. Walking together their demeanour and dress indicated that Nancy was in the pay of Esther, but their shared experience, of a loving man suddenly taken from them, had given them a kind of bond that often overstepped their social positions.

'Now that Wally's gone? I suppose you might say the same as brought you down here – London is where what's left of Wally is.'

'Wally's best boots?'

Nancy smiled. 'Those are his mother's. I don't really need them to remember Wally, but I do want to live where he lived, and go back to work where we worked together.'

'You would go back to working on the trams?'

'The war has given women a chance to get a foot in the door of better jobs. I dare say they'll try to oust us out, so we have to do what we can while we can. I joined the Independent Labour Party, and they're all for getting women into the unions, so if I get back into the depot I'll see if I can help out with the sort of work Wally was doing.'

'Isn't all that kind of thing men's business? I'm not saying that women should not have the vote, but there are so many more suitable things that are more natural to women than what you propose. The way you have helped me has been wonderful – it is that kind of thing that women should do.'

'I did that for you, Mrs Blood, because I knew you when you was a girl and I knew your ma, and I saw how you was with young Kitt when he was a baby. But what I really want to do is to go back to working for the unions and helping with the Family Planning campaign. We're not far off the day when there will be proper clinics; all that's needed is some funds.'

Esther wrapped a large napkin around Stephanie's twill silk smock and helped her to hold a cup daintily and be careful of biscuit crumbs. 'Goodness, Nancy, how shall I ever manage to produce a graceful daughter from this little bundle of fidgets.'

'Same way you got there yourself, miss: a bit of you, a bit of her, and a bit of give and take.'

'I wish that you would stay here.'

'Perhaps I could come down to see you from time to time.'

'And talk common sense to me? Yes, that is if we are still here.'

'Miss, can I suggest something?'

'What then, have you got the answer to it all?'

'I wish I had. I don't know if it would even be feasible for you, but I just wondered if Master Jack ever thought of selling Mere Meldrum, that you should buy it from him.'

Esther looked at Nancy with mild astonishment. 'I could, couldn't I? Why did that never occur to me? I could, couldn't I? My mother's legacy was not large, but I might come to some arrangement . . .' She patted Nancy's arm. 'You are so clever, Nancy. Oh, I feel so excited, just think what an asset a place like Mere would be when Baby is a young woman, what a setting for weekends in the country for her friends.'

Nancy unwrapped and wiped the face of the embryonic debutante of her mother's imagination. 'Ups-a-daisy, Miss Stephy. Now hold your mama's hand nicely or you'll find yourself in knickerbockers and black boots and your curls cut off.'

The child did as she was bid by Nancy, knowing that

394

when she came along here in the morning with Nancy and no Mama, Nancy would reward her with a race along the sand and a search for crawlies, perhaps even with her toes bare.

'Baby will miss you, Nancy.'

'Yes, ma'am, but she's going to be fine, you see if I'm not right. Just let her have her head sometimes, let her be a little girl for as long as she can. Being a grown woman an't no great shakes, is it?'

My Dearest Ess,

Your suggestion is the perfect solution to Mere Meldrum. You could, of course, have had it for your home for as long as you wished, but if it suits you to become its owner, then I shall put it in hand at once. I shall make it over to you entirely for whatever sum you raise on the property Mother left you.

If I may suggest, be guided by Hewetson. He has always looked to your interests very well and from what you have told me of his investment of the income from your property, it must have yielded very well indeed.

I should prefer that the entire matter be handled by Hewetson, as I do not wish to involve my own practice. Mere will be costly to keep up, but as most of those portraits, vases, clocks and pieces of statuary you consigned to the attics are valuable, I suggest that you let him send them to Sotheby's and invest the proceeds. Get him to go over the books with you and the agent: you will see that such bits of Mere as the dairy herd will bring in a fair contribution.

Whatever you do, don't let Mere become a burden. Ask Father for money if necessary, take in paying guests, open it as a hotel – anything, just so long as you make it your – and Stephanie's – home. It is a beautiful house that deserves to be happy – as you do, my dearest sister.

It may be some time before I see you, but I shall carry with me a picture of you there in Lyme creating a new Mere Meldrum.

As ever, yours,
Jack

KATE

Wife of Rev. Peter Warren
Died 22 October, 1917
R.I.P.

Victoria stood in the October chill of the graveyard before the newly erected headstone, a twin to that of its close companion, to the Rev. Peter.

Aunt Kate, unlike Grandmother who had wanted no marker for her old bones, had wanted a 'piece of respectable marble like Peter's' which her successful children had seen to it that she had. Kate, who had not seen her sons for years, would have been proud of them, silk-hatted at a village funeral. In their youth they had been given the same advice as had later been given to Victoria – 'get on out in the world if you wants to make summit of yourself, you won't never be nothing in this here place', and so as Vic and Linty had gone, Victoria was now going.

She had been to look at the weathered cross, carved 'Louise Tylee 1862–88' which, apart from Victoria herself, was the only thing of substance left to indicate that her mother had ever lived.

Unsentimentally, Victoria knew that this was the end of that part of her life. Of the warm, strong environment of her childhood, where women living alone fended for themselves; where homeless children came and went, and some orphaned children came and stayed; and where destitute women, abandoned – as her grandmother had been abandoned – by men who had left them with children to feed and no means of providing for them, had received the unpatronizing charity of The Refuge, as the hospice was known.

She still had relations in the village, but they were not so close that it would hurt Victoria never to see them again. And, much as she had loved her home as a child, she had outgrown it. Kate had taught her her first letters there, and her grandmother had shown her how to deliver a baby safely in sterile surroundings. It had been a home shared with a dozen other children and sometimes more, and several temporary aunts; its floors had gleamed with polish and its shelves and cupboards had reeked hygienically of the Old Lady's disinfectant – Caroline's Holy Water, as the Rev. Peter had once called it.

The links that had attached Victoria to the village and The Refuge were now all broken – Uncle Peter and Aunt Kate side by side; her mother, whose cross had been erected when she was younger than Victoria was now; Grand-mother, who had been mother, father, guide, conscience and mentor, had become a recently sunken mound where snowdrops, scillas and anemones were now as naturalized as the horse-daisies, buttercups and poppies that bloomed after them. The Refuge will continue, Uncle Vic and Uncle Linty, hard-nosed, soft-centred railway contractors, have agreed to become its trustees in Victoria's stead.

She can go. From this village. From this country. The Hague Congress, the petition for peace with its thousands of signatures has made no impression on governments, on the war, on the slaughter of young men. The senseless killing of an entire generation of men goes on and on. The bookshop, the birth-control network, the 'Underground' are all functioning. Red Ruby has said everything she can say. Women have still not got the vote, but it will come soon, she is convinced of it.

Now she feels as free as Tankredi once said that people with revolutionary ideas must be. Tankredi. Recently he had turned up in London and had once again set her alight – this time not only her body but her mind.

Russia! he had said.

And had enthused about his colleague Trotsky, and the

398

remarkable Lenin. Once power was seized a whole new system would be created. The people would take over all factories and all privately owned capital. The peasants would take possession of their holdings and the old, rotten and infected regime would fall.

And Victoria Ormorod, Blanche Ruby Bice, Red Ruby, was afire to be part of it.

> Greywell, Stormont Road, London.
>
> *Mr and Mrs Martin Hewetson request the pleasure of*
> ....
> *to join them at their home for a musical evening followed by supper*
> *to celebrate the twenty-fifth anniversary of their marriage. Dress*
> *informal.*

The evening had been a success, thank the Lord. Otis, knowing what she needed to do to please her mother, had willingly agreed to every one of her whims both as to her dress and the available men on whom she should dance a little attention. Being Otis, that dancing was a perfunctory jig just to show willing.

'I'll be nice to them, Ma. I really don't mind.'

'Otis, when you are co-operative, I always suspect the worst.'

'I want your celebration to be so splendid that none of your acquaintances will ever have done better.'

'Well, at least be pleasant to Mr Cordwallis.'

'I will, Ma. He will go away believing that I am his greatest admirer, and that if his Party would only give women the vote, then I should give him mine at the next election.'

'Otis, you must absolutely *not* bring votes into the conversation.'

And Otis had not done so. She had been a model daughter.

Now that it was finished, the debris of the celebration supper cleared and the hired staff gone, Otis sat, as she liked to do, drinking a nightcap with her father. He rose from his seat and went to ponder over the array of silver-wear displayed on a chiffonier.

'Very nice items, Otis, don't you think?'

'Oh, very. But whatever shall you do with a silver sealing-wax box concealed in a coach and horses, and Ma with a scissors and thimble set – I never saw Ma use a thimble in her life.'

Martin Hewetson grinned at his daughter. She was a delight to him. Not only had she turned out to be intelligent and beautiful, but she had a wicked sense of humour to match his own. To think that there had been a time when he had wished that she had been a boy. Boys might join one in one's profession but, as he had seen in other families, once they left home, they returned only as a duty, whereas Otis, although she had caused such upheaval at the time by going to live under another roof, still had Greywell as her home.

Quite obviously men were attracted by her looks and intrigued by her self-assured manner – certainly Cordwallis had been impressed. Equally obviously Otis liked the company of men. It was difficult for a father to judge these things, but he felt that she had inherited a certain tendency to strong emotion from Em, and perhaps a liberal attitude from himself. An explosive combination but, when the right man came along, they were traits that ought to bring happiness in one with such a generous nature as Otis. What was she now, twenty-three? Only a matter of time before some young man would strike a spark to her fuse and she would be off like a shilling rocket. How happy Em would be in ruffled silk with roses in her hat, weeping gracefully. How she longed to sacrifice her only daughter at the altar of marriage, as she would put it.

Martin wished fervently that it had been possible for him to tell Otis what was going through his mind.

'Your ma will lay out the scissors and thimble whenever the giver of that particular gift is about to visit. It is not so much the small gifts that concern me but . . .' He gave her a purse-lipped smile.

'The windmill!' In unison. And in unison they laughed explosively and on the edge of hysteria or intoxication, at the monstrous gift that had no purpose except to be its incomprehensible and hideous self.

'Oh Pa, it's no wonder I find it difficult to be serious about some of the things that matter so much to some people.' She put her arms about him and pressed her cheek to his. 'And you, my dear pa . . . you are such a *nice* sort of person.'

'Nonsense, child.' He gently patted her back as he had done many times over the years.

Because he was such a nice sort of person, and because she loved him so much, beneath the display of gaiety she had so consummately portrayed all evening, Otis was in torment. She could think of nothing worse that she could do than to betray his trust. She was going away but she could not tell him. After tonight . . .

'Pa. I hope you won't mind, but I am going back to Islington tonight.'

'But it is so late.'

'There are quite a few things I have to do.'

'Always work, Otis. Leave time for other things.'

'I'm sorry, Pa. It will make things easier for me if I go back tonight.'

'But I have given Dawkins the evening off, and you cannot possibly go in a hired cab at this hour. If you must go then I shall come with you.'

Otis knew that it was no use arguing. He would come and she would have to keep going cheerfully.

He came back from telling Em, putting on an overcoat

402

and carrying a travel-rug and one of Otis's tweeds. 'Never mind what you look like, this is warm.'

In the chilly cab they sat close.

'Your mother wasn't pleased.'

'You shouldn't have told her.'

'How could I go out without doing so?'

'Oh dear Pa, I'm such a nuisance to you both. I really do wish that I could be what you and Ma want.'

'What I want is what I have. Two beautiful, healthy women.' He squeezed her hand and kept hold of it. 'Both of whom can twist me around their little fingers.'

Otis fell silent, staring out of the cab window at the quiet roads of night-time Lavender Hill, and listening to the steady clop of the horse's hooves.

'Do you want to tell me, Otis?'

'Tell what?'

'I don't know.'

She should have known that she could not hide behind gaiety. When she was a child she had believed that he possessed the ability to know what she was thinking, until she realized that he was so attuned to her moods that he could detect any change.

When he held her hand between his two, she realized that hers was cold and stiff with tension.

She longed to tell him. About Jack, about Danny Turner, about what they had arranged – but she knew the rules. Only the couriers and the escapee must know. She thought that she knew her pa, but he might easily do something uncharacteristic in his worry over her involvement in such a scheme.

'You know that you can trust me with any secret, Otis.'

She still did not respond.

'I can't bear knowing that you have something on your mind that I cannot help put right for you.'

'You have to let me go, Pa.'

'Dear child, I let you go three years back. It is your mother . . .'

'No, Pa. You have given me the means to be free – the chance to study at college, your support when I wanted to teach and your marvellous lack of criticism – but you haven't let me go as you would if I were your son.'

Now it was his turn to fall silent. Then he said, 'Is it to do with Jack Moth?'

'Jack?'

'He has been in touch with me, in a professional way.'

'I know that he was settling some of his affairs. He's ready to be certified fit for active service again.'

'You see him then?'

'He took me out to dinner – you remember?'

'You realize what a difficult position I am in, of course, knowing his beneficiaries.'

'I heard from Esther that they have come to some arrangement about Mere.'

Gradually and without difficulty she eased herself out of the quicksand of her guilt. They were not now far from Islington where she could be alone, drop her mask and weep for herself and for him.

For the last half-mile they did not speak, her hand, still lying between her father's, thawed. The cab drew up before Lou's unlit shop.

'You *are* still happy here?'

'Very happy indeed, Pa. I like my new school and I am hoping that it will not be long before I am able to work for my Master's.'

'Don't you ever think of what you will miss if you don't have children of your own?'

'Yes, Pa. I do. But I put it out of my mind and hope that when women have a say in affairs, then we shall have the same privileges as men. There is no reason why women with children of school age could not be teachers – at least for part of the day.'

'Who would see to the domestic side of things in Utopia?'

'I dare say it would be worked out as it has always been in

404

primitive and peasant communities – we should see to it ourselves.'

'Is that disillusionment, my dear?'

'I don't believe that I ever had illusions to start with. It is already a fact of life for some of the women of Islington. They have work inside and out of the home.'

'Is that what you want?'

'I don't know, but I want the opportunity to choose. Goodness, aren't we getting serious?'

She kissed him, trying to make it her usual affectionate peck and hug.

'Goodnight, Pa. Thank you for coming with me.'

He tucked the collar of her tweed coat across her bare throat.

'You wouldn't think of eloping or any such thing, would you, child?'

'Eloping? Me, Miss Otis Hewetson BA, twentieth-century career woman, with her own front door.' Her voice was light with jolly derision. She jangled her keys at him. 'Can you ever imagine such a thing?'

Martin Hewetson got back into the cab and waited until he saw her door close behind her.

Can you ever imagine such a thing?

Yes. Since he had drawn up the arrangements regarding Mere Meldrum and a brief will which made Otis a beneficiary beyond anything that their youthful friendship warranted – he could imagine just such a thing.

Jack, head bowed, gaze inward, sat in an exhausted attitude, one hand dangling between his knees and the other holding the nagging wound in his breast. His interrogator, Danny Turner, had left, and Otis had gone downstairs to fetch some food, whilst Jack was left nursing the exposed nerves of his mental wound which was a hundred times more painful than the physical one.

The man was hard, damned hard. Danny, the diminutive name, was, Jack suspected, preferred as sounding more disarming than Daniel. Wasn't he himself Jack to his friends but John Clermont Moth when he wanted the edge on somebody? Had it been necessary for Turner to prise out every detail of Cully's death?

Otis had protested on his behalf. 'Danny, surely you can take my word that we can trust Jack?'

'Nothing personal, Jack, you know that; but we have to know everything, we have to check.'

'It's all right, Otis,' Jack said. 'The man needs to know and it is time that I told somebody.'

'Is it because he is related to George Moth, Danny?' Meaning: Or is it because of Jack's familiarity with me and you have a streak of jealousy? And because you were sceptical so that I almost needed to beg for him to be got away.

'Anybody who has anything to do with the special police branch is bound to be suspect. You understand, Jack? Your father is no fool, he has not penetrated the organization, and it is my job to see that he never does. Look at it from my point of view. You are friendly with Victoria and Otis, your father offers Nancy Dickenson work, then Otis comes to me and says that Superintendent Moth's son wants help . . .'

'All *right!*' Irritably because she had discovered that at one time or another she, and Victoria herself, had not been above suspicion. It was only when Otis and Victoria had shown themselves loyal by becoming conspirators in the 'Underground' movement that they were trusted.

There were others involved but they worked in separate cells where the only link was Danny Turner who had organized the escape routes to America and Dublin. America, having become involved in the war, was now cut off as a safe haven. The only route now was to Southern Ireland.

'All *right*! But I feel cheapened that you cannot take my word for a close friend.'

'Why don't you go out for a while? Go downstairs and sit in Lou's.'

She refused. 'For God's sake, Danny! Aren't I part of this?'

Jack had looked sharply at her oath. She was severe and forceful. Like Victoria Ormorod – who in one character had cleaned the sleeve of his coat and smiled at him across the table on Southsea Pier, then metamorphosed into the fierce Red Ruby – so now it was with her protégée, Otis. The only similarity between this Otis and the silk-clad woman at the Cavendish – she who had devoured oysters with truffles, and soft fresh figs with such sensuousness – was the beauty of her face and figure.

He hated to think of the years that she had lived in this cramped little flat with its gas meter and its stairway directly on to the street, with its below-stairs smell of pastry and meat and apple; he hated to think of her donning the grey skirt and dark-blue blouse to go out every morning. And he hated to think that perhaps the good-looking Danny Turner, with his deceptive devil-may-care air, might have ruffled the white counterpane of the bed that was visible from where he was now seated.

Objectively, Jack, who had experience of questioning and cross-questioning, had been able to admire the man's technique whereby one minute he was asking seemingly casual questions and the next shooting a question that stuck like a barbed arrow into Jack's agonizing memory of Cully's death, until in the end Jack had said, Why don't you let me tell it in my own way. And he had done so, telling not the astute Danny Turner, but relating the whole dreadful episode to Otis.

'You remember you sent me some socks and those Floris chocolates?'

Danny Turner's sharp eyes flicked to Otis as she nodded.

'I gave Cully the chocolates and he sat and ate them one after another with his back towards the rest of our little group, like a child. That's what he was. He did things like that all the time. Although he was large he had a mental age of a young boy. Certain parts of him had never developed beyond that age, so that he had no beard and his hair and skin were almost babyish.'

'Why did you call him Cully?'

'His name was Cullington.'

'I thought you said that you had been to see his parents who were called . . . Pearce, wasn't it?'

'They weren't his true parents, though they brought him up.'

'I see.' Danny Turner smiled disarmingly. 'Sorry, Jack, tell it your way.'

'Some of the men tricked him into doing foolish things – a bit of amusement for them. It was something that riled me, and as I'm bigger than most men, I've always been able to use that to intimidate if I wished.'

Danny Turner smiled encouragingly.

'Normally I don't wish.'

That part of his story took ten minutes, building up for Otis his picture of Cully, of his childlike pleasure at possessing a weapon, and the danger to his own platoon when it was loaded.

'Nobody who ever saw him could possibly have said that it was feasible for him to be in the army.'

'So, by the time you went into this battle, you were the boy's . . . what? Friend? Guardian?'

'There were five or six of us, all trying to keep him out of trouble.'

'But you didn't succeed.'

'No, no. We did not succeed. We failed most horribly – I failed.'

'You shouldn't take the blame of it on yourself, Jack. The blame lies at the door of whoever took the thirty pieces of silver to certify that Cully was fit and able.' Danny Turner's voice was gentle and sympathetic.

'I'm not necessarily taking the blame – I am saying that we failed to protect a child from himself.'

'In the heat of battle, Jack? Nobody could have done more.' Otis's voice was as sympathetic as Danny's. He had already told her part of the story; even so she found his anguish hard to be with.

'What happened was, quite suddenly, we came upon a dug-out with about six or seven of the enemy. It was as though for the first time he realized what was happening around him. He began to cry. We had recently been attached to a new unit composed of the remnants of several others. The officer was a brute. He had a reputation for harshness that he seemed to cherish. After an earlier battle he was reputed to have had men flogged for want of bravery. He was called Roper, which I had thought was because of the floggings – but that was his name. He was probably the most stupid and most vicious officer I ever had the misfortune to serve under. Any man who had served under his command would understand how it was that the Cullys of this world can be certified fit for active service, and how it is that there are men who will justify the sacrifice of 30,000 men to recover a couple of miles of territory.'

There was a small clunk and the gas-fire stopped hissing and the row of yellow flames disappeared. At once the room seemed to drop ten degrees in temperature. Familiarly, Danny opened a small tin on Otis's mantelpiece and took out some penny coins which he dropped into the slot meter beside him. For a moment Jack's attention was diverted by that small act indicating as it did that Danny Turner was no stranger to Otis's rooms.

Soon, though, as he began to pour out his story, he looked only inwards at the images that his memory had obliterated during those long weeks in hospital.

Cully stood before Roper, his face streaming tears and the inner seams of his khaki trousers becoming dark and soaked. 'I can't! Don't make me, I'm afraid, sir. They'm Germans and they wants to kill me,' and so on, sobbing and becoming incoherent.

Roper, his revolver already in his hand, pointed it at Cully's lower belly. 'Bloody, pissabed! Half-witted bastard! Two seconds and you won't need any bloody Germans – I'll kill you myself.' Jack, with his own rifle and bayonet as though petrified and fused to his hands, shouted, 'Come on, Cully. Come on. It's all right, they're gone.' Roper, with spittle of fury spotting his chin, had cocked his revolver. He fired into the air. 'One!' In spite of the screaming of injured men, and the rattle of machine-guns, that single report as the bullet left Cully's rifle seemed to Jack to silence all other noise.

Roper, with a small hole in his cheek and an enormous one behind one ear from which spilled grey matter, twisted and fell as Cully also sunk to the ground, crying hysterically like the terrified child that he was.

Head bowed, with three fingers on her brow and thumb

on her cheek, Otis covered her eyes. Danny Turner, his face showing the stress of listening to Jack's anguished voice, stared at his own knees and drummed his fingers.

'They wouldn't let me see Cully at first, but when I insisted that I was going to act as Prisoner's Friend at his Court-Martial, I was allowed a single visit. Because I was not an officer it was deemed that I could not act in that capacity. However, after a day or two of argument, somebody took the decision that in the interests of fair play, a private who was a qualified lawyer would serve better than an officer with no experience in law.'

Cully stood – as he had been told to stand by Jack – to attention, answering questions truthfully. The proceedings had not taken long. Cully not only admitted cowardice in the face of the enemy, but that he had shot his own commanding officer.

Both charges carried the death penalty.

The presiding officer agreed with the defence that the man was obviously not of high intelligence, but he had been passed as fit for service, and low intellect was not a suitable defence against either charge.

And so Private Cullington was sentenced to be shot by a party of riflemen. There were no grounds for appeal, and in the interest of humanity the sentence should be carried out at first light on the day following the trial.

'I had one more visit. I don't think that he had any idea of what had happened or what was going to happen. I ask you, how does one say: "Listen, Cully, they're going to take you out and shoot you in the morning. Is there anything you would like me to say to your mother? Would you like a swig of rum to help you through?" What can you say to a boy like Cully in those circumstances?'

Danny Turner's voice was thick. 'I've heard enough.'

Jack halted him with his hand. 'No. You have to hear. Not you, Otis. Why don't you do as Danny says and go down to the shop?'

'I'll stay. If you and the boy went through it, it's not much to ask that I sit and listen.'

'The execution party which went out with picks and entrenching tools thought that they were a party of coal-picking volunteers. It was not until they reached the coal-mine and they saw the post and rope that they realized what it was that they had volunteered for. There was no going back, or they too would find themselves facing grave charges. Mutiny? Or carry out a death sentence on one's own comrade? What a choice. From the outcome, it is likely that either every man suffered a fit of tremors, or he determined that he would not carry this particular death on his conscience.

'Cully received wounds in every part of his body except where they would prove fatal. It fell to the officer in charge to give Cully the bullet of grace through the temple.'

'Were you there?'

'It was the least that I could do. It took less than ten minutes. Within hours the execution party was back in the thick of battle, doing mad heroic deeds, blindly winning medals. I was wounded, but I don't remember how.'

There were a few long-drawn-out moments of silence. Then Jack said quietly, bitterly, 'Well, Mr Turner, do you understand why, whatever you decide, I shall never again take aim at a fellow human being? Do you?'

Danny Turner stood up purposefully and held out his hand. 'Nothing personal, Jack. I am doing what I have to do to protect the rest. It's my job.'

There was a moment when it looked as though Jack Moth would not take his hand.

'Isn't that what we all say? It's my job.' Swallowing his bitterness, he grasped the proffered hand.

'Join the pacifists of the world, Jack.'

Part IV

Now the last hurdle was over.

Otis had offered their papers and they had been accepted – Mr and Mrs John Hewetson of Dublin returning home after a death-bed visit to Mr Hewetson's father. Mrs Hewetson, with her lilting Dublin accent, understandably did most of the talking. She could probably be quite pretty under the dowdy coat and hand-made scarf that added to her plump and bulky appearance, but her severe mouth and scraped-back hair stuffed untidily under an unfashionable hat put off anyone with half a mind to have a bit of a crack to liven things up whilst they waited. A lonely pair, with no one to wave them off. Other people passed remarks to one another, or nodded a response to some friend or relative on the quayside. No one expected the tall man and his wife in mourning to do anything but sit and comfort one another in their grief. They were left alone.

The smell of engine oil caused her to feel queasy.

A tall, stooped Mr John Hewetson, nervously guarding his various rush and cloth bags saw the gap between himself and the quayside widen, and felt the vessel shudder as the engine churned and turned her prow seaward. For a moment he dared a look into his wife's eyes. One day, he hoped, he would find there the response he sought.

She, looking inward, saw this journey as the first step in a much longer journey that was going to take her far.

Quietly she said, 'We shall be all right now, Jack.'

He took her hand and looked down at the wedding band

that Danny Turner had provided and which in her own rooms she had jammed upon her own finger as a final defiant gesture that she was still her own woman. Still Otis Hewetson.

Victoria Ormorod had been prepared for Moscow to be cold, but nothing, nothing, in her previous existence had prepared her for the November outside air of this, her first Russian winter.

Since she and Tankredi had stepped down from the train with their few possessions, the days had passed in a whirl of activity. Breathing in deeply, she relished the burning sensation to her bronchia in the same way that she relished the slight pangs of hunger and the alien, deep, deep dry white snow that enveloped the surrounding countryside, and the male-sounding language of which she already had a fair understanding.

She had not felt so alive, so necessary, so involved in anything for ten years. She had not been so totally committed to a cause since the intoxicating and powerful years when she had toured England speaking to huge audiences. Now, conscious of her bulky clothes, of her thick, coarse mittens and shapeless fur-lined boots, she smiled at the image of her younger self, dressed in a sway-enhancing cream skirt, straw hat with a ribbon band, and close-fitting white blouse, as she dramatically removed her calf-skin gloves whilst holding those same audiences in thrilling anticipation.

Nor, until Tankredi's dramatic reappearance into her life, had she realized how physically dull she had become. The men and women who had come into and gone from her life over those years were transient lovers. Only with Tankredi had she ever experienced authentic, wholehearted passion. And passion was not to do only with the body, it was to do also with the soul and the intellect, and it was only when all three were uninhibited that life was worth living.

Now, she had everything.

She was useful.

She had a cause into which she could pour her enthusiasm, the cause that would result in peasants and workers taking control of their own lives in the way that she had once hoped that English women would.

And, one day at a time, often living on the knife-edge of danger, she and Tankredi were back together, living the exciting, passionate lives that fulfilled them.

Dear Jack. It was nice of you to send us a Christmas card. I saw it was your writing and we noticed the postmark straight away and will send this to the address in London and hope that you get it all right. You dont need to be sorry about it, I only hope that you are all right and you havent gone abroad for convalessant or anything like that. I could read between the lines all right when you particular said you hoped that I was keeping very fit and well. It wasn't no wishful thinking what I told you about when I took you to the station and my babe came in November a bit premetur but she is perfect in every way. You can guess all right that Bert is like an old hen with a chick and have made all sorts of plans for her. I still cant hardly believe our luck. I wanted you to know as you was the first one I told outside of the midwife. Weve called her Johnetta on account of you. Folks round here thinks its a bit fancy but they probably puts it down to me and Bert getting above ourselves in our old age what with getting a baby at our age and all. Still, while theyre talking about us theyre giving other people a rest. I dont suppose theres a chance of you coming to Johnettas christening is there. If there was we should be really pleased because we cant think of anybody we would rather have as godfather for her. We dont have to have her done yet and could easy wait till you come back. Dont think weve forgot Arnold just because of Johnetta. We couldn't never ever forget him. We shall tell Johnetta how she had a brother that died in the war and about how him and you was soldiers together. Take care of yourself lad.

  Your grateful and affectionate friend,
  Fanny

Christmas 1917.

Dear May,

A card to wish you comfort at Christmas. I don't know what robins have to do with it, but I thought that it was the pretty kind of card that you would like. I'm glad you agree with me about Wally. It's like I used to say to Mrs Blood, we have to talk about those who have gone before or it's as though they wasn't ever real. I'm glad you were pleased with the painted likeness from Wally's photograph, it was done by a young widow of one of our members. As you can see, she is very good at it and I don't see why she shouldn't get trained at a proper school. A good many of the men in the union think I'm daft, but there's nothing wrong with trying is there? They're still suspicious of a woman wanting to do union work, but because of my Saturdays giving family advice in the Islington bookshop, they tolerate me and if I can get somebody interested in getting this widow trained, then I'm sure I shall squeeze some sort of help for her fees from them. It's kind of devious, but then that's how women have to work don't they? People say that the first year after a loss is the worst, but there's still hardly a morning goes by without Wally don't come to my mind. Funny enough I feel easier in my mind now I know what happened to him. It must have been over in a second. You hear stories about men who was posted 'Missing' turning up, but I knew in my bones that he wasn't just missing, but I couldn't never set my mind to anything properly. One day, when people come to their senses, they will see that men like Wally stood against the tide of things and was true to their beliefs, and that it took courage when the tide was so strong gainst them. And people will be ashamed that honest men was treated so vicious and cruel. I have minutes of meetings and union accounts and that to make up. The Executive's a bit funny about a woman taking part in union work (but they don't mind a good dogsbody) and I know they're only waiting for me to trip up – but I won't, you can depend on that. I shall be over for the day, I wouldn't miss one of your sherry trifles for anything.

Love from Nancy

Quite casually, the French woman – a member of the 'Committee' in the lodging house that serves as headquarters for their group – mentioned that she thought that today must be Christmas.

Victoria slips out into the harsh, snow-rivelled streets to see if she can find a church open, not for any religious reasons, but because she has always sat in a church once a year, on Christmas Day. Her earliest memory is of her atheistic grandmother and agnostic and doubting Aunt Kate puffing smoke-like breath as they joyously sang Christmas carols in the village church.

It is the one day in the year when Victoria allows herself a few minutes of nostalgia and wonders where she will be next year this time. Wherever that may be, she hopes that Tankredi will be there.

December 1917

My dearest child,

  I suppose all this cloak and dagger business is necessary. Until today, when your Mr Danny called at my office with an address for you, it has been most frustrating not to be able to write to you.

  Now that I come to put pen to paper, I scarcely know what to say. 'Wishing you a Happy Christmas'? I do, most sincerely, yet what a strange and ineffectual greeting from a father to a most cherished daughter who was whisked away. I think that Emily will never get over her dashed dream of white satin and cathedral bells, but you know E. – she is never bested so she spreads the romantic notion that you have eloped and are travelling abroad. None can say that this story has not the bones of truth.

  It has been hard to be without you, my dearest, but I have always been of the opinion that women are as capable as men are of living their own lives and succeeding or failing at it, and I have, as you know, believed in their right to do so.

  The letter you sent when you 'eloped' prompted as many questions as it gave answers, but they are questions that I am not able to ask until you and I are together and alone. I know you well enough to believe that your reasons for doing what you have done are sincere – and that is enough for,

    Your most affectionate Pa

Mere Meldrum

Dear Father,

Although I am, naturally, disappointed that you and Effee will not be coming down to Lyme at Christmas-time as I had hoped, I fully understand your wish to take a touring holiday together. I am sure that you will love Scotland. Do you remember that Otis and I spent one holiday bicycling in the area of the beautiful Trossachs? The scenery there in winter must be very imposing.

Thank you for your Christmas present for Baby. I am sure that when Santa Claus has delivered it she will spend many happy hours dressing and undressing her doll and taking it for a breath of ozone along The Cobb, which is still our favourite walk.

You will be pleased to hear, I am sure, that I have become quite a social being of late (for which I have only Nancy Dickenson to thank, she having put me once more on the path to life) and have made many acquaintances in the area, not the least of whom are Anoria and Pamela Hogan, two sisters who write books and paint pictures (respectively).

I am sorry that you feel about Jack in the way that you do, for I feel most content and want everything to be nice. I hope that you will come to realize that Jack is not a man to take such a drastic step lightly. I know him well enough to be assured that there is something grave behind his decision. One day we shall know his story, and until we do I believe in his integrity, courage and honour. I can think of no more suited couple than Otis and Jack, and (whatever 'rash and unwarrantable action' they might have taken) I shall never cease to love them for the fine people they are.

I am arranging a very grand dinner party on Christmas Evening. The invitations have gone out and none have been refused. I believe that people are curious to see inside Mere and what I have made of it. Please come to visit in the New Year, and please give my warm regards to Effee,

Esther

Mere Meldrum

My Dear Otis and Jack,

For one reason in particular I should have liked you to have been to visit here this Christmas, and that is to become better acquainted with Colonel Holman Hay whom you met briefly on the occasion when Baby was christened, and whose estate, as you will probably remember, adjoins Mere. I suppose, having gone thus far, I may as well continue and tell you what I should have told you the moment I received an address for you, and that is that he has proposed marriage to me and I have accepted and that we shall announce our engagement to be married at my dinner party.

Holman is a widower with a young son, his wife having so sadly died in childbirth (oddly enough, the same morning as Bindon died) which means that Baby will soon have a little brother. She has named him 'Boy', but I think that one can hardly have children who are known as 'Boy and Baby Hay'. I have no secrets from Holman. I believe that it was his understanding of the pressures that soldiers may suffer that advanced our friendship. He himself has had to face life with only one hand, but has told me that this is small damage compared to that of many men whose wounds have been caused by mental shock or gassing.

With the changing circumstances of my marriage, we shall need to discuss the future of Mere Meldrum, as in a few months I shall no longer be in residence here. This house has become very dear to me and it is my fervent wish that the day will come when Holman and I will have Otis and Jack as our closest neighbours.

With love this Christmas-time, from Esther and Stephanie

Mere Meldrum

Dear Kitt,

Father will have told you the good news that you are to spend the holidays with Baby and me. What fun we shall have. We have a large tree in the hallway and a small one just for you and Baby in the morning room which we have left for you to trim with decorations just as you wish. There is to be a party for you and Baby and another (very) little boy named Stephen (though Baby insists that his name is Boy).

Mrs Clipper has baked a special cake that is full of cherries which she says is strictly for children only and grown-ups are not allowed to eat it. Dear Kitt, do try to smuggle a piece for your poor old sister who so adores cherry cake.

I want you to promise me that you will not fuss and worry yourself about the journey. You know Ernest well enough and he will probably tell you stories the whole way and when it is time for your return (ages and ages away), Baby and I will travel with you.

I am sure that this will be absolutely the most splendid Christmas, for Boy Holman's father has a whole stableful of horses and ponies and says that he has personally arranged a visit by Santa Claus to the children's party.

Just a few more days and we shall be able to hug one another (unless, of course, that at six-and-a-half you are too grown-up for such carryings-on. Goodness, I do hope not, for I don't know what I should do without a hug from my dear Kitt).

With much love from your sister, Esther

A VIEW OF GALWAY BAY AT SUNSET

Happy Christmas, Danny.
With fondest love, yours, 'O.H.'

Leaflet issued by the North London Herald League pre-1914:

A GOOD SOLDIER

A good soldier is a blind, heartless machine. At the word of command he will put a bullet in the brain of the bravest and noblest man who has ever lived. He respects neither the grey hair of age nor the weakness of childhood. He is unmoved by tears, by prayers or by arguments. He is indifferent to human thought or human feelings.

DON'T BE A SOLDIER — BE A MAN!